Snowbound in Havenport

Nicole S. Patrick
Ruth A. Casie
Emma Kaye
Lita Harris

Timeless Scribes
Publishing

Timeless Scribes Publishing LLC

Print ISBN-10: 1-945679-10-7
Print ISBN-13: 978-1-945679-10-0

Digital ISBN-10: 1-945679-09-3
Digital ISBN-13: 978-1-945679-09-4

Cover image by Joanne Marinaccio at Castle Harbor Photography
Cover created by Jay Aheer at Simply Defined Art
Edited by Deserie Comfort of Comfort Editing
Copy Edited by Michael Mandarano

This edition published by arrangement with Timeless Scribes Publishing LLC.

www.TimelessScribes.com

Havenport Herald

*** Winter Edition ***   *** Volume 04 Issue 01 ***

Get the latest with Candy Apples.
Gossip with a snarky, tart bite…

SNOWSTORMS, AND WEDDINGS, AND MOBSTERS. OH MY!

❄ ❄ ❄

Talk about a crazy weekend. A gossip writer's dream. With everyone snowed in from that unexpected blizzard (Thanks for the heads up, Misty Storm.) you'd think Havenport would snuggle in by a warm fire. I assume there was some of that, but we also had an engagement, a mysterious Russian, a second chance for old flames, and a hint (make that a wallop) of magick.

❄ ❄ ❄

Well-laid plans never seem to go the way you want. Such was the case with a certain someone's plans to pop the question over the weekend. If the weather weren't enough to throw a wrench in the plans, finding out the intended bride's ex-husband isn't yet her ex, was sure to do the trick. Not to worry, our favorite single (or maybe not-so-single) mother is sure to find a way around such a minor inconvenience. And all our hunky veterinarian has to worry about is whether or not she will **Say Yes**.

❄ ❄ ❄

✳ ✳ ✳

✳ ✳ ✳

The police were beside themselves this weekend. What with missing teens and a drug cartel on the loose, they had their work cut out for them. And with the phones not entirely reliable due to the weather, they weren't able to warn anyone of the dangerous Russian thugs running along the coast. Maybe if they had, our lovely historical society president might not have been so happy to help the mysterious Russian who showed up on her dock in the middle of the storm. That would have been a pity, since it turns out they knew each other from way back when. They've sworn to never love again, but then again—**Never Say Never**.

So what caused that crazy blizzard this weekend, you ask? Our own Misty Storm is on the case, but is she telling the truth or devising an elaborate tale as an excuse for not warning us about the biggest weather event of the year? You be the judge. Of course, you'll have to believe in witches, and magick, and things that go bump in the night...like abusive ex-husbands. That's what caused one nervous witch to panic and surround our town with that nasty storm. It took a strong man, with a warm heart, to defrost this chilling situation. Let's all hope the sparks between the two don't set off a heat wave next. So do you believe Misty's story? At the very least, I'm pretty sure there's one witch who will never have to be **On Her Own** again.

✳ ✳ ✳

✳ ✳ ✳

❆ ❆ ❆

While Havenport prepared for the big wedding, our lovely bookstore owner's divorced parents came to town. And when their daughters went to celebrate the big day with their friends, the storm trapped the estranged couple at the bookstore. Alone. All night. Awkward! Maybe you don't know the history there? It's a tragic story—buy me a cuppa at Mellie's Diner one day, and I'll dish all the dirt. For now, let's just say that after a devastating loss, mistakes were made and the marriage fell apart. But I hear time heals all wounds, and while the kids are away, the adults will play. Maybe enough time has passed that these two can finally heal. Or is that just **Wishful Thinking**?

I hope you all enjoyed the weekend as much as I did. Snuggle up and stay warm!

~Candy Apples

❆ ❆ ❆

Contents

Say Yes

by Nicole S. Patrick

❄ ❄ ❄

An unexpected snowstorm shouldn't prevent Havenport's hunky veterinarian Dylan O'Brien from popping the question to the woman of his dreams, right? The ring's bought, the romantic evening set, and it's a matter of Meghan Washburn answering the age-old question. The life they've built together over the past year has been as near to perfect as he could have imagined or dreamed. He's more than ready to settle down and do everything to make Meghan his. Until an unwanted visitor brings more than a frost to the forecast, and Dylan starts to question whether he's the one to give Meghan her happily-ever-after.

❄ ❄ ❄

Dedicated to ~

Joe — Nothing could ever compare to your proposing to me.

110-100

Chapter One

Today is the first day of the rest of my life.

Dylan O'Brien opened his eyes and stared at the ceiling, wondering why that adage had jarred him awake. A wooden plaque hung in Grandpa O'Brien's house with that saying. He and Danny used to try and knock the old thing off the mantel with a homemade slingshot whenever they went for a visit. *Hmm*...interesting random memory. Could've been triggered by his brother's "Happy B-day Old Man" text—the wiseass.

Carefully, he rolled over on the mattress so as to not disturb the vision of loveliness beside him. Sprawled out on her stomach, Meghan exuded sexy, sweet, and beautiful wrapped into one. Her back, the color of cream, had a subtle hint of tan line from last summer's bikini. Although slender, she had just the right amount of curves from her defined biceps to the soft flair of her hips. He thanked God she was tall to compete with his height. And, yeah, those mile-long legs of hers wrapped around him were just fine. He swallowed hard at the tightening below. She shifted, emitted a cute sigh she often did in her sleep, and her lashes fluttered. Those were dark, bordering on black, and so long they practically hit her brows when she was awake. Meghan didn't need any makeup, although she insisted on mascara when they went out. Who was he to argue with her beauty regime? It only made her over-the-top drop-dead gorgeous. She shifted and squished the pillow in her grip. The sheet slid down, exposing the bare curve of her spine. Her tousled brown hair dropped onto her cheek. He knew firsthand it was the softest skin imaginable. A curl rested against her lips. Oh yeah, those sweet, full lips tasted like honey and had been locked against him a few short hours ago.

He'd better stop that train from leaving the station or she might wake up. Again.

But hot damn, he honestly could not get enough of her.

Most weekends, from Friday night until Sunday afternoon when she picked up her teenage daughter, Brielle, from visiting her parents, Meghan Washburn—formerly LaRue—was his alone. No sharing with anyone, especially the Washburns. Since her divorce and change back to her maiden name, her folks thought they owned Meghan. No way. Not the smart, independent woman he was totally head over heels for. Mr. and Mrs. W. might be pillars of the Havenport, Rhode Island, community, but they sure as hell got on his nerves, especially her father. Christ, the man put the *P* in *pretentious*. If Dylan had to hear one more time how Mr. Washburn had made his fortune doing *blah, blah, blah* in Havenport, and how *he* should expand his veterinary practice to a cookie-cutter, lack-of-feeling establishment, he might tell the man to screw himself.

No need to ruin a good moment thinking about him. With the exception of a few fun weekends spent with Brielle, it had been Meghan and him exclusively the past year. Felt good to have someone committed in his life.

They didn't do anything crazy, merely hung around his home, which she had a hand in redecorating to make it his palace. Yes, her business, Haven on Earth Designs, kicked butt. Havenport, and the surrounding towns, were clamoring for her expertise and creativity, and he couldn't be prouder.

He'd found the woman of his dreams. They loved drinking wine, making dinner together, and building the kind of a relationship he'd wished for but never imagined.

And tonight, he planned to make things a bit more permanent. He released a long breath and fixated on the nail pop in the sheetrock ceiling.

And hope to God she says yes.

He offered up a prayer to the patron saint of don't-make-me-screw-up-this-proposal-and-make-an-ass-of-myself, and shut his eyes.

"What's on your mind, my love?" came a sleepy voice near his ear.

Tingles graduated to pulses from where her hot breath invaded his auditory canal straight to south of the border.

"Nothing. Why?" he answered, eyes still closed. He gritted his teeth, commanding the lower extremity with a mind of its own to behave. But her feathery kisses glided across his chest right above his heart, making it difficult to concentrate on ticking off the million things he needed to accomplish before tonight.

"Well," she said, her fingertip making circles around the three chest hairs he possessed. "You're smiling and brooding at the same time, Doctor O'Brien. Are you feeling bad about turning thirty-five? Take it from me, it's just a number."

Slowly, he opened his eyes to her easy grin. A sunbeam shot through the open curtains, turning her hair into fiery streaks of auburn amid the brunette softness.

He laughed and pulled her close. "I'm smiling because a gorgeous, naked woman is whispering in my ear. I'd be ready for the old age home if I didn't react." Nice deflection.

"Uh-huh." She gave him a peck on the lips and pulled back way too fast for his liking.

"More, please." He reached but grabbed air, for she'd scooted shy of his grasp and sat on the edge of the bed. Her hair fell over one shoulder, giving him a view of the spot on her neck he loved to nuzzle. He could feast on her all day.

"How did I get so lucky?" He blurted the words, which swirled around his head at least fifty times a day.

Meghan glanced over her slender shoulder with a smirk. "Flattery usually gets you everywhere, but not today, mister. As much as I'd love to be dirty and stay in bed and ravish you all day, *you* have got to go." She pointed to the door.

"I like the ravishing part, and I can do dirty," he countered, chuckling despite the nervous twinge invading his gut. Yes, time to get his ass out of bed and tackle the day's list before tonight and the big step toward their future. Who would have thought proposing would be so stressful?

"Later, you'll have a proper ravishing." Her eyes flared with unspoken promise. "You *swore* to make yourself scarce. I want tonight to be perfect."

He grabbed her hand before she could stand and brought it to his lips.

"*You're* perfect."

A soft blush invaded her face. "Why thank you, Doctor. Now scoot."

"I'll be out of your hair in less than half an hour."

She leaned back over him, and waves of anticipation flew over his body, careening pulses of heat into his nerve endings. He held his breath. She trailed her lips from his abs up to his collarbone, sending quivers straight to his toes.

"Not without a proper goodbye." Her lips hovered mere centimeters away, then grazed his with the slightest touch. Meghan liked to start with tentative, teasing kisses to drive him mad. He'd learned she turned into liquid fire when he begged.

"Let me in," he pleaded against her bottom lip.

More than a few breathless moments later, his head plopped back onto the pillow, the soft down relieving the pent-up passion in his skull. Meghan gazed down with a satisfied smile and flushed cheeks before she shimmied off the bed and sauntered across the room.

She pulled aside the curtain. "It's flurrying. Dyl, did you hear?"

He blinked. His heartbeat finally slowed to normal, and he forced himself to look away from her perfect behind.

Head. Back. In. Game. He had plans. Big plans. His contact at Newport Jewelers had texted the picture to seal their deal. The engagement ring was an emerald cut diamond of over a carat in size, with side accent stones set in platinum. It had screamed Meghan's name from minute one. Sophisticated, stunning, and classy.

"*Rhode Island Today* mentioned something about a dusting this weekend. But that weather lady is wrong a lot," he commented, his voice hoarse. The digital numbers on the alarm clock showed a few moments shy of eleven. Snow might mess up his ETA back to Havenport after completing everything on his list, but no biggie—his truck could handle snow.

She turned from the window with a frown. "I hope it's not a full-fledged storm."

"I doubt it. November is a bit early for a snowstorm. And if it is, we'll hunker down. I can think of a few ways to stay warm." He winked, and she chuckled. If he timed the errands, he could make it from Havenport to Newport and back by dinner, giving Meghan plenty of time for whatever she'd planned. He had no clue, but suspected there would be dinner involved, if the numerous grocery bags on the counter yesterday were an indication.

"By the way," she said, and tugged on her robe, "where *are* you going today? Should I be worried you'll get sidetracked at Royce Tavern watching a hockey game and forget to come home?"

"What?" he scoffed. "Of course not."

One of her eyebrows arched as if to call bullshit.

He dipped his head, pretending to smooth a wrinkle in the blue faux suede comforter she'd picked to decorate his man-cave bedroom. Yeah, well, last year the Sox *had* made the playoffs and he may have gotten caught up in the last game and forgot to call.

"I'm going to the clinic first. It's open until five and I have to check it at least once."

She shook her head. "On your day off? Your dedication is just one of the reasons I love you, Doctor O'Brien."

His turn to arch an eyebrow. "Care to share the others?"

She laughed. "Maybe later," she said, while picking up their clothes from where they'd been strewn in the heat of the moment last night.

He checked his cell for any texts from work. Nothing. Meghan was right, and even though he'd taken the day off, he felt compelled to check in at Havenport Animal Hospital. Ben, his best vet tech, could handle most emergencies, and hopefully his furry patients would cooperate. However, none of his staff knew the real reason for his day off.

Only three people were aware he planned to ask Meghan to marry him, and those didn't include Peg. Holy

God, his mother would have a cow when she found out he'd kept this secret. He'd need more than a dram of Jameson to place that phone call to Margaret O'Brien, Irish guilt personified. Couldn't be helped. Peg and her church bingo hens would be posting it all over social media in half a second. Those old ladies were relentless with their tweets.

"Then where will you go?" Meghan asked, throwing the question over her shoulder and heading to the closet. Her voice sounded innocent, but Meghan was up to something. He'd picked up on clues—a subtle rise in her tone, or when she inadvertently twisted a lock of hair around her index finger. *Yup. There goes the twirl.*

He frowned. "I may take a quick drive into Newport. Why?"

Dylan swung his feet over the side of the bed and grabbed his dress shirt from where he'd flung it last night. Meghan crossed the room and lifted the sexy red dress she'd worn to Bacchanalia for dinner off the floor and folded it over the cushioned armchair.

"Are you going to pester that poor guy at the repair shop again? I'm sure the table is in good hands." She winked and wound her hair into a sloppy ponytail.

He swallowed the lump in his throat but set aside that surge of emotion. "Actually, there's a vet supply one of my patient's owners suggested. The animal shelter needs supplies." Technically, it was kind of the truth. He had to make sure to report his destination to the office since he was the only veterinarian in Havenport and he owned the practice.

"We'll have a homecoming foosball tournament as soon as she's fixed." Her voice held a teasing tone, but he knew she was half serious. Meghan supported his hobbies 100 percent—foosball being one, hockey, and any Boston-based sports team the others. He'd named the table Bea. A bit creepy, he'd admit, but hey, it *had* been his prized possession.

Bea was now a memory, but Meghan didn't know that. "We'll see. What time would you like me home?"

She crinkled her nose then smiled. "I love it when you say home." She bit her lip. "I think six thirty-seven o'clock should be fine."

"Seven is it." The commute from Havenport to Newport wasn't a far drive, but traffic on the weekends could be tough. He still had to make a pit stop at the florist for Meghan's favorite gerbera daisy arrangement. Dylan dropped the shirt on the bed and shoved on a pair of stray boxers from the floor. "I promise I won't go anywhere near Royce's, unless you need me to pick up takeout?"

A sting hit his bicep. *Ouch.* "You taking lessons from Augusta?" His best friend in Havenport had a habit—a bad one—of punching him when she didn't like his comments. Augusta also happened to be dating Meghan's brother, Evan, and spent way too much time feeding Meghan nonsense about *his* bad habits, as if he had any.

"Or," he said, and stalked her around the mattress with his best devilish grin, "if you're into kinky stuff I *can* stay awhile." He raised both eyebrows and deflected another blow while she scooted around the bed.

Her gaze narrowed. "Just make sure you call before you're on the way."

He grabbed her around the waist and tickled her until she squirmed, begging for mercy. He pushed aside the fluffy collar of her robe and nuzzled the side of her neck, breathing in the sweet, clean scent, which reminded him of peaches and cream. "Don't you know by now that anything you do I love," he whispered against her skin. "Simply being able to spend time with you, especially on my birthday, is enough for me. Please, don't go crazy cooking."

She pulled out of his embrace and crossed her arms against the pink terry cloth. "You're planning to grab food before you get home."

Heat invaded his cheeks. Busted.

No way would he say that Meghan's talents lay in interior design—and *not* cooking. If he'd learned anything from Augusta about all things related to relationships—whether he'd wanted the lessons or not—it was to *never* insult a woman's cooking skills.

"I wouldn't dare." He crossed his fingers behind his back, not ruling out a quick trip to Corky's café for a pastrami sandwich.

She pursed her lips and poked him in the middle of his chest. "You just wait and see. This dinner will be stellar, and there will be no burning of your kitchen…this time."

Yeah, her last attempt resulted in smoke filling his entire first floor. Poor Ed had tried to squeeze out the doggie door, difficult at best for the mammoth shepherd. "You know we have a connection in the Havenport FD, so I'm not worried. Mac can come to the rescue," he teased.

"Very funny. Mac and Savannah will be at Christa and Jeremy's wedding tonight. And besides, I will *not* need the fire department, ye of little faith. Go." She pushed him out the bedroom and closed the door with a thud.

Ed, who must have heard them talking, poked his head around the corner of the hall, and with the *click clack* of his nails, came to Dylan's side. He wasn't allowed to sleep in the bedroom whenever Meghan stayed overnight. An enormous tan-and-black fluffy head with its wet, cold nose butted up against him.

"You okay, buddy?"

Ed whined and placed a slobbering lick on Dylan's bare calf. According to the paperwork from his deceased handler, US Marine Sergeant David Prentice, Ed's real name had been Apollo. Except Apollo had never fit for some strange reason, at least not since Ed had come into Dylan's life so unexpectedly last year when he was found on the animal shelter's doorstep in pretty bad shape. With the help of Augusta—Havenport's resident animal lover and dog groomer extraordinaire—they'd patched and cleaned the pooch, and Dylan took him home. Temporarily. *Yeah, right.*

Ed, as it turned out, was a retired MWD, or military working dog, in the EDD or Explosives Detection Dog unit. Ed, short for EDD, fit as far as names went, and the dog had responded right away. That Apollo name reminded Dylan of the boxer character in that '80s movie who got his ass kicked by Sylvester Stallone.

Ed swung his head around and raised his snout toward the stairs, as if to say, "Get a move on. I'm hungry." No doubt Ed thought he was a person. Albeit with powerful jaws that could snap your neck in two seconds. But they'd all learned that anyone Ed grew attached to, he protected life and limb. The dog had done many tours overseas with his handler before the Marine had passed away and Dylan officially adopted him.

Ed was an integral part of the household, which included Meghan, Brielle, and their own crazy pooch, Rambo. Hell, life without any one of them was unimaginable. But a hundred-plus-pound shepherd and a fifteen-pound miniature pinscher made for a very interesting family dynamic.

"*Woof, grrr.*"

Speaking of the small powerhouse, Rambo darted around his large friend, his favorite stuffed giraffe dangling between his teeth. Both dogs pivoted, then bounded for the steps in a symphony of clods against the oak treads. Those troublemakers would be Meghan's problem today. Dylan padded the hallway into the bathroom and regarded his image in the mirror, smoothing the stubborn wave of hair that never seemed to stay styled. Meghan liked it so he didn't have the heart to cut it short.

"Not bad for a man ready to take the plunge," he mumbled. *Note to self: Stop at the dry cleaners for your one good suit and dress shirt before they close, or the jeans and Navy T-shirt you grabbed on the way to the bathroom will be your proposal clothing.* Hell no, he had no plans to propose to the woman he loved looking like a slob. She was a Washburn and grew up in a very high-society life, so he'd better rise to the occasion. He hoped her stupid father and controlling mother would get on board with this and not give Meghan a hard time.

If she says yes.

After a five-minute shower, he dressed and checked the bedroom. Coast clear, he snatched his dress shoes from the closet and a pair of socks from the dresser, stuffing both into a gym bag. "Babe, where are you?"

"Down here."

She'd put on tight yoga pants and one of his Navy sweatshirts, which brushed the tops of her knees. With her face scrubbed free of makeup, Meghan looked more Brielle's age of seventeen than forty.

"I'm trying to feed these two," she said, struggling to drag a new bag of kibble from the pantry closet. Chucking his gym bag by the front door, he hoisted the sack and padded to the kitchen. Ed's and Rambo's noses pressed into the bag before it hit the floor.

"Step back, you two," she ordered, giving each dog a pat on the head. Ed licked her hand to show his affection, knowing he was in for a nice, big bowl of lunch. The moocher.

"You spoil them."

"That's because I love them and they know it. Right, guys?" Barking in unison, they waited for their bowls to be filled before devouring the food.

Meghan held out a steaming cup of coffee and winked. "You men are a jealous bunch. Don't feel left out."

"You spoil me, too. And *I* love it." He sat at the counter table, moaning at the first sip of the rich, biting brew. "God, that's fantastic. Where did you buy it?"

"That new place off Main Street called Deja Brew. I just discovered it yesterday after grocery shopping. It's a wonderful little shop, and so is the owner. She mixes different brews and has all kinds of things for the tea and coffee aficionado. I spotted a machine that does it all."

He noted the dreamy look on her face. "Crazy expensive?"

Meghan rolled her eyes. "Let's just put it this way. It'd be a nice down payment on a car for Brielle." She huffed and sat opposite him. "She's already hounding me about taking driver's education next semester."

He frowned into the dark brew, remembering those times. "Ooh, I cringe when I think back on Shannon learning to drive. Good luck." His kid sister had been a handful. "At least Brielle is a reasonable kid who actually listens to instruction, unlike my sister."

Meghan nodded. "We'll see."

He took a long sip, put the cup down, and reached for her hand across the island. "You love coffee as much as I love my wine. If you want the machine, then buy it." Although he had a feeling bottles of Pétrus might be fewer and farther in between, especially with the cost of her ring. A small sacrifice knowing she'd officially be his and they'd be a family.

If she says yes.

Meghan drew her hand back and plopped a tea bag in a Red Sox mug.

He regarded the steaming brew. "No coffee? You're missing something epic."

Her nose wrinkled. "Not in the mood. My stomach's been off lately. This ginger blend tea is amazing." She hopped off the chair and threw the bag into the trash.

He loved watching how she moved around his kitchen, bare feet padding across the tiles with those sexy red-painted toenails, and the seashell bracelet he'd bought for her at the Cape last year around her left ankle. She reached for the honey in the top shelf of the cabinet adjacent to the fridge and the sweatshirt rode up. He gulped. Nobody in Havenport could compare with Meghan's beauty and outrageous body.

He cleared his throat to force his head back in their convo. "A few of my patients' owners say there's a nasty stomach flu going around," he said, noting the piqued hue to Meghan's face.

Meghan shrugged. "Probably just something I ate."

Dylan rose and stood toe-to-toe with her, pressing his lips to her forehead. "Well, you're cool to the touch, so I think you'll be fine."

She chuckled. "I thank you for the prognosis, Doctor. Shall I bark or lick your hand?"

He peered deeply into her eyes. "I love you."

She sucked in a breath, and her chest rose beneath the sweatshirt. He bent to kiss the spot where the pulse beat in her neck, and her hands fisted at her sides.

"Love you more," she murmured.

"Not possible. Can't wait until later." He threw the words over his shoulder on the way out of the kitchen. Before he closed the front door, he heard her clapping for the dogs to get moving. Yes, today was the first day of the rest of his life, indeed.

Chapter Two

The ladder shifted under her feet, and Meghan's stomach lurched. Damn, why did she have to feel nauseous again?

"Elle, quick, help!" *Omigod.* Heights always made her nervous. Damn this "Happy Birthday Dylan" banner she'd attempted to tack up for over twenty minutes.

A chuckle came from behind. "I don't know why you didn't let me hang that. I am taller."

"Be my guest." Last thing she needed was to twist or break something before Dylan's special surprise. His sleepy, sexy eyes this morning, and that tousled hair that never seemed to behave, made her tingle. *Phew.* That kiss this morning—talk about sizzle. Who knew at forty her hormones would be in overdrive. Everything about Dylan, from his amazing blue eyes to his frat-boy grin, made her quiver. The feelings hadn't abated one iota in the past year. She was a giddy teenager—worse than Brielle acted with her boyfriend, Jacob, most days. It was embarrassing.

Taking a breath, she released the end of the banner and stepped down the ladder, feeling incrementally better once her feet hit solid ground. They half decorated the house with Boston Red Sox and Bruins streamers and posters for his birthday party. The custom banner had seemed like a great idea, until an eight-foot monster showed up via overnight express delivery. The one wall it would fit fully opened was in the living room over the large picture window.

Easier said than done.

Brielle plucked the end of the banner from the floor and repositioned the ladder. "Might be best if we put those sticky hooks up *first* and loop this end-tie through using a broom or something," Brielle suggested.

"And that is why I rave about my brilliant daughter to everyone in Havenport."

Brielle tossed a lock of her long hair away from her eyelash and grinned. "I think you're just nervous, or you would definitely have thought of it yourself, madam decorator," she teased.

"I am not." Warmth spread to up her neck. Well, she kind of was.

That earned another chuckle. Brielle rolled her eyes, grabbed the plastic adhesives, and shook her head as if to say, "yeah, Mom, preach it." Watching Brielle work, she couldn't be happier at her daughter's enthusiasm in helping to plan Dylan's birthday and keep it a secret.

With mile-long legs, Brielle scaled the ladder, stretched her long arms, and stuck the last hook onto the painted wall. At five-eleven, Meghan figured Brielle had finally stopped growing. Now seventeen, her daughter was striking—supermodel gorgeous, and a beautiful person both inside and out. Her long, pin-straight, shiny hair hit well past the small of her back. Meghan was insanely jealous given her mane's propensity to frizz at the slightest precipitation. High cheekbones and a sculptured nose enhanced Brielle's wide blue eyes. And, Jeez, her French runway model figure, which she got from her father's side of the family tree, equaled stunning. No doubt about it,

Brielle turned heads. But her daughter remained blessedly unaware of the reaction her outward appearance rendered from people, especially boys. Most times Brielle came off as shy, almost uncertain. Except around animals. Then she shined and connected to her furry friends on an altogether different plain.

Fortunate didn't begin to describe how she felt every day that their relationship had grown into more than just mother and daughter. They each held a mutual admiration for each other as women, with a solid respect and genuine friendship thrown into a deep and abiding love. The type of relationship she'd yearned for with her own mother, but Mrs. Washburn, Havenport's resident matriarch, wouldn't dream of it.

After moving to Havenport—or back to Havenport—over a year ago, she'd never have banked on the state of their bond being as good as it stood. And the other amazing relationship in her life, the total head-over-heels-in-love one with Dylan O'Brien, would have been the last thing she'd expected to go along with relocating. But here today, planning the thirty-fifth-birthday surprise for the man she loved—the hunky town vet who every woman in Havenport wanted, but *she'd* landed—was where she was meant to be.

"We could use one of Dylan's hockey sticks," she told Brielle.

"Good idea, Mom. I'll just wait here and check for dust bunnies on the ceiling," Brielle called out from atop the ladder.

"Wise guy," she mumbled and trailed down the hall to the closet next to the powder room. She meant to grab a hockey stick and return to Brielle right away before her daughter did clean the dust bunnies, for Brielle had turned into a neat freak the past year, but a wave of nausea belted her stomach. *Uh-oh.* Throwing open the powder room door, she stepped in and clicked the lock. Heaven forbid Brielle heard the gagging and came rushing in. In a flash, she flipped up the toilet lid and proceeded to lose what had been lunch. The retching wouldn't stop. Eyes clenched, she fought a wave of dizziness by blindly grabbing at the wall and finally connecting to the mounted paper holder for balance.

The clenching in her gut made it hard to breathe, so she tried her best to do it through her nose. Sweat beads formed on her upper lip, the salty taste mingling with the disgusting tang in her mouth. Once the last wave subsided, she turned and flushed with a grimace. She used her shaky hands to splash water onto her face, and rinsed out her mouth.

"Mom, you okay?" Brielle's muffled voice sounded over the running water.

She killed the faucet and took a deep breath. "I'll be right out." What a horror show. She resembled one of those sunken-eyed zombies in the show Brielle watched on her computer. Had she contracted that stupid stomach bug? When was the last home consultation for Haven on Earth Designs? She whipped out her phone from her back jeans pocket and scrolled the appointments in the calendar. Mrs. Nolan had a child, or was it two? In any case, that dated back to September first.

A red *X* sat on the screen next to that date. Just out of curiosity she swiped the screen forward to October, but there were no other red *X* marks next to any dates for the whole month. *Think back.* Her heartbeat sped, thumping a steady beat in her eardrum. *Oh, shit.* She and Dylan had stayed overnight in Danbury for the Fall Festival in that cute B and B in October. And yes, there was lots of wine and lots of sex.

Meghan closed her eyes and gripped the bathroom vanity, trying to suck air through her nose. Lavender from the air mist plug-in wafted into her nose, soothing her stomach a little, until her suspicions started again.

How long?

"No way. It's just stress, or perimenopause," she murmured to her reflection. Yeah, that's a lame explanation. She'd just wait and see. Knowing Brielle waited, she took one last stare at the mirror, straightened her shoulders, and turned the doorknob.

Brielle rifled in the hall closet where Dylan kept athletic equipment, her rear end sticking out from the tons of stuff hanging on the rod. Meghan knew the single light bulb dangling from the ceiling made it impossible to see the myriad of crap inside.

"This place is a mess." Brielle wrestled with a hanger on her way out. "And it smells like the locker rooms in school."

Meghan nodded. "Tell me about it. I've been after Dylan to clean it out before something falls out and knocks someone unconscious."

"What is all this stuff, anyway?" Brielle pulled out Dylan's hockey jersey, which, in her opinion belonged in the garbage can.

"Eww." Brielle pinched her nose between two fingers.

Meghan's hand shot over her mouth and nose. "That's his lucky Havenport Hammers championship jersey," she muffled into her palm. With a grimace, she swapped Brielle the gross shirt for a hockey stick. "Here, use this to hang the banner."

Brielle hoisted the stick over her right shoulder and sauntered back to the family room while Meghan stuffed the jersey back on a hanger and shoved it way back in the closet. *Jeez*, Dylan and his prized possessions. The sports gear was as bad as Bea, the foosball table, whose absence seemed to be causing him separation anxiety. At least the table would soon be fixed and back where it belonged: in the middle of the family room.

More banners cluttered the tiny closet, making it impossible to get the door closed once anyone opened it. Maybe if she did it quickly, she'd have luck—but a giant red Havenport Hammers foam finger got stuck in the jam. She yanked it out and heard the rip. Yeah, the finger needed surgery. *Oh, well.*

All of Dylan's *stuff* played serious havoc with her OCD design tendencies, but his hobbies and interests came with the whole Dr. Dylan O'Brien package, especially since the Havenport Hammers beat the Newport Nooners and named him their captain. The whole team hoisted him on their shoulders and skated around the rink. Dylan's reaction had been priceless.

To ask that he throw out the countless items associated with that game would be criminal. Not that she minded all that much. Watching him skate during those playoff games, getting physical and showing off his muscles, not only made him damned hot to watch, but the whole camaraderie of the team wives and girlfriends made for the best times of her life. Who knew she'd grow to like sports? From high-society cocktail parties in New York, to beer victory parties at Royce Tavern.

Her life had taken a monumental turn for the better—stinky equipment aside.

She froze, hand on the knob, her mind not registering said equipment all over the floor. Lately, all kinds of smells inside and outside the closet *had* made her want to gag.

"Crap." She tossed the finger onto the shelf. Dylan's birthday party took priority. No time to ponder that scenario until there was no other choice. She closed the door when Ed's wet nose suddenly pressed against her palm and stopped the motion.

"Hey, bud, are you looking for your blanket?" The dog whined as if to say yes, and Meghan smiled. The way Ed responded when spoken directly to made him seem almost human. Aside from him being one of the most intelligent creatures Meghan had ever encountered, he was super protective, which made her feel safe.

"It's in the wash." A sandpaper-like tongue swiped at her thumb. She stroked his mammoth head up to the tips of his clipped ears. He grunted before flexing over to sniff Dylan's hockey gloves on the bottom of the closet. Whenever Dylan remained away from the house for a long period of time, Ed, too, experienced separation anxiety.

"I miss him, too. Don't you worry, big guy. He'll be back soon." Ed straightened, and she bent to give him a kiss on the furry head.

A high-pitched yelp pierced the air, and Ed answered with his deep *woof* before he galloped off to his buddy, Rambo. Rambo might be a miniature pinscher in terms of breed and size, but he ruled their roost. Amazing how Ed could easily devour Rambo for a snack with his powerful bite and lethal canines, yet the large pooch was gentle as a lamb around his best friend.

Between the pouncing, food snatching, and hogging the couch, Ed never batted an eye at the abuse. Must be a far cry from the life she could imagine Ed experienced as a bomb-sniffing dog in the military.

The dogs played tug of war in the living room with Rambo's favorite toy. She chuckled.

How lucky could she be?

Between Brielle and the dogs, and, of course, Dylan, this was a life she'd never thought possible after divorcing Jacques. The life she'd always longed for was finally unfolding. A stable home, down-to-earth people with no pretense or care about how many Louis Vuitton bags she had in her closet. A real family.

And maybe a bigger one than you planned?

The back pocket of her jeans vibrated with her cell phone, pulling her out of her reverie. *Unknown caller.* Might be a potential new client. "Haven on Earth, this is Meghan Washburn."

Crackling sounded in her ear. She strained to make out the words on the other end, but the voice faded in and out of the static.

"Hello?" More crackling. "Is anyone there?"

A beep signaled the call had dropped. She frowned at the screen and tried to get the number from her recent list. Nothing came up.

"If it's important they'll call back."

In the living room, Brielle leaned her long torso over the ladder with the string of the sign looped around the hockey stick.

"Be careful. Don't stretch like that or you'll fall."

"Relax, Mom. I got it." Deftly, Brielle hung the banner in place.

"Perfect. I do believe everything is on schedule. Uncle Evan's on his way to the airport to get Margaret." She glanced at her watch. "Her flight is supposed to land at four and is still on time according to the website, despite the stupid snow." She crossed her fingers on both hands. "I don't want to jinx anything, especially when I have to cook."

Margaret O'Brien—*Peg*, as Dylan called his mother— was the surprise along with the surprise party for his birthday. Augusta and Evan would be here, of course, to help celebrate.

What was she thinking by trying to replicate Peg's famous stuffed crown roast of pork for the birthday celebration dinner? She ached to make a good impression with his mother. They'd met briefly last Christmas when her relationship with Dylan was in its infancy. Peg, along with his sister, Shannon, and brother, Danny, couldn't have been more welcoming to her and Brielle. They were loud and warm and the kind of family that made you feel cherished. This weekend she'd make it a point to get to know Margaret. It might be nice to have a mother figure who actually cared. Mrs. Washburn would never win Mother of the Year.

"No offense, but you're much better at interior decorating than cooking." Brielle poked her head and arms through the Havenport High sweatshirt she'd strewn over the banister.

"Truer words were never spoken, sadly. Which is why I need to finish decorating so I can concentrate on *not* screwing up the food. Make sure Augusta gets the cake from Led Zeppoli."

"Already done, Mom." Brielle cooed at the partners in crime who, as usual, were by her side. Rambo held streamers in his mouth while Ed pawed at the tape dispenser. "I'll even get something for these snuggle bunnies. You want ice cream?"

Meghan groaned. "Take them to play in the backyard and hope the snow wears them out."

Brielle chuckled. "Come on, you two."

Grabbing the remnants of streamers and tape from the floor, Meghan took one more look around the rooms. The decor was as good as it was going to get. She grudgingly made her way back toward the kitchen.

"I'm so outta my league here," she muttered, and hoped for the best. There was always takeout from Mellie's Diner as the worst-case, last-ditch scenario.

Chapter Three

Evan Washburn checked his watch and sprinted from where he'd parked his Jeep to the main entrance of Providence airport. An hour late was a freaking miracle. Felt like he'd been on the road forever. Not only did the traffic from Havenport into Providence suck, the roads were becoming more treacherous by the moment, which made people drive like idiots.

Christ, the temps remained frigid. What the hell with this snowstorm? He turned up his jacket collar to block the wind and stepped onto the curb. He yanked off his skullcap and shook off snowflakes as the automatic doors to the airport terminal swished open. Hordes of people camped out on the floor and rows of connected plastic chairs lined the waiting areas. He passed the check-in counter and complaining passengers four-deep in line. Maneuvering around a woman, he came upon two kids dragging their superhero suitcases. One of the rug rats stopped short and turned around, whacking into his prosthetic leg.

"Whoa," he blurted, although he didn't feel the blow, and there was no damage, but damn, he did a quick two-step to avoid colliding with the person walking behind. The woman wore earbuds and scooted around to his left. She turned her head with a sneer, and threw him the stink-eye.

"Not my fault," he announced, and pointed to both creatures staring up at him like he was Godzilla. Being six-four made him a bit intimidating. The boy's brother—presumably, since they had identical features—chose that exact moment to yell at the top of his lungs.

"Hulk smash!"

Evan cringed. He shouted again, and Evan resisted the urge to plug his ears. Then the brat used said Hulk suitcase as a battering ram to his twin's stomach. The brother doubled over in pain and fell over.

"That's gonna leave a bruise," Evan mumbled under his breath, and hid his smirk. *Jeez*, this place was more dangerous than the shithole streets of Kabul, where he'd patrolled with the Corps.

Civilian life sometimes made him twitchy.

"Flight seven eight four from Logan, please use baggage area three," came the nasal voice through the airport intercom.

"What a zoo," he mumbled. The luggage carousel beeped and a red light flashed before it started its slow spin. Looked as if the flight from Boston had been booked to capacity. Throngs of people herded forward to grab their suitcases. One guy hoisted his rucksack and walloped the person standing next to him. People had no concept of respect or personal space. Thankfully his height afforded a view over the top of most heads. Maybe he should have made a sign with Margaret's name on it, instead of standing around like a lost lamb searching for a woman he'd never met.

He pulled out his phone from his coat and swiped to the picture Meghan sent this morning. Not much help there. The best he could make out was a woman with blondish hair, maybe around five-six. A cell number was listed below the picture.

"Evan Washburn?" He was just about to hit the phone icon when the question came from behind. He pivoted on his good foot to a woman staring up at him with a curious smile.

Dylan described his mother as a churchgoing woman in her sixties, and on the matronly side. This woman was far from it. Perhaps this lady was one of his constituents? Being Havenport's town councilman, he'd met a ton of people from the surrounding Rhode Island towns. She kind of reminded him of an older version of Christie Brinkley with her wide smile and blue eyes. Yeah, he had a serious crush on that model back in the day. This woman wore heeled boots with a black-belted quilted jacket, and held her phone.

"Ms. O'Brien?"

She let out a breath, seeming relieved, and put her phone back in her purse. "Yes, I am. I was just about to phone your sister for your number. Please, call me Peg."

"Yes, ma'am." On instinct, he reached for her suitcase, as well as the bag slung over her right shoulder.

"Thank you," she said, handing over her bag. "Those people are crazy." She tipped her head to the crowd. Her eyes twinkled like the shimmering water in his parents' palatial pool. His mother was pushing seventy, and despite various "work" she'd denied having done by her plastic surgeon, Mom wore her age. This woman did not. Dylan needed serious work on his descriptive ability.

Peg smoothed back her hair with long, manicured fingernails in blood red and *tsked* at the crowd. "Such impatience. Thank Jesus my bag came off first."

"I do, too." A guy to his right started an argument and tug of war with a lady and her suitcase. "Might be time to get outta here before this turns ugly." Evan steered Peg with a hand on her back. "I apologize for being late. The weather didn't cooperate with the drive from Havenport."

"Don't apologize. I wasn't waiting long. The plane was delayed. Your lovely sister texted me your picture, but I have to admit I was searching the throngs for a man in running shorts and a tight ass." She winked.

Evan's step faltered, causing Peg's suitcase to teeter onto its side. Heat catapulted to his face and he knew he couldn't hide his shocked expression. *Holy!* He righted the wheels and swallowed hard. He sputtered, and mucus from the damned postnasal drip he'd been fighting all week pooled at the back of his throat. His eyes burned and he fought to catch a clear breath. A second later, she pounded on the middle of his back.

"Are you okay?" She peered up into his face, which he knew was beet red. Good going.

"Look up at the light," she ordered in a voice that reminded him of his old grammar school principal. Yeah, except Mrs. Langston had never complimented his ass in the fifth grade.

Meghan owed him big-time for this favor. Finally able to suck in oxygen after the coughing fit, he waved a hand in her direction. "No worries. I'm fine, I swear. Just getting over a nasty cold, that's all."

A glower marred her face, and he swore she was contemplating checking his forehead for fever. "You need water," she declared. "I spotted concessions up there." She pointed toward a row of vendors set up next to a newsstand. "Be right back."

Before he could object, Peg darted away in a flash of blond hair and boot heels clicking on the tiled floor, leaving him to wonder what the hell just transpired. Augusta was going to crack up when he told her about this calamity. Speaking of which, his phone dinged the barking dog text tone he'd chosen for the love of his life.

Just heard they might close the intercourse.

He arched an eyebrow and typed, *Huh?*

Introspective. Oh hell. Roads. The roads are bad. Hate autocorrect. Love you, though.

He chuckled. Augusta hadn't mastered texting quite yet. His phone vibrated, and Mayor Owen Henry's Office flashed on-screen. "Evan Washburn."

"Evan, have you seen this weather?"

"As a matter…" he started to respond, but the mayor cut him off, as usual. Mayor Henry could be a bit high strung at times.

"Highly unpredictable. Might be prudent to think about limiting the roads in and out of Havenport to authorized personnel only."

Mayor Henry continued to buzz on about ice and wind and power issues. Phone to ear, Evan listened and trudged to a large window, dragging Peg's bags with him.

"Owen, I'm at the airport in Providence. It's coming down at a steady clip here." Question was what the impact might be closing off Havenport with the Saturday-night dinner crowd. Many folks drove in to patronize the myriad of small restaurants in town. Since elected town councilman, he'd made it a point to recognize and encourage entrepreneurs to set up shop in Havenport. Lots of new businesses had opened this past year. However, the safety of everyone in town, as well as visitors, came first.

"Might be a good idea," he answered reluctantly—or tried to, but the mayor clamored on about dispatching extra police and volunteer fire personnel. Evan highly doubted the storm conditions would warrant that type of emergency.

"I'll call from the road. If it lets up in an hour or so we may be able to salvage the rest of the weekend." Evan clicked off the phone and glanced out the terminal window.

His breath fogged the panes. With all the hype about global warming at every Town Hall in the past year, nothing about weather patterns should come as a surprise. But still, this type of snowstorm seemed awfully strange for early November. Not one plane had budged from a gate within sight. The clouds were a dark, ominous gray. It was coming up on six, and the fringes of darkness had begun to fall. *Shit.* Dylan was due home from Newport shortly. He'd better get his ass moving. If he was late bringing Peg home, Meghan would kill him for ruining her surprise. He spotted Peg walking toward him.

"Here you go." She handed him a water bottle and waited while he took a long swig. "Feeling better?"

Evan wiped a droplet of water from his mouth on his jacket sleeve. "Much. Thank you."

"I certainly hope you wore a hat." She shook her head in disgust and peered out the window. "I've seen *plenny* of snow in my day growing up in the Back Bay. Lived in my house for going on *foddy* years, you know. There's something to be said for the Rhode Island *chahm*, but this weather is bullshit."

Evan smirked, liking her Boston accent with "*plenny* of," and he suspected *foddy* was *forty*. This was more like the woman Dylan described. He'd heard Peg was strong; a single mother who'd worked three jobs and raised three kids alone. His stress level subsided a bit.

This Peg, the concerned-for-his-health mother-like figure, he could handle. Cougar Peg? Not so much. You'd think with being in a steady relationship with Augusta he'd mastered how to handle women. Nope. They constantly kept him guessing. He whipped his hat and gloves from his jacket pocket and held them up. "Gloves, too."

"I've heard you Marines are always prepared." She winked and extracted a hat from her pocket, placing it on her perfectly coiffed hair.

He hooted and picked up her bags. "Yes, ma'am. Now, let's go or we won't make it there before Dylan. I do not relish being on Meghan's shit list, pardon the language."

Peg whooped. "Language? Ha! You should join my church group for our monthly poker game. Your ears would melt."

"I'd be honored." He placed a hand under her elbow to ensure she carefully stepped onto the moving treads of the down escalators leading to the parking area. Once on the ground floor, Peg fell into step next to him.

"I'm sure you're exaggerating about your dear sister. I'm just thrilled my son got his head out of his ass and found a real woman instead of the little coed twits he used to date."

They passed another gift shop and newsstand with the metal gates down. Guess some of the airport staff had gone home due to the weather. Evan kept his pace slow and steady, although Peg could probably outrun him, his prosthetic Terminator leg notwithstanding. But damn it was hot in here. Beads of sweat dripped between his shoulder blades down his back. His jeans were starting to rub and stick to the place where his prosthetic and stump met. Thankfully they'd be in his Jeep shortly. "I parked my Jeep in the lot, but I'll bring it around to the double doors," he told her. "No need for you to walk in the snow."

Peg snapped the buttons on her coat closed and arranged her scarf. "Very chivalrous of you. I cannot wait to get to Dylan's place. I acted like I'd forgotten his birthday was coming up when he called this week. He sounded crushed." She snickered deviously.

Oh yeah, Peg shared his sense of humor. However, Dylan wasn't the only person in for a surprise tonight, and the sooner they got to Havenport, the better for everyone. Together they ambled toward a car rental kiosk where a slender woman in a button-down shirt tried to placate an irate customer.

"What do you mean, there are no available cars?" The man's voice rose, and a few people milling nearby stopped to stare. "This *eez* an outrage." He slammed his palm on the desk, causing the girl to flinch.

Evan growled under his breath. That was no way to speak to a lady. The young woman, not much older than Brielle and clearly frazzled at the man's ranting, typed furiously on the console. "I'm sorry, sir, but we're closing. My manager advised no more cars to be dispatched due to the weather."

"I demand to see someone in charge," he shouted, and stamped his foot—a real diva move, given the dude wore an expensive suit and tie. There was something familiar about the guy's build from behind. Stocky, a bit squatty with thick muscles, and a sausage roll at the back of his neck where his cropped hair met his white collar. Almost like a cartoon character. Take Brutus's large head, complete with his five-o'clock shadow, and plop it on Popeye's body. The hairs on the back of Evan's neck stood on end.

Peg let out a huff. "Oh, Lord, not that *chowdahead.* What an ass."

Evan glanced at her sideways. "You two know each other?"

She puckered, like she'd eaten a lemon. "Hell no. What a rude man. Practically pushed me out of the way when I bought the waters." She sneered at the man's back and shook her head in disgust. "Some men think a Rolex and Ferragamo loafers make the man."

His radar heightened a few notches. No way. French accent, loafers, clearly a lack of manners. Yes way, apparently. The man rotated, giving Evan a good look at his profile. Evan's body tightened. "That lousy motherfu…"

Peg placed a hand on his forearm, her grip surprisingly firm through his leather bomber jacket. She stopped him from taking the step forward he hadn't realized he was about to.

"Now, Evan." She cocked her head to the side and regarded him. "I doubt you'd let a fool like that one get the satisfaction of your reaction, would you?"

Evan glanced down at Peg's hand, then covered it with his and gave it a short squeeze. "My reaction isn't what he should be worried about."

Peg's eyes lit with understanding. "Ahh, I take it *you* know him?"

"Unfortunately. And I'd like to know what in the hell he's doing in my state." He eyeballed Jacques now arguing with someone else, presumably the manager. Evan steered Peg toward one of the cushioned chairs near the exit. He propped her suitcase against the wall and placed her carry-on bag on the floor. "I'll be right back."

"Should I have the bail money ready?" she asked with a straight face.

The corner of his mouth lifted. He and Peg were going to be best friends by the end of this weekend. "You don't know me very well...yet. I seldom lose control, at least not anymore. Losing a limb kinda puts things into perspective."

Peg nodded, brushed a piece of lint off her sleeve, and batted her eyelashes. "You know, I took a martial arts class. They'd never arrest a sixty-two-year-old woman," she whispered behind her hand. Her eyes glittered. Hell, she was thoroughly enjoying herself.

"Good to know." Evan let out a long breath and tried not to clench his teeth. Time to face a situation that he'd neither expected nor wanted, especially on a night like tonight. He strolled toward Jacques, who was in the throes of a full-fledged whine session. Oh, joy—Jacques The Jerk all in a tither. His bitch sessions were legendary, had happened quite frequently when he'd been married to Meg. All that huffing and puffing made the French idiot sweat. Profusely. Evan's nose twitched at the sweat dripping from Jacques's forehead down to his unibrow. What a hairy bastard. Never could figure out Meg's attraction to him other than the money, which in truth turned out to be a mirage. Asshole had tried to suck every penny from Meghan's bank accounts, and nearly did. Evan took a breath through his mouth. Damn, the stinking man-perfume Jacques wore had started to ferment.

"Is there a problem, Miss..." Evan regarded the woman's name tag. "Brennan?" Might as well play it off slick, and surprise the a-hole. *Can't wait for that reaction.*

"No, sir," she answered, her attention shifting away from Jacques.

More huffing, then Jacques spun around. "Excuse me, *I'm* talking..."

And just like that, the words ceased, thank the heavens. Jacques's eyes widened and his chest expanded like one of those puffer fish. If Evan wasn't blindsided, and pissed off, he might have found the sight comical. Jacques lifted his chin, attempting to stare down his nose at Evan. A bit hard to accomplish given he topped the wimp by a good five inches. With a dramatic flair, Jacques smoothed out his French-cut sleeves, adjusted the gaudy cuff links, and whirled around on expensive loafer heels, giving Evan his back.

Un-fucking-real. Evan glued fisted hands to his jeans. Oh, he so wanted to pummel that smug face into a sweaty French pulp.

"Cost is no concern," Evan heard Jacques tell the manager. "I need a car. Now."

Evan recognized the manager—Johnny Arnold. Played football for Providence High back in the day. John topped six-five and weighed a good two-fifty. John held Evan's gaze over Jacques's head, ignoring the French-tard, as Augusta called him. Jacques whipped out a wad of bills from his suit jacket pocket, in what Evan could only imagine was the idiot's attempt to get John's undivided attention. Yeah, John didn't seem impressed.

John tipped up his chin. "Hey, Evan. Good to see you, man."

"Same here, John. Problem?" He slanted his head to Jacques.

John barely gave Jacques a second glance. "Nope." Then John smiled, showing pearly whites, which contrasted with his cocoa skin and glossy baldness. "Sarah," he said to the girl, "see if Councilman Washburn needs assistance."

The girl's gaze darted between them, and she gripped her pen. "Oh. Of course."

Jacques sputtered, muttering a few not-so-nice French words under his breath.

"Actually," Evan said, "I'll take care of this one." He made a point to stare at Jacques. "You two close up shop and get home safe."

"What?" Jacques cried. "They're not going anywhere until I get a rental car."

"Sir." John splayed his immense hands on the counter, leaned over, and got real close to Jacques. His deep voice boomed like a cannonball shot, making everyone in the vicinity flinch.

"Have a good evening." And with that, John gave Evan a quick two-finger salute before escorting Sarah away from the counter.

"This is an outrage," Jacques sputtered, his face an unflattering shade of mottled crimson.

Against his better judgment, Evan reviewed the scenario in his head. The weather sucked, Jacques's whining shit had gotten old ten minutes ago, and Peg needed to get to Dylan's, pronto. Oh, and his patience was on empty.

Evan kept his expression blank and regarded Jacques. "Why are you here?"

Jacques seemed to be debating spilling, but must've realized he was up shit creek without a paddle, or without a rental car to be exact.

"I need to see Meghan. Right away." He emphasized the last two words in that French accent that made Evan's eardrums bleed.

Evan crossed his arms. "What for?"

Jacques had the audacity to give Evan a once-over, acting like the goddamned king of France. "None of your business."

Anger shot to his scalp like a bullet. Enough. Like a panther, he tracked forward and got up in Jacques's space, not giving a shit who might be watching. Nose to nose, Jacques was forced to back up against the car rental counter. Hard. That would definitely leave a bruise.

"Listen, you arrogant piece of turd," he said in a low voice. "You're in no position to be withholding anything about my sister. That relationship is over."

Jacques attempted to twist sideways, but Evan made that maneuver impossible with a shift of his shoulder to block the movement. He placed his real foot strategically between Jacques's feet. Effective.

"So you say." Jacques smirked.

Evan frowned at the man and prayed for patience. "What are you blabbering about?" Okay, so yeah, his patience had officially left the building. "I suggest you clarify before you lose the ability to speak."

That must've hit home. Jacques turned a shade paler and swallowed hard. God, a whiff of that shit he bathed in wafted up Evan's nose. He held back a sneeze.

"Meghan and I aren't divorced."

It took a moment for that bombshell to sink in. Meanwhile, trepidation crept into his scalp. "Like hell you're not." His words boomed louder than was probably necessary despite his best attempts to keep it at a low decibel. "What kind of horseshit are you slinging? If you're thinking for one second about trying to reconcile with my sister, or going anywhere near my niece again, you're fucking delusional."

Jacques's expression grew incredulous. "I want no such thing. That woman is a b—"

"Watch what you say," he said between clenched teeth. "Or you'll be eating through a straw indefinitely."

Jacques whipped out his phone from his lapel pocket and sputtered. "I will not be threatened by the likes of you." Spit shot from his lips. "I don't care what kind of pull you think you have in this shitty little state. Bah, Councilman," he scoffed. "I'll have you arrested."

Evan snatched the phone from his fingers. "I repeat, tell me what you mean by you and my sister not being divorced. Now."

Jacques blanched. "I will, *eef* you back up. Ever heard of personal space?"

A tick clamored a staccato beat in his cheek, and it was all Evan could do to not snarl at the a-hole. *Oh, boy.* Meghan owed him big-time for dealing with this fiasco. In fact, he'd insist she host "The Old Man" Washburn every Father's Day from now until he croaked. And given how much of a mean bastard father-dear was, he'd probably outlive everyone.

Evan drew in a breath for control, backed up, and held out an arm for Jacques to move aside. "Here you go, Princess."

Jacques's nostrils flared and he whipped his briefcase off the counter. "*Mon dieu!* You're a brute. If you must know, I have tried to reach Meghan for the past few days, to no avail. You think I'd come to this backward state otherwise?"

He'd let that insult slide for now. "Not caring about your travel preferences. Get to the point."

"Can you believe she has not responded?" Jacques asked, as if thoroughly insulted and thoroughly full of himself.

Was he for real? "Why the hell would she? You're a first-class douchebag in your business. You were a shitty husband, and a worse father."

Jacques recoiled at the choice of words, and it felt like a million bucks to throw all his shortcomings in his smug face. His lips did that pursing action again. Evan rolled his eyes and shook his head, wishing an end to their conversation. Yet Jacques's sudden appearance was probably important. Jacques displayed the antithesis of what a real man should be. With disgust, he regarded the styled hair and Armani suit. He stood sneering and waving his hands like a dandy. He was grateful Meghan changed her taste in wastrels like Jacques and hooked up with a good man.

Dylan was former Navy—at least he'd been a Corpsman—and Evan respected the veteran and veterinarian 100 percent.

Jacques zeroed in on Evan's face. "It's all your sister's fault. She put the wrong date of our marriage on the divorce papers. When I went to get a new license to marry Ginny, they wouldn't give it until it *eez* fixed." He threw up his hands like a stage actor taking a bow. "So there you have the sordid details. Are you quite satisfied?"

"I'd be satisfied if you left the country, or better yet, the planet." Evan was about to turn away when a thought struck. "Let me get this straight. You flew from New York to get papers signed? Why not go through your fancy lawyers, or send them in overnight mail?" Seemed like an inconvenient detail easily rectified, but what the hell did he know about divorce? As far as he was concerned, that disaster of a marriage should never have happened. Meg had sole custody of Brielle, the only good thing to come from their union.

Jacques waved a hand in the air. "Better to do *eet* myself."

Evan's sixth sense kicked like a mule. The same sense which saved his ass in battle more times than he wished to recall. He shook a finger under Jacques's nose. "No, no, no. You've never done jack shit for yourself. What's the real reason you needed to do this in person?"

Jacques's gaze darted down and to the left while he cleared his throat and wiped his brow with some kind of handkerchief thing. Who used those anymore? Evan waited, although time was ticking.

"My wedding is next weekend."

Evan's mouth fell open. Well, well, good old Jacques must be desperate. "And what happens if this doesn't get done?"

Eyes bulging, Jacques's hands fidgeted with the handle of his briefcase. "Ginny will back out and will never finance my restaurant."

Evan almost felt sorry for the desperation coming out of his ex-brother-in-law—almost. His grin spread. "Seems like you're in a pickle, aren't you?"

"Ahem." A throat cleared from behind. Christ, he'd forgotten about Peg. She must have heard the whole sordid affair from Jacques's loose lips. He froze. If Meghan wasn't quite divorced, how the hell was Dylan going to react, and on the night he'd planned to pop the freaking question? Anxiety hit his gut in waves. *Shit.* What a disaster.

"Evan, may I speak with you for a moment?" Peg appeared next to him and he had to give her an A for effort in not sneering or spitting at Jacques.

Evan nodded tightly. "Of course. You. Don't go anywhere."

Jacques scoffed at the same second his cell phone rang. He swiped the screen, put the phone to his ear, and pivoted before Evan heard a French *hello*.

Evan navigated Peg a safe distance away and bent his head while keeping an eye on the a-hole. "Look, I don't know how much of that you heard, but that's my ex-brother-in-law, Jacques LaRue, Meghan's shitball of an ex-husband, whom she hates and wanted dead...not that she's bloodthirsty like that or anything," he added. Yeah, he was a rambling idiot. But, for some reason, explaining this to Peg felt like the right thing to do. "He needs papers signed."

Peg nodded, lips compressed. "So I heard, along with the rest of Providence." She glared at the subject at hand. "It appears he needs it done now?"

A sharp pain pierced between Evan's shoulder blades. What he was about to recommend had *catastrophe* written all over it. "Yeah, and I thi—"

"And," Peg interrupted with a stern expression, once again aiming her focus on Jacques, "it seems this minor detail stands in the way of Meghan being rid of the shitball, as you say, for good?"

Evan's mouth opened and closed a few times but no sound escaped.

Peg sighed heavily and once again placed a hand on Evan's forearm. "I had a shitball in another life, unfortunately. It's obvious you love your sister immensely, and I would gladly help you hide the body," she said with a devious glint in her eyes. "However, I suggest we get him what he needs before he fucks up my son's birthday. Otherwise, they'll never find his body." She smiled sweetly and batted eyelashes, but underneath Evan knew she meant business.

"We could've used you in the Marine Corps," he said with the utmost respect. Maybe this calamity could be waylaid and Dylan's proposal and celebration salvaged. Although a nagging feeling of impending doom hit his gut—and he never ignored that particular sensation.

Peg cleared her throat and donned her coat. She must've taken it off once this little bullshit interlude had begun. His body temp had reached inferno level, so she had to be uncomfortable as well. Peg clucked her tongue at the compliment. Face determined, she rotated toward Jacques, who stood against the wall speaking fluent French to someone on the phone.

"Now, you call Meghan and fill her in. It's only right to let her prepare for an unexpected visitor. Maybe she can stall Dylan's arrival, while *I* inform Mr. Shitball how this request of his will transpire." Peg tugged the belt of her coat tight and licked her lips. "Go." Her eyebrows rose, as if to tell him to get a move on, and he hopped into action.

After an emotionally charged call to Meghan—boy, she sounded spitting mad and stunned—they finally slid—literally—onto the road to Havenport. Evan had no idea what Peg had said to Jacques, but he was quiet as a mouse sitting in the back of the Jeep, laden with Peg's suitcases across his lap. He'd even tried complaining about the heat, or lack thereof, in the vehicle, but Peg gave him a stern look over her shoulder and he shut his trap.

Evan drove on, anticipating seeing the Havenport Town sign.

Holy! The storm seemed to have worsened. Visibility sucked. He could barely make out the street signs and traffic lights covered in the white powder. Thank God he knew his way around Havenport with his eyes closed.

He needed a drink.

Chapter Four

Meghan stared at her cell phone, hands shaking, mind racing.

The backs of her knees hit the couch and she sank onto the cushion. Not divorced? How was that even possible? She had the divorce decree. She'd changed her name back to Washburn, for crying out loud. Now this came up. It was more than a year later and many, many arguments over his lack of support for Brielle. What the hell?

Shock, anger, and a knot the size of Dylan's prized Wade Boggs baseball sunk in her stomach. Then a seething anger grew, sparked by Jacques—the biggest mistake of her life. Spitting mad was a great antidote for wanting to puke.

"OMG, Meg. That roast smells heavenly," Augusta gushed when she glided into the family room, a large cake box from Led Zeppoli perched across her arms. "Phew, it's snowing like crazy. Wearing my new Vera's tonight might have not been my wisest choice."

She was too numb to acknowledge the compliment, Augusta's gorgeous knee boots, or the weather report. All she could muster as tears blurred her vision was to glance up at her friend.

"What's wrong?" Augusta placed the box on the coffee table and hurried to her side.

"This night is ruined." She buried her face in her hands, wanting to crawl upstairs and sleep for a year.

"Don't be silly. You did a terrific job with decorating and the food."

As always, Augusta would make the best of the situation. She'd truthfully never met a more glass-half-full person, but her hearing ability ceased when the ringing in her ears started, along with the panic. What would Dylan do when he found out he'd been sleeping with a married woman for the past year?

Blood rushed from her head, and she clung to the arm of the couch. Oh, jeez, what was Brielle going to think? And Peg? *So much for making a good impression.* Her palms grew clammy. The couch cushions shifted with Augusta's weight.

"You're scaring me. What happened? Is it Evan?" Augusta snatched her hand, forcing her look up into her friend's pale face under all that gorgeous olive skin.

Get a grip, Meghan. Time to stop making everyone else panic. "No, he's fine." She squeezed Augusta's hand and managed a weak smile. "It's…well…" The words stuck in her esophagus. Now was not the time to cry.

Augusta's eyes grew as big as saucers. "Is it Dylan? He's been in an accident. The roads are horrible. Why did he have to go to Newport today of all days?" she wailed.

What? The fog swirling around her head lifted. Oh, of course Augusta would consider Dylan. Guess he told her where he was headed. After all, he was her best friend. Meghan swallowed hard and found the strength to explain.

"Jacques and I aren't divorced." Not exactly graceful, but blurted nonetheless.

Confusion crossed her friend's features. "The French-tard?" Meghan almost laughed at the nickname Augusta had coined for Jacques after they'd first connected about man woes over many gin and tonics at Royce's. No laugh escaped now, though. Just the need to cry hysterically into the couch cushions.

"How is that possible? Did you get a letter or something?" Her eyes narrowed. "Did he call? What an asshole, lying sack of sh—"

"It's my fault." She'd better clarify before Augusta went into a tirade. "Apparently," she began, fighting the bile rising to her throat at the whole shitty situation and her stupidity, "I filled out the date of our marriage incorrectly, and when he attempted to get a new marriage license—he's getting married to Ginny next Saturday, by the way—he couldn't. So he flew here for me to sign the papers in person."

Augusta regarded her in silence, seeming to digest that mouthful. "Are you upset about the wedding?"

A valid question given how protective Augusta was of Dylan's heart and love life, just like she was protective of Evan's. Her face must've shown the horror, for Augusta's shoulders relaxed. She placed her phone on the coffee table and grabbed both of Augusta's hands. "Of course I'm not! I'm totally in love with Dylan and he's perfectly fine, by the way. The last time I spoke with him was an hour ago, but now I have to try and stall his arrival. See why this is a nightmare?"

"Oh, okay. I thought…well, I thought the worst."

Meghan realized what Augusta must have assumed. "Are you kidding? I could care less about what Jacques does with his life. Ginny, the bitch, is welcomed to him."

"Oh, thank you," Augusta exclaimed, and pulled her in for a hug.

The familiar and soothing scent of the coconut shampoo Augusta regularly used tamped down her need to vomit. Helped to have someone to lean on.

"Mom, is that true?" Brielle's question cut through the air like a knife. They jumped apart. Her daughter stood in the doorway leading to the hall with an unreadable expression. Since the divorce—or the almost divorce—and moving back to Havenport, Brielle hid her feelings well, especially those concerning her father. To describe the father-daughter relationship in one word: nonexistent.

Meghan blew out a breath. May as well not sugarcoat things. Besides, Brielle expected—no, deserved—to be told the truth.

"Yes. It is."

Augusta, bless her compassionate heart, vaulted off the couch and to Brielle's side for another hug. She was such a hugger.

"It's okay, honey." An unspoken *I got this* passed between them over Brielle's shoulder, and Augusta nodded in understanding before she held Brielle at arm's length.

"You know what? I'll just go and put away the cake." With that, Augusta picked up the cake box and walked out of the room. Brielle leaned against the ornate moldings she'd picked out last year when Dylan hired Haven on Earth to redesign his house. That had been the beginning of their relationship. He'd agreed to put up the wall, which now separated the family room and the foyer. With one long leg crossed over the other, Brielle waited.

"Come sit?" Meghan asked, motioning to the place Augusta had just vacated. Brielle's hands clenched at her sides, but her face showed no emotion.

Instead of sitting, she strolled over to the picture window and pushed aside the curtains.

"It's snowing like crazy," Brielle said, and rubbed where her breath had fogged the glass. "I hope Uncle Evan and Dylan don't have problems getting here."

Meghan wanted to punch something. *Damn you, Jacques.* If he put a dent in the solid relationship she'd tried to build with her daughter, he wouldn't need to worry about his wedding. More like his funeral.

The carriage clock, an oak and inlaid pearl piece they'd found in that quaint store in Boston, chimed from the front foyer table. Another amazing memory popped up of that weekend. *Oh, jeez*, it was already six thirty. Meghan pushed off the couch and stood next to Brielle to watch as snow blanketed the boxwoods. Dylan planted those along the walkway last spring. They'd all pitched in to help him landscape, even the dogs digging holes they hadn't quite needed.

Those kinds of memories and good times would continue, despite this fiasco unfolding. She'd fight for their happiness with her last breath.

They'd built a life together this past year—she, Dylan, Brielle, and the dogs. A life Brielle could be proud of when she found her own way in the world. A life a hell of a lot more filled with love, support, and understanding than *she'd* ever experienced growing up in the Washburn family mansion. It was no wonder Evan left to join the Marines the first chance he'd gotten. No, Brielle needed the influence of good, solid, honest men like Evan and Dylan in her life. Not a man who went through woman as often as he changed his socks.

"Uncle Evan is on his way back from the airport with Dylan's mom," she stated. "Elle, I need to tell you something." Might as well get this over with before the surprise of her father walking in.

Brielle turned to face her with a curious yet guarded expression, and it broke her heart. She pushed a lock of

Brielle's long hair away from where it'd fallen out of her ponytail. It stuck to the shiny lip gloss she must've put on for her FaceTime with Jacob earlier. "Baby girl, you know I want you to be ecstatically happy in your life every day, right?"

Brielle shrugged and gave her a sly smile. "I know, Mom. I'm totally happier than I was a year ago."

Her words eased a portion of the burning sensation of stress punching in her gut. "How much did you hear of what Augusta and I discussed?"

Brielle rolled her eyes. "Dad's getting married again, and something about divorce papers. You're not still married, right?"

"No. Well...technically...I don't quite know." Although she and Jacques had a horrible marriage, to bash him might destroy any of the rare good memories Brielle might still have.

"Honey, your father and I are through. These papers are a technicality, a mistake I made when I'd filled out the information. He needs it fixed now. He's on his way."

Brielle's mouth flew open. "Dad's coming? Here?" Brielle shook her head with vigor, making her ponytail come loose. "But...but...he can't. Not tonight. *Not tonight*," she repeated to the floor. "Does Dylan know?" she asked, the lines deepening in her forehead.

Meghan bit her lip until it started to sting. "Not yet. But, to be fair, Uncle Evan just called to explain this whole debacle. Apparently, he found your father at the airport trying to rent a car. I plan to sign the stupid papers and the French—err, your father—will be on his way. Right away." Yeah, except with the snow falling like they'd moved to freaking Siberia, she hoped that would be possible.

Brielle gaped at her. "Mom," she started in an urgent tone, "call Dylan now and tell him the situation."

Meghan gripped the windowsill, looking outside for the camouflage paint of Evan's Jeep. Shouldn't be hard to spot amid the white background. "I know. I will. I just hoped that…"

"No, no, you have to tell him *before* he gets here."

Meghan frowned at the frazzled state Brielle was working herself into. It wasn't as if Dylan knew about the party, so no harm, no foul in making the Jacques problems go away. Right? They'd have a good laugh over it when they all shouted "surprise" without Jacques in sight.

"I realize this has the potential…okay, the real possibility of ruining the birthday celebration surprise, but Dylan is a reasonable person."

Brielle moved away from the window and sat down hard on the couch, hands wringing in her lap. "You cannot blindside him, Mom. It's not right. Not tonight."

Making her way back to the couch, she sat next to her daughter, wondering the reason for her desperate and heated reaction. For a girl who showed little emotion, this was unusual. "I know it's crazy, but Dylan does not need to be in the middle of this crap I created. I can handle it."

Brielle grabbed both her hands and squeezed. Emotions Meghan hadn't witnessed before crossed Brielle's beautiful features: hope, love, and even fear?

"Dylan is the one, Mom. You know it, I know it, and *he* knows it. Call him and tell him, then…just…get rid of Dad, quick."

Meghan heaved a sigh of relief, and joy filled her soul at Brielle's announcing what she'd known for a long time. Dylan was the one. "You're right. We'll all have a good laugh over dinner. I'll call him now." She hoped so, anyway.

Panic and dread set in ten minutes later.

"Any luck?" Augusta asked when Meghan found her way back to the kitchen. Her friend had stepped up to help, donning the "Kiss the Kitchen Diva" apron Dylan had given her for Christmas, and stirred bubbling gravy on the stove.

Meghan swiped at the phone, hoping for better results than the past twenty times she'd tried. Still half a bar icon on the screen. "No good signal. You?"

Augusta shook her head and readjusted her hair. She'd pulled her long waves into a clip at the back of her neck. "Nope. Something must be up with the cell tower and this weather. My phone's been searching for service for twenty minutes. The last text I got from Evan was that they were making slow progress from Providence, and nothing from Dylan; went straight to voice mail. However, knowing Dyl, his cell battery is probably dead."

Meghan rubbed her arms. That might explain things. Or, what if Dylan *was* in an accident? Even the weather lady seemed baffled with the freak squalls churning outside. She had to stop thinking ten million miles a minute. Dylan's truck could handle the weather, and he was an excellent driver. *One thing at a time.*

Taking a last look at the beautifully cooked creation sitting on the stovetop, she covered the pan with aluminum foil. The roast had turned out to be a work of culinary art, and the roasted garlic and rosemary stuffing smelled luscious, but she had zero appetite. Her stomach was coiled so tight the thought of one forkful of Dylan's favorite scalloped potatoes made her eyeball the bathroom door in earnest. She checked her watch again.

"This storm is crazy bad. I know the landlines are messed up. My mother left a message on my home machine, something about my father's boat, *Liquid Assets* is missing," she said, rolling her eyes. "Which, frankly, I have no time to worry or care about. But I could swear there were a few other people on the line. It was all crackly, too. Do wires still get crossed in this day and age?"

Augusta shrugged. "Beats me. I know I'll feel so much better when everyone gets here so we don't have to try calling anymore." She wiped her hands on a towel and put her arm on Meghan's shoulder. "Listen, we will deal with everything as it comes. You'll sign the papers, and Evan arranged to get Jacques into the Havenport Inn so he's out of your hair tonight, and then we'll celebrate."

Meghan leaned her head on Augusta's shoulder, thankful for her eternal optimism. "No wonder my brother loves you."

"Yeah, well, he's not so bad, either," she said. "At least the dogs are enjoying the snow." Meghan followed her gaze out the parted kitchen curtains into the backyard. The floodlights illuminated Dylan's expanse of a yard, now covered in a blanket of white. The snow was a bit too deep for poor Rambo, so he barked at his crazy friends from the back deck. Their Christmas tree, an evergreen they'd planted after last year's holidays, sagged under the heavy, wet snow.

"Zeus is a beast." Meghan laughed at Augusta's large pooch pawing at poor Ed, romping around him in circles. Given the weather forecast, Augusta had wisely gone home to get her big man Zeus, a lumbering bloodhound mix, and packed an overnight bag.

The door clicked open, bringing with it a blast of cold air.

"Meggy?" came Evan's voice from the hall.

"Oh, God," she croaked, her throat dry as sandpaper.

Augusta's arm tightened. "No worries. If he acts up, I'll sick Zeus on his French-tard ass." Augusta leaned in and whispered, "Besides, Dylan is head over heels for you. Remember that's what matters."

Meghan swallowed hard and nodded. "Too bad Sniper's not here." Mac and Savannah's mastiff would make Jacques crap his pants. She let out a long breath. "Time to get this done and him outta here." She turned toward the hall. Augusta lightly patted her on the shoulder for moral support.

The walk to the front foyer felt like a thousand yards. The high heels she'd worn to impress Dylan—cream leather ankle straps to match the pink-and-cream sweater set she knew he loved—clicked on the wood floors like a staccato death march. Feelings she'd long buried—like being second page on her ex's priority list, accused of being the nagging wife, the stupid girl too young and naive to compete with an older French businessman—rose fast and furious.

Stop. You've changed. You've matured. You own a business, for Pete's sake, much more successful than any of the failed bullshit ventures Jacques bought and sold. You don't need or want to be the woman you used to be.

Plus, she'd found the love of her life.

Why did she care what Jacques thought, anyway? It'd been a dog's age since she'd laid eyes on his arrogant sneer, and didn't miss it in the least. But when Peg stepped into eyesight, a fissure in her confidence started to crumble into a crater. Evan's expression, normally stoic in the face of stress, said it all. Oh, he was pissed.

Jacques clumped in last, banging his snowy loafers onto Dylan's birch floor. She gnashed her teeth. Surprisingly, he carted a suitcase behind him. And with a sour and annoyed expression on his face, he propped it against the railing in a huff.

At the edge of the foyer, she stood stock-still. Evan stepped inside. He'd turned sideways to allow Margaret access to the warmth in the family room. Yeah, building that nice, cozy, romantic celebratory fire seemed like a great idea before the evening morphed into hell in an Armani suit. Jacques, spotting her at last, tilted his head to the side and checked her out like a piece of meat, the asshole. With a smirk, he licked his thin, weak lips—how that was ever attractive was a mystery—and raised a bushy eyebrow at her in a haughty, come-now-didn't-you-miss-me action. Cue the stomach churning.

Her face must've shown the horror, grief, stress, and nausea all in one, for Peg rushed to her side and Jacques grunted. Had she just elbowed him? No way, but before Meghan could perceive the image real or her imagination, Peg enveloped her in a hug. The cushion quilting of her ski jacket was icy against the thin material of Meghan's sweater. She shivered. After more than a minute's embrace, for Peg didn't seem to want to let go, and neither did she, Meghan loosened her arms.

"I'm so happy to be here. It's all going to be fine, I promise," Peg murmured in her ear, then pulled back to keep Meghan at arm's length.

Jacques momentarily forgotten, she stared at Peg. Dylan's face was shaped the same, and his eyes were a darker sapphire. And, wow, Peg looked fantastic, a whole lot different than at Christmastime. Maybe she'd done a makeover. Her hair hid under a stylish knit tam hat, and thankfully her face held a smile and not the you're-no-good-for-my-firstborn expression Meghan feared. However, underneath, Meghan sensed Peg was troubled, maybe for Dylan driving in this weather, or more likely if his heart would be in jeopardy.

"I love your son, a hundred million percent," she announced, and didn't give a rat's ass what Jacques or anyone thought.

Peg let out a long sigh, her shoulders relaxing. Then she winked. "I know."

And in that moment Meghan knew as well. She'd found not only an ally but also a friend and possibly a mother figure. Like a security blanket, the kind of comfort only a mother could give.

"I smell my roast recipe, my dear. Well done."

Oh shit. The roast. She'd completely blocked out the whole best-impression thing. "I hope it tastes as good as it smells," she said, a little shaky.

Peg swiped off her hat and unbelted her coat, turning around to finally acknowledge Evan and Jacques. "I'm dripping all over my son's floor. Please find a place for this, Evan dear. And you," she addressed Jacques, "whip out that document and let's get this done, shall we? In here will do. Follow me. Now," she ordered, turned, and walked into Dylan's family room. "By the way, Meghan, stellar job in turning my son's frat-boy decor into something spectacular."

And with that, Jacques surprisingly did as Peg instructed, set his briefcase on the coffee table, and opened it.

Meghan's jaw slid to the floor.

Chapter Five

"I'm gonna need new wiper blades after this," Dylan muttered to the windshield. The pair currently laboring on the Suburban cleared a minuscule arch shape for visibility. "Crap."

With the damned whiteout conditions, he'd been lucky to see a fraction of the interstate from Newport. Thank St. Patrick that trucker had spotted him and motioned to follow. The trailer's taillights were a godsend for the crawl toward home.

Carefully, Dylan rounded the corner on the way toward Havenport's center of town, or at least he hoped so. He squinted past the sign for Jefferson and headed to the traffic light. The roads were horrendous. What, was the Havenport sanitation department snug in their beds instead of cleaning the roads to be at least passable? Councilman Washburn was going to get a piece of his mind at the next Town Hall meeting. *Jeez,* talk about slippery.

"Yes, folks, the snow has certainly walloped through Havenport tonight," came the comment from the weather dude from *Rhode Island Today*'s sister radio station.

"No kidding, Captain Obvious," Dylan muttered, and hit the button to turn off the radio. One of the few things he missed about Boston—when snow fell, the city was prepared. This town was like a ghost town. Had Mayor Henry closed Havenport?

The wind gusted, and one of the metal trash containers set at each corner under the lampposts toppled over and rolled a few feet into the street. He swerved to avoid running over the thing. The Serendipity store sign and that of the bookstore next to it were obscured by snow sticking to the letters. The sidewalk in front of Wags and Walks had drifts up to its windows. He turned up the temperature and upped the blower to heat his feet. At least his suit and dress shoes were dry. Might have been wise to pack an overcoat, though, but the extra ski jacket he kept in the back of the truck for after hockey games would have to do.

His watched beeped, as it did every fifteen minutes. Dylan shot a glance at the digital clock on the dash, reluctant to pull his attention off the road, even though there wasn't a soul on the road—except for his crazy ass.

"Driving around in a freakin' blizzard," he muttered to no one but the whistling wind. *Shit*. It was nearing eight o'clock and his cell battery had died over an hour ago. Meghan had to be wicked worried, and he hated that he may have caused her concern.

Stupid ass. He'd forgotten to grab the car phone charger out of the animal hospital van yesterday. He'd contemplated stopping on the road from Newport to call home, but with the weather worsening, the idea of being stuck at some random gas station wasn't an option.

Dylan crept down Main Street toward the more residential part of Havenport. Keeping the speed at barely ten miles per hour still made maneuvering the corners dangerous to say the least. The Suburban pulled left, and Dylan gripped the leather-covered steering wheel. The tires slipped on a patch of flattened snow covering the asphalt.

"Holy shit, this is treacherous." The ring box and flowers on the front passenger seat shifted and the gerbera daisies wrapped in cellophane and pretty pink paper slid off the seat. Before the ring box hit the vinyl Red Sox floor mat, Dylan reached over…and promptly lost control.

Another patch of iced-over roadway made the Suburban's rear end slide and veer sideways. He backed off the throttle and attempted to right the truck, going with the spin instead of against, but to no avail. The rear end fishtailed, and he knew he was in deep shit.

Tension shot to his scalp, and his stomach took a nosedive. He heaved another hard right, but not in time. His body launched forward, followed by a crunch and bang, and the seat belt yanked, cutting into his torso. Then a hard stop.

Dylan swallowed and rubbed his sternum where the seat belt had pulled so taut he knew there would be a bruise later. And, *a-yup*, tachycardia in full effect. The thumping of his heartbeat in his ears broke the frozen silence inside the vehicle. Christ, that was a close one. Another inch and the SUV would've taken out the lamppost and sent it careening into Wags and Walks' front window. Wouldn't Augusta have loved that?

The radiator discharged a waft of steam from where the front hood was bent like a crinkled can. He closed his eyes, trying to slow his breathing, and did a check by feel of his extremities. Other than a nasty case of whiplash he knew would follow once the adrenaline wore off, all body functions seemed fine. What the hell had he hit? He craned his neck to see over the front of the vehicle.

"Aw, come on. Sonofabi…" The wrought-iron bench anchored to the sidewalk was now part of his front grill.

And the snow continued to fall. Dylan closed his eyes again, delving into those skills he'd used as a Corpsman. Assess the situation and make a plan. Luckily, he'd been doing ten miles an hour, tops, or else the air bag would have made a mess.

No phone, no boots—*shit*—and the mile walk home would suck. Maybe one of the stores was still open? Was that a light on in the apartment above A New Chapter? Maybe Olivia was home. But most people were at Christa and Jeremy's wedding tonight, if that was still going on, so probably not. Better just make his way home.

A quick glance out the side windows showed no signs of life. He unclipped the seat belt and bent over the seat back to grab his gym bag. A suit and sneakers would look ridiculous, but nothing he could do about it now. He and Meghan would have a good laugh about it later.

Once he made it home.

Once he proposed.

If she says yes.

Dylan swapped the wing tips for his track shoes, donned the parka, and shoved the flowers into the bag. The ring box squirreled securely in his inner suit jacket pocket, he zipped the coat and opened the car door.

Flakes hit his face and the wind chose that moment to whip into a frenzy of cold, wet grit. Shielding his eyes from the gust, and on a last-minute thought, he reached back into the truck, flipped open the glove compartment, and grabbed his handy travel flashlight. Peg had pounded into his head to be prepared for the worst-case scenarios every time she called. She might be a worrywart at times, but hell, he'd be thanking her for her annoying words of wisdom as soon as he got the chance.

Slamming the car door shut, he beeped the alarm. Why? He had no idea. Not like anyone was going to steal a screwed-up truck. He hoisted the gym bag over one shoulder and started walking home.

Chapter Six

Jacques carted out what looked like an awfully thick stack of papers from his designer briefcase and placed them on Dylan's coffee table. By now, Brielle had made an appearance with a polite hello and kiss on her father's cheek. She gave him the cold shoulder, and his nostrils flared. A sure sign he was annoyed. *Too bad.* He pulled the designer cuffs into place, as if he were running the show, and Meghan wanted to tell him to stuff it.

"Are you ready?" he asked, tilting his head to the document, and she nodded. Might as well get this over with—and quickly.

Augusta came out from the kitchen and walked straight to Evan, who pulled her tight against him, whispering something in her ear. She kissed him and joined Brielle in the doorway. They all glared at Jacques together, like a panel of jurors, and if she weren't feeling sick to her stomach she might have laughed. But, of course, Jacques and his stuck-up, better-than-everyone attitude gave a haughty sigh and clicked his briefcase shut.

Zeus lumbered in and sniffed at his loafers, causing Jacques to back away in horror. Ed, who must have sensed the tension emanating from everyone, growled. Jacques's eyes widened like saucers. Rambo even bared his little doggy teeth and joined in the alpha-male party.

"Don't worry, they won't bite, unless we tell them to," Augusta chimed in, with daggers shooting from her gaze.

Talk about fierce. She gave Augusta a slight smile. Once she turned back to Jacques, she forced her face into a neutral expression. It was damned hard not to sneer.

How in the world had she spent fifteen years with an asshole of Jacques's proportions? His ego and sense of entitlement were incrementally worse than her parents'. No wonder they'd been so against her leaving him. The Washburns and their society save-face attitude.

Money certainly didn't make the man.

Meghan scrutinized the document. Had there been so many pages? She frowned down at the insignia. Was that his lawyer's name? She honestly couldn't remember.

"I'd like to read it through, please." At first glance, the papers appeared familiar. *Supreme Court of New York State, New York County, Meghan Washburn LaRue, plaintiff, Jacques Anthony LaRue, defendant.*

Truthfully, she hadn't the inclination to read the damn thing lately, either.

Jacques hesitated, his face turning a shade paler. "But why? It's all the same." Then he flicked his fingers up against his chin and raised a shoulder in a nonchalant way.

Her eyes narrowed. Oh, he'd done that gesture many times. And usually it preceded a lie. "Hand them over," she told him. Out of the corner of her eye, she saw Evan's hands fist at his sides. Peg, sitting on the couch, looked up curiously.

"Very well." Jacques huffed, but wouldn't look at her, another sure sign something wasn't right.

This wouldn't be the first time she'd done battle with Jacques and gotten her way. But this time, Meghan knew he hid something. The way he'd shifted between each fancy, snow-stained loafer, the profuse sweating—all telltale signs.

But she wasn't that naive housewife any longer.

Meghan flipped through the tome, its contents becoming more recognizable. The penthouse apartment in New York City sold, the bank accounts split, the right to his restaurants she'd turned over, gladly. A no-brainer, since they'd been money-sucking ventures anyway. There was one place she'd make sure to check. The one thing she'd fought for and lost a hell of a lot of things in return to get. About halfway down page six, her lungs burned. She took a few deep breaths because the urge to punch Jacques in his smug mouth took nearly all her willpower to refrain.

"You bastard!" She swallowed hard, and moisture welled in her eyes. Crap, she'd started crying. More angry tears than sad. "How could you?"

At least he had the decency to appear contrite and guilty. A forlorn countenance, one he'd worn at the beginning of their marriage when he'd commenced his cheating and she'd confronted him. When she'd been home with a crying, colicky baby for months, the half-guilt, half-pity expression crossed his features. Back then, he may have cared, but it was plainly not the case any longer.

Evan stepped forward to intercede, but she held up a hand. "How dare you try and rob our daughter out of her inheritance? Wasn't my money enough? Those wineries in France were meant for her from *your* father, her grandfather. You're a disgusting, philandering piece of shit."

Jacques, Brielle, Peg, and Augusta all gasped.

At that moment, the lights snapped out, plunging the house into darkness. The only illumination in the room came from the cozy fire. All three dogs barked, then the automatic gas generator Dylan had installed last winter kicked in, throwing off light from the lamp on the end table and the ceiling fixture in the hallway. The dim lights cast a glow on the monster Happy Birthday Dylan sign hanging over the window. She closed her eyes.

Oh, Dylan where are you? I could use your strong shoulders right about now.

No. This was her fight. Her daughter. All at once, questions fired off from Augusta, who actually called him a French-tard, Peg stood and chimed in, and Evan snarled and advanced on Jacques, ready to take his head off. Then, in the most unusual gesture, the usually calm, cool, and collected Brielle marched right up to her father nose to nose. Only she towered over him.

"Take it all," she told him, voice shaky. "I don't give a shit. Sorry for the language, Mom," she threw over her shoulder. "Why can't you just leave us alone?" Brielle shook her head. "Didn't you hurt Mom enough? You're such a jerk!"

But when Jacques got flustered, as he appeared to be at this very moment in his newly formed role as the enemy in the room, he possessed fast hands. Something no one knew about, and something that hadn't happened to her all that often. But she'd seen her fair share of his waitstaff accept the brunt of his ire. His hand shot out, and they all heard the crack of his palm across Brielle's cheek. Brielle reared back, hand to her face, unshed tears pooled in her eyes, and something in Meghan snapped.

She sprang in Jacques's direction, but the sound of the door slamming shut, the blast of cold air, and a figure—actually, two—appearing in the corner of her eye made her hesitate.

"You're a dead man." Dylan vaulted into the room, Ed tight on his heels, and planted his fist into Jacques's nose with a sickening pop.

Stunned, her ex staggered back and fell onto the couch cushions in a heap, clutching at his bloodied, broken nose.

"Stay away from my family," Dylan ground out, and stood over him. Ed bared his lethal teeth. "And get the fuck out of *my* house."

Meghan was rooted to the spot, unable to process the scene unfolding. She thought she heard "atta boy" coming from Evan, but wasn't sure. Dylan appeared soaked to the skin, like he'd trudged in knee-deep snow, wearing a suit and sneakers? That flop of hair she loved dripped large droplets of water onto his nose, but it was the most amazing sight Meghan had ever seen.

Evan stepped forward at last, and Meghan was honestly a little afraid for Jacques. Two *huge* men—Evan a muscle machine, and Dylan, tall with lean, strong arms that could beat the crap out of anyone on the ice—were probably going to kill him.

Augusta gasped. Zeus, sensing his mommy was in danger, pounced. And Rambo chomped down on Jacques's loafer like it was a bone. Jacques wailed, arms shooting up to block his face, as if to dodge any more blows, but there weren't any. Didn't need to be, especially when Ed vaulted his big, powerful body onto the leather with ears flattened. The dog's eyes narrowed and he growled low and deep, his hindquarters quivering, tension in his muscles, waiting for Dylan's command to attack.

"Heel," Dylan directed. Meghan let out the breath she'd been holding, although she knew Dylan had to be contemplating letting Ed do his best. How dare he touch her daughter? She wanted to give the command herself.

Dylan's fists were clenched, his jaw tight. Ed obeyed, sitting back on his haunches. However, he didn't jump off the couch cushions. *Smart dog.* He positioned his enormous paws an inch from Jacques's legs, crowding him against the end of the couch. Jacques gaped in horror and adhered himself to the armrest, torso leaning away from Ed's large head and large teeth.

"This is an outrage," he bellowed, while cradling the side of his face. Dylan had given him one hell of a wallop. "Meghan, how disappointing. What kind of animals do you associate with now? How low you have sunk on the social ladder. It's pathetic."

It was her turn to gawk. Guess he didn't realize he was an inch away from death. *Stupid ass.* "You're the only junkyard dog here."

Evan trudged to the couch and kicked Jacques in the shin with his prosthetic foot, causing Jacques to howl. "Oops, that was an accident. Fake foot and all." He plucked Jacques off the couch by his collar like a rag doll.

"I don't care if you freeze your balls off—you're getting the hell away from my sister and my niece. I will remove this trash from your home," he told Dylan, "and deposit him on the front steps of the Inn."

"What?" Jacques cried, a nasal gurgle emanating from the swollen mess on his face. "I'm pressing assault charges. Take me to the police station at once."

Meghan leaned in close, right in Jacques's stupid, sweaty, bloody face. Ed growled behind. "Just you try it and I'll have you locked up for child abuse."

Dylan had moved to the foyer entrance. He tilted his head to the door. "Get him the hell out of here before I call the Havenport PD myself."

Evan faced Augusta, and they exchanged a quick nod, a silent understanding. He grabbed the briefcase, stuffed the papers inside, and propelled Jacques toward the front door. Jacques had the audacity to gripe about the papers and his wedding. *Might want to call that off.*

Oh, crap, that meant she wasn't divorced, though.

"Good riddance," Peg said. "Well done, my boy." Ed ducked his head for Peg's scratch behind the ears. He catapulted off the couch and flew into the kitchen with the other pooches. Peg followed.

Meghan felt like she'd been watching a crazy family feud movie. Dylan trailed Evan to the door and out of sight. What a disaster. The pop and hiss of the fire intensified when everyone fell silent. *Get a grip. This is your future. These people are your family. Say something.*

Unexpectedly, a flurry, like butterfly wings—or indigestion—hit her in the abdomen. Well, this was a convenient time to realize what she'd suspected earlier.

The front door clicked shut, and Dylan was back in the room. One glance in her direction and his brows puckered. "I should have tried to call from the road." He reached her side and took her hands in his. His were icy. Well, except for the knuckles on his left hand, which were warm, red, and swelling. "My phone battery died."

Still dazed after coming down from the anger surge, Meghan couldn't think or speak. Not even to ask if he was okay. This was all her fault.

Then she was in his arms and the world shifted to right again. One hand cupped her head and pressed her cheek against his wet coat; the other splayed on her hip, holding her against him. "Meg, I'm so sorry for this crazy stuff," he whispered into her hair.

Wait, *he* was apologizing? When she'd brought her ex into his lovely home, essentially ruining his birthday? Tipping her head back, Meghan gazed up into Dylan's beautifully handsome face. "It's all *my* fault," she whispered. "I ruined your birthday. I thought I could handle Jacques alone and then he'd be out of my life forever."

He swiped the wetness from her cheek with the pad of his thumb. "See, that's where you're wrong. You never have to handle anything alone."

Her heart skipped inside her chest. She tilted her head to kiss his jaw. "Forgive me?"

"Nothing to forgive." He smiled, but it didn't quite reach his eyes, and she grew worried. He squeezed her shoulders. "I'm going to check on Brielle." He broke the embrace and headed to where her daughter sat on the couch holding what looked to be a bag of frozen peas to her face.

Dylan nodded to his mother. "Good thinking with the peas, Mom. And by the way, nice of you to remember my birthday," he said with a wry smile.

Peg shrugged and patted him on the shoulder. "Nice entrance, and you're welcome. You look like a drowned, frozen rat."

He knelt beside Brielle and tenderly lifted the bag and examined her cheek. Meghan's heart skipped a beat.

"Hurt a lot?" he asked Brielle, who shook her head.

"I'm fine. I've got this. Go." Brielle tipped her chin in Meghan's direction, and Dylan stiffened. "You need to talk to Mom in private."

They exchanged a long, silent look, and he nodded. "Yeah, I do."

Now what was that all about? She was about to ask when Augusta fluttered back into the room. She must've gone into the kitchen when Evan left. "The dogs needed to go out," she informed them, briskly rubbing her hands together. "It's getting worse, if that's even possible." She approached the window and held the curtain aside. "Jeez, all the streetlights are out. I hope Evan doesn't take long." She wrinkled her nose, but Meghan knew Augusta was anxious, eyeballing the darkened street for Evan's camo Jeep. "Dyl, where's your truck?" Augusta let the curtains fall back into place and faced him.

Dylan didn't answer right away, but rubbed the back of his neck and sloughed off his ski jacket, tossing it onto the side ottoman on the leather sectional. Underneath was the one good suit he owned, a gray wool blend they'd picked out together last winter before the Havenport Animal Hospital's Christmas party. Water stains rose practically to his knees, turning the color to charcoal. He hadn't left the house dressed like that.

"And why are you soaking wet?" Augusta crossed her arms and voiced the same thing she'd wondered.

The corner of his mouth lifted into a smirk. "Just noticing that, huh?"

Augusta punched his arm, which she usually did when they got into a playful banter. "Yeah, well, your Muhammad Ali imitation took front and center."

"I'm wet because I walked here from Wags and Walks."

"Why would you do that?" Meghan asked.

Dylan dipped his head. "I crashed into a snowbank."

"What!" they all cried, and Dylan turned a shade darker.

"The roads are terrible. There's zero traction and Main Street is a mess, but thankfully the streets were practically deserted. By the way, the bench in front of your store is toast. Sorry," he told Augusta.

Augusta's face paled. "Who cares about that? I'm thrilled you're okay, but now I'm more worried than ever about Evan driving around. I should call him." She fled the room.

"Brielle, my dear," Peg said, while pushing off the couch to stand next to the coffee table. "As much as I love these couch cushions, how about you come with me into the kitchen and take a look at the lovely-smelling roast your mom prepared."

Brielle removed the peas from her face, the red mark fading from where Jacques had dared. Meghan sucked in a breath, still coiled tight with anger.

Guessing where her mother's thoughts had returned, Brielle came over and whispered, "I'm fine, Mom. I swear. You need to talk to Dylan. Tell him." She kissed her on the cheek. Meghan couldn't believe what an understanding, mature woman Brielle had become. "I'd love to help, Ms. O. I'm starving."

Peg swept an arm toward the kitchen. "Can't have that. I'll follow you. I know my son keeps flashlights in every room. I have a feeling we'll be dining by candlelight. How romantic. You two"—she turned to address them—"take your time. We'll holler when dinner is ready to be served."

Oh, God, what if the pork roast only *presented* like it had come out of *Bon Appétit*, but tasted like an old shoe that'd been dropped in the mud?

She swallowed hard. "Um, okay. Thank you, Margaret." All the adrenaline built up from the past half hour dissipated, leaving in its wake another twinge in her stomach. Oh, and how the hell was she supposed to drop *that* shoe on Dylan? That she might very well be pregnant? For the immediate shoe-dropping issues, it was past time to tell Dylan he'd been sleeping with a married woman.

It was now or never. Then, salvage what was supposed to be a wonderful birthday surprise for the hardest-working, most-caring man she'd ever met. She chewed her lip. Peg took Brielle's hand and led her toward the kitchen.

Honesty was her best bet. Their relationship to date thrived on it. No secrets. Only openness, the likes of which she'd never experienced with any man, from the first fateful night when she'd visited his house for a design consultation, broken his prized Boston Bruins mailbox, and opened up about her life.

Tell him everything, like Brielle insisted.

Chapter Seven

Dammit, his hand *hurt*. But seriously, trudging the steps soaked to the skin, worrying about Meghan with this freaking blizzard, the first and last thing he'd expected to see upon opening his front door was Jacques in his living room. No wonder he'd exploded. Couldn't remember the last time he'd lost it.

No man had the right to hit any female. Not on his watch. His hands fisted thinking about it again and the memories it conjured up. Yeah, his sorry excuse for an old man had fast hands, too.

"Are you okay?" Meghan asked, and placed her hand on his arm.

Her question broke him from his nightmare down memory lane. "The question is, are *you*?" He covered her shaking hand with his. "This blizzard is enough and no freaking power, but what was that all about?" He swept his arm out, causing Meghan to step away. He pictured the scene unfolding again. The dogs, and the asshole whining on the couch. Somehow the entire debacle felt like an hour ago, when it'd been ten minutes, tops. "Believe me, it felt amazing to punch that fool, but what *was* Jacques doing here?"

Meghan's face turned a shade paler and she sucked in a breath and stared at the floor. Her mouth opened and closed a few times, like she was about to respond, but then rethought the answer. That worried him. A few silent moments ticked by, but it was enough time to imagine all sorts of crazy scenarios. Had her ex come begging for forgiveness and it all turned sour?

Her eyes shot up and she squared her shoulders. "Sit, please?" She pointed to the couch with a weak smile.

Dylan nodded and sank into the cushions. It felt good to get off his feet. That last half mile trudging against the wind had been brutal. He untied and removed his soaked sneakers. The blue nylon-and-mesh material turned almost black from being drenched. Fat lot of good they'd done in the snow. His feet felt like two blocks of ice.

Might be best to keep busy before what he suspected was a shoe about to drop.

Meghan paced the room in front of the bay window. There was an enormous—wow, more like ginormous—Happy Birthday Dylan banner hanging on the wall. The fire popped and hissed, a large piece of wood fell onto the grates with a thump, and embers shot into the air.

But she remained silent. The only sound her sexy high heels clicking on the wood floor as she strode back and forth. She'd dressed in his favorite sweater set, the one that hugged her slender curves in all the right places. Were those fake eyelashes? Smudges of mascara had formed under her eyes, an indication she'd been crying. Her hands were clenched, wringing at her stomach while she moved.

He groaned silently, waiting for an explanation. The ring box burned a hole in his pocket. Not exactly the way he'd envisioned popping the question. He cleared his throat. "So, you planned a surprise for my birthday?" Yeah, maybe another question, a deflection from the first one she hadn't addressed, would somehow break the ice.

She turned and faced him, expression confused. He shrugged and pointed to the banner above his head. "That's one hell of a banner."

A sad, cynical laugh escaped her throat. "I know," she replied, and his gut clenched at the wetness pooling in her eyes. "I wanted it to be perfect. But then Evan found Jacques at the airport and…and…I…well, he brought him here, obviously." She rolled her eyes.

That gesture, so Meghan, and so the other Washburns in his life, gave him a thread of hope that things might— just might—go back to the way they were this morning.

Before all the chaos, and possibly broken knuckles.

"I swear to you, there was no other choice," she added quickly. "I would never have allowed him access to your home otherwise."

"Why did you?" He tried to sound calm, but a seed of doubt had planted in his skull. Why would Meghan want to reconcile with a man who hit women? Was there something he didn't know?

"He needs the divorce papers resigned," she explained.

Tension built between his eyeballs. "But you're already divorced."

She flinched. "Well, apparently I messed up the first set by putting the wrong date, and he can't get remarried now. Then he tried to screw Brielle out of her inheritance. All those months negotiating the wineries and château in France—I gave up a lot to make sure Brielle got what was her due. My parents won't leave anything to her." She shook her head in disgust.

Wineries? *In France?* He gulped. The ring, which cost him Bea, seemed like a Cracker Jack box item compared to the kind of wealth she'd been accustomed to.

"And then," she continued, pushing her hair away from her forehead, "I lost it. But it was Brielle who stood up to him, which provoked him to do what he did. That bastard."

Dylan frowned, concentrating on Meghan's account of the events and not the second thoughts swirling in his head. "I came in at that last part. And I, well, I lost it, too. Which, to be honest now that I think about it, wasn't the best example in front of Brielle, but…Meg, he crossed the line."

Disbelief crossed the planes of her face. "He deserved it. If you hadn't, I would have."

"So he wasn't here to reconcile?" *Slide that over to the plus column, right?*

"Reconcile?" She snorted and shot to his side. "As if I would ever, ever consider that an option. Besides," she said, a little breathless, and knelt at his feet, "I love *you*. I…I'm just a stupid twit, and apparently *technically* still married. You've been living in sin with a married woman this past year. Your very Catholic mother is going to hate me," she whispered.

Dylan boosted Meghan onto his lap, and she shivered. "Yeah, I know, I must seem like a block of ice." He felt infinitesimally better she wasn't getting back with Jacques. He wasn't happy with the married part, and hell, he could never compete with property in France, but he still wanted to ease her angst. "First of all, my mother does not hate anyone, except the asshole who sired me. And second, I'm an adult. Plus, if what I smell is her famous roast recipe, she's happy *someone* wanted to emulate her cooking because no one else does."

She rested her head against his shoulder, and he felt her body relax, which was a good thing. "Your mother has been amazing and supportive, especially at the airport. Evan told me she put Jacques right in his place."

He chuckled. "Margaret O'Brien could put the fear of God in Jesus."

"Dylan," she said, and her head came off his shoulder, determination set into her mouth, "I need to make sure that divorce decree is right—for Brielle. Are you upset? I just hope it doesn't take too long." She bit her lip.

Yes, I am upset, because I want you to marry me. Not be Mrs. LaRue. But Mrs. O'Brien. He tried to keep a neutral expression. "Of course not. I mean, we're fine the way we are. I like just us, and I'm in no rush." *Coward.*

Meghan slid off his lap and looked away. "Just us, yeah. Me, too." Then she cleared her throat and clutched both his hands in hers. He tried not to recoil at the pressure on his left knuckles. "I can't believe you got snowbound and had to walk, you poor baby. The cell service stinks. I hope your truck is fixable."

He waved a hand in the air, but realized it was the one that hurt and he winced. "I'll have Mac take it to his garage in the morning." If this blizzard ever stopped.

"Oh, jeez," Meghan cried, looking at his injured hand. "Chalk this up to my mind being mush and the stress. You need an ice pack." She went to move, but he stopped her.

"It's fine." Doubt the size of his Irish potato head, as Shannon always said, crept into his gut, and he just couldn't shake it. Guess his proposal plans were shot to shit. He wished he could called Danny and dump his insecurities on his brother. Yeah, Danny would listen and probably call him an idiot. Now wasn't the time to give in to self-doubt, not when Meghan had outdone herself for him, for his birthday. "I think I'll go take a shower while there's still hot water. Then I can enjoy your cooking." He winked and stood.

She blinked. "Oh, okay. I'm going to check in the kitchen." She tilted her head back and gave him a tentative peck on the lips. He caught a whiff of the sexy peaches-and-cream scent and wanted to crush her to his chest, bury his nose in her soft neck, and tell her to get rid of everyone. Screw the dinner. They could be alone. But that wasn't going to happen.

❄ ❄ ❄

A half hour later, a wet, freezing Evan stomped in, much to Augusta's joy. Meghan's brother held his love close, and Augusta melted into his embrace. Dylan had come downstairs in sweats, hand bandaged and hair still wet and curling at the back of his neck from his shower. He kissed Peg on the cheek, teased a bit about Meghan's roast smelling better than hers, and they all sat at the table at last.

The candles, long tapers in red left over from Christmas, burned slowly and even in their crystal holders on the dining table. Peg joked that he finally had a civilized setup and remarked that Bea was missing, but how she was thrilled there was so much more room without it.

"Oh, it's just temporary," Meghan chimed in during dessert. "She's…err… it's getting fixed in Newport. I told Dyl we'd have a homecoming party for her." She reached over the table and gave his uninjured hand a soft squeeze. For some reason, she couldn't wait for the large, Boston Red Sox–embossed championship-size entertainment piece to be put where it belonged, smack in the middle of the family room.

The entire table grew silent, or at least Augusta, Dylan, Evan, and Brielle did.

"You are a more tolerant woman than I am, my dear Meghan," Peg said with a wink, and dove into another forkful of birthday cake. "And this cake is out of this world. I must get to Led Zeppoli before I leave. Not that I think there will be any flight departing out this weekend. Wicked storm, huh?"

"Oh, yeah. Roads and airports all closed tight. The Inn, too," Evan said with a smirk.

"The Inn, Uncle Evan? Then where did you put you-know-who?" Brielle whispered. She'd confided to Meghan she wasn't ready to speak her father's name. Not tonight, and probably not for a long time.

Evan stretched his muscular arms overhead and looked like he was the proverbial cat that ate the yellow canary. Augusta rolled her eyes and elbowed him in the ribs.

"Hey!"

Her friend's lips flattened. "Tell them, or I will. Not to put a damper on your cake festivities, Dyl, but it's nothing more than what the French-tard deserved."

"Evan, what did you do?" Meghan asked, picturing Jacques dead in a ditch somewhere.

Evan scratched his flattop head and closed an eye, mirth making his shoulders shake. "Let's just say the Havenport Elderly Center has a visitor tonight. Oh, and they received a generous donation for their willingness to take on a stray, drowned French poodle. I thought the lady at the front desk would keel over when I pulled the wad of cash out of Jacques's suit jacket."

Meghan's jaw hit the table. "You didn't."

Evan's eyebrows rose and fell in mischief. "Uh-huh. I did."

Dylan rose from the table, placing his linen napkin next to his plate. "You're a crazy man," he commented, but for some reason the jest didn't quite fit the tone. He turned toward the kitchen. "Ed needs to go out one last time, and I'm feeling the effects of my snow trudge. Mom, I love you. I know Meghan has everything set up in the guest room, and you," he said to Augusta," know where to find what you guys need to hunker down. Just pick a place, and let's hope this stuff blows outta here tomorrow." He leaned down and gave Meghan a gentle kiss on the lips. "I love you."

"Love you more," she said against his lips, and everyone in the room *awwed*, though she *thought* she heard her brother make a gag noise.

Dylan's eyes took on a sad, uncertain glean, but it disappeared in a second. Perhaps she'd imagined it. It had been an awfully long ordeal.

"Not possible," he replied, and whistled for Ed, who shot out from the corner of the room and followed his master.

Chapter Eight

Outside his bedroom window, the snow continued to fall at a steady clip. Dylan couldn't sleep if his life depended on it. Didn't help that Meghan insisted on bunking with Brielle, especially in light of the whole "living in sin" ridiculous theory of hers. Guess he couldn't blame her, though. Not exactly the best example to give a daughter.

But would she be his stepdaughter? That was the million-dollar question.

Ask and see if she says yes, you putz.

How the hell could he possibly compete with a winery in France? No, scratch that, *wineries*? Hell, he could barely afford the Pétrus he enjoyed on the rare occasion, and those bottles weren't even the expensive vintage.

Groaning like an old man—thirty-five to be exact, for it'd passed midnight two hours ago—he slipped out of bed and threw on a pair of sweats, a shirt, and his sneakers, which were stiff from drying out the past few hours. What was he thinking? That Meghan would want the town vet barely able to keep his employees paid on time each month? The Havenport Animal Hospital generated *some* profit, but he was certainly not raking in the dough. However, money or prestige never mattered before, right?

Quietly, he padded down the steps, passing where Evan and Augusta were comatose on the pullout sofa, toward the kitchen. The electricity hadn't come back on, and to conserve his generator they'd killed most of the lights with the exception of an under-cabinet LED, which cast a dim glow into the kitchen. Zeus was splayed in the hallway, snoring like an old man, and Rambo had tucked himself into his hind legs.

Dylan stepped over the two. Ed, who'd positioned himself against the front door like the protector, slit one eye open but didn't raise his head. Yeah, his buddy had had too much ice cream and cake to move.

Dylan grabbed his jacket from the peg near the back door and stepped onto his back deck. Crisp air hit his lungs, and he welcomed the shock. His sneakers pressed into the snow, which they'd cleared a few times so the dogs could go out easily.

The night sky was dark with a few twinkling stars, but otherwise it was kind of peaceful. He wondered when the snow might let up. Well, at least with tomorrow being Sunday, they'd all dig out and prepare for the week ahead.

"Dude, I'm not one to interfere…"

Dylan nearly jumped out of his skin. "Damn, you're stealthy for someone with one leg." He gave Evan a sideways glance, heartbeat jacking to mach speed, but he knew his friend wouldn't take offense. They'd grown to respect and admire each other over the past year. "And on crutches, no less," he muttered. "Why do I get the feeling you might be about to?"

Evan rubbed his head. He still insisted on wearing the Marine Corps flattop and his shoulders filled out a Marine Corps fleece paired with flannel pajama bottoms. He hadn't bothered to don what he called his Terminator leg, so Evan had used a pair of crutches to get around, a pair he always kept in his Jeep.

"I'm wondering why you haven't asked Meghan to marry you yet?" He propped himself against the deck column and waited.

"Beat around the bush much?" Dylan said, half joking, because he knew it was a legit question, and he knew how protective Evan was of both his sister and his niece.

Evan's lips flattened. "Not my style, Doc. You love my sister or not?"

Dylan's brow puckered. "Hell, of course I do. I told you and Brielle that when I approached you with my intentions."

Evan seemed to be contemplating that, and nodded. "So you did, which I respect, and I know it made Brielle super happy. What's stopping you? The shitball Jacques coming here? He's a nonentity, believe me."

Dylan chewed on that comment and looked away. "I know he's nothing to her anymore."

Evan nudged him with the edge of his crutches, right between his ribs, forcing him to turn back. "Then what are you waiting for? Never took you for a nervous one, Doc, even though you're not a Marine."

Dylan couldn't help his teeth from gnashing, knowing Evan and his wiseass, tough-shit way sought to provoke a response. Only he wasn't about to take the bait. "I could ask you the same question about Augusta. She's itching to settle down." Nice deflection.

Evan's jaw ticked. "Don't you worry, Corpsman. I'm working on it. Difference is, there's only the two of us to consider, and I sure as shit wouldn't want to waste her time if she were raising a daughter by herself."

Dylan jolted back, stunned. "You think I'm wasting Meghan's time?"

Evan shrugged. "I didn't before. But you acted strange at dinner, and I know my sister felt your vibe. Everyone did. And we were here for you, bro. I could've been keeping my woman warm in my own bed during this blizzard, instead of blowing out candles."

Now who felt like a selfish prick? "I can't compete with wineries and Armani, and…hell, maybe she deserves more." There, he'd said it. Out in the open. Exposed. His fears and insecurities told to Mr. Sensitive Councilman Washburn.

His admission gave Evan pause, it seemed, for he'd finally shut his trap for a long moment.

"I'm going to tell you a story," he began.

"Will it be quick, or will I freeze my ass off first?" He blew his warm breath into his hands.

Evan snickered. "You know I'm no fan of the old man."

Dylan nodded. Not many people in Havenport were.

"We tolerate each other. Barely. Growing up, the atmosphere was strained, to say the very least," Evan continued. "I cannot recall there ever being a time we saw eye to eye. Hell, I'd provoked most of his ire, to be plain." Evan gazed out into the snowy yard. "I hated the wealth and the pretentious crap. It made me want to vomit. So I left. But it wasn't like that for Meghan, or so I thought. Being older, she'd left for college in New York when I was still getting into fender benders with Dad's Bentley." Evan shook his head. "I was dead wrong. She'd hated it as much as I did."

"But she married *him*," Dylan responded, his voice hoarse with emotion.

"Because she had no other choice," Evan ground out, and looked him square in the eye. "She made a mistake. The old man showed up and threatened to pull her out of school if she didn't make nice with the French asshole who said he was interested in coming to Havenport with his winery expertise. Promised to make my father millions with the rich soil in Rhode Island." Evan grimaced. "Horseshit! Merely a ploy to suck Meghan in to get at her trust money, and he nearly did." Evan glanced out at the darkness and shook his head in disgust.

"She never told me," Dylan whispered. And here he thought she'd shared all of herself.

Evan shrugged and swiped at the snow piling on top of the deck railing. "Not her best moment. We all have them. After Brielle came, Meghan tried to fit into that high-society world. I knew it was all bullshit. Who she is—*really* is, the true Meghan, stronger on the inside than twenty-five Marines suited for combat—I've witnessed lately. *Here.* With you."

Dylan let that doozy of a comment sink in. *Because of me?* "You're serious."

Evan rolled his eyes. "Please don't get a large noggin, Doc. It's because you helped her understand that being a strong woman is all about what's on the inside." He patted himself on the sternum. "She loves you, man. You either bask in that and count yourself the luckiest sonofabitch on earth, like I do with Augusta, or not." Evan adjusted his crutches and turned toward the house. "Take my observation for what it's worth and make your move. Or give her the freedom and courtesy to keep being who she is, without you."

Silently, Evan trudged back toward the door.

"Gunny?" Dylan called out, and Evan turned. "Copy."

Today was the first day of the rest of his life, and he'd better make it so.

❄ ❄ ❄

The warmth of the down comforter was a safe, soft cocoon. Her nose was the only thing exposed, and it was cold. She cracked open an eye to a large, wet snout breathing into her face. *Note to self: Pick up a bag of those toothbrush-shaped treats at Wags and Walks.* "You need a doggy mint," she muttered, and stretched her arms overhead. She peered out at the break in the curtains of Dylan's guest room to see gray skies. At least it had stopped snowing.

Ed pulled at the comforter, bringing with the movement a blast of cold air.

"Brr...stop that."

Guess the electricity wasn't on yet, for there wasn't any warm air blowing through the vents and the room felt like an icebox. A quick tug of war ensued, and Ed, of course, won. "Okay, I'm getting up. Didn't anyone downstairs think to feed you? Where's Dylan?"

Dylan. *Oh, boy.* She closed her eyes for a split second then sat up. Not a happy camper last night, not that she could blame him. But today she planned to make up for it. Prove to him that their life together was the most important thing on the planet.

Stay away from my family. Her stomach fluttered with the memory. Yes, Dylan *had* voiced that heated sentiment last night, and he must believe he still meant it. Ed gave her leg a nudge, and she petted his head. "I'm on it. Let's go get you some food and me some coffee." He gave a short bark and bounded out of the room.

Standing, she gripped the bed as a wave of dizziness shot to her head, but it passed quickly. Yeah, today she needed to get to a drugstore to confirm what she already knew. "I better get those papers signed." Time to call Dad's lawyer again. She donned her pink, fluffy robe over her pajamas and threw on slippers.

She opened the bedroom door and stopped short. "What on earth?" Had Rambo gotten into something he shouldn't have? A trail of yellow, pink, and lavender petals littered the floor, setting course down the hallway. She followed the colorful trail to the stairs, noting they extended on each tread. She peeked over the railing. Okay, more scattered on the wood floor leading to the kitchen.

Curious, she made her way to the first floor. She reached the bottom step and her mouth trembled. Rambo and Zeus had large black bows around their necks.

Then Dylan stepped into view with a tentative smile.

"What's all this?" she asked, anxious.

He gave her a sideways grin, the one which melted her heart on many occasion. "Technically, today is my birthday, so I figured we'd continue the celebration."

She blinked and swallowed hard. "Oh, okay. Sure." His outstretched hand enveloped hers and he tugged her off the last step. The smell of freshly made coffee, bacon, and eggs hit her nose. Her stomach growled. "Guess I'm hungry, but let me cook for you."

Dylan shook his head. "Nope. But I will need you to close your eyes."

Her steps faltered. "Why?"

He blocked her view of the kitchen with his wide shoulders. "Just trust me," he asked, and brought her hand to his lips.

She rolled her eyes. "Fine." She huffed. "Lead the way, Doctor."

Meghan felt his smile against the back of her hand before he tugged her forward. If felt disorienting to walk with her eyes closed, but she took baby steps and followed the low and deep sound of his voice. "Just a few more steps."

They stopped, and his hands rested on her shoulders from behind. Had they turned around? "Which way am I facing now? Dylan?"

His hot breath hit her ear, and she shivered. "Open your eyes, my love."

She did, and her jaw slid open.

Standing in a row in the kitchen, in their PJs, were Brielle with Rambo at her feet, Augusta, Evan, and Peg. Ed, last in the line, sat back on his haunches with a large chain dangling from his massive neck. Each held a sign with one word on it.

Will. You. Marry. Me?

Her breath caught in her throat. No words formed. All four of her friends…no, scratch that, *family* looked on anxiously. Brielle had the brightest smile on her face.

She craned her neck back at Dylan, whose grip had tightened on her shoulders. He seemed positively nervous, and bit his lip. "What…you…"

"Come on, Meggy. Please put the man out of his misery," Evan jested, and she heard his grunt where Augusta must've elbowed him in the ribs.

But she couldn't move. Could only stare into Dylan's face with love overflowing in her heart. Then he whistled for Ed, who approached and sat at her feet. Dylan removed the chain from around his neck, pulled off what had been dangling, got on one knee, and placed the most stunning ring on her finger. She gasped.

"Will you marry me, Meghan?"

Tears blurred her vision. "Yes."

His whole body relaxed. He shot to his feet and crushed her to him. Then he cupped her face and gently kissed her. "Oh, thank God," he murmured against her lips. "I love you."

She tipped her head back and looked deeply into his eyes. "Love you more."

"Not possible," he replied.

"It might be possible in eight months, give or take," she whispered, bit her lip, and placed his hand on her stomach, hoping her hint wouldn't make him rethink his question.

His eyes widened, followed by his face splitting into a grin the size of Ed's head. "We're gonna need a bigger house for the crew over there." He tipped his head to the people and four-legged creatures who were their true family.

The room erupted in applause, and they all approached with congratulations, hugs, and more love than she ever thought possible filling her life.

About the Author

NICOLE S. PATRICK has always loved to read, and in her teenage years, she "borrowed" her mom's books to sneak away and become lost in the world of romance. After more than ten years in the corporate world of tech recruiting and HR management, she decided to stay home and raise children. But with so many romantic stories and characters floating around in her head, when the kids napped, she was compelled to put those words on a page and pursue this crazy dream of becoming published. Nicole writes romantic suspense and her heroes are those alpha males in uniform. She lives in New Jersey with her real-life hero, her husband, and her two sons.

❄ ❄ ❄

For more information about Nicole, please visit her website at www.NicoleSPatrick.com

Also by Nicole S. Patrick

❄ ❄ ❄

<u>Timeless Tales – Short Stories</u>

Letter From St. Nick featured in Timeless Keepsakes

Poseidon's Strength featured in Timeless Escapes

The Colors of Courage featured in Timeless Treasures

From This Day Forward featured in Timeless Vows

<u>Havenport – Novellas</u>

White Christmas featured in Christmas in Havenport

Hometown Hero featured in Welcome to Havenport

A Spirit's Bond featured in Haunted Havenport

❄ ❄ ❄

Never Say Never

by Ruth A. Casie

❄ ❄ ❄

Pam Dawes has always done what was expected by her high-society parents and friends. Look where that got her. Husband number two is quickly becoming a bad memory. She's through with men. Never again.

Mikhail Ivanovich Stephanov, doesn't care what happens to himself—revenge for his family is all that matters.

When a freak storm brings down communications, Pam's the only one who can help the mysterious Russian who washes up on her dock. Sparks reignite when they realize they'd met years ago. Mik's more than willing to put his vendetta aside, until Pam becomes the target of the Russian thugs that have infiltrated Havenport's coast. He'd die to keep her safe.

They'd both sworn to never love again. Will they learn to never say *never?*

❄ ❄ ❄

Dedicated to ~

Staci, Cori, Chris, Ari, and Kait for their unwavering support and enthusiasm. They spur me onward.

Olivia, Alex, and Caylee for their limitless smiles, hugs and kisses.

DM Comfort and her spot on editing. You've made this a better book and me a better writer.

Paul for his unconditional friendship and love. He always has my back.

Emma, Lita, and Nicole who keep me focused and on target and tolerate my bursts, the good ones and the not so good ones.

Chapter One

"Another great cup of tea. I love spending time and catching up, but I can't stay for a tea-leaf reading. I spent more time at the gym than I planned doing squats and exercising with fifty-pound weights. With this snow, I want to get home before the roads get bad," Pam said.

Pam Dawes sat with Marta Aleksandra Valentinovna, the proprietor of the Russian Bear, Havenport's exotic tea room. Pam swore by Marta's honey-lavender tea, not the free tea-leaf reading that came with it. Why examine her future? Marta would only confirm what she knew. Bleak. Bland. Empty.

"Oh, no, you don't. The last time I read your leaves was a year ago, which is much too long. You can spare five minutes for a reading." Marta drew her black pashmina wrap close. The twinkle in her silver-gray eyes morphed into a solemn expression. For all the jokes about tea-leaf reading, Marta took her work very seriously.

"We have plenty of time. It's only snow flurries. Humor me. Pick up the cup with your left hand and silently ask your question."

"I don't have a question," Pam said, taking up the cup as instructed.

Marta raised her chin and flashed an icy glare.

"All right." *Don't offend her.* The quicker Marta got the reading over, the quicker she could leave. Was she really a nonbeliever or was she afraid to hear what Marta would find hidden in the tea leaves?

Sitting with Marta, Pam, who worked hard to outwardly give the impression she feared nothing, squirmed in her seat. The reading last year was eerily close to the truth. *A lucky guess. That's all it was.* A coincidence, or perhaps the reader had inside information. How else would Marta know the Havenport Historical Society board's closely held decision? Marta showed no surprise when the board nominated Pam as their next president. The woman had a cat-ate-the-canary smile when Pam told her she'd accepted.

That coincidence could never happen twice.

Pam sighed. A few more minutes with Marta wouldn't hurt. Perhaps a diversion would get her out of her mood. Her marriage to Merle, husband number two, was over years ago. The legalities lingered, but with the finality only weeks old, she looked back on her marriage and wondered how she'd got into this situation again.

Love wasn't part of the equation. If anything, it was all calculation. Her rebellious days were tamed, and in the end she did everything according to her social position—married the right man who had the right business acumen and belonged to the right family. As a result, she'd expanded her already extensive bank account and became a prominent personality in Havenport, if not Rhode Island, society.

Her mother said love found people over time. It found Merle…with someone else. Good for him. He was a bastard, but he found his love. As for her? She accepted that love had lost its way where she was concerned.

Just once she wanted to be the object of someone's attention, not her money or social standing, and have a relationship like her best friend. In love at least, Rachel followed her heart rather than her head.

Heart. Did she have one? It didn't beat with excitement or anticipation. These days, she raised her heart rate training at the gym for the Tough Mudder challenge. She'd been the weakest person on the team when she started six months ago, and now trained four days a week for the May event. She worked her way out of the training basement and became one of the top two women on the team. Great benefits came with her improved upper-body strength. Made carrying shopping bags so much easier. She coughed over a chuckle.

Pam stared at the small pool of liquid and twigs in the bottom of her tea cup. Her question? *Coward*. She didn't have the nerve to ask, and didn't really want to hear the answer sitting in her heart. She didn't need a third strike. No. Never again. Her life was fine. She was fine. No longer would she assume the part of the victim. Heroine. That's the role she wanted.

Bring on the reading. She'd figure out the question later.

With a counterclockwise motion, she swirled her cup three times, then inverted it over her saucer. After a minute, Pam turned the cup upright and handed it to Marta who studied the pattern made by the leaves.

"Notice how the tea leaves scatter in the bowl. There is meaning to where they land on the cup. The rim is the present, the side shows events close at hand, and the bottom the distant future."

Pam studied the leaves along with Marta, but gave up. Where Marta perceived prophecy, she observed sludge.

"The tea leaves form pictures. Overall, your leaves reveal good fortune. The anchor, palm tree, and triangles."

Marta pointed to the dregs in her cup. "The anchor means success in business or in love."

"Yes. My attorney congratulated me. My divorce settlement from number two is final. It was a fantastic success. I walked away with my bank account intact," Pam said.

"Don't be so sarcastic," Marta snapped, although a smile smudged her lips. "Palm trees are a positive omen, also success—in anything you do. For single people it means marriage."

Pam examined the inside of the cup. "Hmm. Triangles. Is there a ménage in my future?"

"Don't be ridiculous. Triangles indicate a boon of some kind." Marta tilted the cup. "Ah, heart shapes—a lover, and much success. I've never seen a grouping of leaves like this. They keep pointing to marriage."

"Oh, no. Not again. I couldn't take another marriage. I'm not putting my attorney's kids through college. This last divorce probably bought him a new Lamborghini."

Marta ignored her and kept studying the delicate china cup. "I'm not sure if this is the letter *M* or *W*," Marta said.

"Is the *M* for *man* and the *W* for *woman*? Does that mean my lover could be…"

Marta didn't rise to Pam's bait. Instead, she pulled her shawl closer and focused on the contents in the small cup. "No, it represents the first letter of *his* name, whichever letter it is. The image of the letter sits near the rim. You'll find out soon." Marta tipped the cup in another direction. "There also appears to be an aura of crisis closing in on you. Perhaps these small axes hold the answer."

Pam peered into the cup. All she made out were twigs, lines of them. "Axes? Too late. I divorced Merle, although I contemplated axing off his more manly parts when I found him in a compromising position on the sofa in the boathouse with his secretary."

The scandal was in black and white in the *Havenport Herald*, thanks to Candy Apples. Pam took a deep breath and faced the gossip in the newspaper full-on. She had nothing to hide, except Merle's rejection and deception. They cut deep along with the humiliation. She shrugged away the thoughts and again looked inside the cup.

"What about these lines? Do they mean anything?" Pam asked.

"They signify a journey. These seem to be straight and reach toward the handle." Marta straightened in her chair quickly, so quickly she almost head-bumped Pam. "You need to go home. Now."

"I didn't need the reading to tell me that." Pam stood and pointed toward the cup. "Before I leave, take one more look. I'm sure you can see a best-selling book with a hot cup of honey-lavender tea in front of the fireplace in my future."

"As a matter of fact, I do." A broad smile lit Marta's face. She handed Pam a package of tea and glanced out the window. Marta crunched her brows together and bit the side of her cheek. "Snow is in your future; lots of snow. Are you going to the lodge?"

"Yes, tomorrow. Why?"

"Nothing. Be careful. Now go." The woman shooed her out of the shop.

Pam drove out of town along Constitution Boulevard and turned onto Manor Road past the entrance to Havencroft Manor. Edythe Emerson and her husband had donated the estate to the Historical Society last year and provided a trust to help fund its renovation.

The capital campaign Pam launched for the Historical Society to raise the rest of the needed funds exceeded the Board of Trustee's expectations. The success of the campaign catapulted her to board president, and while the fund created a solid financial foundation, Pam's goal was for Havencroft Manor to be self-sustaining.

When a couple asked to have their wedding at Havencroft, Pam knew the grand Victorian manor would be the perfect setting and lead to financial success.

That must be the wedding Marta saw in the tea leaves. Pam's cell phone rang through the car's system. She glanced at the incoming number and let out a slow breath. An able manager, her assistant, Ina, had called twice: once while she was in the gym and again before she reached the tea room.

"Hi. Has the florist arrived? And the heaters? I still can't believe they want part of the ceremony outside in this weather. Oh, and have someone clear the snow off the patio." The bride's mother was crazy, but with the light snowfall and the garden lights, the patio atmosphere would be magical.

The bride's mother insisted the fireplace was the perfect spot for the ceremony. Floor-to-ceiling windows flanked the oversize stone fireplace and looked out on the patio. The blushing bride and the gallant groom would be surrounded by the snowy wonderland dressed with small twinkling LED lights. Even she thought the spot was romantic.

"Pam, stop worrying. The florist got here a half hour ago. The snow is wreaking havoc on the incoming flights and forced her to wait at the Providence Airport for the flowers to arrive. All the flowers and heaters are in place. You won't believe how terrific the room looks. I had the groundskeeper clear the patio. He'll shovel again before the ceremony. With the huge windows, we don't want the wedding guests distracted by the snow-shoveling brigade. We want the guests' eyes glued on the happy couple. Are you stopping by to check everything?"

"Me? I admit I love planning weddings as long as they aren't my own. No, I'll wait to see the picture in the *Herald*. I'll catch up with you later. Call if you need me."

Pam ended the call and drove along Manor Road past other estate entrances. Some of these grand homes were set far back from the road; others behind man-made knolls. Either way, the stately houses were hidden from probing eyes. Some of the most influential, privileged people in Rhode Island had a Manor Road address.

As one of the founding dynasties, the Dawes family was included in those privileged few. The position came with a burden of keeping up with her peers on all levels.

She'd had enough. Under the guise of saving her marriage, she'd invested two years into finding out what made her tick. In the end, she didn't like what she found or whom she married. It was easier than she'd imagined, breaking away from the constant parties, aimless travel, and shallow relationships, including Merle. Pam stepped out of the limelight, took back her maiden name, and ran as fast as she could into obscurity, determined to move on, this time in the right direction.

Pam turned onto the Dawes Manor drive. It was six o'clock. The snow had been falling all afternoon and didn't show any signs of stopping, which was fine with her. The garage door opened, and she parked her Land Rover, put the car keys on a peg, grabbed her tea, and hurried through the colonnade that attached the house to the garage. It was a godsend in bad weather.

The house stood on a knoll and from its perch above the tree tops had a majestic view of the water. Her mother hated getting caught in the wind that swept up from the water and roared unchecked through the courtyard. She insisted on an enclosed breezeway between the garage and the house. Mom, who was a stickler concerning outward appearances, didn't care that a breezeway would be an architectural eyesore with an old Victorian manor. Instead, her father built an enclosed colonnade from the garage to his game room that protected the courtyard and made it useable.

Pam entered the game room. Nervous energy, like electric sparks, raced along her nerves at the sight of her ski equipment ready to load into the Land Rover for her trek to the lodge in the morning. With any luck, this weather would provide enough snow for her to enjoy her first ski of the season.

Husband number two's all-white ski gear hung on its peg like an empty astronaut suit waiting to be filled. He'd left it behind with other things, and established his new house with his new wife in Key West. No need for ski clothes there. She'd packed all his ski clothes and was ready to donate them to the pro shop at the ski lodge.

Over the past year, she'd looked at his things and couldn't bring herself to toss them. It wasn't because she loved him or wanted him back. She was stuck in this place of nothingness and couldn't go in one direction or another. One day, she'd broken out of the haze and began reorganizing her life. She worked with the Historical Society, the town library, and weeded out the things Merle left behind.

Once through the game room, Pam entered the house. Usually her housekeeper, Helen, greeted her. Today the house was empty. Helen was visiting her friend in Providence and wouldn't be back until Monday.

After putting her coat in the closet and tea in the kitchen, she made her way to the family room. The soothing view looked down on the private cove with its boathouse, dock, breakers, and ocean beyond. As a child, she'd rested her elbows on the windowsill and stared at the clouds and made up stories about their shapes. As a young adult, she'd stared at the water and dreamed of the places she would travel. Now, as a grown woman, the view comforted her as she sat by the fireplace and read.

Merle's telescope was by the window. To watch the stars, he told her. Except the lens focused on a bungalow on the outcrop of land by the cove. The bungalow his secretary lived in after her divorce. To help her out, Merle said.

Pam turned on the fireplace, thankful she had insisted on installing a remote-controlled gas unit. She grabbed the throw and curled up on the reclining wingback chair with a book. She let out a deep sigh. Life didn't get much better than this.

Chapter Two

Pam read the last page and closed the book. *The Plot Thickens*. The writing duo and her good friends, Beth Holmes and Jarred Watson, always delivered. The story's heroine was brave and fearless, and the hero supportive and strong. She shook her head. Fantasies, all of them. *If only life imitated art*. She chuckled at the turned phrase.

The mantel clock struck the quarter hour, nearly eight o'clock. With daylight long gone, she put the book on the end table and stretched in the soft light. Before she could curl up again and watch a movie, her stomach rumbled. She padded into the kitchen and heated up the tomato bisque and toasted the grilled cheese croutons Helen left her.

She bypassed the kitchen table—too many empty chairs—and put her food on a tray and brought it into the family room. Small ice missiles bombarded the windows as the snow came down harder and faster. Pam turned on the television to drown out the noise. A red banner burst across the screen.

"We interrupt our regularly scheduled program to bring you breaking news from the Northeast Weather Bureau," the announcer said. A digital map of Rhode Island indicating the movement of the storm flashed behind him.

"Winter storm warnings have been issued for the eastern shore area of the state for tonight and tomorrow. As you can see on the map, one to three inches of snow is likely to fall over parts of inland Rhode Island. Heavier totals of up to five or six inches are expected in a narrow corridor over the eastern shoreline where the storm has appeared to have stalled. The National Weather Service is keeping an eye on this weather system. There is a strong weather system behind this winter storm that should sweep this snowstorm out to sea by tomorrow morning. More news at eleven."

Not a terrible storm, if you're not a bride and it's not your wedding. Pam dialed Ina. On the second ring she disconnected. The woman would call if she needed anything. It was just a little snow, a phenomenon that happened often in New England, although this storm was earlier than usual.

A public broadcasting program resumed. Pam brought a spoonful of warm soup to her lips and took a deep breath. The mildly spicy aroma of the creamy tomatoes and the melted cheddar cheese croutons smelled like her childhood and reminded her of sitting with Rachel Emerson, her best friend at home in Havencroft Manor. Over the years, the two girls had spent their time after school in Havencroft's breakfast room bent over their homework, snacking on soup and grilled cheese, talking of their latest crush, and planning their futures.

Their futures. Marrying a prince of a man, having children, seeing the world. Pam took a deep breath. That was a lifetime ago. *Get a grip*. Next, she'll believe Marta's tea-leaf predictions.

The television snapped off a split second before the house lights flickered and failed. Even with the huge windows, the room plunged into darkness. The flickering flames of the fireplace provided the only light. Pam sat in the quiet room to let her eyes adjust and listened to the snow pelt the windows.

She grabbed her cell phone, switched on the flashlight app, and made her way to the hall closet and the emergency lantern. Everyone who lived on the coast had lanterns stowed around the house, used to storms with their intermittent blackouts.

Emergency lights came on in strategic areas in the hall and on the stairs. The backup generator was programmed to start up three minutes after the power loss and would light select areas of the house. Husband number one lit essential rooms, the master bathroom and wine cellar. It never ceased to amaze her where his priorities were. Every so often he'd trip the electricity to force the generator on so he could glow in his genius.

She had more realistic priorities and lit the kitchen (to keep the fridge on), colonnade (to get to the garage), garage (to get to the generator controls), and dock (to keep the emergency lights on). The backup generator went on more often than she liked, but she wouldn't dial down the system. Before she reached the hall closet, the generator kicked in and the lights were on. Back in the family room, she glanced out the window.

It was almost a whiteout condition. The wind off the water made it look like a blizzard. This was not a five- or six-inch storm. By the time this ended, it would be twelve or eighteen inches, maybe more.

She checked her computer. Nothing. Her cell phone was on but it didn't have a signal. The cell tower must be out.

She tried the landline and got a dial tone. Relieved, she called Ina.

"Pam, we're all right. The ceremony was beautiful. The men kept the patio relatively clear considering it was still snowing. The lights went out but the generator went on without any problems. Who would have thought there'd be a snowstorm now? How are you?"

"I'm on the backup generator here, too. Is everyone all right? Do you need anything?"

"We're fine. One minute, Pam. Christa, I'll be right with you…" A crackling noise and other voices interfered with the call. "Pam, you there?"

"Ina? Is there someone else on the line?"

"I hear you now." The interference cleared. "I've got to go. They're calling me. I'll speak to you later. I'm having everyone stay put. I plan to be here all night if I have to." They ended the call.

Satisfied everyone was safe at Havencroft, Pam made honey-lavender tea and brought it into the family room. A sense of satisfaction bubbled up. She stared out the French doors every so often and got glimpses of the windswept landscape and the dock.

The blue emergency dock light twinkled in the distance. Gust after gust of wind swirled the snow into drifts. Winds like this were concerning. Thankful the yacht club was closed and most of the boats were in dry dock, she didn't have to worry about an inexperienced sailor in this part of the cove. The Maine-like coast at Dawes Manor was rocky and treacherous. A wrong turn and a boat could slam into the rocks and sink.

The weather appeared fierce, but she looked past the danger and saw the beauty. A chill ran across her shoulders, even though the doors were tight. Axe-like images in her tea cup swirled in front of her. *Is this the crisis Marta predicted?*

She rubbed her arms, more to ease her tension than for warmth. The comfy wingback chair beckoned to her. Without electricity, the furnace would be out. Her only source of heat was the fireplace. Axes, palm trees, anchors, triangles, hearts. *Pfft.* With a sigh, she curled into the chair. She drew the blanket over her and closed her eyes.

Chapter Three

Pam could feel the warmth of his lips a breath away from hers. In the distance, a pulsing sound filled her ears—a heartbeat? Pam ignored the sound and concentrated on his lips, sure they would be warm and their touch velvet. The beep grew louder. Her eyes flickered, and like a sheet of water tumbling down a waterfall, her dream collapsed.

She moved the blanket that covered her face and stretched to snag the alarm clock.

"Okay, I'm up," she said, the beep more insistent. "Dammit." She brought her hand down to search for the offending timepiece, but found empty air until her hand smashed onto the end table.

"Shit!" she screamed. Her eyes flew open. She pulled her arm away and cradled her hand to her chest. Wide awake, she blinked and tried to focus.

She stared at the coffered wood ceiling in disbelief. This wasn't her bedroom. Her heart jumped from her chest to her feet. It was—the family room? How'd she get... It all rushed back: electricity out, backup generator on. Yes, the family room.

The mystery solved, her heart moved back to her chest. She relaxed. The constant beep still sounded. A bright pulsing light behind her washed out the glow of the fire.

She peered around the side of the chair through the French doors. The flying snow hadn't stopped. The blizzard was still in full force. The defused emergency dock light flashed like a lighthouse beacon through the windswept snow.

The dock protruded from one side of the channel that led to the cove. It took more than a thump against the dock to set off the alarm. With the forest reaching the water's edge at places, the weather could have brought down one of the tall pine trees.

Pam climbed out of the chair and rushed to the security pad to shut off the alarm. She turned the beacon's switch from pulsate to steady and kept the dock light on.

The echo of the alarm quickly faded. The silence welcoming until… She turned toward the French doors and concentrated on the sound of the wind and something else, the distressed sound of a large boat motor.

Jeez, the cove was treacherous. A seasoned sailor would have a difficult time managing the current and rocks, especially with this wind. No. No sailor would be out in this mess.

Pam rushed to the window, swung the telescope toward the dock, and searched through the swirling snow for something recognizable. Anything that would tell her what was out there.

Through the thin patches of the dense falling snow created by the shifting wind, the dock light lit up the wind sock straining in the storm. The wind attacked the dock broadside. She moved the telescope in a slow search grid. After a few seconds, the wind cleared the way; she glimpsed a green streak and refocused the telescope.

Another snap of wind and a green-and-yellow flag filled the lens. The Havenport Yacht Club burgee. She straightened. Who kept their boat in the water this late in the season? How had the boat gotten loose from its mooring?

She put her eye to the telescope and concentrated on the flagstaff at the boat's stern. Pam pulled back on the magnification and stared into the snow, determined to find the house flag and identify the boat's owner. Nothing. She strained to see through the storm and continued to search.

There. Was that a red mark? The wind caught the cloth and spread the swallow-tailed flag out, as if the cloth were pinned on a clothesline. A red *W* on a white background—the Washburn house flag.

Now she saw the outline of the boat and watched as the stern went wide. The motor ramped up. Startled, she scanned the length of the boat. If the throttle was thrown wide open someone had to be on the boat.

If the stern went any wider, the boat would be parallel with the shore, and if it got caught in a crosswind, the boat would be pushed across the narrow rock-lined channel. The boat and whoever was inside would be doomed. She grabbed her cell phone. No signal. She couldn't wait. The boat needed to be secured to the dock, and fast.

Pam rushed through the house to the garage. She pulled on her boots, a wool scarf, gloves, her winter nylon coat, and fastened the hood in place. Ready for the wind and snow, she grabbed the heavy-duty torch kept by the door and stepped into the frigid weather.

With her head tucked down, she set off into the full force of the storm, following the line of trees that ended a few yards from the dock. Even though she'd bundled up tight, the cold went through her. The snow pelted her face like tiny knives hitting their mark. The strong blasts of wind hit her hard and forced her to step back in places. She leaned into the wind and pushed on.

Pam stopped at the end of the tree line. The last twenty yards were wide open, no trees breaking the wind. Superstorm Sandy had taken those down. The wind and icy snow continued to pummel her. She adjusted her scarf over her mouth and nose.

The driving snow made the boat difficult to see. The sputtering motor grew louder, and she heard the boat knock against the dock.

Pam braced against the wind and pressed on. Finally on the pier, Pam raised her head and confirmed the boat was the Washburns' prized all-wood 1949 Chris-Craft 46-foot cabin cruiser, *Liquid Asset*. The boat bobbed like a cork in the choppy water. The wind had shifted and brought the stern back in line; the boat's port side rubbed against the pier.

"Who's onboard?" she bellowed as she searched for any lines to secure the cruiser. Nothing. The forward action of the motor kept the bow of the boat wedged into the pier.

She needed to climb on board and find the lines to tie down the stern and bow. That would be a challenge under the best conditions, and this weather was anything but the best. The motor sputtered, the gas almost gone.

The wind was too powerful to tie the boat to her dock. If the wind hit the boat in the right way, she'd lose the boat, whoever was on board, and her dock.

A strong westward gust caught the stern and pushed the boat toward the channel. The forward force of the motor kept the bow in place. *Liquid Asset* was at a forty-five-degree angle to the dock. She froze in place. If the stern pivoted away more, the boat would lose its precarious grip and wind up smashed into the rocks.

Chapter Four

Pam lifted the lid of the dock box. The fishing rods had long been removed. Under a tarp she found a length of nylon rope and pulled it out. There were heavy-duty clips on both ends.

"Damn." This was the lead her father used to attach his yacht, *Nauti-Buoy*, to the winch that pulled the boat into the boathouse. She threw the line into the box. She needed something longer. Pam turned toward the boathouse tucked into the protected cove. The water wasn't as agitated, and nor were the trees flailing.

Pam looked at *Liquid Asset*. Only slightly larger than *Nauti-Buoy*.

"Hold on. I'll be right back," she said to no one. She picked up the lead and hurried to the boathouse ten yards away. She hadn't been in the large building in the past three years.

Out of breath when she reached the building, Pam punched in the code, the date of her first divorce. She opened the door and threw on the lights. The large open area with two empty slips flooded with light.

She'd worked with Dad and navigated *Nauti-Buoy* into the boathouse countless times. Now she went into autopilot: clipped the lead to the rope on the winch, set the winch on release, opened the boathouse door, and braced for the wind.

Thank God. The boat remained pinned to the dock. Racing toward the distressed boat, she pulled the rope and listened to the hum of the winch as the line played out. After years of the machine standing idle, would the force of the wind and drag of the current be too much for the old equipment? Without any help, she had no alternative.

The boat inched forward, its engine sputtering badly. This could be an advantage. Her first challenge? Clip the rope onto the boat's bow eye. She'd worry about the rest later.

The engine coughed and stopped. The east wind pummeled her and the boat. She reached for the eyelet and tugged on the boat, as if that would make the large yacht move. The whine of the winch stopped. A quick glance toward the boathouse and she located the problem. The line, stretched to its maximum, sagged in the snow. The boat drifted away from her in the current. She had to act now, before the boat drifted any farther. She would have only one chance.

With her left hand on the clip, she reached for the boat eyelet with her right and tugged on the rope with all her might. Inches short.

The clip had to go through the eyelet. The rope would reach if she pulled up the slack. One deep breath, then another. She let go of the boat, grabbed the line with both hands, and in one movement, pulled the line taut and smashed the clip against the bow eye. The sound of the clip's *click* and moan of the strained rope was her reward.

A smile spread across her face, but enjoying her victory would have to wait. Pam raced back to the boathouse and hoped for the best. She stood at the control panel and turned on the master switch. The equipment's light went on. She moved to the winch and flipped on the power. The grind of the motor pulled the line tighter. Nothing happened. She had to be patient. It would take a lot to move the yacht.

A movement by the bow drew her attention. A line dropped over the side. A minute later, another line dropped over the stern. She moved from one foot to the other like an impatient child. This might actually work. Waving her hands wildly over her head, she hoped whoever was inside the boat saw her. She felt more alive than she had in months.

The line stretched and creaked. She brought her attention back to the winch. The drum turned at a snail's pace.

The boat scraped against the rubber bumpers along the dock. If the boat hugged the dock, she could reel it into the boathouse like a prize fish. That was a big "if" in this weather. There were a few things that could go wrong: the rope could snap, the winch could pull loose, or the boat could fishtail and slam across the neck of the channel and break into pieces. Pam tossed those thoughts out. The direction of the wind was critical. She concentrated on the wind sock. It shifted and the bow dug into the dock, keeping the boat in place.

"Come on, a few degrees to the east." A slight change in direction brought the stern in toward the dock, but not enough to free the bow. If she could get to the wheel, she could steer the boat away from the dock.

Little by little, the winch tightened the line.

The stern inched toward the dock and the hull cozied against the pier, freeing the bow. A movement on the boat's bridge drew her attention. Someone was up there, but who? Open on one side, the bridge at the top of the yacht housed the command center with all the steering and engine controls.

"Hello," she shouted. "I'm going to pull the boat through the channel into the boathouse." Pam didn't see or hear any acknowledgment. No surprise. It would be difficult over the sound of the wind and winch.

Pam ran back to the boathouse and accelerated the winch. The boat moved steadily toward her through the narrow passage. As long as the wind didn't change direction, the tension on the line and drag of the yacht would keep the boat on course to pass into the cove. Keeping the line tight and tying down the boat was the easy part.

The yacht continued its graceful procession through the channel. A flurry of snow puffed in front of the boathouse. Pam checked the wind sock. It swung toward the south. She turned toward the boat and watched in horror as the stern swung toward the dock and set the boat on a collision course. She threw the winch's lever to high, demanding it give her all its power. The line strained, but the boat moved faster than the line. The boat came at her sideways.

A shadow on the bridge staggered into view, struggling with the wheel. She couldn't make out who it was, didn't have time. *Please let him straighten the boat.*

The stern and bow came back into alignment, taking the middle of the channel. Whoever was up there knew how to handle the boat.

The cruiser slid through the channel. Pam's hand hovered over the winch, ready to cut the power. The bow needed to clear the channel. *Just. A. Little. Farther.* With the boat into the cove, she turned off the winch and the boat glided toward the boathouse.

The line went slack and dipped into the water. The wind shifted and pushed the boat from behind. Forty-six feet of cabin cruiser picked up speed and headed for the boathouse.

Damn. She had waited too long. Large boats didn't scare her. Pam had been around them all her life. But she was running out of options, fast. A list of ideas raced through her brain as she evaluated each one, then tossed it aside. Nothing stuck. She needed to slow down the advancing boat or else it would crash into the boathouse and take the boat pilot and her. The engines were the key.

The cranking of the ignition echoed in the air. She peered at the bridge and once again tried to make out the person at the wheel. Over and over, she heard the determined attempts of someone trying to start the engine. It had her on an emotional roller coaster. The engine had to catch. Each *click*, *cough*, and *sputter* had her hopes up, only to be crushed when the engine failed. She didn't give up.

"With all that is holy, start, dammit. Start," she said under her breath, her fists tight at her side.

The yacht rushed toward the boathouse, only feet away from the door. She stepped back, her mind racing for the best way to minimize the damage and save the pilot.

The person in the boat kept at the engine. Over and over, the grinding noise of the ignition continued until a welcome sound exploded in her ears.

Relief surged through her. She stepped forward, ready to grab the dangling lines. From the revs, she knew only one of the twin screws operated at full throttle. The boat slowed from what must have been the full reverse thrust of the boat's propeller. As quickly as the engine burst into life it died, but it was enough. The boat glided with a stately grace into the boathouse. Pam rushed forward, grabbed the bow line, and secured it to the cleat. She hurried to the stern and secured that line, then hit the switch and closed the boathouse doors.

Shaking from the adrenaline rush, she pulled herself up the ladder onto the main deck. Looking up at the bridge, she called, "Who's on board?"

Above the rattling of the wind, there was a low moan from the bridge.

Pam scaled the ladder to the bridge, pushed through the tarp, and entered the small command center.

An unconscious man, soaked without a coat or shoes, lay sprawled across the instruments. She pulled off her hat and scarf, grabbed a discarded tarp she found crumpled at his feet, and covered him. The man lifted his head.

Chapter Five

Mikhail Ivanovich Stephanov struggled to open his eyes and focus on his savior. His eyelids, as heavy as his mother's potato pierogies, settled for peeking through thin slits. A warrior with a porcelain complexion, long dark hair, and ruby-red lips gave him a concerned stare.

He swam for his life to catch the drifting yacht headed out to sea. Once back on board, he brought the boat around and set course for shore. Frozen to the bone, he hunkered under a marine tarp he'd found in a deck locker. His body had shut down to conserve what little heat he had left. Exhausted from his ordeal and colder than Siberia, he passed out.

Roused by the boat banging against the dock, he stumbled to his feet and forced his sluggish mind to assess the situation and take action. The weather had worsened. Visibility was zero. He realized the gravity of his situation when the glare of the dock light blasted through the snow. Keep the boat straight, start the goddamn engine, and move the boat away from the rocks.

Two fuel cans stood by the engine. He had poured their contents into the two Chris-Craft 300 engines earlier. Now he squeezed the drops that were left into the starboard engine. It would have to be enough. One shiver after another overtook his body.

He was an experienced sailor and smart enough to know he needed to be at peak performance in this blow, with a boat this size, and close to shore. He would either die smashed against the rocks or drown in the sea. Neither option appealed to him. He preferred dying in his sleep an old man. In his line of work? He let out a scratchy chuckle at that fantasy.

He went back into the enclosed command center and spied her rushing about on the dock. Maybe he would still make it out of this alive. He pressed the ignition over and over. The engine whined and coughed.

"Come on, baby. Start for Papa." He gave it a rest then tried again. He was unprepared when the engine caught and the boat lurched backward. He tumbled like a new foal on unsure legs onto the wheel, then everything went black.

"Who are you? What happened?" the woman asked. "And what are you doing on the Washburns' boat?"

A woman's urgent but sweet voice reached his ears. His eyes focused on her red lips and tried to make sense of her question. The sound of her quick intake of breath excited him. Perhaps she would kiss him before he died.

The engine off, the boat bobbed in the water. Lines creaked as they tightened. The wind howled in the distance. Intuitively, he knew the woman was alone. Impressive.

A shudder rushed through him, and he pulled the tarp closer.

"We've got to go to the house. There's no heat here," she said.

Who was his savior? And where was he? He stared at her, searched her face. She didn't hide her thoughts. That was refreshing. The woman had no idea what to do with him. He felt the corners of his mouth pull. With those red lips and long hair falling over her shoulder, he could think of a few things.

His savior left and returned minutes later with an unopened bottle of whiskey.

"It's all I found."

She helped him sit in the pilot chair and held the bottle to his lips. He took a long draft. The amber liquid burned going down, but oh, how it warmed his belly. He began to feel alive. In the shadowed space between them, he smiled his gratitude.

Her hand quivered as she brought the bottle to his mouth, licking her lips as if she, too, tasted the whiskey.

He covered her hand with his and guided it to her target. He held her with his gaze as she gave him another drink.

"I'm Pam. Pam Dawes," the woman said.

He blinked and tried to keep his teeth from chattering. Dawes. The name lingered at the edges of his mind. He forced his mind to work. The face was familiar, but it didn't match the name.

"Mik." His voice sounded like a frog's. "How? Where?" He removed the bottle from her trembling grasp and took another swig.

"You're at my home in Havenport; the boathouse, actually. Lucky for you the yacht set off the dock alarm. With this storm, you could've crashed into the rocks." Pam searched his face. "Your color is better. Wait here. I'll be back in a few minutes."

He had no intention of going anywhere at the moment. He raised the whiskey to his lips and watched Pam leave the bridge.

❄ ❄ ❄

Outside, the blizzard raged. Pam couldn't move away from him fast enough. First things first. She wound her scarf around her mouth and nose, then pulled down her hat. Her goal: reach the garage and bring the Land Rover to the boathouse. She had no idea how to move the man down the ladder or what to do with him when she did, but she'd figure that out later.

Her heart hammered. A familiarity filled the space between them. He wasn't a stranger, but she couldn't place him. His disheveled condition didn't hide his stature, wide and tall. His wet shirt clung to him, exposing rough-hewn muscles that looked as hard as stone. Protector came to mind. She sighed. She didn't miss how his eyes studied her, whispered to her. Familiar, she had heard it before.

Deep snow drifts piled up in odd places made going across the property difficult. The east wind blasted off the water toward the house. Everywhere she looked, the familiar landmarks were obliterated, replaced with a landscape that was as white and blank as an unpainted canvas. Pam raised her gloved hand to shield her eyes. The ferocity of the wind left her breathless and forced her to take the longer route to the garage.

No way could she cut across the exposed area facing the water, even with the colonnade. The house would be her protection from the wind. Forced to keep her head down, she followed the low stone edging and walked up the driveway to the garage. She disturbed the snow as much as possible. Her plan: get the car and follow her footprints back to the boathouse.

She was pelted with ice that clung to her eyelashes and hair, and her fingertips were numb by the time she entered the garage and turned on the blue emergency light. She rummaged through the donation bags she'd planned to deliver to the lodge until she found what she needed. Satisfied, she hit the automatic door. Still no power. A seasoned pro at not using the noisy automatic garage door—in her youth the skill had been priceless—she manually opened the door. Pam grabbed the Land Rover keys from the peg on the wall. A quick glance at her cell phone showed there was still no service.

Shit. Shit. Shit. Her limited survival skills, the ones her ski instructor had taught her, were all she knew. She was on her own.

"I can do this," she repeated over and over under her breath. Perhaps if she said it enough she would believe it. Pam started the Land Rover, flipped the switch to heat the front seats, and pulled out of the garage.

Snow blew everywhere, creating large drifts that made the landscape she could walk in her sleep unfamiliar. *You can do this* echoed with authority in her head as she pointed the car in the direction of the shallow divots that remained of her footsteps.

❄ ❄ ❄

Mik threw off the tarp. His sluggish mind, much like the boat engine, kicked into gear. He ignored the cold and concentrated on what he needed to do next. From his vantage point out the bridge window, the boat was docked inside the boathouse. A miracle they weren't killed in the process.

The slip protected him from the wind, but he needed to get someplace warm. He suspected there were living quarters upstairs in the boathouse, and headed for them.

He made his way to the main deck and found his discarded coat lying in a puddle of water, saturated. He didn't have much in his pockets. What he found he stuffed into his pants pocket and left the useless coat where he'd found it. Mik made his way to the boat ladder and found his shoes nearby. Grateful for something dry, he slipped them on.

He struggled to make his numb hands hold on to the ladder and his feet work as he went down. In the end, he thanked all that was holy that he'd gotten off the boat without falling flat on his face—or worse, into the water.

Dawes. He climbed the boathouse steps. He still couldn't place her. He didn't like not knowing. It wasn't like him to not remember a beautiful face. Her lips mesmerized him and reminded him of Merle Whilton's wife...Pam. He stopped in the middle of the staircase as a vivid recollection of Pam Whilton's face appeared in his mind. Dawes was her maiden name. Relieved his memory had thawed, he continued on.

At the top of the stairs, he stood in a spacious open room. The reflection of the dock light on the falling snow streamed through the oversize windows and lit up the space. The room looked comfortable and the fireplace inviting. If only it were lit. The kitchen occupied the far wall.

His mind churned as he made a quick assessment of his surroundings. Layers of dust were everywhere, and not just from the fall and winter seasons. No one had used the room in years.

But there was a bigger oddity. The room waited for someone to return. An empty glass on the table, a newspaper left open on the sofa, and slippers next to the chair. The place hadn't been closed down, but rather abandoned.

The glare of headlights streamed through the window. Mik shaded his eyes. He raked his hand through his damp hair. *Shit.* This was a disaster. Best not to be seen snooping around up here. He made his way down the stairs.

Chapter Six

Pam pulled the Rover close to the building. She grabbed the package off the passenger seat, got out of the car, and left it running with the heat blasting. She opened the boathouse side door. The wind blew behind her. Pam grappled to keep hold of the knob, but the wind almost pulled it out of her hand. The man caught the door before it slammed against the wall. He pulled her inside and closed it behind her.

"Thanks." She glanced from the boat to him. "I wondered how I was going to move you down the ladder."

"The whiskey got my heart started. I thought it would be drier and warmer down here than up there." He motioned to the boat.

She expected to find him huddled on the bridge, cold and weak. Instead, he stood by the winch, his wet oxford shirt and dark slacks sticking to every part of his muscular body, as if nothing was out of place. Her gaze traced down his long body, then snapped back to his face.

"Your shoes are dry." She pointed to his feet.

He stared down at his feet then at her. "They're the only dry clothing I had. I must have kicked them off before I went in the water."

So you went willingly into the water, was on the tip of her lips. She'd save that discussion until after she got him to the house. The weather worsened by the minute, and she didn't want to be stranded in the boathouse. She'd rather die than be in here. Even after all this time, the humiliation was hard to bear.

"I didn't want to waste time going into the house. I had this in the garage." She handed him the package.

He tore off the paper and unfolded a piece of fleece material. The embroidered picture of two Westies stared at him. He tilted his head and looked at her, a question on his face.

"The blanket is not a fashion statement, but it's warm," she said, her hands fluttering. McDuff and McBeth, her Westies, were long gone. It didn't seem right to throw away their favorite blanket. Over the years, the blanket made its way from the house, to the game room, and finally, to the garage.

Pam took the coverlet out of his hand and swirled the blanket around his shoulders. Still soaked, she was surprised to feel heat from his body. In the darkened space between them he smiled, showing straight white teeth and an unnerving attitude. The light in his dark-brown eyes was almost sensual.

"Thanks." He pulled the material close. The broad set of his shoulders made the blanket look like a warrior's cloak.

A warmth rushed up her neck and gathered at her cheeks. Her gaze never left him. Her fingers itched to run through his dark, wavy hair. It must be his maddening hint of arrogance that enticed her.

Was he a player? Two divorce decrees locked in her attorney's desk proved she knew the type all too well, handsome and overconfident. This man didn't appear to be like that. Like she would know. Really? Based on what? *Get a grip, Pam. Get him warm, into Havenport, and out of your life.*

"It was all I had available until we reach the house. Are you ready? The car's outside." She made her way to the door.

Pam reset the dock light and flipped off the lights. Mik went to the car as she locked the boathouse and scooted into the driver's seat.

"I believed automakers installed seat warmers and heated steering wheels to make more money. I'll have to rethink that." A deep, low moan escaped his lips.

Pam grabbed the steering wheel with a death grip. Mik's unexpected deep moan made her girlie bits come alive. They'd been dormant for some time, well before husband number two bit the dust. She gave Mik a sideways glance and saw the ecstasy on his face, and for a split second wondered if he sounded and looked that good in bed.

Jeez, where was her mind? She didn't know the man. Delirious. That's it. Or desperate. What else explained her reaction?

She put the car in gear, kept her eyes on the road, and headed for the house. The sooner she got Mik on his way, the better.

The heavy snowfall gave the landscape a pristine appearance. She glanced at Mik. Distracted for the moment, the Rover hit one of the raised rocks. She veered to the left, overcompensated, and sent the car into a skid.

Mik grabbed the wheel and steered into the skid.

"Foot off the break," he said, his voice calm and in control. The car slowed and came to a stop. "You okay?"

"Driving in the snow is nothing new to me, but thanks for your concern. I can take it from here." She knew better than to get distracted. Somehow, all she thought about was his muscular chest in that wet shirt. *Desperate.* It almost made her laugh.

Mik let go of the wheel and settled back in his seat. She followed the fading tire tracks and paralleled the trees.

Blizzards rarely hit the coast, but this storm was something else with its whiteout conditions. The usual landmarks were hidden behind a wall of white. Sporadically, she made out crude outlines that confirmed she was headed in the right direction. In this mess it would be easy to get turned around.

"We're not far. The house is on the other side of this line of trees," she said. Her heart thudded against her ribs as she thought what might happen once they moved away from the protection of the trees and were at the mercy of the erratic gusts. They could wind up back at the dock, out the drive onto Manor Road, or over the cliff.

She pulled away from the trees. The Rover shook as the full force of the storm slammed against it. She crept forward. If her passenger was concerned, he never let her know. He remained relaxed and calm, as if they were out for a summer Sunday drive.

The short drive turned into a challenge. Even though she knew the estate like the back of her hand, the tire tracks disappeared and the windshield wipers iced over. She took aim and moved the car forward.

Out of the darkness, a solitary blue light flickered through the blowing snow and confirmed Pam was headed in the right direction. In a matter of minutes, she pulled into the garage.

"Door-to-door service," she said as she got out of the car. "Need any help?"

"No," Mik said as he followed her.

She led him through the colonnade and opened the door to the game room. Pam turned to her guest, startled by his ashen color and quivering body.

"Are you all right?" she asked. Pam put her arm around Mik to help him before he collapsed.

"Oh, my God. You're ice cold." She moved her palm across his arm, chest, and thigh. "We need to warm you up before you go into shock."

Pam led him through the house, up the grand stairs, and into her bedroom.

"Is this your plan to warm me?"

She followed his stare to her very large king-size bed. Instead of responding to that silliness, she darted to the bathroom, pulling hand towels and bath sheets off the heated towel rack.

"Take off your clothes," she said as she entered the room.

Mik stood in front of her, a shit-eating grin on his face. "I'm going to enjoy your method of first aid." He started to strip.

Chapter Seven

A rush of heat went up Pam's neck as well as down to other places. A quick picture filled her head.

"It's a pleasant thought, but not what I meant. Take off those wet clothes. Here." She shoved the warm towels at him. "Leave your clothes outside the door. When you're done, you'll find clothes in the last closet."

"I look cute in pink silky things," he teased, already drying his hair.

"No. My former husband left some clothes, and I haven't gotten around to tossing them out." She looked him up and down. "I think they may be snug on you in some places, but they should do until the power comes back on and I can dry your clothes. Meantime, I'll find something to warm your insides."

He answered with that playful smirk again. Her girlie parts went crazy.

"Soup," she said, shaking her head.

He gave her an innocent expression.

"And here I hoped," he said. He took the towels from her. "Anything warm would be good."

"When you're done, I'll be in the kitchen." Pam started to leave. He grabbed her arm.

"I appreciate your help. I know I wouldn't have survived—"

"We did it together. I needed another pair of hands to manage the boat. Besides, you impress me as too stubborn to let a little wind and cold water stop you." She closed the bathroom door behind her and waited. For the first time, she was thankful husband number two put the master bath on the backup generator.

❈ ❈ ❈

Mik emptied his pockets. He didn't have much, a few bills and some change. He put that on the desk. He removed the Glock from the pocket of his cargo pants, then stashed it under a stack of towels in case Pam decided to take him up on his offer. A cold sweat covered him, and not from the frigid cold.

Never. He made a bargain. That part of his life was dead. He glanced toward the door. Not since Natasha.

He stripped off the rest of his clothes. His body shook as shivers ran up his back. The hot towels made quick work of getting him dried off. He wrapped a large towel around his waist and another towel around his shoulders. *God.* He closed his eyes and a deep moan escaped his lips. He never thought he would be warm again. He put the wet clothes outside the door, then stood still for several minutes until the chills subsided.

❋ ❋ ❋

Pam stood on the other side of her bathroom door. Mik's deep moan made Pam smile. Yeah, she knew just how good those warm towels felt when you came in from the cold. The door opened a crack. His hand snaked out and dropped his clothes on the floor, then retreated. She shook her head, picked up the wet mess, and took them to the laundry near the kitchen.

She checked his pockets and found nothing, which didn't surprise her. A glance at the labels revealed they came from a high-priced ready-made store.

So much for playing Sherlock Holmes. His clothes gave nothing away, not even a laundry mark. She learned that from one of the television shows, or perhaps from one of Beth and Jarred's novels. With the dryer set, she moved to the kitchen and poured two glasses of wine.

❋ ❋ ❋

After a quick, hot shower, Mik towel-dried his hair. He opened the door to the closet. A sea of white clothes greeted him. He rubbed the shirt material between his thumb and forefinger. Nothing here was cheap, either.

He opened the first drawer of the built-in chest and passed on the underwear. Commando would have to do. The bathroom was warm, but his ass was getting cold. He concentrated on the next layer. The pants he chose—short in the leg and too big in the waist—hung low on his hips. The T-shirt fit tight across his chest. The oversize sweater wasn't oversize on him. He opened the top drawer. The jewelry section was empty except for a gold band. He examined it. No engraving. No "I love you," initials, or a date. Next to the band he found handkerchiefs embroidered with the letter *M*. He closed the drawer, then slipped his money in his pocket and tucked the gun into the small of his back.

Mik put the folded towels on the rack and caught his reflection in the mirror. *Damn, he looked scary.* He opened the mirrored cabinet, looking for something to help tame his hair.

Expensive face creams, dental floss, cotton swabs, and toothpaste filled the bottom shelf. Aspirin, decongestant, and a bottle of over-the-counter cough medicine crammed the next shelf. The top shelf held prescriptions, an old opioid, an equally old antibiotic, but the third vial grabbed his attention—an antidepressant. The thirty-pill prescription was over a month old, and from what he saw, more than twenty were left. He put the pills back and closed the mirror.

The light from the bathroom spilled into the dark bedroom. A jewelry cabinet stood against the wall. A name tag from the Havenport Historical Society lay on a nightstand on one side of the bed. President of the Board of Directors. Pam Dawes.

He slipped out the door and headed to the kitchen.

❄ ❄ ❄

Slouched against the wall by the kitchen window, a glass of wine in her hand, Pam looked out at the horizontal snow and the faint blue glow of the dock emergency light in the distance. She couldn't see anything else.

There were times when she enjoyed living on the edge, pushing boundaries, shocking people, but after all these years, she knew better. Now a stranger—a naked one—showered in her bathroom. The thought made her smile.

Her internal argument said she couldn't have left him wet and half-dead on the boat or to fend for himself in the cold boathouse. There was something familiar about Mik. Or did she create that in her mind as an excuse because something drew her to him? He made her feel alive. Was she that desperate that anyone who floated into her life was fair game? She laughed at her own pun.

She picked up the phone. A call to the police would get Mik on his way. Static. She tried her cell phone. No service.

Trust your instincts, her mother told her, but she rebelled against that at every turn. Instincts. Instead, she followed her father's advice, plans and strategies. She'd learned the hard way that plans and strategy hadn't worked for her. What made her think she could change now?

Something nagged at her. Nothing about Mik surprised her. She pushed away from the wall. She knew him, but from where? How absurd. He must look like someone she'd met at a party or one of Merle's client events. They had been in Russia four or five years ago. She couldn't bring the events or the faces back. *Don't look for connections where they don't exist.*

Pam had a lot more important questions for her guest. First, what was he doing on the Washburns' boat? Second, why didn't he have a coat? She was sure he didn't go out in this weather without it. Third, why had he been in the water during a snowstorm? And fourth, how did he get to her dock?

Anchors, palm trees, and triangles swirled in front of her. A smile touched her lips. She should tell Marta her thoughts about the letters were right: *M* and *W*—Mik and Washburn.

She took out the artisan bread and various cheeses and made grilled cheese sandwiches. The rich, cheesy aroma wafted through the kitchen as they cooked on the grill pan. She moved to the stove and stirred the soup.

A movement by the kitchen door made her turn. He filled the entrance with his tall, well-proportioned body. Wide shoulders topped a trim waist and narrow hips. He had dark, wavy hair, distinct cheekbones, and an angular jaw. Strong arched brows and thick dark lashes that should have been illegal framed rich brown eyes flecked with gold. She stared at the most perfect man she'd ever seen.

Chapter Eight

Mik crossed the kitchen and stood next to her at the stove. He waved his hand over the pot, wafting the aroma to his nose, then took a deep breath.

"Smells good." He picked up a piece of bread from the counter and dipped it into the pot.

"Be careful. You'll burn your mouth."

He gave her a sideways glance, the tomato-drenched bread poised in his hand. Pam actually looked alarmed. It had been a long time since anyone worried about him. He stuffed the bread into his mouth.

"Delicious." He stood over her as she poured the soup into large bowls, then floated the toasted croutons on top. Mik took the bowls and brought them to the table.

"As a child, I'd come in from the snow and have hot tomato soup and a gooey grilled cheese sandwich, my comfort food," Pam said, and set a platter of warm grilled cheese sandwiches on the table for them to share.

"I did much the same, except not tomato soup. Hot borscht with a boiled potato." He kept eating.

"Beet soup is good, but not the best for dunking grilled cheese sandwiches."

"I would agree. Borscht goes well with *pirozhki*, a small bun stuffed with meat. My mother made the best."

Mik and Pam sat in silence, eating and remembering.

He understood a bit about her. They'd spoken for hours at a Tatanov party in Moscow years ago. He entertained her while his boss met with her husband, Merle, and Steffen Burkett, a mutual friend. There was a lot to Pam Dawes Whilton, a beautiful woman who could hold a conversation about a variety of subjects and gave you her undivided attention. They spent the evening talking and laughing. Two people who fit together well, but whose lives were set on different courses.

The internationally well-known Dawes family, and Pam, the headstrong heiress, owed their fortune to old family money. Pam had not gained wealth from either husband, Huntley Andrews or Merle Whilton. The twice-divorced woman had some feelings for one of the men, Whilton he suspected. The man's clothes remained in the closet. Was that the reason for the antidepressants? Had she put that behind her? He hoped so.

She was smart and showed resourcefulness in saving him and the yacht. He came away with the same impression when he'd first met her. She wasn't part of this job. He'd have to be on his toes.

"You told me your name is Mik. Is that short for Michael?" She took a section of grilled cheese and dunked it into the soup.

He added no airs to her list of attributes. He had sat with rich and famous people who carried their affectations to the casual areas of their lives. Pam sat with him eating as if they did this every day. It was a warm and comfortable feeling.

Danger flashed in his head—*opasnost!* He pushed the warning to the back of his mind for now. He wanted to enjoy their meal together. He glanced at her from under thick eyebrows, and his body warmed in places that had been ice since Natasha. Yes, Pam was more dangerous than he'd first thought.

"No, not Michael, although it is a derivative form. Mikhail." He didn't offer the rest of his name. She wouldn't remember it, and that would protect her.

"Russian?" No alarm in her voice. How refreshing. The mere word *Russian* usually raised an American's hackles. "Where?" she asked.

"Volgograd." He waited for the usual questions. Americans were familiar with Moscow and St. Petersburg. Even the smart ones didn't know about the other fashionable areas in Russia.

"On the Volga River. Volgograd is a beautiful modern city. At times it's hard to visualize the bloodiest battle in human history took place there," she said.

"Yes, the Battle of Stalingrad was the turning point of World War II," he said.

She nodded. Not an empty nod, but one that said there was intelligence behind her eyes. "Have you been away from home long?" She wiped her mouth with a cloth napkin and placed it next to her plate.

He shrugged. "Quite some time." Why had he mentioned Volgograd? The World War II battle there was nothing compared to three years ago, the bloodiest day in his life. He glanced at his hands, half expecting to see Natasha's blood, relieved he found nothing. With a compulsion, he hid his quivering hands in his lap.

Volgograd came rushing back. What was it about Pam Dawes that loosened those memories he'd worked hard to keep locked away?

"The Volga is the longest river in Europe and used to be known for its sturgeon," he said, the neutral statement safe.

"Ah, Russian *caviar*," Pam said with an over-affected Russian accent. She leaned close. "My comrade. Tell me about the cold *Russsssian* nights and the warm *wodka*."

"*Lozhimsya spat' golym i derzhim drug druga v teple.*" He leaned closer and whispered in her ear.

She didn't pull back. He found the heated flush that went up her neck charming. Was it his hot breath against her ear or...

Pam turned and faced him. Their lips a breath apart.

"You go into bed...naked...and keep each other warm," Pam said. Her stare didn't waver. "Surely you don't mean that as an invitation."

A cool sheen dampened his forehead, and excitement raced through his veins. Her breath bathed his face. Smoky, seductive eyes stared at him. For the moment, they were back at the Moscow gala, sitting alone on a small sofa in a ballroom. He blinked and returned to the sand-colored kitchen.

"No. *We* go into bed. You have the wrong conjugational form." He put his hand around her neck and pulled her toward him. Slowly, her eyes closed. He bent closer, then lightly, very lightly, kissed her lips.

❄ ❄ ❄

Pam's heart dropped to her feet, then slammed into her chest, but not before stopping at her girlie parts to shock them into life. What the hell was she doing? She had no idea who this man was. Just because there was something familiar about him didn't mean...

She opened her eyes and stared into his. The mystery in his eyes enthralled her. *Shit*. She didn't care who he was.

The picture of him standing at the kitchen doorway popped into her mind. His body screamed…what—sex? Oh yeah, that's what it screamed. And she'd played right into his hands, acting like a stupid schoolgirl. She pulled away from him, picked up the dishes along with her self-respect, and took them to the sink.

"What did you do in Volgograd?" She kept her back to him. *Get it together, Pam. You're playing with fire.*

"I worked for a shipping company."

She faced him. The gears in her head spun and settled into place.

"Tatanov Maritime." She rushed toward him, almost giggling with relief. "You're Mikhail Ivanovich. I thought you were familiar. We met in Moscow." A broad smile transformed his face. "You knew who I was all along."

"Yes, but not right away. Your face didn't match your name. I've thought of you often, especially when I received word of Steffen's passing." Mik stared at the table. "He liked to drink vodka. His Russian accent was worse than yours."

The more she and Mik spoke all those years ago, the more she realized he had those qualities she admired in Steffen, her best friend's fiancé. Their body types were similar, and while that didn't hurt, it was the character of the man that attracted her. Steffen stayed true to Rachel to the end, but that was another story. She let out a heavy breath. That meeting was all a long time ago.

"Have you left Tatanov? You were Tatanov's right-hand man." Merle had been working on a steel deal and took her to a reception at the Metropol Hotel. She was his arm candy.

The Metropol, an old pre–World War II building, was opulent and breathtaking. She and Mik talked for hours, which made Pam the envy of every woman in the room. Mik's attentive ways charmed women, a trait ladies couldn't resist. Then Natasha, Tatanov's niece and secretary, arrived. The beautiful, vivacious woman stayed at his side the rest of the night.

Pam glanced at his hand. No wedding ring. That didn't mean anything. Not all men wore a band, but somehow she thought Mik would.

"My job ended." It was a bland, unemotional statement. While she didn't keep tabs on the handsome dock foreman, she did watch her business interests. She had no idea there were changes at Tatanov Maritime and wondered what else Merle had kept from her.

"I'm sorry to hear that."

"Tatanov was encouraged to sell the business and leave the motherland."

"And you?"

He shrugged his shoulders. "I found another job."

The haunted look in his eyes told her there was more to the story. But she was more interested in how he got here, to Havenport, in the Washburn yacht, in a blizzard without any coat. He wasn't going anywhere. She had all the time in the world to find her answers.

Chapter Nine

Mik carried his wine into the family room while Pam straightened the kitchen. He sipped his drink and made a quick survey of the surroundings. The large windows would give a grand view of the cove and ocean on a clear day, but he preferred solid walls, especially at his back.

Several conversational areas filled the large space. He chose the sofa near the fireplace where he could see the doors, all of them.

"What did you do after the shipping company closed?" She came into the room and topped off his glass of wine and hers. He didn't object.

"I went into the Spetsnaz GRU, similar to your American Special Forces."

"Like our Navy SEALs?"

He took another sip and relaxed into the sofa. "I started out there, but the state had a special need for my services." As perceptive as Pam was, he had no intention of telling her his intimate knowledge of the Tatanovs' business dealings which gave him a special skill that interested the Special

Forces. "They sent me to Siberia then thought Afghanistan was a more appropriate mission for me."

"A bloody, horrible war," she said.

Not nearly as bloody as Volgograd. He took a bigger gulp. "As my father would say," he said, and beat his chest with his fist, "strong like bull."

His over-affected accent made her burst out laughing. This was the Pam Whilton he remembered, the woman who smiled often and laughed freely without a care in the world. He wanted to hear her laugh again and often.

"I survived." He tossed the comment out as if it were nothing. He joined the military with every intention of dying. Instead, he learned and grew strong.

"Yes, I can see that." She still laughed.

"Then I left the army." The suicide missions for which he'd volunteered made him strong and deadly.

"Your parents must be happy to have you back safe."

How naive. She had no idea of the reality in which he lived. No one did.

"My parents passed on before I left for the service." He had buried the guilt for their deaths a long time ago.

His mother and father had been with Natasha and the Tatanov family the day of the massacre—collateral damage. Natasha was barely alive when he found her. She died in his arms, his hands covered with her blood. Too late to help her or his parents, he made a vow to wipe out everyone involved in the murders, to wipe out the Soika Pack.

Pam turned to him. The pain on her face made him sorry he said anything. He forgot how sensitive and caring she was. It had drawn him to her those years ago.

"I'm sorry. I don't know what to say."

He took her hands. "It was a long time ago." The Special Forces taught him how to plan, kill, and survive.

His vow to avenge his family's murder became more than an empty threat. It was his new mission. Today, three gang members remained. Every day he planned and plotted.

He looked into her eyes. She rattled him to his core. He brought his fight to her doorstep and put her in great danger. He couldn't let anything happen to her. Protecting her was important, and a part of him said surviving wouldn't be bad, either, if it was with her.

He rubbed the soft skin on the back of Pam's hand and wondered if he could start his life over. He let out a deep breath. What would an heiress want with a murdering dockhand like him? The wealthy didn't mingle with his kind.

"Without any ties in my country, I decided to travel, so I came to America and started a yacht piloting business." It was his cover story and close to the truth. He couldn't tell her much more and hoped she didn't press the issue. Lies only meant more trouble.

"Why were you on the Washburn boat?" Her direct question startled him, but he knew she would ask.

"I've known Evan Washburn a long time and stopped to see him. When he got the weather report he asked me to do him a favor and take his father's boat down the coast. Out of Havenport, he said, before the storm hit."

He pulled her close and tucked her into his side. She didn't argue.

"Before I reached the breakers, the weather turned. The wind came up fast and the snow flurry turned into a blizzard, as if someone turned on a switch. I came about and raced to the safety of the yacht club. The water turned more violent the closer I got to shore."

"That's so unusual," she said. "The water is calmer on this side of the breaker."

"I was counting on that, but when the engine stalled I got tossed around like a leaf in the wind. I took off my coat and opened the engine compartment. A wave broke over the stern and pulled me over the side. It felt like it took me hours to work my way back onto the boat. I got the engine working and tried to call the harbor patrol, but the phone was dead. I must have collapsed. The next thing I knew, I banged up against your dock."

He hoped she accepted the story. From what he remembered, Pam wasn't the gullible type, but he couldn't tell her the details he'd left out for her own good.

"Lucky you bumped into my dock and set off the alarm. If that hadn't gone on, you and the *Liquid Asset* would be toothpicks."

He looked deeply into her eyes. "I'm well aware. How should I reward you for saving my life?" He played with a curl over her ear.

"All a part of water safety. The fine print on my lifesaving card states I cannot demand compensation when saving someone's life." She bit the side of her check, but while she held back the smile, she was unsuccessful at controlling the smile that lit her eyes. He couldn't help but smile with her.

She settled back next to him. "Although I may make an exception where you're concerned."

"Make sure they are mutual benefits. I hate one-sided deals."

Pam let loose with a throaty laugh. They sat like that for a while, staring at the fire. Cozy and comfortable, as if sitting together was something they did every day.

❋ ❋ ❋

Pam didn't know how long they sat watching the fire, silent and content. She got up and took the empty glasses. "More?" she asked.

"Sure." He stood.

"No," she said, and pushed him back. "I can do this myself. You stay here, near the fire and keep warm. I'll be right back."

Pam headed into the kitchen and retrieved a bottle of wine from the wine fridge in the middle of the kitchen island. The green button flashed on her landline. She picked up the phone, not so sure she wanted to contact the outside world as she glanced toward the family room. Her world had suddenly gotten full, and even pleasant.

Pam put the phone to her ear. Static. The crackling noise on the line subsided. No dial tone. She had to speak to the town council about emergency preparedness.

"Hello, is anyone there? This is Police Chief James Kantor."

"James, Pam here."

"Hello. Hello. Jeez, Marge, when does the phone company expect the phones to be up and running? They said they were working on it, but I can't get a dial tone. Taylor, you there?"

"Roger, Chief," Taylor said.

"At least you're coming through loud and clear," James said.

"James, it's me, Pam Dawes."

"We need to alert the community," James said. "Agent Lyons wants to put out an all-points bulletin, but we can't do that with both the landlines and cell towers compromised. This storm is wreaking havoc on a lot of fronts. I don't want to panic people, not with them locked down by this storm. The houses along the waterfront are our first priority. That's the last place the boat was seen. We'll go house to house. I've arranged for a town plow to lead us. We'll tell everyone we've come to make sure they're all right and ask if they've seen anyone who needs help. We can't tell them there's a dangerous Russian criminal at large. The FBI already lost one agent. Hello, hello. Taylor. Are you there? Shit." The line went dead.

Pam put the phone down. James couldn't be right. Mik… She couldn't be that wrong. Okay, people change, but not that much. She closed her eyes.

Her brain screamed *Help, James*, but her heart told her things weren't as they seemed. She uncorked the bottle. Her head swam trying to decide what to do. The answer wasn't so simple.

Chapter Ten

Be objective. You know very little about Mik and less about why he's here. Some of his story stretched even Pam's vivid imagination. Was it a coincidence that Mik showed up and James was on a manhunt looking for a Russian? Yeah, right. Even she understood the odds of that happening were slim to none.

The blaring alarm wailed and jarred her out of her thoughts. She rushed into the family room.

"What's going on?" Mik asked, and the color drained from her face. He had gone through some sort of physical change. He stood in front of the fireplace taller, his chest broader. Her glance swept from his face to his balled fists at his side. It was his commanding expression that both startled and soothed her. She had seen his soft side and didn't expect any hard edges. His body, his attitude, screamed protector.

"It's the dock alarm. The light should go on any..." The dock light came on, but all she was able to make out was a wall of snow.

"I didn't expect such a blizzard," he said. "The wind must be thirty-five or forty miles an hour. What—"

"Shhhh." She held up her hand and tilted her head in deep concentration. "Never mind. I thought I heard a motor. Besides you, I can't think of anyone who would be out in this."

She smiled to bring down the tension. Pam turned off the alarm, then went to the telescope and searched the area near the dock to make sure no one was there.

"This limited visibility makes it difficult to see anything. The alarm is sensitive." She continued to search the area. "This type of wind creates a lot of debris in the water." A chill went down her back. Why was she making excuses to him?

Mik, brows furled, walked toward the telescope.

"Mind if I—"

"Be my guest." She swept her hand toward the telescope and sat on the arm of the sofa. If she couldn't make out what was happening, she doubted he could.

❋ ❋ ❋

Mik took his time and peered through the device. He swung the scope toward the water and searched the horizon.

"How you can make out anything in this mess is beyond me," Pam said.

He swept the scope toward the trees, adjusting the lens as he scanned. After a few minutes, he stood back and raked his hand through his hair.

If he left now, she would be vulnerable. He had walked away and let others fend for themselves. Not Pam. He took her in his arms.

"I need you to trust me." He spoke softly, almost lovingly.

She pulled away to search his face. "What—"

"Everything I've told you is the truth." Bringing her back close, she needed to understand, and he had little time to explain. He knew what to expect from the others. She was the wild card. And that may possibly get them both killed.

"But you didn't tell me everything." The warmth in her eyes morphed into sadness, and finally, into indifference. *Damn, he had hurt her. He had to make her understand.*

"No, I didn't. But you must trust me. I'm the good guy."

The soft curves of her body turned into hard angles. "How many times have I heard that before? Twice, to be exact. You know how that ended." She tried to step away.

He wouldn't let her go, not yet.

"I need you to do what I say. No matter what happens. Do you understand?"

A lot rode on Pam's actions. He needed her cooperation. He used everything he knew to convince her, from the way he spoke to the way he looked her in the eye with unquestionable confidence. *Trust me.*

Her ice-queen glare melted a few degrees.

"No, I don't understand. You're some man that floated into my life in a blizzard. I can't think of anything stranger than that. Can you?" She pulled from him and walked away.

The snowfall lightened. He stared out the window and studied the area. Siberian hunting and survival skills. He never thought those skills would come in handy again. From the house's high vantage point, he concentrated on the landscape and made out faint variations in shading, in patterns as the snow whipped around objects. A moving object. What he would give for his infrared glasses. He went back to the telescope.

He tracked the moving objects and estimated two people by the dock. The hunted had become the hunters. Until now, that hadn't mattered. He walked to the sofa. It wouldn't take them long to find a way around the line of trees.

"What's out there?" Pam grabbed the telescope and searched. "I can't see anything."

Strategies rushed through his head. He scanned the room. The lights were out, but the fire burned brightly in the hearth. The smoke from the chimney announced an occupied house. It would draw the men. He couldn't let that happen.

"There are two people by the dock. I have to get to them before they come here."

"What are you talking about? Who are they?" She stepped away from the telescope. "Who's coming? Mik, what have you gotten yourself into? Let me call the chief of police."

He pulled the Glock from the small of his back.

"What?" She grabbed his arm and pulled him around. "What type of boat pilot carries a gun? Dammit, Mik, who are you?"

He took a calming breath, put the gun in his pocket, and searched her face, keeping his emotions in check. Her furled brow and intense eyes burned into him. She deserved an answer, but his time was running out.

He held her by her arms and used every ounce of his training as an elite soldier to make her understand the gravity of the situation. If he had had a choice, he never would have brought this to her door. Now his mission depended on convincing her to cooperate.

"There isn't time now. I will tell you everything. I'm going outside. I must find where they are and keep them away. Keep you safe. Do you understand?"

"I…I want to believe you, but…" Some of the stiffness left her body. He dropped his arms.

"You must make your decision to trust me or not. I'm going to stop them. When I leave, turn off the lights, lock the door, and don't open it no matter what happens. Do you understand?"

He hated himself for getting her involved. Her eyes showed concern, but she nodded.

"Good." He headed for the front door.

"Wait, you can't go out in this weather without a coat, and not by that door. Follow me." She led him to the game room where the ski equipment was neatly arranged. Pam pulled a man's white ski parka and pants off a peg and handed it to him.

"Your husband liked white." Mik smiled.

"It screamed purity to him, which he was anything but. Gloves should be in the pockets. Do you know how to ski?" She was already reaching for a pair of skis. Mik nodded.

He put on the pants and jacket. He picked a pair of ski boots and slipped them on, then took the skis and turned to leave.

"Wait," she said, and rummaged in an equipment closet. She came out with ski poles. "Here. You'll need these."

"You think of everything." He took the poles. She didn't let go.

※ ※ ※

"Stay on this side of the tree line. They continue to the right along the water. You'll be in the woods. No one will find you there. The trail ices over quickly. You'll need the poles to help you along. If you follow the coast for about four miles, you'll cross a bridge and be on the Havencroft property. They have a larger boathouse. It hasn't been used in years. The door knocker looks like a set of keys. The third key from the left unlocks the door."

"I'm not leaving you," he said, and she put up her hand and let out a deep sigh.

"Yes, however, it's the safest place for you. I'm well protected in the house. You needn't worry about me. This is the way we came in," she said. "It leads to the garage. It's closer to the tree line."

Mik's face lit in a beaming smile. Her hand rested on the doorknob.

"Before you go..." he said. "I didn't lie to you, only omitted things I can't tell you. And before you ask, I have no one in my life. I didn't want anyone in my life, until now."

He took her in his arms and stared at her face as if memorizing it. His lips twitched into a sexy smirk.

A wild trembling rolled through her. She wasn't an innocent. She knew what was brewing, but this was different. This was to be savored, not forgotten. Her heart beat wildly against her chest. Her eyes fluttered closed as he kissed her tenderly. His kiss went from soft to desperate, to urgent.

He broke away and leaned his forehead against hers.

"Come back to me," she whispered.

Mik's eyes filled with longing. He felt it, too, and her heart soared as if she was coming down a diamond trail, full out.

"For tomato soup and grill cheese sandwiches." His voice was soft.

She opened the door. She didn't want him to leave. He turned back to her.

Mik glanced back and gave her a single nod.

"The door," he said, and waited.

She closed the door, afraid she'd never see him again.

❄ ❄ ❄

Mik waited until the click of the tumblers falling into place reached his ears, satisfied no one could get into the house through this door. He checked his gun one last time, then walked to the garage. The room could fit a dozen cars but held four: a BMW Z4, a Cadillac Escalade, the Land Rover, and a vintage red Corvette. He could easily imagine Pam riding in the Corvette or the Z4. He didn't think the Cadillac suited her style.

He had no intention of going to the other boathouse. Did she think he would leave her alone? Unprotected? He had every intention of finding the men who were after him and settling this vendetta once and for all.

With each step he took toward the far wall, he went deeper into stealth mode until he was fully focused on his mission. Plastered against the wall next to the window, he glanced outside and saw the halo of the blue light in the distance.

The emergency light went out. He was eager to thank Pam for that later, if there was a later. In a matter of hours, over tomato soup and grilled cheese sandwiches, life had become more important to him. Not his life. Pam's.

Chapter Eleven

Pam raced to the kitchen, turned off the light, then went to the closet and killed the house emergency lights. She peered through the telescope. What had Mik seen by the dock? She swept the area looking for anything out of place—a movement, a shadow, anything. The wind buffeted the snow, sending it swirling, making it dense in some places and thin in others. A blast opened a path. She focused the lens on the dock before the wind shifted and everything was again buried from view.

Shadows moved. She increased the magnification and saw a small motorboat tied to the dock. She rushed to the control panel and shut the emergency light.

She didn't search for Mik. From her vantage point, the trees hid the cliff walk. Instead, she swung the telescope toward the boathouse. Nothing. Whoever came off the boat must be coming up along the trees.

The sound of an incoming call on her phone blared overly loud in the quiet of the room. She fumbled with the device. Finally, communication with the outside world.

"Hello," she shouted into the receiver. The cacophony of voices made her think of waiting for a town hall meeting to be called to order.

"Hello, this is Pam Dawes."

"Hello, James. James Kantor, can you hear me? Stan Peters here. Are the roads clear? James? Are you there?" Stan wasn't the only person on the line. She made out other voices. Havenport's phone system had turned into a party line.

"Stan, this is Pam. What's going on?" she said.

"This is Stan Peters. Will you all stop talking at once." The noise continued.

"This is Officer Taylor. Wait, Marge. Yes, the situation is serious, but I don't think anyone is out on the cliff walk in this storm… I'm trying to reach the chief? Chief, if you copy, the footbridge along the cliff walk between Havencroft and Dawes Manor collapsed…covered with ice…the harbor patrol was coming back empty from searching for Washburn's cruiser when the bridge came down. The two Blake kids went cross-country skiing at the cliff walk hours ago and no one has seen them. One more thing to worry about."

"Taylor?"

"Chief. I copy."

"Has anyone reached the phone company? And no, Stan, the roads are not clear. Everyone, please, off the line. We need to keep it clear for police business."

Pam made out the clicks on the line as people disconnected. Perhaps if she stayed on it would be clear enough for her to speak to James in confidence. The line went silent.

"Taylor?"

"Yes, Chief."

"Go to the office. We're starting a house-to-house search along Manor Road. Bring Matt Lyons with you. Tell him we haven't found the Russian yet, but we'll keep looking."

Pam waited for Taylor and James to get off the line before she hung up. Her stomach churned. She needed to warn Mik about the cliff-walk bridge. If he skied down the trail, he'd come up quickly to the bridge. In this blow, he wouldn't see the collapse until it was too late. She'd never forgive herself if anything happened to him.

She hurried to the game room and pulled her ski clothes out of her luggage. Hot pink was not a smart choice. Throwing them down, she went through the ski shop donation bag, yanked out the white all-in-one ski suit Merle had bought her years ago, and made quick work of putting it on. Satisfied after one last check, she went into the garage and locked the door behind her.

Pam picked up her skis and poles and, as an afterthought, slipped the utility key ring with the Swiss Army knife into her pocket. She went out the garage side door. The overhang and half wall protected the entryway, keeping it relatively clear of snow. Her heart pounded at the sight of the small ruts that remained of Mik's ski tracks.

The view from the house had been deceptive. The snow had gotten deeper than expected. Large snow drifts were everywhere. Pam put on her skis and followed Mik's tracks.

She moved cautiously down the incline, the row of pine trees on her right. The flying snow made it difficult to see, and the total darkness moved that to impossible. With less than three feet of visibility, it didn't leave her much time to react to obstacles, but she was familiar with this terrain.

Up ahead, the path split. She stopped at the crossroads. One path led to Manor Road and the chief of police. The other path led to Mik. Head or heart? The symbolism wasn't lost to her.

Pam pushed off on the path that led to Mik. Committed now. There was no turning back. The snow must have been blowing harder than she first thought, or Mik had gone off the path into the woods. The closeness of the pine trees left little room to maneuver. She didn't find any tracks, not even filled ones. She had no idea where he had gone.

She used a skating technique to get her across the flat area faster, but she couldn't keep the pace for long.

The utility shed came into view. Her head went into rescue mode. She unlocked the door and grabbed a coil of rope. A lifeline she hoped she didn't need. After she slipped the coil over her head, Pam started up the path's steep incline that crested a few yards before the end of the forest and started the downhill slope toward the bridge.

After a few minutes her legs shook and burned from the exertion. Still no sign of Mik. Her heart pumped faster as she got closer to the end of the forest. She imagined him hanging on to the cliff, or worse, far below on the rocks.

The last rise before the bridge was more severe with the ice and snow. She was forced to sidestep up the incline. She demanded her body move faster and pushed herself to the crest. Tucked for the downhill, she raced toward the bridge until something big and dark stepped onto the path. She flexed her ankles, knees, and hips, pivoted to the right, and came to a full stop inches in front of a man.

"Where does this go?" The man's thick Russian accent hit her like a bucket of cold water. She hadn't thought the intruders would be Russian. She took a few seconds to catch her breath and connect the dots. Which Russian was James looking for?

"This is a trail along the coast. Eventually it goes into Havenport," she said. "What are you doing here? Is that your boat at the dock?" Her breath came in spurts and she fought to remain calm and in control.

The man pulled himself to his full height and breathed deeply, expanding his chest. "How do you know?" His voice was menacing, his sneer uninviting.

She put her hands on her hips. "My dock alarm went off. I came out to find out why. This is a dangerous part of the cove. Expert sailors have gotten caught on the rocks."

He came out of nowhere. One minute the man was standing in front of her, and the next he was sprawled in the snow. Mik pushed her behind him and stood over the intruder.

"So you are here," the man said as he got to his feet. "We fished Pavel out of the water. He never learned how to swim. Drowning is one way to get away from him. But you can't run from us." He brushed off the snow.

Mik let out a loud laugh. "Run, Igor. I followed you and the others to every hellhole you've crawled into. One by one I picked you off. You and Boris are the last."

"We may be the last of the Soika Pack, but there is still our director who you'll never reach. The director's identity has been cleverly hidden. Even I don't know who it is."

The Soika. Her heat beat even faster, if that was possible. Merle spoke of the deadly Russian crime group. Their trip to Moscow had been to quell his fears of their involvement in Tatanov Maritime.

"Now you are a wanted man in many nations, including this one, dead or alive. We saw to that. I would have thought seeing Natasha, holding her dying in your arms, would have been enough to convince you we meant business." He glanced at Pam, then back to Mik. "Need we show you again?"

In a movement that was quicker than she'd thought possible, the man was behind her with a knife at her throat.

She and Igor faced Mik. His face gave nothing away. She was tired of being a victim, anyone's victim. She wasn't about to become Igor's.

With a practiced ease and burst of energy that surprised even her, she put the palm of her right hand between the knife blade and her throat. Better to cut her hand than her throat. With smooth movements, she pushed the knife away as she cocked her left elbow, drove it hard into Igor's stomach, and stepped away. More surprised than incapacitated, Igor doubled over.

Mik stepped in close before Igor recovered. He let loose a left jab. Igor's head flew back, his jowls quivered, and his eyes glazed. A right cross that exploded from Mik's shoulder sent Igor to the ground, unconscious at Pam's feet.

"That was a stupid thing to do. He could've killed you. Let me see your hand." Mik grabbed her hand. The knife had barely cut through her ski gloves.

She pulled away from him. Pam wasn't sure if she was more pleased that she had defended herself or that Mik was genuinely concerned.

"We can lock him in the utility hut," she said, and gave him the rope coil. "But you must leave now."

❄ ❄ ❄

Mik heaved Igor over his shoulder and waved away the rope.

"What are you doing here? I left you safely in the house," Mik said as they trekked up the path. Pam carried his skis.

"I came to warn you. The bridge collapsed. It's a five-hundred-foot drop onto the rocks. I was afraid you wouldn't see it in this weather."

"How do you know about the collapse?" *Opasnost!*

The easy conversation earlier in the evening, the closeness and growing bond with Pam, was all he wanted. He'd allowed himself to dream of another life. Until the dock alarm went off and the real world came crashing down. He had to face reality. Pam was a tease, their closeness only an illusion. He and Pam traveled on different paths. He had done too much, watched too many die, some by his hand.

"We can lock him in here," she said, stopping in front of the utility shed. He waited as Pam undid the padlock. He dumped the unconscious Igor on the ice-covered floor, closed the door, and reset the lock.

"The police are looking for you. They're going to the houses along the water looking for the boat." Pam held his stare.

"Then you better go back. You can tell the police I forced you—"

"James, the police chief, knows me well. No one forces me to do anything. Think of something else." Her hostile glare didn't intimidate him or make him feel guilty.

"You didn't answer my question. How do you know about the collapse and the police search?" He scanned Pam's face for a reaction. The ferocity of the wind seemed suspended as the silence between them hung in the air. Worse, he didn't know what to expect and braced for her answer.

"I heard it on the phone. The lines were crossed, like an old-fashioned party line. James mentioned Lyons hadn't found the boat or the Russian."

"I need to get you back to the house. I can't worry about you and search for Boris," he said.

"Boris? So there were two people on the boat. They must have separated. There aren't any footprints leading to the boathouse. Maybe we should split up."

"No. I followed Boris here. He must have left Igor as a lookout, which means he's up ahead. He's aware I'm here and will come after him."

He searched her eyes. They didn't lie. Perhaps he had it all wrong. Maybe their closeness wasn't an illusion. The idea gave him strength. He'd only find out when this was over.

"I want you to go back to the house and wait for me there."

"But the bridge? It's dangerous in this weather. I need to show you where it collapsed."

"No, you don't. I'll be careful. Now go. I'll meet you at the house as soon as I can."

She nodded. He waited while she skied out of sight, then put on his skis, turned, and headed toward the cliff.

Chapter Twelve

Mik skied out from the trees and down the slope. The edge of the cliff, where the ground fell away, came up quickly. He turned his skis at a forty-five-degree angle, executed a classic hockey stop, and slammed his ski pole in the ground inches before he toppled over the edge. Snow battered his face. It didn't hide the rocks five hundred feet below. He suspected the height of the cliff and the driving winds, along with the sprays of water, caused this section of the path to be under a thick layer of ice. Pam was right. If she hadn't told him about the bridge collapse he'd be at the bottom.

Unable to pull his ski poles out, he moved away from the edge and scanned the forest. Boris wouldn't be far. He had no alternative but to go and find him. But it would be difficult to maneuver in the tightly packed woods wearing skis. He stamped on the heel lever at the back of the binding and lifted his foot out of the ski. As he lifted his other foot, two hundred and fifty pounds slammed into him, sending him crashing to the ground. His skis flew over the edge.

"You think your new friend is safe." Boris straddled him and glared down with his one good eye. Mik and Boris had met before. Another altercation with a knife left Boris with a deep knotted scar across his face and blind in his left eye. It made their meeting personal.

"Igor is waiting for her, and you know how he enjoys a woman's company. You remember how he entertained your family and Natasha."

Boris grabbed Mik's collar and stood, dragging Mik with him. Mik didn't need to be reminded. The pictures in his head were on a closed loop that played over and over. It kept him going in his mission to eliminate Soika.

"I see you remember. I thought you would." Sweat ran down the large man's face. Boris traipsed around office buildings. Fieldwork was not his forte. It was getting hard for Soika to recruit new talent with someone taking out the staff.

Mik grabbed the hand on his collar and held it in place. He brought up his free hand out of Boris's line of vision and pressed his thumb into Boris's good eye. This fight was his to win.

Boris shoved Mik away and grabbed at his eye. They stood facing each other, whipped by wind, pelted by snow, close to the edge of the cliff.

"Pavel is gone," Mik said. "Igor? He's on ice at the moment." Boris answered with a dark stare. "The only people left are you, me, and your director. Tell me who it is and I won't throw you over the side."

"You make me laugh. I'm a dead man if I tell you."

"You're a dead man if you don't. One way or another I'll find out who the director is, and when I do, let's just say your ears will be burning. Your name will be everywhere." Mik's voice was quiet and laced with an undertone of cold contempt. "The name."

Boris let out a roar and charged him like an injured Russian bear.

❋ ❋ ❋

Pam turned off the trail toward the shortcut to the house. She and Mik were two lonely souls. Was that the essence of their bond? It came from her heart.

She continued through the woods, and warmed at the thought of his kiss. The sexual attraction seemed as strong for him as for her. The way he gazed at her, wanted her.

Neither husband had ever stared at her the way Mik did. Or were they all playing the same game, the right family with the right connections? That's what her husbands wanted, but what did she want?

"Mikhail Ivanovich." His name rolled off her lips as a slow breath escaped her, sending a stream of vapor into the air.

The wind let up as she stepped out of the forest and into the field not far from the drive. Although it was still dark, she easily made out shapes of bushes and benches hidden beneath the snow.

The vibration in her pocket startled her. Thank God. The cell tower must be operational. Hopefully the power would be back online soon. She fished the phone out of her jacket pocket.

"Hello?"

"Pam."

She let out a long sigh of relief.

"James. You must be busy." Head or heart echoed in her mind.

"What a mess. The cliff-walk bridge collapsed. The two Blake kids are missing. I'm on the Havencroft side and can't see a thing. We're heading over to you to check the bridge from your side."

Was this part of the chief's plan? But if the boys were in danger...

"I'll head over to the bridge and wait for you there."

A muffled crack broke the silence. She felt vulnerable out in the open. A second report. It wasn't a backfire or a firecracker. *Mik.*

"Pam. Are you all right?" James screamed through the phone.

An invisible hand covered her mouth and adrenaline pumped through her veins. Her lungs demanded air, but she was frozen in place. A shiver up her spine loosened fear's grip and she broke free. "I shouldn't have left him."

"Who, Pam? Answer me."

"The bridge. Come quick." She stuffed the phone in her pocket, turned, and raced toward the cliff.

❄ ❄ ❄

Mik struggled with Boris for the gun. There was no honor, no code in this fight, just winning. Mik liked short and brutal fights. It raised the fear factor and his reputation. The fight continued as they spun and slid on the icy path and inched closer to the edge where the ski pole stood like a lone flag in the ice.

Boris tripped and fell, taking Mik with him. Still, they fought for the gun. Their hands stretched over the edge. Mik slammed Boris's arm over and over against the sharp rim trying to shake the gun loose, but Boris hung on. The gun went off.

Their grip loosened, and still they struggled. With a final tug, the gun went off again. Their loose grip and the firearm's kickback sent the gun flying out of their hands and down to the rocks below. The fight didn't stop. Both men got to their feet and searched for an advantage.

"You think you're the only one with a vendetta? With each of your kills, I vowed I would finish you," Boris said as his arms went around Mik in a giant bear hug. It was Boris's preferred maneuver.

The vise tightened around Mik's upper chest. Unable to breathe, he stayed calm and bent his arms at his elbows and pumped both up. He knew it wouldn't free him, but it raised Boris's grip and gave him room to work. Mik eased his right hip to Boris's left, shifting him off balance. Mik planted his foot behind Boris's, and in one swift movement fell to the ground, taking Boris with him.

Boris broke his grip and rolled to his feet. Unsteady on the ice, he stepped backward. The big man's arms windmilled as he tried to gain his footing.

Mik stared in shock as Boris screamed and teetered on the edge. All of this was for nothing unless he got the director's name. Mik scrambled on all fours and caught the thug's hand as Boris fell over the side.

Boris's legs worked against the cliff face, searching for a ledge. He flung his free hand up over the edge, scratching at the ground, clawing for something, anything, to use as an anchor. He found nothing.

"Stop moving. You'll get us both killed," Mik said as he lay along the rim of the cliff. He wouldn't let Boris go, at least not until he got the information he needed.

"Tell me your director's name," Mik said. Boris stopped scrambling and smirked at the request.

"Or what? You'll let me go?" His voice had an air of finality. Boris yanked on Mik.

Lying precariously at the edge, Mik grabbed for the ski pole with his free hand. Boris tugged again, and Mik slipped over the edge. He hung on to the pole with one hand and held Boris with the other.

"We're both going to die. At least let me die knowing who ordered the executions." Mik couldn't take his eyes off the ski pole as little by little it bent below his hand. His other sweaty and cramped hand held Boris. He fought against the spasms that demanded he relax his fingers. Boris's grip slipped.

"Grab my arm with your other hand," Mik said.

"Forget about Tatanov and Volgograd," Boris said.

"I can't," Mik said. Boris's hand slipped more. "Grab my arm," Mik demanded.

Mik wouldn't give up. He crushed the man's fingers and held on. Boris's panicked look turned to acceptance.

"I told them you were dangerous." Boris opened his hand and slid from Mik's grip.

Mik didn't take his eyes off Boris's face as he fell away.

"The name," he shouted.

"Cat—" Boris called, his voice lost in the wind.

"Cat?" Mik mumbled, his arm still stretched out reaching for Boris. His hand slid down the ski pole toward the hand grip. The wind buffeted him, and his eyes teared. Pam had thrown him a lifeline, but it was too late. At least he would die knowing she was safe.

"Mik." He looked up. Pam's frantic eyes searched his. "Hold on."

"Don't touch the ski pole. Any movement and it will come loose," Mik said.

Pam looked around. "The rope. I'll be right back." She hurried off before he could say anything.

"Cat?" It didn't matter now. He hung in the air, afraid any movement would be his last. He had failed. How ironic. For years he courted death; didn't care if he died. He stared up where Pam's face had been. Now all he wanted to do was live. He stretched his free hand up and tried to grab the edge of the cliff. Covered with ice, there was nothing to latch on to. He kept searching.

His hand, sweaty and cramped, inched down the bent pole. Maybe the pole's handgrip would stop his slide. He chuckled. Wishful thinking.

Would it be best if he let go before Pam returned rather than her watch him fall? He closed his eyes. That would be kinder, but he wanted to see her one more time. He wanted her face burned into his brain when he died.

"Mik."

He looked into Pam's steady, confident eyes. She squatted at the cliff edge. He didn't ask about the rope. The fact that she didn't have it was answer enough. A cramp worked down his arm. His fingers spasmed and begged for relief. He fought the sensation.

There was so much he wanted to tell her. How strong, how funny, how clever she was. How he wanted to spend the rest of his life with her.

"The rope was too short," she said.

"My love, *moya lyubov*," he whispered, and saw the determination that burned in her eyes. "Move away from the edge."

"Give me your hand." Pam reached for his free hand.

His other hand slid down the ski pole all the way to the grip. With a pop, the pole pulled out of the ice.

With a firm slap, Pam's hand grasped the forearm of his free hand and held him fast.

Her face was a mask of concentration. There was no way she could lift him over the edge. That she was able to hold him at all impressed him. She would always impress him. God, give him more days and he would honor her forever.

"Pam. Let go. I'll only drag you to the rocks with me." He let go of the bent pole.

She grabbed the other side of his arm with her free hand.

"I'm strong like bull."

He smiled at her bad Russian accent and ached at the thought of losing her.

She strained, slowly straightened her legs, and took a step backward. He was almost eye level with the edge. He marveled as she pulled him higher.

Chapter Thirteen

A large, meaty hand grabbed his free wrist. "Pam, on the count of three."

He stared into the face of Matt Lyons and let out a sigh of relief.

"One, two, three." Lyons and Pam hoisted him over the rim.

Before Mik could go to Pam, Lyons pulled him aside.

"You enjoy hanging around." Lyons dusted off Mik's clothes like an expert valet and tugged on the white ski jacket. The agent's casual joke didn't match the ashen color on Lyons's face or his quivering hands, which didn't come from the strain of the rescue.

"You gave me a few gray hairs." Lyons stood back and finished adjusting Mik's clothes. "You owe me. What is this now—three markers?" Lyons glanced at Pam. "And her. You owe her big-time. By the way, she did a nice job."

Mik gulped deep breaths to clear his head and stop his legs from shaking.

"I thought you Russian guys wore black." Lyons took another step back, the agent's expressive face once again casual and irreverent. Lyons needed as much time as Mik to recover.

"*Spasibo, moy drug.* Thank you, my friend." Mik couldn't manage to say anything else.

Lyons moved away, and Pam stepped in to fill the empty space. Mik grabbed her close into his arms.

"I thought I'd lost you." Her muffled voice was barely discernable against his embrace.

He pulled back and looked into her eyes. "Strong like bull. I never would have let that happen."

Under the cold-chaffed skin on her face she blushed, and it warmed his heart. "Strong like bull almost had a heart attack. Please, enough excitement for tonight?"

This woman continued to amaze him. Continued to make him want things he'd buried a long time ago. He yearned to tell her things, dead and buried things he'd never told anyone. He didn't want any secrets, missions, thoughts about Russia, the Tatanovs, Natasha, or the director. He wanted Pam. But would she want him? Her comments about husbands one and two…the realization struck him between the eyes.

James and Officer Taylor peered over the edge of the cliff. "Who's down there?" The chief waited for him to answer, breaking him out of his reverie.

"Boris. Boris Badenov, like in *Rocky and Bullwinkle.*" That was the Lyons Mik knew, unable to be serious for long. But he was glad for the humor and distraction. Pam relaxed in his arms and caressed his back through the wet, cold snow gear.

"Okay, Lyons, quit the kidding." James let out an exasperated sigh. "Between the storm, power lines down, phone outages, and Russian mobsters, I'm at the end of my patience. Thank goodness the Blake boys called their parents. The Peterses took them in when the snow got bad. That was the good news for the day."

"Lyons is not that far from the truth." Mik decided saving Lyons from the chief was worth at least one marker. "Except Boris isn't as cute. Boris had so many aliases no one knew his real name. Interpol nicknamed him Badenov, and it stuck. We found out he was Boris Raspopovich. He, Igor, and Pavel are part of the Soika Pack. The Russian drug cartel."

"It's a cute story, but I'm cold. Let's move out of this weather." Lyons turned to Pam. "Mik can fill you all in at the house."

They walked past the empty utility hut, its door wide open.

"You found Igor." It was a statement rather than a question.

"You hit him hard. We carried him to the car. He never came to. My team has him," Lyons said. That eased Mik's mind. With Igor in Lyons's custody it would be easier to interrogate him and find out about the "cat."

The snow stopped falling. It was an hour or so before dawn, that time when the sky is light, and dark shadows still cling to surfaces. They tramped out of the forest into a blaze of electric lights illuminating the grounds and inside the house.

"The power came back on a few minutes ago," Lyons said.

The flashing red lights bounced off the snow and sandstone house. Three police cruisers welcomed them at the front door.

Mik breathed in the cold air and appreciated the silence. Lyons, Mik, and Pam stood at the door. A rush of concern pulsed through him, and he pulled Pam closer.

Pam faced FBI Agent Matt Lyons. "Look, he was…"

"Stop. No need for you to defend him. He's one of the good guys, one of us. Not a fugitive or a criminal. Certainly not with Boris or Igor. Mik's a member of Interpol's Incident Response Team. I know. I was with him when he was in Afghanistan for Interpol." Lyons held her attention. "I didn't see the Washburn boat at your dock. Did we lose it?"

"*Liquid Asset* is in my boathouse." They all stood at the manor entrance. "It floated to my dock and we locked it inside to protect it from the storm." Pam opened the door and ushered them into the foyer.

"That's a relief," Lyons said. "I wouldn't want to explain to Washburn that we lost it."

"Mik, what is this about?" Pam asked.

"Last July, Agent Lyons ran fingerprints related to a drug bust against the I-24/7 network. The database came up with a match. Lyons contacted me at Interpol when his search turned up with an outstanding warrant for the men issued in my country. I came to America to assist the investigation. I knew the men and spoke their language."

"Mik speaks more than their language. He understands these men inside and out. I knew he'd been waiting for them to surface for a long time. It was a match made in heaven," Lyons said. "Together, we traced the suspect and his two friends to Havenport. Mik volunteered to wear a wire and go after the men."

"The chief helped plan the sting. Pavel was at the marina packing *Liquid Asset* with drugs they planned to deliver up the coast," Mik said.

"The Washburns?" Pam said. "They wouldn't… Impossible."

"Whoa, Pam. Evan Washburn worked with us." Lyons tried to calm Pam. The war veteran had been eager to help, and the agent was adamant about including the young councilman even though Lyons had his hands full keeping Evan from working directly with Mik.

"Washburn played a corrupt councilman. The fact that Washburn was a politician added to the draw. He made the *Liquid Asset* available to Soika, along with a pilot. We provided Mik. We wired the boat, but with the storm, the signal went out. Mik was on his own."

"When Pavel saw me," Mik continued, "he started the engines and threw off the lines. Before I had both feet on the deck, he was swinging."

"He landed some pretty solid punches from the grunts and groans we recorded before we lost the audio." Lyons gave Mik a dazzling smile.

"In the scuffle, Pavel went over the side, and I went in after him. The weather was bad and getting worse. Visibility was down to zero. One minute he was up ahead of me, and the next he was gone. I swam and searched but couldn't find him anywhere. I was moving further away from the boat, a dangerous move in the thickening fog. I gave up the search.

"I swam like hell for the boat and struggled back on board. Communications and navigation instruments were out. I headed toward what I hoped was shore. I must have passed out. I woke up when the boat bumped into your dock. The rest you know."

"Before I head out to speak to Igor," Lyons said, and faced Mik, "was he able to give you the information you wanted?"

"Not exactly. Before Boris died, he said something. It sounded like *cat*. Igor may still be my best lead, even though he swore he doesn't know." Mik sat on the sofa and reached out to Pam. She snuggled willingly into his arms.

"Sure, you go on. Show your appreciation. I'll close the door on my way out. Pam, take care of our comrade. Mik, call if you need a ride into town." Lyons headed out the door.

"You look tired. I should leave." He brushed the hair off her forehead.

"No. I couldn't sleep after all this. Let's just talk," she said, her head on his shoulder.

His smile played at the corners of his lips. Her eyes were already half-closed.

"I heard James say they were looking for a Russian." She didn't face him.

"And you thought they were searching for me." A flash of red raced up her neck and painted her cheeks. He kissed her forehead. "I don't blame you. I didn't give you much information."

"And then the gun," she said.

"What do you want to know?"

"What happened to the Tatanovs? I thought their shipping business was doing well." She let out a deep sigh and sank into his arms.

"Tatanov built his business from nothing. My father was one of his first employees and got me a job. Keep it in the family, he said."

"So he was a good man," she said. Mik nodded.

"Tatanov was rough in his business dealings. I thought he was more honest than others," Mik said. "Over the years of working closely with Natasha, I fell in love with her. Both families were happy.

"Three years ago, the Soika Pack sent a group of thugs and stormed the office. My father and Tatanov were destroying papers when I reached him and tried to make them leave before the attackers arrived. I got my father out, but Tatanov was a desperate man.

"I haven't much time. I leave it to you, your father, and Natasha. Keep the business going. Your loyalty will be rewarded. Now go, before those thugs come."

"Tatanov may not have done things exactly within the law. I remember the phone calls Merle had with him," Pam said.

"My father, Natasha, and I worked to keep the business together. She came in the evening and did the bookkeeping, and my father and I took care of the day to day.

"Little by little, I uncovered what looked like criminal dealings, except it wasn't Tatanov. Someone was using his shipping business to transport drugs, interfering in the Soika Pack's territory."

"That must be why they took Tatanov," she said.

"Yes. I kept digging to find out who had set him up. Eight months later, a car drove up to the office and Tatanov got out, a sick and broken man. Before the end of the week he sold the company to his competitor for pennies on the dollar and made arrangements for the family to leave Russia. The night before their departure, the family planned a quiet dinner and invited my parents and me. Earlier in the day, I'd uncovered the traitor. I stayed late at the office and went over every piece of information. I needed confirmation. I didn't want to believe it, but the evidence was there. There was only one person who had the opportunity. One person who had the information the Soika Pack needed to crush Tatanov. For what reason would someone betray him? Power. Money. I had to hear it from her lips.

"They were all at dinner. I couldn't wait to confront the traitor. I pulled into the drive. Gunshots rang out. I rushed into the living room. My parents...they were dead. I stared at Igor as he shot Tatanov, then turn and aimed at me. Before I could move, Natasha threw herself at Igor. The gun went off. She crumpled to the floor, and he ran."

"You don't have to tell me any more," Pam said, so quietly he questioned whether she had spoken at all.

"She told me to leave quickly, before they came back. There was blood and bodies everywhere." He raised his eyes toward Pam. "I couldn't help her. I couldn't help any of them. The woman I loved betrayed her family—and mine. She died in my arms. I swore I would never love again. It took me a long time to come to terms with her treachery. I hated myself for not seeing the signs sooner, for not protecting my family."

They sat in silence for some time.

"We have that in common. Betrayal. I trusted both husbands to be honest and trustworthy. You think I would have learned my lesson after the first disaster. No. I made the same mistake a second time. Then you came along and I followed my heart, not my head."

"For a long time I haven't cared about anyone. But today I would have killed anyone who hurt you. I have a lot to reconcile in my head." He kissed her forehead.

She looked up at him. "We both do. We can help each other."

"I'd like that." He cupped the back of her head with his hand. Her eyes fluttered closed, and his heat rose. With a gentle tug, he drew her closer. His body ached to be touched. He kissed her, and the very air around him felt electrified.

She broke the kiss, stretched over him, picked up the remote, and closed the shades, throwing the room into darkness. "I vowed never again."

He rolled on top of her and looked into her eyes. "*Nikogda ne govori nikogda*," he said, his voice deep with passion.

She let out a soft chuckle. "No, never say never."

About the Author

RUTH A. CASIE is a *USA Today* bestselling author of swashbuckling action-adventure time-travel romance about strong empowered women and the men who deserve them, endearing flaws and all. Her Druid Knight novels have both finaled in the NJRW Golden Leaf contest. Writing with the Timeless Scribes, Ruth also writes contemporary romance with enough action to keep you turning pages. She lives in New Jersey with her husband, three empty bedrooms and a growing number of incomplete counted cross-stitch projects. Before she found her voice, she was a speech therapist (pun intended), client liaison for a corrugated manufacturer, and international bank product and marketing manager, but her favorite job is the one she's doing now—writing romance.

※ ※ ※

Ruth loves to hear from readers, too, so drop her a line at Ruth@RuthACasie.com or visit her on Facebook: facebook.com/RuthACasie. She's also on Twitter: @RuthACasie. If you'd like to receive her newsletter and receive a free book, please sign up at www.RuthACasie.com. Thanks!

Also by Ruth A. Casie

❄ ❄ ❄

Medieval Romances

The Druid Knight Series
Knight of Runes
Knight of Rapture
Knight of Redemption – Coming Soon
The Druid Knight Tale: A Short Story Expanded

The Stelton Legacy
The Guardian's Witch
The Highlander's English Woman

Medieval Novella Collection
The Maxwell Ghost featured in Once Upon a Haunted Castle

❄ ❄ ❄

Collections

Timeless Tales – Short Stories
Medieval Romances
Mistletoe and Magick featured in Timeless Keepsakes
Whispers on the Wind featured in Timeless Treasures

Contemporary Romances
Second Chance by the Sea featured in Timeless Escapes
Forsaking All Others featured in Timeless Vows

Havenport – Contemporary Novellas
I'll Be Home for Christmas featured in Christmas in Havenport
The Game's AFoot featured in Welcome to Havenport
The Witching Hour featured in Haunted Havenport

On Her Own

by Emma Kaye

❄ ❄ ❄

Finally free of her abusive ex-husband, and the magick that bound her to him, Jennifer Venkat returns to Havenport for a wedding. She never planned on going back to the scene of so much pain, but she couldn't help but think about the man who'd helped her through it all. Will she rekindle the spark she felt with the groom's best man, or is she not yet ready to risk her heart?

Braeden Tiede can't wait to see Jennifer again. Ever since their one weekend together, he hasn't been able to get her out of his mind. She's been through a lot, and he's determined to prove he's nothing like her ex. But is he man enough to be there for her when she needs him the most?

When Jennifer receives threatening messages, her latent power turns a gentle snowfall into a raging blizzard. Snowed in and terrified, Jennifer can't control her magick. Can Braeden help Jennifer through her fear, or will she run from her past and destroy any hope for their future?

❄ ❄ ❄

Dedicated to ~

My family. I can't think of anyone with whom I'd rather be snowbound.

Nicole, Ruth, and Lita. Love you guys.

My readers. Thanks for joining me in Havenport. I hope you've been enjoying the town and its residents as much as I have.

Chapter One

"Turn left," the too-pleasant robotic female voice said.

Jennifer Venkat cursed the GPS. "*What* left, you stupid piece of... Argh." Every few minutes her faceless nemesis would tell her to take a turn where no street existed. The darn thing lost its signal about a mile ago, and she had no idea how far she still needed to go. According to the Internet map she'd glanced at when planning her trip, the pine trees should have given way to the manicured lawns of the rich by now, but all she saw was the faded yellow double line curving this way and that through tall trees. With her windows rolled up to keep out the cold, she couldn't use the sound of the waves crashing against the rocks or the salty smell of the ocean to give her a clue how close she was to the million-dollar homes that lined the coast. She hadn't been back to Havenport in over a year, and back then she hadn't spent any time in the wealthier district near the hotel, but she knew it bordered the ocean.

Thank goodness Christa's wedding wasn't until tomorrow evening.

She slowed to a crawl, squinting at a street sign. Jefferson Avenue. She swung a right. The name sounded familiar. One of these streets must lead downtown, right? If she could make it to Main Street, she could find the small A New Chapter bookstore and buy a map or ask directions or something. Better than wandering around like a dope waiting for her stupid GPS to magically start working.

Magick. She shuddered. Enough with the *jaadoo*, the Hindu version of magick her mother once practiced. After all the emotional and physical abuse her ex-husband, Carlos, had heaped on her in the name of magickal domination, she wanted nothing to do with that kind of power ever again.

The ringing of her phone made her jump. Who would be calling? Her phone was buried deep in her purse, so she couldn't check. She gnawed on her lower lip, a pit of indecision twisting her stomach. Should she answer? She'd just gotten a new number, again, after Carlos flooded her last phone with threatening texts. Hoping he hadn't somehow tracked her down already, she pressed the talk button on her steering wheel. "Hello?" *Please don't be him.*

"Jen? Hi, it's Christa. Just got your message. I'm so happy you can make the wedding."

She released a breath in a noisy gush and flexed her hands on the steering wheel, releasing her death grip and forcing feeling back in her fingers. The knot in her belly loosened. "Christa, hi. Yes, I'm on my way."

"That's awesome. I'm so glad. I take it the bail hearing went well and Carlos is behind bars where he belongs? Savannah's been keeping me informed, but we've been playing phone tag lately."

Jennifer nodded, immediately realized Christa wouldn't be able to see her gesture, and responded, "Yes. He'll be locked away until the trial. No bail. His last attack put it over the edge. Of course I'm grateful Tim wasn't hurt, but having Carlos lose control like that in front of a police officer certainly helped my case. Without Tim's testimony, I have no idea whether the judge was going to rule in my favor. He seemed to think I'd made it all up in order to get the upper hand in the divorce. Carlos had done such a good job of appearing 'healed' in front of everyone. Except me, of course. I can't tell you how many people looked at me like I was overreacting."

Just thinking about what she'd gone through the past year sent her blood pressure boiling. She rubbed the scar by her left eye. He'd practically killed her, and no one believed her until he lost his temper in front of a police officer. When the tire iron Carlos had aimed at her head hit the officer on the shoulder instead, he'd sealed his fate.

Thank goodness.

"Oh, Jen. I'm so sorry. At least your divorce is finalized. And once we get through the trial, he'll be locked away for good, and neither of us will have to worry about him ever again."

She massaged her naked ring finger, reveling in the feeling of freedom at having shed the cheap piece of jewelry. Not that she'd worn his ring in the year-plus since she'd begun divorce proceedings, but with that part of her nightmare officially over, she no longer felt the phantom weight of those shackles. "I can't begin to describe how good it feels to have my disaster of a marriage behind me."

Jennifer spotted the bookstore she remembered from her last visit. A parking spot down the street opened, and she slid her sedan into the empty slot. She put the car into Park and leaned back to finish her conversation. She twisted her neck to the side to ease some of her tension from the long ride. Her chakras were seriously misaligned. She'd have to work on balance once she checked in to the hotel.

"So, on to something more pleasant. How's everything with you? All set for the wedding tomorrow?" The wedding was a safe topic. She refused to ask what she really wanted to know. After all, if Braeden wanted anything to do with her, he would have called, right?

Christa spoke a mile a minute, happiness bubbling over in her tone. Less-than-perfect cell reception meant Jennifer didn't hear every detail, but she couldn't miss the joy in Christa's voice.

When she came up for air, Jennifer said, "I'm so happy for you. You and Jeremy are a wonderful couple. I know you're going to have a beautiful life together. I'm so honored to be invited. I…" She searched for the right words. "I don't know how I can ever thank you for all you've done for me. For forgiving me after all I put you through."

"Nonsense," Christa replied. "You saved my life."

"After putting you in danger in the first place."

"You didn't know what Carlos planned to do. And it's not like you had any choice in the matter. He's the one who kidnapped me. You're the one who helped me escape. At no little risk to yourself, if you remember."

She certainly did. That Christa managed to forgive Jennifer's part in it all amazed her.

Nightmares about those days haunted her sleep.

Her eye twitched. The wound had healed, but thinking about those days still had the power to make it throb, bringing back the remembered pain of Carlos's boot smashing against her temple.

To think he'd actually made her happy in the beginning. Little had she known her happiness stemmed from a spell he'd found in *On Magick Most Powerful*, a formidable book of *jaadoo* meant for Jennifer. If only she had recognized it for what it was and guarded the book instead of showing it to him. He'd seen its potential and used its *jaadoo* to benefit himself in all sorts of ways.

Money, power, love.

Not real love, obviously. Even *jaadoo* as powerful as that book contained couldn't produce real love. But it could create a feeling so close that the unsuspecting victim wouldn't notice the difference.

She hadn't.

After dating Carlos on and off for a few months, mostly to dissuade her parents from setting her up with yet another eligible Hindu male, she'd been on the verge of breaking up with him when tragedy struck and nearly her entire family—parents, grandparents, great-aunt—died in a horrible accident that changed her life forever. In the midst of her mourning, Carlos cast his spell. She thought she'd finally recognized all his wonderful qualities, when she was actually blinded by a magickal cloud of obsession.

He'd tricked her, all right. And when the book got tired of his greed, it found a way to abandon him, finding its way to Christa. And all his conniving had fallen apart.

Jennifer had been under his thumb by then. The fake love had worn off, and she'd realized how many ways he'd taken advantage of her. But digging her way out felt impossible. She'd been in too deep. Married to a monster and alienated from her brother, her only remaining family. Not until Carlos took Christa hostage in an attempt to regain the *jaadoo* had she realized she had to take a stand. She'd lived with the abuse, but she couldn't sit by and let him hurt an innocent woman.

To her shock, Christa had reached out the hand of friendship and Jennifer had taken it, gladly.

"...see him in his tux. You won't be able to stop drooling."

Drooling—what? "I'm sorry. The, um, service is terrible." *Cell service, her attention span—same difference.* "What did you say?"

Christa laughed. "I thought that might get your attention. I said Braeden looks fantastic in his tux."

A blush heated her cheeks. Thank goodness no one was around to see it. She must look like an overripe tomato. "Oh, yes. I'm sure he does." She gasped. "I mean, I'm sure you picked out lovely outfits for all the groomsmen. I assumed Braeden would be in the wedding party, being Jeremy's business partner and best friend, and all. And so of course he'd be..." She let her ridiculous rambling die off to the sound of Christa's laughter. "Very funny."

"I'm sorry." Christa's laugh indicated she wasn't in the least. "I can't help myself. You two are so obviously interested in each other, I can't for the life of me figure out why you haven't hooked up."

Her cheeks flamed hotter. If she only knew.

Jennifer wasn't proud of the affair she'd had a year ago. Even though her weekend with Braeden had been the best time of her life, she'd been married at the time. Just because she'd been tricked into the marriage by *jaadoo*, and had already filed for divorce, didn't excuse her behavior. She'd never admitted the affair to anyone, and judging by Christa's comments, Braeden had kept silent as well.

✻ ✻ ✻

Braeden Tiede came to an abrupt stop in the living room doorway. Who was Christa talking to? Hooked up with whom? He could have sworn he'd heard his name before he got to the door.

His thoughts turned to the last person he'd hooked up with. Hard to believe it had been over a year. But when his mind kept returning to the way her dark-brown, almost black, hair looked spread across his chest, or how her cheeks would turn a fiery red when he spoke dirty to her, and how her Indian accent thickened when she answered in kind, and…

Well, no one he'd met since could hold a candle to Jennifer. So he'd taken a break from women to concentrate on work. With his business partner, Jeremy, so wrapped up in Christa, Braeden took charge at the office to make sure their move to Havenport happened smoothly and by deadline. They'd wanted the move complete before the wedding, and they'd just barely managed.

Jeremy bumped into him from behind. "Hey. What're you doing?"

Braeden held a finger to his lips and pointed to Christa, who continued to laugh and tease whoever was on the phone.

Then the connection Christa shared with his best friend kicked in. As if sensing her fiancé's approach, she turned and locked eyes with Jeremy. She continued her conversation, but anyone could see her attention focused on her lover.

He sighed. Damn, the mushy shit was about to commence.

He didn't know whether he wanted something like the two of them shared or not. He wanted to be happy, sure. He could even get into the idea of being with one woman for the rest of his life. But the way they were so consumed by each other? Sometimes he thought it was overkill. That kind of feeling couldn't last, could it? And when it faded, what would be left?

Yet sometimes—especially when he thought of Jennifer and their one perfect weekend…

But that was over. The outside world had nudged its way into their short-lived fantasy, and damn, life was a bitch.

He'd wanted to take care of her, he really had. But she'd pushed him away. And after everything he'd learned from the bits and pieces Jennifer had let slip, he doubted whether he was man enough to be what she needed. And if not, he'd be the biggest sort of asshole if he got in the way of her finding someone who was.

Much as he wanted to.

Christa said her goodbyes and hung up the phone. After a long—like, get a room already long—kiss hello with Jeremy, she finally turned to him. "Hey. You'll never guess who that was."

"Who?" But from her teasing smile he knew his thoughts had led him down the correct path already.

"Jen. She's on her way to Havencroft Manor."

He shoved his hands in his pockets and rocked back on his heels. "She's coming to the wedding? I thought this place scared her off after..." He clenched his hands. Everything had come to a head here so he couldn't blame her. "But he can't get to her anymore, so she has no reason to worry." Just thinking about Carlos made him want to punch something.

Jeremy appeared to have the same reaction. He kept one arm around Christa, but his other hand opened and closed like he was prepping for a fight. "He'd be a fool to try it. Then again, I wouldn't put it past him. He's not the sharpest tool in the shed."

The soft tap of claws on the wood floor preceded Daisy's entrance to the room. The Gordon setter shoved her head under Braeden's hand, demanding a petting. He smiled at the dog, remembering her part in apprehending Carlos after Jennifer's ex had kidnapped Christa. The way the bastard had screamed, Daisy's bite must have been as vicious as it looked. Ah, good times. He hoped the bastard walked with a limp for the rest of his miserable life.

"Actually, she says it looks like Carlos is going to be out of the picture for good. After his last attack on her in August—"

Braeden stopped petting Daisy and focused on Christa.

"What happened in August? I thought he was locked up in a nuthouse for another few years. Or at least until the trial. How'd he attack her in August?" Seriously, if he didn't find something to punch soon, he would go mad.

Christa blushed and picked at a button on Jeremy's shirt. "She didn't want anyone to know. She only told me when he got out on the off chance he decided to come after me again. She wanted me to be prepared. Savannah called me, of course, but Jen didn't realize that. So when they caught him, Jen called me again so I wouldn't worry. That's when the story came out."

"What happened?" Their friend Savannah, a trial lawyer, used her connections to keep them all up to date on Carlos's case, but she'd never mentioned any of this to him.

"He snuck out of the hospital. He'd managed to convince them all he was doing better. A model patient. Blah, blah." She rolled her eyes while waving her hand in the air. Then her gaze dropped and she frowned. "They stopped worrying about him, and he used their lapse to escape. He came after her at work. He had the bad luck of not seeing the police officer standing nearby watching everything."

"And?" Jennifer was all right. He knew that. But his heart pounded like he'd run a marathon.

"And Jen has taken some self-defense classes. She held Carlos off long enough for Tim to intervene. That's when Carlos took a swing at him."

Jeremy laughed. "Stupid. He'd probably be free by now if he hadn't. They got him for assaulting a police officer with a deadly weapon."

Braeden raised a brow. "Trying to murder his ex-wife wasn't enough?"

"You'd think, right?" Christa said. "But Carlos always managed to convince people he wasn't an actual danger to anyone. He must have some personal magick. Charming power."

"Now *that* I find hard to believe. The guy was a raving lunatic." He gestured to his eyes. "You could see the crazy in his bloodshot, bulging eyes. One look and you could tell he belonged in the loony bin."

"Sure. When we met him," Christa replied. "Strung out from losing the power of *On Magick Most Powerful.* The way he abused the book's power took a toll on him. He was in major withdrawal that summer."

Jeremy hugged her closer to his side. "You never told me magick was so dangerous."

She nodded. "When you abuse it, yes." She stood on tiptoes and kissed his cheek. "I don't abuse it."

"Why didn't I know all of this?" He couldn't blame Jennifer for not calling him. Not after the way they'd left things. But he thought his best friend would have given him a heads-up.

"She called you, but when you never got back to her…"

"She never called." He smacked his forehead. "Damn. What number did she call?" He'd given up his home number when he decided to move to Havenport.

Christa shrugged.

His shoulders slumped. Jennifer had reached out to him. And for all she knew, he'd ignored her.

Great. Just the impression he'd wanted to make.

❄ ❄ ❄

A bell jangled when Jennifer opened the door to A New Chapter. She breathed deep. The smell of books always cheered her. A cuckoo clock decorated the fireplace mantel, while a roaring fire bathed her in a comforting heat. The worn-down furniture and Oriental rug were just as she remembered. Soothing. Peaceful.

Light glimmered through the store's front window. Rows of books beckoned her. Maybe she'd pick up a romance or a cozy mystery to while away the time tonight. She could spend an hour or two here and get to Havencroft Manor in time to grab a bite to eat before bed.

A vaguely familiar-looking woman with long blond hair and a wide smile sat at a table piled high with books. She chatted to people standing in line while signing one of the books. A poster behind her head read Award-Winning Author Winnie Boyle above her picture.

Wow, she actually looked like her picture. How many people used current photos for that type of thing? Then again, Jennifer would plaster her photo all over the place if she looked like the author. Gorgeous. And the name struck a chord. Had she read something by her before or recognized the name from the library stacks? If only her brain wasn't so fried. She considered stepping up to the table, but hesitated. What if she didn't want to buy one of the books? She'd feel terrible and end up getting one anyway, out of guilt.

"Welcome! Let me know if you need any help. I'll be right over here," a woman's voice called out from near the cashier's counter. Probably the owner. They'd met a few times when Jennifer was last in town. Olivia…something. A first name was all that stuck.

"I'm good, thanks," she called back. She rushed over to a rotating map holder and flipped through the contents. Best to find what she needed and get back on the road. The Havenport townsfolk could be the chatty type. She had no wish to get stuck listening to a rundown of all the small-town gossip.

She doubted much had changed since she'd been there last.

Except for her.

She'd been a mess back then. Married to Carlos, but just beginning to fight her way out of her miserable, destructive relationship. When had that been?

It was November now. So last September, or thereabouts. Two months after Carlos kidnapped Christa and put Jennifer in the hospital with two broken ribs for trying to help Christa escape. Thank goodness Braeden, Jeremy, and the others had arrived, or Carlos would have done much worse.

Jeez, the months all melded together after a while. Hard to believe it had already been over a year since the whole mess.

Yes. Definitely September. School had just started when she'd come back to town. Carlos managed to land in a low-security mental facility rather than jail while waiting to go to trial for kidnapping. And who could blame the courts on that one? He'd been raving mad about needing the *jaadoo* back. He'd clearly gone over the edge.

She must have been somewhat crazy, too. Thinking the connection she'd felt to Braeden could have developed into something lasting…a foolish dream. She should have known better. But she'd come back to Havenport with just that in mind.

One weekend, albeit a perfect one, was all they'd managed.

Carlos, once again, stepped in and ruined everything. A habit of his since the day she'd met him.

The jury was still out on whether she could truly blame Carlos, though. Yeah, him showing up and threatening her all over again was the spark that lit the fire, but she and

Braeden were doomed from the beginning. She was too damaged, carried too much baggage. How could she expect anyone to step into such a situation?

If they'd known each other ahead of time, maybe. But that wasn't the case.

Memories of their weekend would have to be enough.

Damn, she should have known coming back here would get her feeling all maudlin and jumpy. She expected to bump into Braeden around every turn. He'd be at the wedding, of course. Jeremy was his best friend and business partner. But she had no reason to expect he'd be at a bookstore the day before his best friend's wedding, now did she?

Wishful thinking on her part?

As much as she regretted things not working out between them, she knew it had probably been for the best. Still, the urge to see him again made her hyperaware of everyone who walked by in case he showed up.

No. Stop it. She squashed the tiny ray of hope that things would be different this time. She had a long way to go before she'd have her act together. Braeden was a good man, but not many people could handle dating a woman with her kind of drama. She wouldn't ask it of him.

If he wanted a repeat of their weekend, though…

Jeez, what was she thinking? She wasn't that kind of a woman. She still felt guilty from their last weekend and she wanted to do it again?

Yes.

If only she wasn't always so honest. A good, healthy dose of denial would come in handy about now.

Selecting a map of Havenport that seemed to encompass the outlying mansion area, she wandered over to the romances. Within minutes she had a nice selection to choose from. She'd love to get all eight, but with the divorce and the ton of debt heaped on her by Carlos's reckless spending habits, she had to keep an eye on her money.

She settled on two historical romances and a thriller before replacing the others on the shelves. On her way to pay, she cast another glance at the author and got a good look at the books spread around her. She recognized one of the covers. Winnie Boyle! Yes. Now she remembered. Winnie's 'Lost' series of historical romances was fantastic. Jennifer had read *The Lost Duke*, *The Lost Heiress*, and *The Lost Heir*.

Her gaze caught a title she had yet to read. *The Lost Bride*. She stepped closer and picked up a copy to read the back cover. Oh, yes. Perfect.

"That's my latest. It's part of a series, but they don't need to be read in order." The author tapped a copy of *The Lost Duke* with her finger. "This is book one if you prefer. I—"

Jennifer held up a hand to forestall the sales pitch. She didn't need convincing. "I've read the others. It's one of my favorite series. I didn't realize you wrote a new one, though."

"I can sign it for you, if you like." Winnie beamed, her pen poised above an open copy of *The Lost Bride*.

Jennifer nodded. "Thanks," she said, taking the book and immediately flipping it open to view the signature. *May you always find your way. Enjoy! Winnie Boyle*. Seemed like a good omen. She'd been lost for a while now. Finding her way back would take some time, but she was working on it.

She read the first few pages as she waited in line to pay. Several others stood in almost identical poses before her. Each with an open copy of a Winnie Boyle romance. Thankfully, they all kept the woman behind the register busy enough she didn't try to engage Jennifer in a lengthy conversation. Making it out of there without an overview of Havenport gossip proved easier than she'd have guessed.

When she got to her car, she unfolded the map across the dash and figured out a route to Havencroft Manor, the old mansion that recently opened up as a wedding venue and hotel. She tossed her cell in the cup holder, surprised to see she'd missed a call. No message and an unfamiliar number.

She'd once raced to pick up her calls, hoping to hear Braeden's voice on the other end. Not anymore. Carlos made it a habit of terrorizing her over the phone and had the uncanny ability to find her number every time she switched.

Braeden never called anyway.

Nerves flickered in her stomach. Would she see Braeden tonight? He'd be staying at the hotel, right? Or would he arrive tomorrow?

Well, she'd find out soon enough.

Chapter Two

Braeden straightened his tie, checking the knot in the mirror. The rehearsal dinner didn't start for another hour, but Christa had mentioned Jennifer was due to arrive any minute and he wanted to "just happen" to be in the lobby when she arrived.

Pathetic?

Sure. But he didn't think he could wait another minute to see her. Freakin' butterflies assaulted his stomach. Macho as shit, right? But he couldn't think of any other way to describe it.

She'd been in his thoughts almost constantly since last summer. He'd dated a bit, but no one moved him like her.

This crazy attraction had to be some kind of a by-blow of seeing her as the damsel in distress. No way he could have fallen so completely for a woman in such a short time. His memories were playing tricks on him. Building her personality and beauty up to unreasonable proportions. The sooner he saw her, the sooner he'd recognize she wasn't so special and he could put her out of his mind.

He checked his watch. One last glance in the mirror to be sure his hair hadn't flipped up in the back like it sometimes did, then he headed out the door.

Most of the guests would be situated out in the renovated carriage house that stood about thirty feet out the back between the main house and the dock, but the wedding party was in the main building. With snow expected tomorrow, he was glad he'd be able to stay inside and warm the entire time. Although if Jennifer wanted company over in the carriage house, he'd brave the weather.

He took the main staircase down to the foyer. Christa planned to use the stairs to make her grand entrance for the wedding tomorrow night. He hadn't missed the opportunity to tease her about tripping on her dress.

Thoughts of the wedding ended when he made it to the ground floor and looked toward the registration desk.

Jennifer.

Damn, his memory was spot on. Absolutely freakin' gorgeous. Dark windblown hair fell in her face and a bulky winter coat disguised the curves he remembered so well, but her flawless skin glowed and her jeans clung to her sweet legs, doing nothing to hide the rounded fullness of her rear end. He paused to admire the sight.

She struggled with a black-wheeled bag that seemed hell-bent on falling over. He rushed the last few steps and grabbed the handle. Her gaze shot to his face, then quickly dropped. But not before a hint of a blush stained her cheeks.

"Braeden," she exclaimed. "How nice to see you."

Distracted by her sweet, delicate Indian accent, he blurted, "Hey." *Jeez*, freaking genius comeback. He was surprised she didn't throw her panties at his head, overcome by his charming wit. "Here, I've got this."

Their fingers brushed, and the electricity he remembered seared his hand. So much for thinking their crazy attraction was a figment of his imagination.

He eased the recalcitrant bag out of her grasp and dragged it toward the desk. Tracy, the clerk, regarded him with a flirtatious smile. He'd dealt with the same woman when he'd checked in earlier that day.

"What can I do for you today, Mr. Tiede?" She batted her impossibly long—*fake?*—eyelashes at him.

"My…" He hesitated a second, trying to come up with the right word, "…friend would like to check in."

Tracy's smile faltered, but she quickly upped the wattage back to full beam. "Name?" she asked in an efficient manner.

"Jennifer O'Malkey," he responded.

"It's Venkat now, actually. I've reverted to my maiden name." She whipped out her ID and slid it across the desk to Tracy, who took it with a practiced swipe.

Maiden name? So the divorce must be finalized. Not that he'd viewed her sham of a marriage as any sort of deterrent, but the thought of her being finally, truly free filled him with a sense of accomplishment. And hope.

Maybe now *was* their chance.

"You'll be out in the carriage house, second floor. I'll have a bellhop escort you over," Tracy said.

"I'll show her the way." He glanced at the clock over the receptionist's head. He had plenty of time to see Jennifer settled and make it back to the ballroom for the rehearsal. He kept a firm grip on her luggage when she made a move to take back the handle. "I've got it."

She hesitated only a second, then nodded. "Thank you."

He tipped his chin at her unbuttoned jacket. "You might want to button up. There's a nice path to the carriage house, but it's open to the water and can get a decent breeze."

"Oh, I didn't realize we had to go outside." She put a hand on his arm. "Do you want to get a coat? It's quite chilly."

"Nah, I'm good."

He opened the patio doors and immediately regretted his macho I-am-man-cold-doesn't-bother-me attitude. A frigid breeze whipped his suit jacket open. He kept a firm grip on the door so it wouldn't go crashing against the wall. Christa would kill him if ugly plywood sheeting covering shattered glass ruined the backdrop of her wedding.

Once Jennifer cleared the doorway, he shut the door carefully behind her and led her toward the path to the carriage house.

They didn't speak as they hurried along, paying careful attention to the slick pathway, the soft crash of the waves against the shore competing with the wind whistling among the trees. He hunched his shoulders and stuck his free hand into his pocket. Thankfully the walk wasn't long, and they reached the entrance in no time.

Jennifer swiped her key card to get them into the building. She held the door for him this time, and he let out a sigh as the warm air embraced him. Much like he wished Jennifer would take him into the comfort of her arms.

Given the way she fidgeted with her purse and avoided his gaze, he wouldn't bet on it.

✳ ✳ ✳

"I can take it from here. Thank you." Jennifer reached for her luggage, but didn't go so far as to grab the handle. Touching him, even so briefly as to take the bag from him, wasn't a good idea. Not when they were one floor away from a private room with a queen-size bed.

He looked just as good as she remembered. She'd begun to have doubts. She must have exaggerated his good looks, right?

Wrong.

His russet-brown hair was a little longer, but swept back off his forehead in slightly wavy, almost tousled, perfection. His charcoal-gray suit hugged his biceps and made her mouth water from the memory of the way those arms flexed as he rose above her, staring deep into her eyes and...

Yeah. Better not get too close to any available horizontal surfaces.

"I have to go to the rehearsal. Why don't you come with me?" He pulled his cell out of his breast pocket. "I'm sure it would be fine with Christa and Jeremy."

She quickly covered his phone with her hand. She needed time to think. "I'm exhausted. I've been driving all day. I'm just going to take a hot bath and read a book for a bit, then get to sleep."

His gaze heated, and she sucked in a breath. She took a quick step back and lowered her gaze. "Tomorrow. I— I'll see you tomorrow at the wedding."

Coward that she was, she grabbed her bag and made a beeline for the elevator bank she'd spotted at the far end of the hall. She could feel his gaze on her as she punched the up button about a million times. Finally the elevator arrived with a ding, and she dashed inside.

Her room was easy to find, once she calmed down enough to read the numbers on the doors. Room 2108 was far enough from the elevator she wasn't likely to hear people getting on and off all night, just as she'd requested. She was a light sleeper, so she always tried to get a room that would be as quiet as possible. The key card turned the light green so she nudged open the door with her hip.

She walked in to the overpowering smell of new carpet. Christa had mentioned the Historical Society's renovations, turning Havencroft Manor into a quaint hotel that could sustain itself with seasonal guests, were barely completed in time for the wedding. Early November was a bit off season, but Christa had booked all the rooms for her big day.

The room was full of charm with the outside wall of warm red brick, a window overlooking the boathouse, distressed wood flooring, and a queen-size bed that dominated the room. A fluffy white comforter and pillows piled high enough to hide the headboard invited snuggling in for a long nap.

Once she got used to the carpet smell, she noticed an underlying scent of cinnamon and apples. The air freshener spritzed its cloud from its perch on an end table, but didn't quite mask the new room odors. They'd have to air the place out come spring if they really wanted to get rid of the stench.

For a hotel, though, it wasn't bad. She'd suffered through much worse while married to Carlos. She shuddered just thinking of the places she'd been forced to live with him. Talk about rank odors…

She shoved the thought aside and put her clothes away. Disentangling the garment bag designed to cleverly wrap around her wheeled luggage, she took out her dress for the next evening and hung it in the closet. It hadn't wrinkled too badly. She might get away with not ironing it.

After a leisurely bath scented with a few drops of rose oil, she dried off and dressed in jeans, T-shirt, and cardigan. She grabbed the clicker and flipped channels. Nothing caught her attention, and she didn't want to waste her money on a pay-per-view movie.

Her stomach growled.

Room service? She glanced around the small room. She could eat at the dainty writing desk in the corner, but the silence was beginning to get to her. Thoughts of Braeden and what she should have said earlier instead of behaving like some shy little schoolgirl dominated her brain. She always reacted much better in her imagination than she did in reality.

More's the pity.

Christa had raved about the bruschetta they served at the hotel bar. Vegetarian options weren't always easy to come by when traveling. She should take advantage. She grabbed her jacket and a book, then headed out the door. She'd grab a quick bite, read a little, then get a good night's sleep.

The minute she walked into the bar, she knew her plans were doomed for failure.

Braeden, Christa, Jeremy, and a rowdy bunch clustered around the bar, glasses raised as they toasted the couple to be.

Before she could duck back out, Christa spotted her. With Christa's jaunty wave and a shout, Jennifer realized she was stuck.

❄ ❄ ❄

Braeden gave Jennifer a moment to accept she wasn't getting out of Christa's clutches anytime soon. No one wanted to refuse the bride-to-be the night before her wedding. And Christa seemed determined for Jennifer to be a part of tonight's celebrations.

Someone tapped him on the shoulder. He spun around to find a grinning Jeremy holding up two shot glasses.

Braeden grabbed one, tapped it against Jeremy's glass, then downed the drink. Fire burned straight to his gullet. He sipped his beer to calm the blaze.

A distinct buzz sounded in his ears. He swayed, squinting at Jeremy through a haze.

Jeremy grabbed his arm, preventing him from toppling over. "You okay? How much have you had to drink?"

"You know what?" He slammed his glass down on the bar and held up one finger, waving the wobbly digit in Jeremy's nose. "I..." He squinted at his finger, wondering why he was pointing at his business partner. "You... No. I am gonna to do something." *There. Take that.*

Jeremy laughed and clapped him on the back, sending him sideways against the bar stool. "Fantastic. Glad to hear it. What are you going to do?"

What? Oh, yeah. He meant to do something. He snapped his fingers, or tried to. "I am going to find Jeffiner an' kiss 'er," he slurred. He put a hand to his temple. "As soon as the room stops spinning."

"Is he okay?" Christa appeared at his side. "I didn't think he'd had much to drink."

"The bride!" Braeden slammed a hand on the bar. "Another drink for the lovely bride." His words came out odd, slurred. "Know what?" He switched his gaze back and forth between Jeremy and Christa. "Maybe I shouldn'a taken my allergy med-meshin this morn. I don' feel too good." He hiccupped.

"You didn't." Jeremy shook him. "Shit, man. What were you thinking?" He turned to Christa. "Last time he mixed alcohol and his allergy meds, he ended up in the hospital. It messes him up."

"Forgot I took it." He squinted at all the frowning faces surrounding him and whispered in a loud voice, "I think I might be a little drunk."

"Yes, I believe you're right," said the most beautiful voice he'd ever heard.

He swung around unsteadily, one hand on the bar stool to keep his balance. "Jennifer." He reached a hand to her, pleased when she immediately took it. Her hands were soft, like... He couldn't come up with a comparison. He frowned.

"Name something soft." He held her hand to his mouth and brushed his lips against her knuckles. "Your skin is perfect. So sweet, so delicate."

A fiery red blush stained her cheeks. He traced the line of her jaw with a finger. "You're beautiful. Even when you're looking at me like I've lost my mind."

Jeremy grabbed his shoulder in a firm grip and hissed, "Dude, now's not the time. We should get you to your room."

He pouted as Christa grabbed Jennifer and the pair wandered away toward the end of the bar.

He moved to follow, but Jeremy grabbed his arm. He lowered his voice and whispered in his ear, "You're way past the point of being able to do anything with those lines, dude. Save it for tomorrow when you're sober."

Christa's mother, Sondra, chose that moment to approach. "Hello, darlings. Braeden, your aura is screaming at me from across the room."

She put her hands on his shoulders and stared him in the eyes.

Both of her. Man, Jeremy was right. He shouldn't have had that shot. "I'm sorry, Sondra. I think I should go throw up about now."

"I don't think so, dear." She shook her head and patted his arm. "Christa and Jeremy are counting on you to be at your best tomorrow. Besides," Sondra said, grabbing his chin and turning him to look at Jennifer, who had wedged herself into a corner of the bar, "you have more important issues to deal with this evening."

He tried to focus, but his sight wavered. Was the book upside down? He swayed.

Sondra placed her hand against his forehead, chanting under her breath. Warmth fanned out from his forehead and through his body. As the feeling spread, the buzz from the alcohol and medicine combo lessened. With each word, the warmth increased and the drunken stupor eased. With a satisfied smile, she kissed him on the cheek. "There now, darling. I like that young lady of yours. But judging from the unease in her aura, I'd say she's not too impressed by your drunken behavior this evening. Tread softly."

She turned to her daughter. "Don't stay up too late, sweetheart. Tomorrow's going to be a busy day, and I'm not spending it trying to wake your hungover ass up."

Christa rolled her eyes. "Gee, thanks, Mom."

He felt a ton better. His head clear, his body steady. He chuckled at Sondra and Christa's back-and-forth. He'd witnessed it many times since meeting Christa's mother almost a year ago. The two were very close, but you'd think animosity ruled their relationship if you went by the way they spoke to each other. Sondra was a character, but she was also one of the most generous people he'd ever met.

As the mother-daughter combo continued their friendly bickering, he turned his attention to fixing the crappy image he'd presented to the one person he most wanted to impress.

Shit. Fierce frown, stiff spine, book clutched so tight the pages crumpled. He didn't need to be an expert on body language to recognize he was in a world of hurt.

Jennifer was pissed.

❄❄❄

Jennifer pretended to be absorbed in *The Lost Bride*. She'd been staring at the same spot for several minutes without reading a word, her attention more on Braeden than the page. She doubted she'd fooled anyone, though. The lighting at the bar was pretty dim.

She cast a sideways glance at Braeden again.

How much had he had to drink? Did he do this often or was this a special occasion? And if the rehearsal was special, what about the wedding itself?

She hated to compare him to Carlos, but drinking always set her on edge. Survival instinct kicking in, she supposed. After a few drinks, Carlos acted like a different man. On the rare occasions he remained sober, he at least *tried* to keep his anger in check.

What would alcohol do to Braeden?

Braeden's eyes continuously flicked in her direction as he laughed with Christa and Jeremy. She stiffened her spine and buried her nose in the book.

Then realized she held it upside down.

Her cheeks heated, and she bit her lip. Turn it over? Wouldn't that draw more attention to the fact it wasn't right to begin with?

Shoot.

She dropped the book onto the bar and grabbed a menu from the small stack just within reach. Her stomach rumbled. Last thing she'd eaten was a package of almonds around two o'clock. She glanced at her watch. Nine. No wonder her head spun with hunger.

But would she be able to keep anything down? After watching Braeden do shots with Jeremy, not only was her stomach empty, but it twisted with worry as well. Would Braeden turn into a monster like Carlos after one too many? She didn't know if she could handle the answer. She'd turn around and leave, but Christa had asked her to hang out, so she was stuck. Might as well get a bite.

While Jennifer pretended deep interest in the menu, Sondra grabbed Braeden's face between her hands, and after a look charged with magickal energy, released him and gave his shoulder a shove.

In her direction.

She blinked to dispel the residual glow from Sondra's spell. Intense. Braeden's chakras had been wildly off-kilter, but with one flash of Sondra's power, they whirled into alignment.

It didn't take him long to cross the room. As it was a Friday, the bar was crowded, but no one paid him any mind.

"Hey," he said when he stopped at her side. He hitched his ankle around a bar stool, pulled it out, and rested his hip against it. "Good book?"

"Yes, it's lovely, thank you." She tilted her chin toward the menu, affecting a calm she didn't feel. With a flick of her wrist, she signaled the bartender. "Can I get an order of bruschetta, please. And a seltzer with lime. Thank you."

He gave her an appreciative once-over and nodded. "Sure thing, miss. I'll get that to you right away." She placed the menu back in its spot, leaving her hands empty and nothing to focus on but Braeden.

The smell of tequila wafted off him. She flinched.

"I didn't actually drink much tonight," he said.

"Not my business." The lie was too familiar to take seriously. Carlos always claimed sobriety, even when he was so drunk he could barely stand. She kept her eyes locked on her image in the mirror behind the bar. Focused on keeping her hands from trembling, steeling her nerves in case he leaned in close, sneered in her face, raised his fist.

"I'm not him." He made no move to touch her. He leaned his elbows on the bar, steepled his fingers together, and stared at his hands. "I know he hurt you. Not just that day. Or after you left him and he tried to force you back. Before that. Before you even came to Havenport."

She jerked in surprise. Heat rose in her cheeks once more. Damn, but she'd tried to keep that secret. She wasn't proud of it. Even less so that she'd stayed with him for so long, despite the abuse. Yeah, the spell had played its part, but...if she were honest, she'd been too ashamed to admit what was happening. Her head knew the blame lay with Carlos, not her. He'd abused her. She'd done nothing to deserve his anger. He was sick, twisted by the power of misused *jaadoo*.

In the beginning, she'd loved him. Or thought she did. The *jaadoo* had created an obsessive, blind devotion that would have made a normal man uncomfortable. Carlos had reveled in it. And by the time the *jaadoo* began to wear off, she'd been so deep with him, and created such a chasm from her old life, she had no idea how to bridge the gap.

Braeden took her hand gently in his. "I admire your strength."

"What?" Strength? She had so little. She must have misheard. Music blared, people laughed, conversations were shouted, not to mention the way his thumb stroked back and forth against her palm had all her nerve endings focused on his touch. She shook her head.

He tilted his chin to speak in her ear. "Standing up to Carlos like you did. You saved Christa." He squeezed her hand. "She told us how you freed her, even knowing what that asshole would do to you if you were caught. That took guts."

His warm breath on her neck made her shiver. "Not so brave. What else could I do? It was my fault she was there in the first place."

He nudged her shoulder with his. "You were brave. You know Christa doesn't blame you for your part in luring her to Carlos, right? She'd never have invited you to her wedding if she did."

"I suppose."

"It's true. She says if it weren't for you she'd never have made it out of that basement." He touched the scar above her eye. "You paid a hefty price for helping her, but you did it anyway."

He lowered his hand to trace a finger along her jawline. Her breath quickened. Her gaze darted up to meet his in the mirror.

Tears blurred his reflection, but she couldn't help seeing the understanding in his gaze. The compassion. The admiration. He turned away.

No, not away. Toward her. She shifted to face him and their lips met in the barest brush of a kiss that tickled and warmed her soul.

The kiss stole not only her breath, but her heart as well.

Chapter Three

Braeden didn't press his luck. He retreated from the kiss before things got out of hand. They were in a crowded bar, for one. For another, Jennifer was close to losing it. Even though she faced him, her body angled toward the exit and she'd slipped her arm through the strap of her purse. If he pushed too hard, she might retreat from him altogether.

He sent a prayer of thanks to Christa for inviting Jennifer to the wedding. If not for the invite, he had no doubt she would never have come to town again. And he'd have spent the rest of his life wondering what could have been.

Now at least he stood a chance of finding out.

Her eyes glistened with unshed tears. *Shit.* He hadn't meant to make her cry. Her hands clenched together in her lap. He took them in his own, massaging them until she gradually let her fists open. "Please don't cry," he whispered.

She sniffed, tugged one hand from him, and used a paper napkin to wipe first her eyes, then her nose. "I'm done. Not sure why I'm turning into a watering pot." Her laugh was rough, but there.

The sudden urge to tell her a joke tripped up his tongue. Anything to turn her feeble humor into a full-on belly laugh. Of course he came up blank, so he simply grinned encouragement. "There's that beautiful smile. Much better."

"Beautiful?"

He kissed the tip of her nose. "Yes, beautiful."

The garlicky scent of bruschetta intruded. Jennifer sniffed again, but this time with appreciation. His stomach growled. The bartender gave them settings for two. "Share?"

She nodded and they made quick work of the savory dish.

"Christa was right. That was delicious." She held a hand up to her mouth, unsuccessfully hiding a huge yawn.

"Talking about me?"

He swiveled his stool to see Christa, with Jeremy close behind.

"Just complimenting your bruschetta recommendation," he said, then clapped Jeremy on the back. "Heading to bed?"

"Yeah. Got a little something going on tomorrow— something in the evening, I think. Can't remember exactly, but it'll come to me."

Christa bumped him with her hip. "Nice. Just a little something." She rolled her eyes. "Not that there'll be anyone around for the wedding if the weather doesn't cooperate. I can't believe it's going to snow again tomorrow. Seriously, we've had flurries all week. And now more for the weekend. I can't remember the last time it snowed this early in November."

Jeremy hugged her. "I knew I should have banned the Weather Channel. They always give the worse case scenario. Besides, it's not supposed to be so bad in town. Don't worry so much. The airport will probably be a mess, but the important people are already here."

Braeden grinned. "Aw, shucks. Thanks."

Christa laughed. "Fine. You're right. I know you're right. Nothing's going to keep me from marrying you tomorrow." They kissed, but Christa pulled away before the PDA got out of hand and pointed her finger at Jeremy. "But *you* can't see the bride before the wedding." She checked her watch. "And we've got only about twenty minutes before midnight."

"We have to run," Jeremy interrupted. He grabbed Christa's hand and practically dragged her from the room. Before they were out of sight, they were in each other's arms. Jeremy grabbed Christa's butt, startling a high-pitched giggle from her. The door shut behind them.

Jennifer's face held a rosy glow. "They look happy."

He nodded. "They are." He was happy for them. And not jealous at all. *Liar.* "I've known Jeremy forever. I've never seen him so head over heels for anyone."

"How did they meet?"

"Christa used to work as a graphic designer in our ad agency. They flirted for a while, finally hooked up, then Christa found that damn book, *On Magick Most Powerful.* Someone…" *Shit*, why did he bring this part up? *Idiot.* "Carlos started stalking her so she took off. A little less than a year later, she thought she'd ditched him so she returned. You know what happened then." That Fourth of July was one of the worst days of his life. Christa kidnapped, then Jennifer savagely beaten trying to help. "Everything worked out in the end, thankfully."

"Uh-huh. That's great." Jennifer's eyelids drooped, and she leaned heavily on her elbow.

"You look wiped. Let's go." He signaled the bartender and paid the bill, including a generous tip.

He grabbed her purse and eased her off her stool.

"I'm good. I'll just go back to my room," she said, her words slightly slurred with exhaustion.

He shouldn't have kept her so long. She'd driven hours to get here today. He should have known she'd be exhausted from the trip.

"Yeah, I don't think you're gonna make it. I'll help you up." The last thing he should do was escort Jennifer to her room when he couldn't stop picturing her naked, but he also couldn't just leave her here. From the moment he'd met her, she'd sparked his protective instincts. Tonight was no different.

He helped button up her jacket, and they made their way outside to follow the path to the carriage house. Christa had a point about the weather. He sniffed the air, his senses telling him the snow would start this evening rather than tomorrow. No big deal. Sondra would preside over the ceremony as planned, both families were already checked in at the manor, and there was nothing to prevent the wedding.

And nothing to keep him from spending more time with Jennifer.

Several times on the walk Braeden resisted the urge to sweep her off her feet and carry her the rest of the way to the carriage house. He'd bet the hero in the book she'd pretended to read earlier would do something dramatic and romantic. Braeden wouldn't mind if Jennifer saw him as a romance hero, but he refrained from giving in to the impulse.

First off, he didn't think she'd appreciate the gesture.

Second, while he was confident he could carry her with ease, ice patches dotted the pathway and he didn't relish the idea of slipping and dropping her onto the hard bricks. He'd imagined any number of ways to seduce the woman of his dreams, but none of them involved dumping her on the cold, hard ground.

Besides, she was obviously tired. He may have the itch to renew their amorous relationship, but he had yet to figure out if she felt the same. And he had no interest in forcing his presence on her if she didn't. She'd had enough of that type of man. He wanted to prove he was nothing like her ex.

❄ ❄ ❄

Jennifer's steps slowed the closer they got to her room. Should she invite Braeden in? Stop him at the door?

She didn't know what she wanted. The kiss at the bar had stirred her blood in a way she hadn't felt since the last time they'd been together. But was she ready for a repeat of that night?

The cold shocked the weariness out of her body. She was wide awake and feeling twitchy. Not exactly in a good place for making important decisions.

And she considered anything to do with Braeden important.

The most urgent decision was to determine what she thought of Braeden's character. His drinking tonight scared her. Carlos's abuse was still too recent, and he'd been ten times worse when he drank.

Yet, other than seeming a bit wobbly on his legs, he hadn't frightened her. Well, maybe a little. But not because of anything he did. More because of anticipation of what he could do. What Carlos would have done.

"Do you drink a lot?" she blurted. Nice. She might as well accuse him of being an alcoholic.

He shrugged. "Once in a while. A beer or two after work maybe. I only had a few drinks tonight to celebrate."

The knot in her stomach got bigger. He was lying to her. Had to be. A few drinks wouldn't make someone slur their words. Before Sondra stepped in, he'd been barely coherent. She stepped away from him to swipe her key card and gain access to the building. "Oh." She bit her lip, then mumbled, "Seemed like more than a few. You were pretty drunk." She should let him respond, rather than sniping at him and disappearing, but her courage fast deserted her. She stopped in the doorway, blocking his entrance.

Was he staying in this building or the main? Her getaway would be far less dramatic if he unlocked the door and followed her in. "Anyway, I better get going. Thanks for walking me over."

She tried to shut the door in his face, but he put out his foot and blocked her move. "Wait a second. Why are you mad?"

"I don't like being lied to," she said. She put her chin up, refusing to let her gaze drop. Her legs trembled like jelly, the knot in her stomach tightened, but she somehow managed not to quail. She hadn't stood up to someone in a long time. Carlos had beaten the fight right out of her. She held her breath. Part of her was amazed at her daring. The other part knew deep down Braeden wasn't any danger to her.

"I haven't lied. Are we going to do this in the doorway, or can I come in? We're letting all the cold in."

She cast a glance down the long hall lined with doors leading to guest rooms. Silence ruled the building. People likely wouldn't appreciate them having this conversation in the hall while they tried to sleep.

She opened the door wider and emerged back out into the cold night, letting the door close behind her back. A few snowflakes drifted to the ground.

He frowned but stepped aside, then nodded. "Want to walk down to the boathouse or back up to the manor?"

She hovered with indecision. She'd enjoy the privacy of the boathouse, but there'd be people about in the main building. The bar wouldn't close for another hour or so.

Did she trust him or not?

"Boathouse."

His eyebrows raised in surprise, but he tucked her hand in the crook of his elbow and turned them toward the waterside.

The snow increased its pace, falling quietly, daring Jennifer to disturb the silence. A thin dusting soon covered the grounds, not yet sticking to the path. They walked in silence, snow drifting down on them. God, she loved the snow. So peaceful. Some of her tension eased. Despite being unnerved by Braeden's drinking, she wasn't scared. He wouldn't hurt her.

She had to stop letting Carlos ruin her life without even being near.

They reached the boathouse, which was all closed up for the season. The porch wrapped along the outside, leading to the large dock. The snow melted on the weathered wooden slats, but made the boards slick and wet.

He switched his grip to wrap an arm around her waist. "It's a bit slippery. Careful." He stopped at the end of the ramp where the railing ended. "Let's stop here. I don't think it's safe out on the dock without a railing in this weather."

Waves lapped against the rocky shore below the dock. Tide looked to be out. There wasn't much to look at with the snow clouding their view, but the sound of the waves and the smell of the water calmed her. She felt bolstered, almost as if she could actually stand up for herself.

Maybe she could.

"I didn't lie. I had a beer and a shot. I didn't even drink at all at the rehearsal dinner."

"Uh-huh. So why were you slurring your words when I first arrived at the bar?"

"If I were that drunk, I'd still be slurring. Do I seem drunk now?"

She shook her head. He didn't appear inebriated at all. "No. But Sondra did something. And that doesn't change how you were acting when I first saw you drinking a shot at the bar with everyone."

"I agree. I was out of it for a bit there. Sondra came to my rescue."

"So what are you saying, you're a lightweight?" Her snarky tone dwindled by the end of the sentence. He didn't deserve her sarcasm. Maybe he'd been drunk. Maybe not. But when he looked at her, even if through a blurry, alcohol-induced fog, there hadn't been a hint of anger in his eyes. No violence, no disdain, nothing like Carlos. She grinned, suddenly finding it funny she'd ever compared the two men. "Can't hold your alcohol?" That alone would have garnered her a punch from Carlos.

Braeden grinned. "I can handle myself. Usually." He leaned against the railing. "The weather's been crazy lately. Have you noticed?"

She nodded. "Of course. Just last week I was out in the afternoon without my parka. Today…" She held out a hand, a snowflake landing on her glove. "…it's snowing. Figuring out how to pack for this weekend was a nightmare."

"Yeah. Well, it's been playing havoc with my allergies. I've been taking medicine for the past few days. It doesn't mix well with alcohol, which is why I usually don't drink at all when I take it. I wasn't thinking when I did a shot with Jeremy. Sondra saw the problem right away and sobered me up quick."

Quite the story. Sounded almost made up. But she didn't think so. She believed him. After a deep breath and a moment watching the flakes fall softly into the ocean, she turned to Braeden. "Would you like to come up to my room with me? Maybe talk awhile?" She rubbed her upper arms and shivered. "It's getting kind of cold out here."

✻ ✻ ✻

Braeden could have shouted with triumph, but resisted the urge. "Sure. That'd be nice."

He breathed a sigh of relief when the warmth of the carriage house welcomed them in. Jennifer led him up the stairs and down the hall. He spied a soda machine. "Want something to drink?" he asked, pointing to the machine.

She nodded, so he bought them a couple sodas before they continued to her room.

Nerves hit him hard as the door closed behind him. This wasn't just some one-night stand. He was crazy about her. And she was vulnerable. He'd known that last year when they had their fling. Known, but hadn't resisted the temptation of being in her bed for the weekend.

He'd regretted his lack of control after the fact. She may have come on to him back then, but he should have resisted. Saying no hadn't even occurred to him until she'd declared the weekend a big mistake.

That had hurt. He'd tried to pretend he didn't care, but he'd failed. Then guilt overtook the hurt because she'd been in a bad place and he'd slept with her anyway.

Her room was decorated similar to his, with a king-size bed taking up the majority of the space. Soft, airy, white bedding with a mound of pillows he knew he'd sink into. A pair of chairs with a small table between them sat in the corner. A flat-screen TV sat atop a mahogany dresser.

He strode straight to the chair farthest from the bed and took a seat. After setting her soda on the table, he opened his with a *hiss* of carbonation and took a long swig. "Do you believe me about tonight?" Should he bring up Carlos? The specter of her ex hung over every move he'd made tonight. They couldn't ignore the issue forever. Better to dive right in and get it over with. "I know how

Carlos was with you, and I'm guessing he'd get worse when he drank."

She gasped. Her hand shook as she picked up her drink. He took it from her to open it. "I shouldn't be surprised," she responded. "You saw what he did to me when Christa and I tried to run."

"Yes, I did."

She took the bottle back from him, and he let his hand linger under hers before releasing the drink. She flinched at the contact.

Aw, crap. After all they'd been through—the kidnapping, her beating and recovery, the sex—did she honestly still think he was like that asshole ex of hers? He thought they'd gotten over that hurdle last year when they'd spent the weekend together.

Apparently not.

Could he blame her? He might have been woozy from the mix of alcohol and medicine, but from her perspective would that matter? To her, drunk idiot equaled abusive asshole. Had he set their relationship back by acting like a drunk idiot?

He wrapped both hands around his own bottle. "I would never hurt you. I hope you can believe me someday." *Go slow. Have patience.* He couldn't blame her for being gun-shy. Somehow, someday, he'd prove she could trust him.

She nodded, then sat in the seat beside him. "I know," she whispered.

He must have looked skeptical because she repeated, "I know," in a firmer voice. "It's just hard to shed the self-preservation mode that's taken over since I married him. Walking on eggshells, curbing my thoughts, trying to do things just the way he liked…"

He forced his hands to not crush his drink. It wasn't easy. He wanted to rush out, find Carlos, and beat the ever-living shit out of him.

Since he was trying to prove he wasn't a violent man, he needed to curb those instincts.

He detested the way she'd been treated. It was unthinkable anyone could use a woman that way. And it killed him to think of Jennifer being in that situation. He imagined it would take a long time for her to recover fully, if she ever could.

Could he be man enough to be there for her? Did he have the kind of patience and compassion she must need?

"You're different. I can feel it. I'm not afraid when I'm with you."

"Then why do you shy away? Sometimes it seems like my touch scares you."

"No." She shook her head. "My heart knows, my mind knows, but my body's still trying to catch up. I'm a mess." She leaned forward and cradled her head in her hands.

He went down on one knee before her. "Hey, hey. It's okay." Would she welcome his touch? He longed to take her in his arms. Hug her and make her feel safe. But he was just as likely to make her feel less safe with physical contact.

But if what she said was true and it was just a matter of her body figuring out what her mind already knew, then maybe he needed to give her body a chance to warm up to him.

He scooted closer to wrap an arm across her shoulders. She didn't flinch. In fact, she leaned into him, tucking her head into the crook of his neck.

"I'm sorry," she whispered.

"Don't be."

❋ ❋ ❋

Jennifer surreptitiously wiped a tear from her cheek while going for a delicate sniff that sounded more like she was trying to suck a milkshake up her nose. Desperate to wipe up the mess she was certain was flowing out her nose, she kept her head down, tucked under Braeden's chin, while scoping the room for a tissue.

One miraculously appeared in front of her face.

She plucked it from his grasp and leaned away in order to blow her nose. "Thank you," she mumbled around the tissue, her nose only partially cleared. "Give me a sec." She stood and made her way into the bathroom. The tissue went into the garbage before she took stock of her image in the mirror.

Okay, her hair had seen better days and her mascara wasn't nearly as waterproof as the tube claimed. She pulled a few makeup-remover wipes from her cosmetics bag and did her best to clean up. Touch-up or natural?

Vanity gave way to exhaustion, so she simply ran a comb through her hair, brushed her teeth, and returned to the bedroom.

The appreciative smile on Braeden's face told her he didn't mind the natural look. "Better? You look great."

She waved away the compliment. "No makeup, clothes a wrinkled mess...yeah, I'm a knockout."

"Don't get me wrong. I like the makeup and all, but you don't need it. And I like knowing you're not hiding..." He broke off, twisted the top off the empty bottle of soda in his hands, then tried to take a sip. He frowned, and placed it on the table.

She ignored the almost-reference to the bruising her makeup used to conceal and asked, "Do you want another?"

He shook his head. "Not really." He smiled sheepishly and spread his hands wide before settling his elbows on his knees and leaning forward. "Honestly? I'm kinda nervous.

Not sure what to do with my damn hands." He stared at them for a second, then clasped them together.

She blinked in surprise. "Nervous?" He always appeared so composed, unruffled. "Why?"

"Shit, Jen. This is new territory for me, you know? Usually if I'm in a beautiful woman's hotel room, I'm not sitting in the awkward chair." He blushed, the color rising from his throat and swiftly turning his cheeks a deep red. "Not that I spend a lot of time in women's hotel rooms. I mean, I'm not a monk, but—"

Her laughter started as a giggle, but quickly turned into a full-on belly laugh when Braeden reared back, eyebrows raised to his hairline, eyes wide, and mouth pulled into a tight, affronted line.

She held up one hand, the other clutching her stomach. A few deep breaths and she wrested enough control over her humor to say, "I'm s-sorry. But really, you just sounded so...so..." She shrugged.

His tight-lipped frown relaxed into a self-deprecating smile, and her heart melted.

She sank into the chair next to him. "So, in case you're wondering, I'm not nervous. You don't need to be. Besides, you've been at my bedside before."

An awkward silence followed. She'd never really thanked him for helping her when she had no one. She cleared her throat. "It meant the world to me, you know."

He cast her a quizzical look, eyebrows raised, head tilted to the side. "What?"

"That you stayed with me. You know, in the hospital. And then after, when the police were asking all those questions and you found that lawyer willing to help me pro bono. I was so overwhelmed, and I don't know what I would have done without you." She clutched her hands together in her lap and kept her focus on her twisted fingers. She rarely talked about those days, but this was something she needed to get off her chest.

His warm hand covered hers, instantly diminishing the chill that had settled over her. She allowed her gaze to inch up the corded muscles of his arm, along the wide breadth of his shoulder, across his square jaw, until finally reaching his eyes. The warmth and understanding there settled the unease that had filled her. Somehow the horrors she'd been through almost seemed worth it if they brought her to this wonderful man.

He leaned in close. His breath fanned her forehead as he gave her a gentle kiss. Her lips parted on a sigh. He smelled delicious. She had to fight the urge to bury her nose in the crease of his neck and breathe him in.

"After what you did for Christa, I'd say we're even."

She tamped down her disappointment. "Ah. I see."

He tensed, his back straightened, and the hand that had just begun to massage the base of her neck tightened, then slowly lowered. He backed up and sat on the bottom corner of the bed. "What do you see?" he asked, his voice as tense as his body.

All the unease that had been slowly draining instantly sprang back. She rubbed the back of her neck where the warmth of his hand still lingered. A knot squeezed painfully, a headache hovering as she tried to think what she'd said wrong. "Nothing." At his grunt, she continued, knowing he wasn't going to let this uncomfortable moment pass. "It's no big deal. I wondered why you'd been so good to me. Was it Christa or Jeremy?" She got up to pace before him, waving away her own question. "It doesn't matter. Christa's a sweetheart, and I really appreciate it, but it was my fault she was put into that position in the first place. It was the very least I could do to try to help her out of it."

He jumped to block her path, forcing her to stop or run into him. He grabbed her by the upper arm to steady her when she teetered from the sudden stop.

"I did not stay with you through all that because of Christa or Jeremy." He nudged her chin up with his finger so she was forced to look into his eyes. "I stayed because I was drawn to you. I admired you."

She opened her mouth to refute the ridiculous statement, but he shushed her with a kiss that left her panting and unable to say a word.

❄ ❄ ❄

"Yes. I did and I do. I know you're doubting yourself now after what Carlos put you through, but you shouldn't." Frustration had Braeden on edge. How could she not see her strength?

"I'm a mess." She pulled her shoulders back and took a deep breath. "But I'm working on it."

He chuckled. "Then you're going to be okay."

She grinned in response and licked her lips, bringing the fact that a king-size bed stood less than a foot from them to the forefront of his brain. She must have come to the same realization because her eyes flicked to the side and a blush stained her cheeks. He should go, but first, just one little taste to tide him over.

He leaned in slowly, allowing her time to back away. Instead she tilted her head and wrapped a hand around the back of his neck with just the barest amount of pressure to bring him forward. Not that he needed any encouragement.

He savored the flavor of her on his tongue. She opened to him without any hesitation. Her lips were soft, pliant, and tasted of mint. He couldn't believe how much he loved her.

He broke the kiss, breathing hard. Her eyes were wide, lips parted, and her chest rose and fell to match the pace of his own.

He loved her?

"Is something wrong?"

The hesitation in her voice gave him pause. The emotions rattling around in his heart were too new. He needed time to process. Maybe this foreign emotion was the result of pent-up lust rather than genuine love. How could he straighten out his thoughts with that bed beckoning him out of the corner of his eye and her looking at him with eyes clouded by passion?

"No. I'm good. But I should probably go. Wedding tomorrow and all. We should get some sleep."

She bit her lip. Damn, he wanted to be the one to do that.

"Oh, okay. I am tired." Her yawn emphasized her statement.

Leaving was the right thing to do. So why couldn't he make his legs work? "Yeah, me too. I really should go." He looked out the window at the inch or so of snow that had gathered on the grounds, and shivered.

She followed his gaze. "You're in the main house?"

He nodded. "Yeah. Looks like it stopped snowing. I should head back before it starts to come down again."

"You'll be wide awake by the time you get to your room, what with the cold walk. You...you could sleep here, if you want?"

Oh, he wanted, all right. They both stared at the bed. "Are you sure?" he asked after a moment. "Just sleep." He could do it. He could. The night would be a slow form of torture, but he'd rushed her once before and he wasn't going to do it again. "Don't get me wrong. I'd like a whole lot more." He gave her his best lewd grin. "But we kind of rushed things last time, and I'm not looking for a fling. I'd like to see where this is going."

Her blush didn't help cool his libido but rather fanned the flames of their attraction. The color set her face aglow. She looked amazing.

When she nodded her agreement, he pulled the throw folded at the foot of the bed and spread it where he'd be sleeping. "I'll use this and you can get under the comforter." A barrier of some sort was wise.

She used the bathroom first. When he came out after his turn, the only light was that filtering in through the window. Jennifer had the comforter tucked up to her chin. "Want me to close the drapes?"

"No, that's okay."

He slipped into bed. They lay in silence, but he was pretty certain she lay there as wide awake as him. He rolled over onto his side to face her, bent his elbow, and tucked it under his pillow to support his head. She followed suit.

"I like the moonlight. I find it soothing if I wake in the middle of the night."

"It's beautiful," he agreed. Her face lay half in shadow, but the moon traced silver lines in her hair and bathed the other half in a gentle light.

"My *naani*—grandmother—loved the night sky. She used to let me stay up late when I was little. She'd point out the constellations and tell me their stories."

"I never really knew my grandparents."

"None of them?"

"Nope. My father's parents died when I was a kid so I don't remember much about them."

"What about your mom?"

"She was an orphan." He never talked about his mom, but felt the urge to open up to Jennifer. "Her mom was an addict. Her father was never in the picture. My grandmother overdosed when my mom was thirteen, so my aunt, who had just turned eighteen, raised her best she could."

"Wow. That must have been so hard for them both."

"I don't know much about it. Only what my father's told me."

"I can imagine it was painful for your mom to talk about."

And now the real downer of the evening. "I wouldn't know. My mom died when I was three. I don't remember her. And my aunt followed in my grandmother's footsteps before I was born."

"Oh, Braeden." She scooted closer and hugged him best she could one-handed. She managed pretty well. Her curves fit perfectly against him, even through the thick padding of the comforter. "I'm so sorry. I can't imagine what that must have been like growing up."

"It is what it is." The sentence sounded pretty laid-back. Surprisingly, the flippant attitude he always assumed when the subject of mothers came up wasn't as hard to maintain as usual. Telling Jennifer felt natural, like he was purging some of the pain he'd carried around most of his life. But he was still ready to change the subject away from his childhood. He'd much rather learn more about hers. "Sounds like you were pretty close to your grandma. Did you visit her often?"

"*Naani* lived with us." She sighed. "Most of the year, anyway. She'd usually go home to India for a month or two each winter. But traveling that far was getting harder and harder at her age. I wish she'd given it one more year, though, then she might still be alive."

He knew her parents had died in some kind of accident, but didn't know the details. He wanted to know more, but wasn't going to push. "You don't have to talk about it if you don't want."

She twisted her fingers in the throw that covered his shoulders. "No, it's okay. *Naani* died with my parents…along with my aunt and uncle, and two of my cousins who were visiting at the time."

Shit. She'd lost that many people all at the same time? "I'm so sorry. What the hell happened?" *Great move, asshole.* Could he be any more insensitive? "I mean…"

A gentle smile curved her lips. "That's okay. It's pretty shocking. I had only recently moved into my own place, otherwise I would have died along with them. Carbon monoxide."

Oh, man. He was definitely checking his smoke alarm batteries when he got home.

"My aunt had a habit of cooking certain dishes until the smoke alarm went off, so on those nights, my uncle would turn off the alarms. He sometimes forgot to turn them back on before bed…"

She didn't need to finish. He pulled her tighter against him.

"Anyway." She sniffed.

He couldn't tell whether or not she cried so he tucked her head under his chin and rubbed his hand up and down her back soothingly.

"So now that we're both thoroughly depressed…"

"I know this is weird," he said. "But I actually feel a little better. I've never talked about my mom. Hard to believe, but maybe it's not such a bad thing to speak about this shit."

"Yeah, I suppose so." She yawned. "It's tiring, though."

He tried, and failed, to suppress his own yawn.

Her body vibrated as she chuckled, then yawned again. Within moments, her deep breathing told him she'd fallen asleep.

He held her close and drifted off.

Chapter Four

Jennifer adjusted her sari until happy with the drape of the purple-and-gold fabric over her shoulder. Carlos had trashed most of her good clothes, insisting she not wear her more traditional garb while they were married. He'd even bought the ridiculously skimpy white dress she'd worn for their pathetic courthouse wedding.

She'd missed the soft lines and beautiful colors, and started the replenishment of her wardrobe with this beautiful outfit. She hoped Braeden appreciated the style. He'd never seen her in anything other than casual clothing—jeans, shorts, and the like.

Regardless, this was how one dressed for a wedding, and she wouldn't be comfortable in anything less. She bit her lip and twisted side to side to inspect her image. Hair up or down? She lifted the heavy strands off her neck, then let them slide though her fingers. Down. She'd caught Braeden admiring her hair more than once.

She added a necklace and decided she was fit to be seen.

The wedding wouldn't start for another half hour, but she had to make her way across to the big house, and while the snow had stopped during the night, it had started up again this morning and been coming down steady ever since. It would be nice to have a little time to warm up before the ceremony. And if she got there early enough, she might be able to sneak in a coffee.

She peered out the window at the gently falling snow. A thin film of white covered the walkway. The snowblower had come through less than half an hour ago. They were keeping the paths relatively clear. Should she wear her boots and switch once she got in the main house? Where would she stash them?

The snow continued to fall, thicker now. If it kept up like this, she'd ruin her shoes on the way back. She slipped off her shoes and changed. Lipstick, ID, and a handful of cash went into her clutch. The room card wouldn't fit, so she tucked it into the inner pocket of her winter coat, picked up her shoes, and headed out.

The cold hit her the second she opened the door, but she didn't mind. There was something about the air during a snowfall she'd always loved. Clean, crisp, and bracing. She took a deep breath. The air fogged on her exhale. No one else was about.

A snowflake landed on the tip of her nose. She giggled, the sound overloud in the preternatural calm of the evening. It was just about six o'clock. The sun had set less than an hour ago. That was the only thing she didn't like about winter: the short days. The cold exhilarated her. Snow made her feel safe and serene, like the world had wrapped her up in a fluffy white comforter.

She took her time along the path to the main building. Twinkling lights in the trees and bushes gave the manor grounds a magickal feel. The good type of *jaadoo*. Not the kind Carlos abused.

Despite meandering along the path like she had all the time in the world, it didn't take long to reach her destination. A porter opened the door and pointed her in the direction of a coatroom to change her shoes and hang her jacket.

Guests hung out in groups in the entry hall, occasionally breaking off and heading into the grand ballroom where the ceremony would take place. She peeked into the room. White chairs with cranberry-colored bows lined up in rows before the huge fireplace flanked by floor-to-ceiling windows. A faint hint of smoke mixed with the sweet scent of the flowers bordering the entrance.

Snow continued to fall. Someone shoveled the patio while another man set up heaters along the perimeter, directed by what looked like Christa's mother. She wondered what that was all about.

A bridesmaid, dressed in a floor-length cranberry-colored dress, brushed past. Her heels clicked along the polished floors. Her head swiveled side to side as she searched the room. She made it all the way to a set of French doors leading to the patio before coming to a stop. Her hand rested on the handle, but she didn't open the doors. She stared out for a minute before swinging away and marching back to Jennifer.

"Is everything all right?" Jennifer asked. A disturbed bridesmaid wandering about the place less than fifteen minutes before the wedding couldn't be a good sign.

"I was looking for Christa's mom, but she seems to have her hands full." The woman gave Jennifer the once-over. "I'm Reina. You're Jennifer, right?"

She nodded.

"Any chance you know how to sew, sugar?"

"Quite well, actually. Why?"

Reina grabbed her arm and led her from the ballroom. "Perfect. Christa has a rip in her dress. We're desperate for someone to work some stitches. I'm a disaster when it comes to mending." She paused. "You don't mind, do you?"

"No, of course not." She followed along in Reina's footsteps. They jogged up the stairs and down a hall. Laughter echoed from a room at the end.

Reina shoved the door open, and Jennifer followed her inside. Christa perched on the edge of the bed, surrounded by bridesmaids. A photographer hovered around the edges, snapping pictures at random as the women joked.

All heads swiveled toward them. Christa popped up, arms outstretched. "Reina, did you find a needle and thread?"

Reina held up a small sewing kit. "Absolutely. Plus, one better." She stepped to the side so everyone could get a good look at Jennifer. "I found someone who can sew."

Christa beamed. Her gown gaped open at the back, the long sleeves falling off her shoulders and halfway down her arms. Her veil lay draped across the dresser in front of a flat-screen TV.

Jennifer took the sewing kit from Reina and fished out a needle and white thread. "What needs to be sewn? I'm sure I can get you all fixed up in a flash."

"Thank goodness," Christa said. "I'm hopeless when it comes to this stuff, and no one else wants to take a stab at the problem." She twisted, one hand to her hip. She plucked at the fabric at her hip where the dress gaped, given the unzipped back. "It's just a small hole in the seam, but I was afraid to zip up in case tightening it made everything worse. What do you think?"

Jennifer leaned over for a closer look. The gap was about an inch long. No one would even notice, but Christa had a point about stretching the fabric and making the tear worse. "That's not too bad. Thankfully it's below the lace." She straightened and gave Christa a wide smile. "You look lovely."

She was the picture of a radiant bride. Despite the small setbacks, her face was wreathed in smiles. Happiness oozed off her aura to the point even Jennifer could sense it with her limited magickal sight.

Christa's soft, shimmery white dress had an overlay of lace ending in a roughly V-shaped fall at the front, then again in back. The lace flowed about three-quarters down the long sleeves. A satin bow cinched at the waist.

At the moment, the gown gaped at the sides with the zipper undone. From under the lace, the skirt flowed softly to puddle at her feet. Along the seam, low on the hip, the small tear marred the perfection of the dress.

Jennifer threaded the needle. "You probably want to pull off the dress while I make the repair." At Christa's uncertain look, she continued, "I don't want to risk puckering the seam if I have to twist it around to reach while you're still in the dress."

"Oh, yes. Sure. Makes sense." Christa trilled a short laugh. "I'm just so nervous, I'm not thinking straight."

She stripped while Reina ushered the others into the hall. "Come on, ladies. Let's give the bride a moment. I don't think she meant all her fancy undergarments to be on display for the lot of you."

Jennifer chuckled. "I promise not to look."

"Here you go," Christa said, handing the dress over.

Jennifer averted her eyes as promised. While Christa slipped into a dressing gown, Jennifer dealt with the wave of longing that swept through her. The silky dress glided through her fingers as she searched for the small tear. Would she ever have a real wedding of her own? Her marriage to Carlos was a farce. She didn't have any fond memories of that rushed, city hall ceremony. Could she get past all the baggage Carlos had heaped on her and find her way to a love like Christa shared with Jeremy?

Her heart told her she'd already found the man she wished could fill that role in her life.

"Can you fix it?" Christa asked, interrupting her thoughts.

She made quick work of the rip. *Easy.* "Here you go."

Christa slipped back into the gown, then turned her back to Jennifer. "Do you mind?" she asked, clutching the bodice to keep it from falling off.

"Not a problem." The back was mostly cut out with the zipper coming up to the small of Christa's back and a button securing it between the shoulder blades. Jennifer zipped it up and secured the top, hiding a tattoo of a delicate fairy sitting on a crescent moon. She spent a few minutes on the row of tiny buttons disguising the zipper.

Christa spoke over her shoulder. "Do you mind if I ask whether or not you intend to stay around after the wedding? I know it's none of my business, but Braeden's really into you and I'd hate to see him hurt if you plan on jetting the second the weekend's over...like last time."

She bolted upright. *Seriously? That's what Christa thinks?* She sputtered, "I—I..." Christa knew the whole sordid story. Did she really think Jennifer just left on some whim without a care for anyone else? She cleared her throat. "Is that what you think of me?" she whispered.

"Oh, no." Christa spun around and sunk to her knee before Jennifer where she sat on the edge of the bed. She grabbed Jennifer's hands and squeezed. "I'm sorry. Everything's different now. I know that. It's just..." She bit her lip. "I probably shouldn't be telling you this, but Braeden fell hard for you. He never talked about what happened after you got out of the hospital, but he was devastated when you left."

A pit formed in her stomach. "I had no idea. I was so messed up back then. I wasn't good for anyone. And

Braeden, well, he deserves so much more than someone with the kind of baggage I carry around."

"Don't underestimate him. He's a good man. He'd do anything for someone he loves."

Jennifer believed it. She felt it in her soul. If Braeden gave his heart to someone, he'd be there for her no matter what. Hell, he'd barely known Jennifer a year ago, yet he'd gone out of his way to help her out of trouble. And she'd been a virtual stranger.

She could only dream of what it would be like to be loved by such a man. She'd spent a lot of time in therapy trying to believe she hadn't deserved what Carlos did to her. Rediscovering her sense of self-worth wasn't easy. But had she come far enough to believe she could ever deserve the love of a man like Braeden? Could he ever love her?

She just didn't know.

❄ ❄ ❄

Braeden smiled for the camera, shoulder to shoulder with Jeremy, while Jeremy's younger brother, Dean, flanked his other side. The camera's flash made him blink. Bright dots floated behind his eyelids.

The photographer insisted on getting shots of the male side of the wedding party before the ceremony. The damn flash had been going off nonstop for the past half hour. His head was beginning to ache.

"Just a few more," the photographer said. "The bride requested a picture of her future father-in-law and his sons." He'd been pulling out "the bride wants" statements every few shots, forcing them to go along without complaint.

Well, not entirely without complaint. "Dude, we've been at this forever," Dean moaned. "Don't you need to get some pictures of the ladies getting dressed or something?"

Jeremy punched Dean's arm. "Relax, man. Almost done. Besides, you might as well get used to it. Lila's likely to demand the same when you two get married. And with a ring burning a hole in your pocket, it won't be too long now."

Braeden punched Dean's other arm. "You're going to pop the question? When?"

Dean grinned, his usual expression whenever his girlfriend's name came up. They'd just celebrated their first anniversary on Halloween, but they'd known each other for a lifetime. "Not sure yet. Waiting for the right moment."

"Gotta get her drunk first. Good idea," Jeremy quipped, then ducked out of reach of Dean's fist.

Braeden laughed as he watched the two brothers spar in mock anger. The photographer got in a few shots while they weren't looking. Braeden was happy for his friends, but didn't relish his position as fifth wheel. Nothing was quite so annoying as happily coupled friends when your own love life wasn't so settled. Of course, after last night, he felt much more optimistic about the future in that regard.

His headache faded as he thought of the night before. If someone had told him he'd enjoy spending a night with a beautiful woman, no sex involved, he'd have thought they were crazy. Yet that's exactly what had happened. And he'd loved every minute of it.

"Now." Jeremy threw his arm across Dean's shoulders. "Smile pretty for the camera."

True to his word, the photographer finished up a few minutes later. Braeden heaved a sigh of relief.

Jeremy thumped him on the back. "It's not nearly over. We're having another photo shoot after the ceremony."

Dean groaned right along with him. Jeremy laughed. "If it makes you feel any better, the ladies will be joining us. Jen won't be in the pictures, but she can hang out if you want."

Braeden must have made some kind of lovesick puppy-dog face at her name, because both Jeremy and Dean laughed.

"What?" he asked, trying to play it cool.

"I couldn't help but notice you are in an extraordinarily good mood today."

"It's your wedding. I'm happy for you."

Jeremy ignored him. "And since you weren't in your room when I called this morning…"

"And you and Jen closed up the bar last night…" Dean added.

"We couldn't help but come to a certain conclusion about where you spent the night."

"Not to mention that goofy grin's a dead giveaway, dude," Dean said.

He straightened. "Nothing happened last night." Great, just what he needed. His friends teasing about Jennifer when all they did was talk late into the night. What if she didn't realize they were only kidding around?

Dean winked. "Right. Nothing happened."

Jeremy made a motion of zippering his lips, then grinned.

"Seriously. We talked. That's it." Not strictly true, but close enough. Gentlemen didn't kiss and tell, after all.

"If you insist." Jeremy cuffed him on the shoulder and with a serious expression said, "Seriously. No worries. We'd never say anything to Jen. She's great. We wouldn't want to screw it up for you. Besides, seeing that panicked, slack-jawed look on your face just now was plenty enough for me." He grinned, then strolled over to the mirror to straighten his bow tie. He'd selected classic black tuxedos with red bow ties and cummerbunds to match the bridesmaid's dresses.

Braeden relaxed and buttoned the jacket of his rented tux. He'd never been so thankful to be a man. His sister had been in a number of weddings and always complained about being forced to purchase a bunch of ugly dresses she'd never wear again. His tuxedo would be returned to the rental agency in the morning. He did own a tux, but the style didn't quite match, so he'd rented this one for the wedding. Jeremy had spent multiple weekends working extra hours because Christa had a dress fitting or needed to prepare something or other for their big day. The groomsmen met once for measurements and picked the rentals up a few days ago. Done.

Braeden would just as soon elope to some luxurious location with a handful of friends and the girl of his dreams. He wondered what Jennifer would want.

Since when did he start daydreaming of eloping? True, he'd shared more with her last night than he ever had with any other woman, but that didn't mean they were on the road to marriage.

Must be all this wedding nonsense. Got a guy to thinking. And that never got him anywhere good where women were involved. But Jennifer was different. He'd pushed aside the idea of being in love with her when it occurred to him last night, but deep down he knew he was a goner. Maybe marriage wasn't nonsense after all—with the right woman.

At five thirty, they headed downstairs. The wedding started at six and they needed to usher people to their seats.

Every time a woman walked through the doors, he perked up until he realized it wasn't her. At least eavesdropping provided a much-needed distraction. One couple was having an entertaining debate on the merits of karma. Apparently, some obnoxious French guy was rude to them on the airport car rental line. They left the airport laughing at the fit he threw when they got the last rental car. The rest of the guests seemed obsessed with reports the police were chasing some Russian mobsters in connection with a drug deal gone south. A few years ago, he would have sworn nothing interesting ever happened in this sleepy little harbor town, but lately... He just hoped no one got hurt before the police caught up with them.

Gossip didn't keep his interest for long as the arrivals slowed and Jennifer still hadn't arrived.

Should he have called her today? He fiddled with the phone in his pocket. Maybe a quick text. *I'm here, where are you?* Or would he seem too needy?

Shit. He'd never had such problems with women. Call, don't call. He never second-guessed his interactions with the opposite sex. But then, he'd never worried much over a woman's reaction or what she thought of him either way.

He cared a lot about how Jennifer viewed him. Hell, he'd spent all night listening to her and couldn't wait to hear more. He doubted he'd ever tire of the sexy lilt of her voice.

"Braeden."

Ah. His heart picked up a beat. He swung to find Jennifer smiling shyly at him. She took his breath away. "You look beautiful," he blurted, realizing he'd never seen her dressed up before. She looked gorgeous in jeans and tight tops, but this dress was something special. The deep purple and bright gold showed off her glowing skin. Her hair flowed straight down to the middle of her back. The drape of the sari over her shoulder got his imagination working on how easy it would be to unravel the whole thing. He tamped down on that line of thought before it went too far. He had to stand up with Jeremy in a few minutes and didn't want to give the guests anything to talk about other than the beauty of the bride.

"Thank you. You look very handsome yourself."

He offered his arm and escorted her up the aisle, his chest puffed with pride.

❄ ❄ ❄

Jennifer stood with the rest of the guests as the last of the bridesmaids walked down the aisle and the music changed for Christa's grand entrance.

She'd already seen Christa in her dress, but the effect was greater as she came down the aisle, train and veil trailing behind, her mother at her side. She wondered what had happened to Christa's father, but was quickly distracted when the pair reached the front of the room.

The groom's expression was just as it should be. Lovestruck, eager, and dumbfounded at his good fortune. Jennifer imagined every woman present longed for someone to look at them that way. She sure did.

Jeremy stepped out to greet his bride, and Sondra placed Christa's hand in his. Then Sondra proceeded forward and turned to face the couple. She took a white cord and draped it once around Christa's wrist, then across to wrap around Jeremy's, binding their clasped hands together.

Sondra raised her hands above their bound wrists and said, "With this cord, I bind your fate, your faith and love shall ne'er abate."

A glow emanated from Sondra's hands and spread over the couple's grasp. The rope shimmered, and as

Sondra released the ties, the glow transferred to Christa's and Jeremy's clasped hands and spread to encompass their whole bodies. Jennifer gasped at the powerful *jaadoo*.

The bridesmaids all shared her astonishment, eyes wide, darting glances at the guests to see if anyone noticed. But a quick scan of the room showed very few seemed to notice anything out of the ordinary. Not to say they weren't all enthralled at the beauty of the moment, but the physical aspects of the *jaadoo* went unnoticed. For the first time in a long time, Jennifer embraced the *jaadoo* within her, pleased she could witness such a wonder.

She'd avoided meeting Braeden's eyes once the ceremony began, but couldn't help casting him a glance now. To her surprise, their gazes met immediately. He gave her a grin and a wink before turning his attention back to the front. His attention brought a glow of its own to her heart.

The rest of the ceremony passed in a haze of beauty and passion. She'd never been to another wedding like it. The vows were heartfelt and teary-eyed, the exchange of rings quick and sweet, and the kiss long. She laughed along with everyone else as Sondra tapped Jeremy on the shoulder with a raised eyebrow and a cleared throat to break them apart.

Guests cheered as the newly married couple skipped down the aisle and disappeared around the corner. The groomsmen followed with their bridesmaid counterparts. She waited her turn and left along with the others, merging with the crowd toward the cocktail reception.

Braeden stepped to her side as she left the ballroom. "There's a little more to the ceremony. Would you like to come with me?"

She lay her hand upon the arm he crooked her way. "Okay."

He led her back into the ballroom where a crew scurried to stack the chairs onto moveable racks and a band set up in the corner.

"Is the reception in here? How will they ever get everything ready in so short a time?"

Braeden pointed to where a man pushed aside a partition, revealing the rest of the great room where tables crowded together. "Everything's all set up in there. They'll just spread the tables out and distribute the centerpieces." He pointed to the far corner where dozens of flowers crowded the floor.

"Clever," she said. With all the flowers flanking the great fireplace and the floor-to-ceiling windows showcasing the flurries outside, she hadn't even noticed they occupied only half the room.

Braeden led her to the patio doors. She stopped him with his hand on the handle, shivering at the idea of stepping into the winter wonderland outside. "Shouldn't I get my coat first?"

"No need. I'll keep you warm." He winked and wrapped an arm over her shoulder, then guided her through the door.

Expecting to freeze the moment she stepped out into the night, she stumbled to a stop and stared around in amazement. A bubble of warmth and light engulfed the patio. The heat lamps she'd seen Sondra organizing earlier radiated warmth and kept the snow from collecting and the air from freezing her breath. They worked so well, in fact, she suspected Sondra of adding a spell of protection to the area. Powerful *jaadoo*, but not above the matriarch's ability.

"Amazing," she whispered.

Braeden grinned. "One of the members of the Historical Society in charge of the manor tried to convince Sondra to have this part of the ceremony inside, but she was having none of it. She says this is a nature blessing so it has to be outside. Granted, I don't think anyone expected this kind of weather so early in November, but nothing's going to stop her."

No kidding. Jennifer couldn't remember the last time they'd had snow in the beginning of November, let alone enough to accumulate.

Sondra clapped her hands for everyone's attention. Christa and Jeremy stood in the middle of the patio, hands clasped, Sondra at their side. The wedding party, Jeremy's parents, his niece and nephew, and a few people Jennifer couldn't name formed a circle around them. Braeden led her to an empty spot between a bridesmaid she believed was Jeremy's sister, Theresa, and Reina, the bridesmaid who'd requested her help sewing the bride's dress earlier.

"Welcome, sugar," Reina said with a smile. She held out a hand, wiggling her fingers in invitation to take hold.

The circle joined hands. Sondra conveyed her approval with a smile and a nod.

"Welcome, friends. We join together in nature to ask The Goddess's blessing on the union of my daughter, Christa, and her new husband, Jeremy. Please open your hearts and spirits to the beauty of The Goddess. Blessed be." She raised her hands to the heavens and turned to face away from the couple. "Hail, the Guardians of the North…"

Jennifer watched in rapt attention as Sondra invoked the Guardians, bringing power to the blessing she placed on her daughter's marriage with a beautiful, heartfelt sentiment. Memories of her own mother's many nature ceremonies brought tears to her eyes. Though the language differed, the meaning remained the same. If life had gone differently, Jennifer would have enjoyed a similar ceremony at her own wedding.

At length, Sondra stilled and they all bowed their heads as a feeling of deep calm and acceptance permeated their circle. With a sigh, the circle reluctantly dispersed and couples fell into loving embraces. Braeden put his arm around her, and she rested her head against his chest. She should have been chilled, standing outside in the snow for such an extended period, but instead warmth surged throughout her body.

The photographer called for the wedding party to gather around the newlyweds. Braeden hesitated.

She nudged his arm. "Go. I'm heading in to the cocktail reception. I'm starved. I'll see you when you're done."

He raised her hand to his lips and kissed her knuckles. "I'll see you in a few minutes. Try not to miss me too much." He winked.

"I'll try." She laughed, her knees weak from the romantic gesture, but she managed to keep to her feet.

She grabbed a glass of chardonnay at the open bar, filled up her dish with an assortment of delicious-looking appetizers, and found an empty seat. She popped a cranberry brie bite in her mouth and pulled out her phone as she savored the sweet, tart treat.

Seeing she had a large number of texts, she opened the app, expecting she'd been mistakenly included on a group text.

You think you won?
Think again.
You're mine.
I'm coming for you.

She dropped her phone from fingers numb with shock. Panic blurred the edges of her vision. She sucked in a tortured breath, aware she'd stopped breathing. The room spun out of control. If she hadn't already been seated, she would have fallen.

The texts had to be from Carlos. How had he gotten her number?

He had to be bluffing. They couldn't have released him. Not yet. Not after everything he'd done.

But he'd managed before.

She grabbed the edge of the table, the cloth bunched in her hand. Her glass tipped, but the cold splash of champagne over her fingers barely registered.

Carlos was out. And he was coming for her.

Chapter Five

Braeden paced the length of the patio as the photographer requested pose after pose. Eager to join Jennifer inside, the picture portion of the wedding seemed to last hours. Seriously, how many pictures did they need?

He had to admit, though, the backdrop was fantastic. The snow continued to drift down through the night air. Trees were lit with thousands of twinkling lights, turning the bare skeletons of the dormant trees into magickal works of art.

Being friends with Jeremy and Dean made it impossible to ignore the magick surrounding them. He didn't have the gift, but the women his friends loved proved time and again magick existed. Standing on the patio watching the snow fall while cocooned in a blanket of warmth, he had no doubt magick was at play in the evening.

"Okay, that's it, everyone. Thanks so much. I'll be taking candids at the reception, but we're done with all the formal shots."

"I spent a lot of time picking the menu for the cocktail hour, so let's hurry up so we don't miss out. See…"

Sondra cried out as if in pain. She gripped her head, stumbling. Jeremy caught her before she fell.

The wind howled. The gentle snow raged to blizzard proportions. Even their little bubble couldn't resist the power of the storm.

"What the hell?" Dean could barely be heard over the screaming of the wind. He pulled Lila to his side, backing up toward the building.

The women's dresses whipped around their legs. Christa struggled to keep her veil from flying away. Jeremy wrapped his arms around her, tucking her head against his chest and pinning the veil against her back.

Everyone stared.

"This isn't natural," Sondra shouted. "Everyone inside. We need to figure out what's causing this."

His thoughts immediately turned to Jennifer. Something similar had happened during the time they'd spent together a year ago. A mild rain had fallen the entire weekend, but when she'd left, a torrential downpour sprang up with no warning. She'd confessed to him that strong weather made her feel safe. The Weather Channel had a field day speculating on the cause when none of the usual indicators were present for such a storm.

What could have caused her to feel so unsafe she'd call forth such an extreme blizzard? He scanned the room, searching for her among the guests. Most crowded the windows, marveling at the sudden ferocity of the storm.

It didn't take him long to spot her, his suspicions confirmed in an instant.

She slumped in her chair. Her face pale, eyes wide with fright. A glass tipped over on the table before her, its contents spreading over the white tablecloth. He ran the last few steps to kneel at her side.

"Jennifer?"

She turned to him with wide, glassy eyes. Her hands shook. "He…he…"

He could only be one person. How the hell could Carlos have reached her here? Last he heard, the bastard was being held without bail. The trial date wasn't even set yet. There was no way he could have been let out so early. "Carlos? What did he do? He can't possibly be here." He searched the room for any sight of the bastard.

She shook her head. "No. Not here. Not yet." She pointed to a phone teetering on the edge of the table.

He picked it up, swiping the screen to turn it on.

"Zero seven zero four," she said.

July fourth. The day they'd met. He pushed aside the pleased, self-centered thought the code had anything to do with him. It was more likely a reminder of the day she'd finally stood up to her evil ex. He tapped in the code, bringing up a series of texts. He cursed. No wonder she freaked.

You're mine.

I'm coming for you.

And at least a dozen more.

The number wasn't programmed into her phone, but who else could it be? How the hell did Carlos get her number? The only one he knew who had that information was Christa, and she would never have betrayed Jennifer's trust.

He'd look into the how of the matter later. Somehow the asshole found out. Whether sent directly by him, or a friend doing his dirty work for him, Carlos knew precisely how to terrorize his ex-wife. Was the bastard ever going to give up?

How was he supposed to handle this?

Kneeling here like a slack-jawed idiot probably wasn't high on the list of ways to deal. He shoved the phone into his pocket. If any more texts came through he'd deal with them first.

"Hey, it's gonna be okay. He's messing with you. There's no way he's getting out of jail anytime soon. He can't get to you. You know that, right?"

Jennifer hugged herself, rocking back and forth, her gaze off in the distance somewhere beyond him. He reached forward to tilt her chin his way. She flinched.

No, nothing so minor. She reared back as if he'd struck her.

He fell back on his heels. "Jennifer?"

She started, blinked, and swiveled to face him. "Braeden? I—I'm sorry. I—"

He shook his head. "It's okay." *Nothing about this is okay.*

He held out his arms and took her into his embrace. He stroked her hair with one hand and rubbed her back with the other. Gradually her trembling eased.

"The storm, Braeden. She needs to stop the storm," Sondra said. The entire wedding party hovered around them.

Jennifer mumbled something he couldn't hear with her face buried against his neck.

He tried to pull away enough to discern her words, but she clung tighter. "Jennifer. Sweetheart. What did you say?"

"Snow. Safe."

"Why?"

"He can't get to me. The snow will keep us safe."

Sondra took the seat next to him and leaned forward. "You have to stop the storm."

Jennifer shook her head.

The lights flickered, then went out. They plunged into darkness.

❄ ❄ ❄

Jennifer concentrated on the comforting presence of the storm. The buzzing of the wedding guests soothed her. Crowds were safe. Even safer to be in a building, in a town, cut off by a blizzard.

The power had gone out hours ago. Generators kept the bare minimum of power going, so no one would freeze this night. Candles covered the tables and every nook and cranny along the walls. The manor staff must have scrounged up every candle they could find. Guests had gone to their rooms and brought back the handful of flameless candles that decorated all the suites. The effect was romantic. Magickal.

The reception continued despite the storm. Thank goodness. Destroying Christa's wedding had not been her intention.

To be honest, she wasn't sure she'd be able to stop the storm if she tried. She hadn't consciously created it. In her panic over Carlos's texts, her *jaadoo* sparked and the blizzard began.

The band played, the singers at times difficult to hear without their microphones. The guests appeared not to notice. The bar remained open and everyone seemed determined to dance the night away. The woman in charge of the manor, Ina, was a wonder. She flitted around, taking care of everything before anyone even noticed a problem.

Braeden hardly left her side. She leaned against him, sharing his warmth, taking comfort from his strength.

"Want to dance?" he asked.

"Okay."

He took the glass of soda from her shaking hand and placed it on a table with what remained of his beer. So casually he put down his drink. Carlos would have downed the alcohol whether nearly full or with only a sip remaining. She couldn't remember a time her ex ever voluntarily left a drink unfinished.

She had to stop comparing Braeden's every move to Carlos. They were nothing alike. She knew it. So why did she continue this torment of looking for similarities?

Braeden swung her onto the dance floor to the tune of "What a Wonderful World."

"You remember Savannah Moore, don't you?" He pointed to a pretty brunette laughing and twirling around with a tall mass of a man on the other end of the dance floor. Jennifer recognized her as the attorney who helped Christa through the whole Carlos debacle.

"Yes. She's the attorney representing Christa in the kidnapping case."

"Right. She's also been keeping an eye on what's going on with Carlos at any given moment. Keeping Christa informed, warning her when Carlos was free, that type of thing. Just in case he decided to go after Christa again."

She formed an *O* with her mouth but no words escaped. Lovely. Just what she needed. A reminder she wasn't the only one whose life had been turned upside down by her despicable ex's violence.

"She assured me there's no way Carlos can make good on his threats. He's been denied bail, and once you add in the cop's testimony about Carlos attacking him when he got in the way, there's no way he'll be found not guilty once the case goes to trial. He's not fooling anyone anymore. He'll be going to jail for a long, long time."

"That's wonderful." She tried to inject her words with the enthusiasm Braeden likely expected, but she'd been down this road before. Carlos was a master manipulator. He'd convinced any number of people of his innocence, that he wasn't capable of the crimes of which he'd been accused. She hoped the courts, the psychiatrists, all of them had learned their lesson, but she couldn't be sure. They'd seemed convinced the first time, but had fallen under his spell.

Spell was the operative word here. Carlos had very little innate power. He'd stolen what he had from *On Magick Most Powerful*. Without the book, he'd lost it all. But that didn't mean he hadn't found some other magickal resource. And she knew from experience his willingness to forgo the entire concept of *ahimsa*, or the witch's rede of "and ye harm none." He viewed *jaadoo* as a means to get what he wanted, damn the consequences to anyone else.

"You don't seem convinced."

Guess she'd failed at her show of enthusiasm. "I'm sorry. I understand what you're saying, but Carlos got his hands on some powerful *jaadoo* before. Who's to say he won't find some other source?"

"Sondra."

She furrowed her brows. "What?"

"After he got out the last time, do you really think Sondra would take any chance of that maniac getting near her daughter again?"

"But what could she do?" True, Sondra was amazingly powerful, but even she had her limits. And it was doubtful Carlos would let her get close enough to use any of her power on him.

"I don't suppose you remember seeing Sondra at his bail hearings?"

She nodded. "Of course. Who could miss her? Christa had an entire cheering section in the courtroom, and Sondra was right up front." Many of them had been nice enough to wish Jennifer well, but she'd been painfully aware of her own lack of a support group. She'd thought she caught a glimpse of her brother before the trial began, but he never entered the courtroom. She'd gotten a crick in her neck continuously checking to see if he'd slipped in. Nope.

And Braeden—she tamped down her hurt he'd never bothered to show up at all. She'd been shocked he hadn't at least shown up to support Christa, while she'd hoped he'd be there for her as well. It was on the tip of her tongue to ask him, but the words locked in her throat. She couldn't think of an excuse that would make her feel better, but a lot that would make her feel worse. She wasn't so sure she wanted to know.

"Well, she wasn't exactly sitting idly by in rapt attention. Christa said Sondra cast a series of spells upon him."

"A series of spells? If she could manage that from across a crowded room, why not just bind his power?"

He shrugged. "I'm not entirely sure. But Christa said Sondra had to be careful about the whole 'do no harm' thing. I guess it's a no-no to cast a spell on someone without their permission."

"True. You're not telling me Carlos gave his permission?"

He laughed. "Not even close. That's what made it difficult, apparently. All her spells had to affect how others see him, but not directly affect him."

She nodded. Made sense. That type of spell work would be difficult and take more than one incantation. "Tricky. My mother would have been able to pull it off."

The song changed, and all around them people bobbed and weaved their way around the floor. Braeden tilted his head toward their table and she nodded. Weaving their way through the dancers took some time. Braeden stopped every few steps to respond to someone or other. Being Jeremy's business partner and friend, they traveled in the same circles, shared a lot of friends. She imagined a large number of the people here tonight would also attend Braeden's wedding.

Her heart flip-flopped. Stupid. Bad enough seeing Braeden in his tux, standing up at the altar during the ceremony, but picturing him as the groom could only lead her heart into trouble.

❄ ❄ ❄

Several members of the wedding party crowded around the head table where he'd left his drink, so Braeden led Jennifer to the bar. She stiffened as they waited in the short line.

"I'll have a seltzer with lime." He turned to Jennifer. "You?"

Her fists unclenched and her frown relaxed into a soft smile. "Soda, please."

They took their drinks, and he led her to a study reserved for the bridal party. He took a quick peek to make sure they weren't disturbing anyone else looking for some alone time, then proceeded into the room. The light of the full moon reflected off the piles of snow outside. Enough filtering in to lend shape to the dark room.

Jennifer strolled to the windows and stared out at the effects of her magick. She appeared calmer, but the snow swirling about and piling up outside begged to differ.

The fire that blazed earlier had burned down to glowing embers. A stack of logs to the right of the fireplace stood ready for use. He set to work rebuilding the fire. Soon enough, the wood caught and set the room aglow with its light and warmth. Jennifer moved to take advantage, holding her hands out to the blaze.

He did the same, though he wasn't the least bit cold.

"You never mentioned your mother was a witch."

She shrugged. "I find it difficult to speak of my parents. But, yes, she was a brilliant *daayan*, or witch, as you say. Very powerful. I wish I had taken the time to learn more of the craft from her." She gestured to the window. "Then maybe I could figure out how to stop the mess I started outside."

"My guess is the storm will calm down once you're convinced you're safe." Not just from Carlos, but with him as well. The way she avoided his gaze made him wonder if Carlos wasn't the only threat she felt. Could she be afraid of him, too? What threat could he possibly pose to her? After last night, she had to know he would never hurt her. Never force her to do anything that made her uncomfortable. "Does the weather always get like this when you're upset?"

A frown crinkled her forehead. "I suppose, to some degree. I can't say I've ever caused anything this severe. Or out of control."

"So this has happened before, just to a lesser degree?" With everything Carlos had put her through, he wouldn't be surprised if bad weather had followed the couple wherever they went.

"A few times. When my parents died, last summer…" A fiery blush tinged her cheeks. "When I was ten and…" She broke off, staring into the distance as if remembering all the awful things that had ever happened to her.

He wanted to pull her into his arms, comfort her, but she'd wrapped her arms about her waist. Closing herself off to any such overture.

"What about when you were married to Carlos?" He hesitated, unsure how much to say.

A tear leaked out of the corner of her eye and slipped down her cheek. She swiped it away. "My natural abilities were stifled during our marriage. The spell he'd cast on me prevented any of my power occurring organically. I suppose I could have cast spells if I concentrated, but he wouldn't let me practice the craft. Using *jaadoo* might have diminished those enchantments holding me under his sway."

He couldn't resist laying a comforting hand on her shoulder. He expected her to shrug and walk away. She'd done it before. Instead she tilted her head and rubbed her cheek against his hand. He took that as his cue to move in closer. He stepped in, wrapping one arm across her lower back and moving the hand on her shoulder up to cup her cheek. "I'm so sorry."

"I'd rather stop thinking about this now," she said. She licked her lips, drawing his attention to her mouth. "I don't want to think at all." Her voice lowered to a whisper. "Kiss me."

He was only too happy to comply.

Chapter Six

Jennifer leaned into the kiss, wholly into the intimacy of the moment. As a distraction technique, the move was completely successful.

The kiss was perfection. The gentle brush of his lips against hers, the warm weight of his hand in her hair, the strong length of his body just close enough to drive her to distraction. Her lips parted on a sigh. He deepened the kiss, tilting her head to allow for better access.

A log fell off the pile with a crash, startling them apart.

She gave a shaky laugh, and he grinned. The firelight flickered over his face, accentuating the strong line of his jaw, the even, white line of his teeth, the soft pout of his lips. Dreamy. That's what she'd call him.

He slowly lowered his hand from around her waist, letting it linger on her hip before tracing up her side to join his other hand in framing her face. His thumbs swept unhurriedly back and forth across her jaw. "Damn, you're beautiful," he said.

She *felt* beautiful when he looked at her with a gleam in his eyes and admiring grin. It had been a long time since she'd felt that way. A mere two days in Braeden's company and she was starting to believe him.

"Look," he said. He dropped his hands and pointed out the window.

The snow had dropped off to the gentle pace from before her panic attack. The three-foot drifts swept up against the building didn't go away, but the trees no longer swayed violently in the wind and visibility improved tremendously.

Braeden tugged her to him so her back nestled against his front. He rested his chin on top of her head and wrapped his arms around her middle. "Should I be happy or worried my kiss has such a calming effect?"

"Worried? Why?"

"*Calm* isn't the response one hopes for when kissing a beautiful woman."

She laughed, and he joined her. "Not to worry. My pulse is racing, believe me. I'm anything but calm. But you have chased away the hysteria."

He kissed the top of her head. "Good. Because your kiss definitely does not inspire calm in me." He moved, brushing his body against her back. The bulge of his erection was impossible to miss. Her blood heated and a delicious tension trembled along her limbs.

But was she ready for this?

A sudden wash of cool air replaced his heat as he moved away from her. He took hold of her hand and led her to the couch before the fire. "Here, let's have a seat."

He sat in the corner and pulled her down beside him. She curled her legs beside her and tucked against his side, resting her head on his shoulder. A girl could get used to nights like this.

"Tell me about the rest of your family." They'd only talked about his mother last night.

"My dad's retired. Moved down to Florida a few years ago. One of those CCRC places where you buy into a house and the level of care progresses as you need more. I go visit him a few times a year, holidays and such."

"And your sister?"

"Evie has no idea what she wants to do with her life. Never graduated from college, even though she went for six years. She shows up now and then hoping to get a handout. I try to help her where I can, but she needs to figure it out on her own. She's stubborn. She won't take advice from anyone, least of all me."

"Sounds like you worry about her."

"I do. But Dad cut her off a while ago, and I can't say I blame him. Give her a little and she just asks for more." He shrugged. "Not much I can do until she grows up."

"My brother's the opposite. Driven. Successful. Mitra knew what he wanted to do from the time we were in high school and never wavered. He got his degree, went to law school, and is a partner at his firm. The youngest partner ever. He's perfect. Even fell in love the right way."

"The right way? What's the right way to fall in love?"

"He married a lovely woman. The child of a friend of the family. Perfect Indian wife. Just the kind of girl my parents wanted me to be." It still rankled. Her parents never pressured him to conform to some ideal. They had no reason to. He was lucky enough to want the very things their parents wanted for him. Unlike her. She'd never been happy with the role she'd been expected to play.

"Bit of a rebel, were you?"

"Not intentionally, no. I just wanted to be myself. Do the things that made me happy. Those things just didn't fall in line with what my parents thought were appropriate for their daughter."

"Do you mind my asking? Jennifer's not exactly a common Hindu name. If your parents were so traditional, how did you end up with such a nontraditional name?"

Did she mind? No. She'd been asked the question often enough. "They were sticklers in some respects; not so much in others." She shrugged. "When it comes to my name, they named me after my mother's childhood friend. She died of breast cancer the year I was born. My mother wished to honor her memory. She sometimes said I reminded her of her friend."

"She must have liked that."

"Not always. Especially when it came to men. Jennifer had terrible taste in men, apparently. My parents often lamented my own judgment in that respect. Of course, they were right about Carlos. I think I knew it, too. I would have dumped him eventually if he hadn't cast his infatuation spell on me."

"I'm surprised your mother didn't sense the spell. Christa says a trained witch can sense these things."

She nodded. "She would have, if she'd lived." Her throat tightened. She'd never said so much about her parents. But she wanted to share with Braeden. "I was barely interested in Carlos at first. I dated him more to tick off my parents than because of any genuine interest. But then my parents died and I couldn't deal with the drama of a breakup. And he was sweet at first. Helpful. And I was in such a state of shock. From the time the police showed up at my door to let me know about their deaths, until after the funeral, I walked around in a fog. Carlos took advantage and cast his spell while I was weak. If I hadn't been so out of it, my innate powers likely would have fought against the spell. As it was, he caught me while I was down, and by the time I started coming out of it, the damage had been done."

And she still struggled to repair the damage. She got the feeling Braeden could be key in her recovery, but was she selfish to expect it?

❄ ❄ ❄

"Tell me more about these 'innate' powers." From things Christa had said—and this storm certainly reinforced the idea—Jennifer had a lot of power built up within her. He wanted to know more.

"The *jaadoo* runs on the female side of my family. My mother was a strong *daayan*. I inherited my power from her, though not her talent."

"Like Christa? Her mom's really powerful."

"I suppose. But I don't have quite the same kind of gift."

"How do you mean?" Magick wasn't the same for everyone? That's the first he'd heard of it.

"Well, Christa can sense magick and work spells. That's why the book, *On Magick Most Powerful*, chose her as its guardian."

"Didn't the book choose you first? Before Carlos got his hands on it?"

She shivered.

"Cold?" He leaned forward and put another log on the fire, stoking the flames until a decent amount of heat built.

They both leaned forward, hands out for warmth.

"I love it when it's like this. Snow coming down outside, blazing fire inside."

He nodded but kept silent, waiting for her to continue their conversation.

"My mom taught me how to do a few spells, and I can follow instructions like anyone else. No big deal. But I generally have no idea when there's *jaadoo* at hand. Unless it's something truly special, like during the ceremony."

Huh? "Magick at the ceremony? You mean when we went outside?" He hadn't gotten the impression the blessing was particularly powerful, magick-wise.

She shook her head. "No. The joining ceremony. Even I could see the love that bound Christa and Jeremy together. It was beautiful."

"I wish I could have seen it from your point of view." The moment had felt magickal, but in the normal everyday way of weddings. "So that was unusual for you?"

"Yes. My mother, though, she could sense another *daayan* a mile away. Me? A *daayan* could walk up, tweak my nose, and I'd still have no idea. No intuition, nothing. I do, however, have an immense connection to nature." She waved a hand toward the window. "The weather, for example, tends to react to my moods."

"I noticed."

They both laughed and watched the snow fall.

She sobered. "I'm not gifted like my mom. One more way I disappointed her."

"Don't think that way. I'm sure she was proud of you."

She rolled her eyes and huffed. "Hardly. But I'd like to think if we'd had more time, maybe I could have done something about that."

"No doubt."

"Thank you." She frowned. "She did love me, though. I know she did. I like to think if my parents hadn't died..."

He waited, but when she simply stared out the window, he prompted, "If they hadn't...?"

"I might not have been so weak." He started to protest, but she held up a hand. "It's okay. I was weak. My grief overwhelmed me. Carlos fed off my anguish and used the book of magick to press his advantage."

He squeezed and released his fists, trying not to make it obvious how much he wanted to punch something.

"What about your brother? Where was he during all this?"

"Mitra? Oh, taking care of everything in his usual perfect manner." She pursed her lips. "Except me, of course."

"Why?"

"I can't say that I blame him. He was so close to our parents. I mean, they doted on him. Their deaths must have been even more of a blow to him."

"That doesn't explain why he'd be mad at you."

"I don't know if he is. I may have just been an easy target to lash out at."

"When did you speak with him last? At the trial? Have you reached out since your divorce went through?" Braeden sensed her wavering. He'd pushed too far.

She gave a shaky laugh. "You don't want to know all this. I think I said too much already last night."

He cuddled her closer to his side. "I *do* want to know it all. All of it. Not just the happy details, but everything you want to share with me."

She inched back so she could look up at his face. "Really? Why?"

"Why?" His voice practically squeaked at the end. *Why?* How could he explain it to her? He stared into the fire. "Because I care about you. I've never felt this way before, so I'm a little unsure what it all means, but I know I can't get enough."

"Even after last night? None of that scared you off?"

"Not even close."

The faint sound of a cell phone reached his ears. "That's not my ring." He patted his jacket until he pulled out her cell.

She snatched it before he had a chance to check the caller. The color drained from her face.

"You okay?" He grabbed her phone and looked at the number. Unknown caller. "Want me to answer? If it's him, I can tell him off for you." He planned on notifying the police as soon as the storm subsided. Carlos's texts were a clear violation of his restraining order. But he'd had no luck making an outgoing call. Reinforcements would have to wait.

She shook her head and took the phone back, swiping the screen to answer the call. "Hello?" she said, her voice shaky.

He tilted his head close to hers to listen in. Intermittent spurts of static disturbed the otherwise silent line.

"If this is you, Carlos, you can go to hell. I'm not afraid of you anymore." Jennifer poked the end button and dropped the phone into her bag.

❋ ❋ ❋

Okay, so I lied. Jennifer's hands shook so badly she stuck them between her legs and clamped her thighs tight in an effort to still them.

Braeden rested a hand on her knee. "Are you okay?"

"Sure. Bad connection. I couldn't hear anything." She released her hands and grabbed hold of Braeden's. His warmth spread through her, giving her courage. "And I don't care. I'm not going to let him do this to me anymore." She straightened her spine and tossed her hair out of her face.

"Good for you." He darted forward and gave her a quick peck on the cheek.

"That all you got?" She smiled. With him by her side, she could get through this. Not because he would take care of everything, but because of the way he looked at her. The confidence in his gaze helped her realize she could do it on her own.

He grinned and leaned forward.

Her phone rang again. She jumped, but with a remarkably steady hand she pulled the cell out of her purse. She swiped the phone and held it to her ear. "I meant what I said, Carlos. I'm not afraid of you anymore. So stop calling."

"I'm glad to hear that, but it's not Carlos."

She gasped. "Mitra?"

Braeden's eyes widened. *Your brother?* He mouthed the words.

She nodded and stood to pace the room. "Is everything okay? I'm surprised to hear from you." Understatement of the year.

Mitra sighed. "I can understand why. I…" He paused so long, she checked to make sure the phone was still on. "I want to apologize."

She nearly dropped her cell. Braeden hovered at her side. "You what?" Her voice squeaked at the end.

"No need to sound quite so shocked. I have been known to admit my mistakes in the past."

"Really—when?" She shouldn't tease him, but he'd caused her not a small amount of heartache the past few years. Forgiving him wasn't easy, though she knew she would, in time.

His laugh was harsh. "I suppose I deserve that. Tanvi is standing here next to me, assuring me I do."

"Oh." She fought her disappointment. "So your wife is behind this?"

"No. Please believe me. This was my idea. I've been trying to reach you for a while now."

She checked her display. She hadn't checked before answering, but she recognized the number as one that had been showing up the past few weeks. "Why haven't you left a message? I would have called you back."

"I didn't quite know what to say in a message."

"How about, 'Hi. It's Mitra. Please call me.'" She toned down the sarcasm in her voice, but not completely. Each time the phone rang, her heart clogged her throat for fear Carlos would be on the other end. Knowing Mitra was reaching out to her would have made a world of difference.

"I'm sorry. I suppose I should have. I hoped you would see my number and call back."

"I might have, if I'd realized this was your number. I thought Carlos was trying to get to me again."

Mitra cursed, and her eyes nearly popped out of her head. She couldn't remember the last time she'd heard her brother use a swear word. Tanvi was probably smacking him upside the head even now.

Braeden put a hand on her arm. *You okay?* he mouthed.

She nodded and slipped into his embrace, tucking her head against his shoulder, the phone to her other ear. "That's a new one for you. Your vocabulary's expanded since I've been gone."

"You're definitely not going to go easy on me, are you?"

She grinned. "Nope." This was too much fun.

Braeden gave her a nudge. "Give him a break. You've been hoping he'd come around. Don't blow it."

"Who's there with you?" Mitra asked.

"Braeden Tiede. He's…" She paused, her face heating. What exactly was he to her?

"You're dating him now? That's great. He seems like a good man."

She pulled out of Braeden's arms, staring at him in confusion. He gave her an inquisitive look in return. "When did you ever meet?" As far as she knew, the two had never crossed paths.

"At Carlos's hearing. The first one. For the kidnapping."

Her confusion increased. "You only came once, and Braeden wasn't there at all." This made no sense.

"We couldn't exactly walk back into the courtroom after the judge ordered us in contempt of court and barred us from the building. I would have been there if at all possible."

"Contempt?"

Braeden stiffened. "You didn't know?"

"Know what?" She tapped her cell's display and placed the phone on an end table. "I'm putting you on speaker. Sounds like the two of you have something to tell me."

Braeden stepped toward her. She backed away, placing a wing chair between them. She held up a hand. "I'm getting really confused. When did either of you come to the hearings? And why would you be in contempt?"

"I figured you knew. Heck, we were so loud, I assumed everyone in the courtroom heard the whole thing." Mitra's voice crackled over the speaker, making him difficult to understand, but she caught the drift.

Now that she gave it some thought, she remembered some kind of commotion when Carlos entered the courtroom that first day. But he'd been acting so crazy, shouting about magick and spells, she just assumed it was all a big act to lay credence to his insanity plea.

"Mitra and I didn't spend a lot of time together," Braeden pitched in. "We happened to be standing next to each other in the hall when they were bringing Carlos to the courtroom. You, Christa, Jeremy, and just about everyone else had already made their way inside."

"That son of a bitch…" She'd never heard Mitra's voice so angry. "…thought he'd get cute with us. While his lawyer walked toward the door, he——"

"He what?" she asked.

"Let's just say he made a few comments neither of us appreciated," Braeden said. His mouth tightened into a furious frown, eyes narrowed, tension evident in the set of his shoulders.

She knew only too well the types of things Carlos liked to spew in his hate-filled rants. She'd let this one go. "So how does Carlos acting like the jerk he is cause the two of you to be banned from the courtroom?"

"We may have stooped to his level for a moment," Mitra replied.

"My fault," Braeden said. He curled his hands into fists. "I should have kept my cool, but the bastard knew how to push my buttons. He taunted, and I responded."

She put a hand over her eyes and sighed. "Ah. I see. You attacked him. And you, Mitra? You, too?"

"I got a few punches in before the guards pulled us off him."

First the cursing, and now the violence. She'd never have guessed.

"The guards pulled us apart and threw us out of the building." Braeden dropped onto the sofa and put his head in his hands. "When I came back the next day, they told me I was banned from the building. If I tried to come back, I'd be held in contempt of court and serve jail time."

A burst of static crackled from the phone. "You're breaking up. Perhaps we could talk more another time. Tanvi would love to have you both for dinner. She'll make biryani. Your favorite."

Tears stung behind her eyelids. "I'd love that. I'll call you this week."

They said their goodbyes and she hung up, her heart lightened at the thought of being welcomed back into her brother's home. They had a lot to work through, but the effort would be worth it.

She sunk down next to Braeden. He slid his arm behind her back, and she rested against his side.

"I'm so sorry. I thought you knew why I couldn't be there. I wanted to be, to show my support. It killed me to have to stay away. I should have known something was wrong when you never called me after our weekend."

"I assumed you took me at my word when I declared the weekend a mistake. I cursed my stupidity many a lonely night."

"I should have been there for you. You shouldn't have had to go through that all alone."

"I've always been on my own." She dabbed at a tear at the corner of her eye. "When my parents died, when my brother turned his back on me, when I was married…"

"You don't need to be anymore. I love you."

Was she dreaming? Projecting what she wanted on what he said?

The look in his eyes filled her with warmth. She believed him. He loved her. Just as she loved him.

"I know this is hard for you. You haven't been given a lot of reasons to trust people. But I'm telling you now." He brought her hands up to press them against his heart. "I love you. And if I have to spend every day of the rest of our lives proving it to you, I will. You've been alone a long time. But no longer."

"Or maybe I'll spend the rest of our days proving it to you." She rose onto her tiptoes and kissed him with all the love and passion that overwhelmed her whenever he was near. "I love you."

She wasn't on her own anymore.

About the Author

EMMA KAYE is married to her high school sweetheart and has two beautiful kids that she spends an insane amount of time driving around central New Jersey. Before musical theater and tap dancing classes entered her life, she decided to try writing one of those romances she loved to read and discovered a new passion. She has been writing ever since. Add in a playful puppy and an extremely patient cat and she's living her own happily ever after while making her characters work hard to reach theirs.

❄ ❄ ❄

For more information on Emma, please visit her online at www.emma-kaye.com, on Facebook at www.facebook.com/emmakayewrites, on Twitter at www.twitter.com/emmakayewrites or on GoodReads at www.goodreads.com/emma-kaye.

Wishful Thinking

by Lita Harris

Stressed and overworked, Patty Baxter takes a much-needed vacation to visit her daughters in Havenport. With her career in jeopardy, and a tragic anniversary fast approaching, the last thing she needs is to face her ex-husband.

Facing a life-changing decision, Alex Baxter decides to visit Havenport the same weekend. He knows he ruined a good thing with Patty, but he's hoping she can forgive him, if only for the sake of their daughters.

❄ ❄ ❄

Dedicated to ~

Ruth, Emma, and Nicole—thank you for being there.

Chapter One

"Yeah, sweetie. I'll be there before dark. I know, I know. Be careful. Jeez, you'd think that you were the parent. I've managed to keep you and your sister alive, you know."

Patty Baxter revved the engine of her SUV and jumped onto Interstate 95 South. She missed the speed of her former faithful coupe. But getting stuck in a ditch one too many times during the Boston winters proved the limitations regarding lack of road clearance, front-wheel drive or not.

"I just want you to pay attention to the road. I don't care if your new car has hands-free capability," her youngest daughter's voice boomed through the speaker.

"It's not a car, dear Olivia. It's an SUV. There is a difference." She ran her glossy, plum-manicured fingers around the steering wheel, embracing the power of the vehicle. Much like she felt about herself—powerful and in control.

She wouldn't dare tell her girls the vehicle was a status symbol. Not because she had the money to burn; she didn't—the payments were a bit more than she wanted. But she had to work that much harder for her commissions.

Something she didn't mind doing. Independence had blossomed within her since the alimony stopped. Though she managed her money well, she feared being poor.

"I'm getting off the phone. I have customers, and you have to focus on driving," Olivia scolded.

"Will Brianna be there by the time I arrive?"

"Possibly. Who knows with her. See you when you get here. Love you."

"Bye." She tapped the off button and the radio resumed playing her eighties rock classics. Steve Perry sang of broken hearts and missing his favorite girl.

She thought back to the day her then-husband surprised her with Journey concert tickets. Set at an outdoor arena in New Jersey, Steve sang and Alex proposed. Her body lightened from the elation of her love finally asking her to marry him. She thought her life would be full of magic like that night—forever.

Well, Steve left the band, and Alex left her.

"Sorry, Steve, you've got to go for now." She switched the station. Oldies, country…no, not in the mood for those.

"Have you ever been lonely?" A woman's sultry voice filled the vehicle. Patty slowed the SUV and moved to the right lane.

"Are you talking to me?" She laughed, knowing full well the radio person wasn't talking to her, but how would anyone know?

Or would they?

"Call in if you want to be part of the conversation: 800-555-2030. I'm waiting to hear from you."

Patty repeated the number. "I'm calling you. This voice command is great!"

Ring. Ring. Ring.

"Hello. What do you want to discuss tonight?"

Her shoulders jumped with excitement. "Am I really on the radio?"

"Yes, please turn down your volume."

"Oops, sorry. I've never called a radio station before."

"No problem. It happens all the time. We can hear each other better with your volume down."

She tapped the steering wheel control. "I love this SUV!"

"Hello? What would you like to discuss?" The sultry voice turned a bit sour.

"Sorry, did I say that over the air?"

"Yes. So what's your topic?"

"Ex-husbands."

"That's a common topic on this show." Laughter in the background.

"I mean they—hey, don't cut me off, you ass." The vehicle swerved and she composed herself. A stream of red brake lights lit the night as traffic grew heavy. She should have left earlier. She'd wanted to, but her damn boss called an impromptu staff meeting, which had nothing to do with her.

"Sorry. My topic. Yes. Where to start?" Her fingers relaxed on the steering wheel and she stared at the traffic. "Never mind. *Gotta* go."

The call went dead, and she changed the station. What good would it do her to bash her ex on the radio for everyone to hear?

None.

A decade later and her heart still ached. The love would not go away no matter how many distractions. She plowed through each one, smarter and stronger than the last complication of her life.

If it weren't for the girls, she wouldn't have gotten through the heartache. Every time she thought of the night Alex told her he was leaving, the emotional punch to her gut hurt as it did the first time.

She tapped the button again. "Call Brianna." The traffic eased, and she breathed a sigh of relief. Punctuality was important; one of her traits that set her apart from the other salespeople. If her ex had taught her anything, it was that she learned to treat people well—in business, anyway. Odd how that lesson came from him. She also picked up management skills from helping run his company. If only she'd insisted on being an actual partner. Her life could have been easier if she were her own boss instead of putting her future in the hands of someone else.

"Brianna. Not available. Leave the message." *Beep.*

"Why do you even have a phone? You never answer your calls. Anyway, I'm almost to Olivia's. I was hoping we could all have dinner. See you soon. Love you."

The lanes opened, and she pressed the gas pedal to the floor and turned up the radio blasting Poison.

The louder the music, the less she dwelled on the emptiness in her life.

She needed a change.

The roads opened up once she got past New Providence. She liked the town but didn't have time to stop. Maybe she'd take the girls there for lunch while they were all in town. She could afford some time away from the office. Her manager made it easy to work remotely, and since her vehicle had built-in Wi-Fi, she was never out of touch.

She drove through Bristol, only a few miles away from Havenport. The few trips she'd taken to Rhode Island since her daughter reopened the bookstore made her fall in love with New England all over again.

The summers visiting her aunt Susan and uncle Matthew were the best. People thought her a local because she'd picked up a bit of the dialect. Bristol, with its homes from the 1600s and its location close to the shoreline, wrapped her in a blanket of comfort she never felt in New Jersey, and definitely not in Florida. Too much sun for her down south. Four seasons is what she needed. Spring renewed her. Summer provided energy from the sun.

Winter was a blanket of warmth from fresh-fallen snow and quieted the night. And fall gave her a little bit of everything.

She pulled into a seafood parking lot and rolled down her windows. Then leaned back and closed her eyes, soaking in the smell of clams and scallops emitting from the restaurant fryers. Her mother would challenge her to a scallop-eating contest. Patty always won. Paid for it later, but won nevertheless. She opened the moonroof and focused on the stars.

"I miss you, Mom. Love you. I hope you and Dad are ice-skating in the heavens."

Buzz.

Damn phone.

"Hello?"

"Patty, Peter." She giggled like a seven-year-old girl every time he said that. It sounded funny and made her smile. They'd worked together for eight years and she trusted her coworker wholeheartedly. He wouldn't bother her while on vacation if it wasn't important.

"Hi. What's up? Did I forget to do something before I left?" She ran through a mental checklist. No. She was good. All clients notified that she would be away. Her most anxious clients had her cell number so they could call her if the stock market began to tank.

"Are you driving? Pull over if you are."

Peter's trembling voice scared her. He wasn't one to upset easily.

"I'm pulled over. What's the matter?"

"Johnson is gone," he whispered.

"What? He seemed fine at the meeting. He even made us stay late. What's the deal?"

"I guess the Feds will let us know."

"What?" She shut off the ignition and switched the call to her phone.

"Listen, I don't know what happened. Except the Feds came in with warrants. Grabbed everyone's computer…"

She glanced at her work laptop on the passenger seat, and her stomach sank. Johnson had used her computer before she left.

"And Johnson?"

"Took him out in handcuffs. He didn't even fight them. I guess that meeting was supposed to have us believe the company was doing well and we didn't have to worry about anything despite market conditions."

She never trusted Johnson. His only redeeming quality was that he'd hired her when no one else would. He took her in as an assistant and encouraged her to become a full-service financial advisor after two years. Other than that, he left her out of the boys' club. At first she thought it was because of her advancing middle age, but she realized her age didn't matter—what did make a difference was that she was a woman.

Her best guess? Her ex-husband's name carried a lot of weight in networking circles. Alex had his own boutique brokerage firm and a knack for securing big-money clients.

"Do I need to come back?" She squinted, puckered her lips, and moved the mouthpiece away, whispering, "No, no, no, no, please. I need this vacation. Pretty please."

She'd finally made top producer and busted her ass to get that award. Now it was time for her and the girls—at least for a week.

"They haven't said anything yet." Peter's voice raised a bit.

"No word as to what's going on?"

"No, but we know they don't come storming in like that unless it's about money. Someone did something they shouldn't."

Peter was right. Unfortunately, they'd seen it happen to other financial advisors. Dipping your hands in client money usually brought trouble. She was proud of her attention to detail and conscientious nature. Another thing Alex had taught her. *Record everything.* Write down every conversation, even if you were just calling a client to thank them for a Christmas card.

"Did they arrest anyone else?"

Peter hesitated. "Not that I know of, but I'll keep you informed."

"Okay. Wait, what about my laptop?"

He hesitated again. "Hold on to it. Don't give them anything unless they ask for it. Or if someone from compliance calls looking for it."

He was right. Never give anyone more than they needed to know. Too many times being helpful and going the extra distance muddied the waters and confused people, making her liable for more than she should have been.

Time to hold back unless asked. That included dealing with her daughters.

"Okay, Peter. Thanks. Keep me informed. I'll keep my work phone on in case you need to get in touch with me."

"Who knows. This could be some kind of mistake."

"Hmm, maybe." She ended the call. *Maybe, but doubtful.* She knew how Johnson operated. Sneaky. It wasn't unusual to find him working from someone else's computer. Something she didn't like, but he was her boss. What could she do?

A huge sigh escaped her chest, and she looked up to the stars. "Mom. Please let this be nothing. On to the girls."

She kicked on the ignition and pulled out onto the road.

❋ ❋ ❋

Salt air filled her car close to Havenport. It was going to be nice spending a few days with Olivia and Brianna. She missed them terribly. The girls were her anchor. Brianna forced Patty to challenge herself when life got tough. And Olivia taught her to always hold on to love even when doing so seemed impossible. It was for that reason she kept communications open with Alex.

Deep down she knew they would always love each other in spite of the choices they had made.

They got together as often as possible, but Brianna changed places every month, trying to find herself. Olivia was married to her job and rarely left the store. Patty didn't mind traveling, and Boston wasn't so far away.

She'd planned this getaway well in advance so the girls couldn't make any excuses. The book and metaphysical stores were doing well. Olivia had done a good job increasing the business of both places. Aunt Susan would be pleased to see what her niece had done to expand.

Olivia had an experienced and loyal staff, which meant she could steal time away from the stores. Of course, profit-sharing had a way of enticing employees to do their best. That was Alex again. *Treat your employees like you want to be treated. They come first.* With that philosophy, your customers will always be there.

She rolled down the window to catch a better whiff of the sea air. It didn't matter that it was November and snow flurries littered her windshield. The fresh air smelled different in Havenport, lighter and sweeter. Even though Boston had its harbor and own distinct atmosphere, nothing comforted her like the weathered docks of where she spent summers as a young girl.

The dry, sparse slats looked like they would collapse any minute under the slightest weight, but they survived each storm. It didn't matter if split boards were replaced with new—it only took one winter to make the dock look like it had been around for a hundred years.

She remembered the last time Alex walked along the docks with her, his hand firmly wrapped around hers. They'd had a steak dinner at Royce Tavern, only it was called something else back then. She couldn't remember.

That night had been perfect. The weather not too cold, her mink coat and Alex keeping her warm. Their relationship steady. He wasn't working as much. His company was doing well and he opened two more satellite offices: one in Boston and the other in Providence.

Their plan had been to relocate from New York and spend the rest of their lives in New England. That fell to pieces with each step she took down the boards that night.

She remembered the sorrowful look in his eyes before the words escaped his lips.

I'm leaving.

She couldn't remember anything past that moment. Thirty years ripped out from under her. No warning. No discussion.

"We're in for some snow this weekend. Nothing much to worry about." The radio announcer broke her thought.

A soft snowfall with a fire and tea, curled up on a couch watching a Cary Grant movie sounded appealing, and she had the girls to keep her company.

It wasn't only the weather that made her want to hide from the world. November fourth was coming up. Each year she did her best to keep herself busy on that day so she wouldn't think about the pain. Whatever that took: volunteering for a rescue shelter, sitting in a movie theater watching the loudest action movie—something she would never view on a normal day. Anything to silence her mind.

She laughed. Losing Alex was hard, but nothing came close to the emptiness she felt at the loss of Hayley.

Patty slammed the gas pedal and cranked up the radio. *Can't do it today. Nope. Don't think.*

After all, she had to figure out her next move. Chances were, her company would be shut down if Johnson was found guilty of embezzlement. He didn't have any partners, and the cowards in her office would jump ship by the time she got back.

If there was an office to go back to.

But life changed, and she'd come out of worse situations. Her mother, Emily, had taught her well. *Everything in your life is temporary. Appreciate what it is and for how long you have it.*

Her mother could turn the worse scenario into a loving life lesson. Like the day Patty's father died unexpectedly. Michael wasn't sick, and Emily wasn't prepared to care for a child on her own, yet she managed.

Patty learned from a young age you were in this on your own. Anyone who jumped into her car of life was welcomed for as long as the trip lasted.

"Call Olivia."

Ring. Ring.

"Hello, Mom." She could tell by Olivia's rushed tone she was busy.

"Hi. I'm almost there. Did you want me to grab you anything to eat before I get to the store?" Her stomach rumbled.

"No. I'm good. I have leftovers in the fridge. Plus, Brianna is right behind you so we can grab something when she gets here. Feel free to get something for yourself to tide you over."

"Okay, dear. See you soon." She didn't want to come across as a pain and didn't need Olivia to entertain her. Patty simply wanted to spend time with her girls. Her therapist said she needed to come to terms with losing Hayley. Having Olivia and Brianna around would be a safe place to do that.

She pulled up to Mellie's Diner and put the car in Park. *Hmm, not busy.* She pushed the door open to the smell of burgers and fries, the ever-present aroma of most diners she'd been in.

Resist. No fried foods. Job seeking against fresh-faced recent college grads, the pressure was on to look her best. The waitress plopped down a platter with a bacon cheeseburger and fries with gravy in front of a customer at the counter.

"I'll have what he's having, except for the bacon and cheese. To go."

One burger and a few fries couldn't hurt—right?

Chapter Two

Patty popped a mint into her mouth and headed into the bookstore. Soft classical music filled the air, as did the smell of coffee and chocolate chip cookies. A staple of the bookstore. The aroma reminded her of Mom's kitchen at Christmas, when she and the girls would help with the holiday baking.

Olivia had done so much with the store since Patty's last visit. More books filled the shelves. The romance section was twice the size it had been. Must be a result of book signings.

A sign promoted the next event. The Winnie Boyle book signing was one of the reasons she'd decided to visit her youngest daughter this week. Winnie was the one author that could write about stuff Patty could barely dream about. She didn't have the imagination for romance but she liked to believe it possible. She'd become cynical since her Prince Charming turned out to be an overgrown, arrested adolescent ass.

She cringed every time she thought of his young wife cozying up next to his middle-aged body. Sure he worked out, but nothing would wipe away the twenty-year age difference between the two. It had to be for his money. Why else would a young girl want his tired ass?

She yanked the belt on her wool coat, having burned the mink long ago, and held her head high as she walked through A New Chapter.

"Olivia! Where are you, sweetie?"

"Here."

"Where?" Patty scanned the room, only noticing books and new accessories like bookends, pens, and a globe in the middle of the floor.

"Yoo-hoo."

She walked toward the counter, nearly tripping over the frayed, Oriental rug. "Olivia?"

"Here." Her daughter popped up from behind the love seat situated in front of the storefront window.

"Do you hide there often?" Patty slid off her coat.

"Only when my mother is looking for me." Olivia smiled, the friendlier of her two girls. A little too serious for her young age. An old soul—always had been. But a joy to be around.

As much as Patty loved her, Brianna, on the other hand, could be a pain in the ass at times. Temperamental, selfish, self-centered, and unreliable, much like Alex. But then, those were the qualities that made him a successful businessman, yet they were the same qualities that made him a shit husband. Traits she'd overlooked until he left her for Tiffany.

That was when she stopped being stupid and blind to his faults. Unfortunately, that cynicism downsized her dating pool.

"You need to crawl into the window seat if you really want a good place to hide." She'd done that when her mother brought her up to visit as a child. At first, Emily would spend hours trying to find Patty so they could get on the road. Her hiding place worked until her mother found her one rainy day. She had protested going back to New Jersey, but they had to get back to see her father. Emily never liked being apart from her husband.

That's what Patty thought marriage was. A never-ending desire to be with the person you love.

Memories.

Bullshit! That's what it was.

The frayed rug would never be discarded. It represented a part of what the store had been. Aunt Susan's solace while Uncle Matthew unselfishly gave himself, bringing medical care into third-world countries long before there was a name for what he did.

He would always bring his wife a part of the culture where he'd spent time working. His way of letting her know he thought about her while away.

Why did she see undying love in her own family yet it eluded her and her daughters? Well, maybe not Olivia. Max seemed okay, but he traveled back and forth between Havenport and Pennsylvania, and her youngest didn't look like she searched for commitment.

And Brianna, *sheesh*, pity the poor guy that ended up with her. If she found a man who could stand up to her ability to steamroll over people he might have a fighting chance.

But maybe her oldest had it right. Don't let anyone take advantage of you.

Probably her fault. She set the mood for how the girls perceived relationships. She tried her best to be strong and civil around Alex for their sake. But sometimes his bullheaded nature just pissed her off and, well, all bets were off, civility be damned. Though the past year their relationship had grown kinder.

"Any word from Brianna?" Olivia asked as she walked over to Patty.

"No. I thought you would hear from her first. She finds it much easier to talk to you."

"Mom." Olivia kissed Patty. "That's not true."

She sat on the love seat. "Don't soft-soap it. I know it's true. She's too much like your dad, and I accept that."

She tried hard with her oldest, she really did. Whenever they had time, she attempted to give Brianna individual attention, but something between them got under each other's skin. Only Brianna was more vocal about it. Patty knew they loved each other but she didn't have the unconditional relationship with Brianna that she had with Olivia.

"I have my issues with her also, so don't feel like you're alone in her madness."

She took Olivia's hand. "I know. It's—well—it's hard most times."

"I know. But I do think she's trying. She's been calling more often and even offered to help me with the book signing this weekend. I told her I could use the company, especially with Max gone."

Patty pursed her lips and chose her words carefully. "He is gone quite a bit, isn't he?"

Olivia nodded. "He hasn't been able to find enough work here to keep him going all year. There's always work to be done at his family's farm, so he tries to manage both."

"Or is he afraid…" She didn't dare broach the commitment question. It wasn't like when Patty got out of school, married and pregnant. That's what a woman did back then. Sure, she bucked the societal expectation by going to college first, even if it was a community college. She was the first woman in her family to go to postsecondary school.

The first thing she did when Alex left her, after she had her alimony secured, was go back to school and get her bachelor's degree in business management. She figured she helped her husband all those years, why not make it official?

"Mom, I know what you're thinking."

"You do? Tell me over a cup of tea. Green or jasmine?"

"Jasmine, please." Olivia took the thin china cup decorated with pink English roses and a matching saucer. Aunt Susan left them behind knowing full well her service ware would be taken care of. Olivia only allowed the Chadwicks to use the set. Their bond to the past and present. "I know you're thinking Max is too laid-back. Not motivated. Happy sitting at the bar throwing back a few drinks."

Patty struggled to fight off a smile that screamed, *I told you so.*

She didn't like telling her daughters what to do. She didn't want to be like her mother, who warned her marrying Alex was a mistake. As right as her mother had been, it was Patty's mistake to make and find the lesson in, no matter how deeply buried in the chaos her divorce brought.

It wasn't easy to be the ray of sunshine her daughters deserved—to be a calm, rational, scorned woman who'd lost the life she'd helped build.

✳ ✳ ✳

"Finally. You got in late last night. I heard you steal in after midnight." Patty tossed a chocolate chip cookie to Brianna as she stomped down the stairs from the upstairs apartment.

"I need more than a cookie. It was a tough drive here." Brianna scoffed down the sugary energy. "And thanks for putting that cot out for me, even if it was in the hallway."

Patty covered her mouth to stifle a laugh. "You mean the dog's bed?"

"What?"

"Mom's right. That cot belongs to Ty. I'd never put out a special bed for you, especially when you were supposed to be here for dinner last night. The dog lives here. He gets a permanent bed." Olivia poured steaming black coffee into the biggest mug at the coffee/tea station and handed it to her sister.

"The traffic in Connecticut sucks. No matter what road you take—ninety-five, Merritt—there's always construction or some pothole big enough to swallow Mars. I hate driving through that state."

"Well, you're here now and have time to recover before heading back. How soon can you be ready?" Patty gently patted Brianna's arm, careful not to drop a smidgen of coffee and cause an under-caffeinated meltdown so early in the day.

"For what?" Brianna inhaled the hot lava without flinching.

"Breakfast. I'm taking my girls to breakfast."

"Food? You're kidding me. Ready in five. Let me get some underwear on." Brianna ran up the stairs, her bare butt cheeks peeking out from her oversized T-shirt.

"What went wrong with her? You two were raised in the same house. Same set of rules."

Olivia held up her finger. "Ah, yeah, but I followed the rules."

Patty hung her head and laughed. "That's true. You were always the one with the most sense, even though you were the youngest. You get that from my mother's side."

Olivia leaned over and kissed Patty. "I know, just don't tell Dad. You know how sensitive he is about that side of the family."

Her daughter was right. The divorce had brought out the worst in her usually good-natured, loving parents.

Something changed between them when Alex abandoned their little girl and her young daughters.

She was grateful they were there for support. Her mother, at least. Her father died a few years after Alex left. No matter of financial support would ever absolve her ex-husband from deserting his family. She heard those words a thousand times in her head over the years. It didn't matter how deep her father was beneath the dirt. His words rang as loud as if he stood next to her.

Brianna bounced down the stairs, fortunately having put on jeans to cover up her bottom. Patty could never figure out what the attention-seeking was about. If anything, Brianna had more opportunity than Olivia. College, living with her father, which gave her immediate access to his money.

But Alex never said no to Brianna. He never said no to Olivia, either, but she never asked him for anything except for the store. Even then, she'd structured a business deal. It wasn't like she'd asked him to hand her money that would never be paid back.

Olivia's maturity and knack for business constantly amazed Patty. She couldn't have been prouder.

Patty checked her cell phone. A text from Peter read *urgent*. Way too early in the morning to deal with the job. She was in Havenport to be with her girls. The job could wait.

Her time would be best spent planning out her strategy instead of worrying about the fallout of Johnson and his company. She would be fine. Her records were impeccable—nothing to hide. She was a compliance godsend: paperwork in order, all conversations documented, and never had there been a client complaint.

It could also be a sign that it was time for her to move on. Life could get lonely up in Boston. Even though she could be in Havenport in a few short hours, it wasn't like she could hop in the car and grab a cup of tea with Olivia whenever the mood hit her.

"You okay, Mom?" Olivia called out.

"Of course. Not much of a morning person. You know that."

She wasn't lying. Even when the girls were small and she a stay-at-home mom, she would lie in bed, praying they would fall back to sleep for another half hour.

"Coffee! That's what's missing. I need my morning brew. You girls ready?"

Olivia tore open a box of books taking up space on the counter. "One minute."

Patty walked over to her daughter and grabbed her hand. "Can you please stop working for a minute? You haven't been still for even a second since we got up."

"I have to…"

"Bull. Let's go." Brianna pulled the box from her sister and placed the stock on the floor. "Come on. I'm starving."

Patty held the front door open as Olivia and Brianna filed out. Crisp salty air filled her lungs. "Ah."

She inhaled deeply and waited for the soothing rush of calm to reach her toes. She didn't know what, but something was about to happen.

Her intuition was rarely wrong.

She took her time strolling behind the girls as they headed down the quiet street. Not much going on except for the year-rounders. There wasn't much of a draw in the off months to pull in tourists, and since the fishing industry was drying up, tourism kept the economy humming.

Patty's eye caught a vacant store next to Led Zeppoli. *Hmm, the bakery has a steady customer base.* Her mind immediately went into overdrive with ideas of what could fill the empty storefront. *Hmm. What does this town need?*

Idle time didn't work for her; she had to stay busy. It kept her sane. That's why she'd made top producer for the year at her firm. Not that it would matter much once Johnson got indicted. But she was getting ahead of herself. Maybe it would turn out to be nothing.

Yeah, no. He was guilty. She was surprised it took this long for him to be caught. Not that she knew exactly what Johnson had done, but his secretive style—never disclosing facts at staff meetings, and not allowing anyone, even his assistant, Grace, to talk to his clients—didn't exactly inspire trust.

Enough about that.

"I hope you two are starving. I am." She held the door.

❄ ❄ ❄

"I love this place," Patty squealed as she slid into the booth and peeled off her tailored coat.

"So do I. It's a frequent haunt for me and Max." Olivia glanced out the window to the apartment across the street. "He's been gone for two weeks and it feels like two months. It's easier for him to take fewer but longer trips back to see his parents in Pennsylvania."

"Don't you go with him so you can get to know his parents?" Brianna asked.

"No, just the one time. The store needs me. He does ask me to go, but I'm not making enough money to justify hiring another employee."

Patty caressed Olivia's hand. "Honey, you have to take time for yourself. I know the bookstore has become your home. We can't even get you to move out of that tiny upstairs apartment. You barely have room to turn around without knocking something over or banging a hip."

"I like it and it makes me feel safe, especially when Max is away."

"Is he living with you?" Brianna asked.

"No, and he rarely stays over. I just like my space."

Patty was afraid the search for Max's biological father had pulled Olivia in closer to him than she'd realized. But at nearly twenty-two, she had time to put off serious relationship decisions.

"Oh, look. Flurries." Patty pointed to the window.

"It's nothing. We're supposed to get a few inches this weekend, but nothing to worry about. The salt air keeps the snow levels down. How long are you staying, Mom?" Olivia opened the menu.

"I was thinking of staying until Saturday morning or afternoon."

"Why don't you stay through the weekend? Leave on Sunday?" Brianna asked.

Patty felt Olivia kick her sister under the table. She knew what was going on. Brianna was trying to convince her to agree and stay longer because Alex would be arriving. Brianna used every opportunity to push their parents together. Olivia had long given up hope, but not Brianna.

"I do like visiting with you girls, but I need to find a job. I don't like how the current one is going. And I don't need any matchmaking getting in the way. I know what you're up to."

"Where are you going to look?" Olivia closed her menu.

"I really like Boston, but other than the people I work with, I don't know anyone well enough to keep me there."

"Florida?" Brianna asked.

"No, I think maybe I'll go back to Jersey. I still have

the two-family I got from the divorce. One of the tenants is moving out so I can take that unit."

"But, Mom…" Brianna stopped short.

Olivia kicked her sister again. "It sounds like a wonderful idea, Mom. You'll be close to the city, surrounded by old friends, and you can go down to the shore anytime you want. Yep, sounds perfect."

"Yeah, I think so. I'm starving. What are you girls having? My treat."

"That's okay, Mom. We can split the bill," Olivia offered.

"No, I insist. After all, you're letting me stay in that quaint apartment."

"That's her word for *cramped*." Olivia laughed.

"It is too small. Why didn't you look for something bigger?" Brianna waved the waitress to their table.

"Because I like it."

"I'm sure Dad would kick in more money for an apartment if you asked him. Just tie it into the business somehow," Brianna said.

"Can we just order? Thank you." Olivia cleared her throat as the waitress approached their table. "Morning. I'll have an egg-white omelet, no cheese, tomato, spinach, mushrooms, and onions. No hash browns or toast."

Patty pointed to Olivia. "I'll have what she's having."

"Well, you lightweights. I'll have scrambled eggs, sausage links, hash browns, and multigrain toast." Brianna slapped the menu closed. "How can you not have the hash browns? That's the best part of breakfast."

"My hips tell me otherwise, so it's time to back down on the carbs." Patty wished she didn't have to worry about her weight. A constant battle. People thought she was naturally thin. She wasn't, and it took work to stay that way. At times she envied Brianna, who could eat anything and not gain an ounce, but she wasn't blessed with those genes.

She would love nothing more than to indulge in a plate of steaming, crisp hash browns, but she was diligent about watching what she ate.

"Why do you keep looking up at that apartment?" Patty added two teaspoons of sugar to her coffee.

"That's Max's place. I thought I saw something walk past his living room window. Must be the sun off the glass." Olivia shrugged her shoulders and slid her finger into the teacup handle. "It's probably nothing."

Without looking up, Olivia ran her finger inside the rim of the handle. "Mom, has Brianna told you what else is going on this week?"

Patty looked at Brianna. "No, she hasn't."

"Your turn." Olivia raised her teacup to her lips, waiting for her sister to drop the emotional bombshell.

Patty knew that look all too well. Her youngest would lock every muscle in her body. Look down and brace herself for the fallout.

"Um, yeah…Mom, Dad will be here tomorrow." Brianna gave Olivia a side stare.

Olivia's ability to ignore Brianna was perfected. She wasn't fazed one bit. Patty, however, still had the ability to catch her off guard.

She smoothed her paper napkin across her lap. "Oh that. Yes, I know."

"And you're okay?" Olivia put down her cup and turned to Patty.

"Yes. Me and your dad, um, have come to an agreement. A truce."

"A truce like you two can sit at the same holiday table and share a meal without you hurling cranberry sauce at him?"

Patty laughed. "You make it sound like I do that all the time."

"Once was enough. I thought Grandma Emily was

going to throw you out of her house for good after that lack of restraint."

"And that happened before the divorce." Patty laughed.

Brianna shot her a look.

Bad timing. Her daughter had a knack for taking a situation too far and goading Patty, waiting for a reaction. The mention of Alex didn't have the same effect on her it once did.

"I guess you will have to wait and see what happens."

Oh, well. It'll be interesting.

Chapter Three

"That was a delicious breakfast. I always enjoy going to Mellie's. Do know that diner has had the original owner since I was a kid visiting Havenport?" Patty hung her coat on the rack behind the book counter.

"Didn't know that, Mom." Olivia rushed to the coffee setup and refilled the carafe.

Patty was lost. The possibility of losing a job at her age hurt, and she didn't know where to go. She couldn't let on to the girls how she struggled with her self-worth. Financially, she was okay, thanks to her shark-toothed divorce attorney.

In a moment of weakness she had called Alex, just for advice on how to market herself for a new job. She had the skills. That was one thing her ex had been good about—he taught her and the girls about business. Sunday-morning breakfasts revolved around reading the stock markets and research reports. Patty never understood how Alex got the girls to listen and pay attention to what he taught them, but she was glad it worked.

She was proud Olivia took over Aunt Susan's bookstore and was keeping her end of the agreement with her father. Business or college? Patty knew that Olivia would be the one to start her own business. She was especially proud when Olivia announced the opening of Serendipity, the adjoining shop.

"Oh, you're back." Marcie burst into the room. Olivia's decision to take Marcie on full-time was the best hiring decision she'd made.

"Hello, dear. How are you?" Patty hugged Marcie.

"It's been a while since you stopped in."

"I've been busy, but I'll be here a few days. Right, Olivia?"

Her daughter nodded as she rung up a customer. The store was getting busy, and Patty took it upon herself to help out and straighten books on the tables.

Noise from the creaky staircase caught her attention, and she followed the sound. She was a bit tired so she'd have to fit a nap into her day. Insomnia kept her from getting a good night's sleep, especially when away from home.

"Holy Jesus, Olivia!" she yelled from the stairs. Her scream ricocheted off the bookcases.

"What's the matter?"

"This stair. My heel is caught. The wood split."

She fought to wiggle her foot free from the spontaneous wood vise, taking care not to break her favorite heels.

Olivia ran up the staircase panicked with beads of sweat on her forehead.

"Are you going to stop twisting your heel like you're drilling for oil in the tread?" She lifted Patty's ankle and slid the shoe from the clutches of the step. "Here. Maybe it's not a good idea to wear these on the staircase."

"Well, I can't be bothered to carry multiple pairs of shoes with me."

"Mom! You're in New England. You will always need sneakers, at least some type of weather-resistant footwear up here. You know how the winters are."

"This weekend is going to be fine. The weather report claims only a few inches. Five to six. That's a dusting. Plus, it'll blow right through. No storm is ever so bad that I can't wear a pair of heels."

So much for a quick nap. She walked over to the snack table and poured a cup of coffee. She coddled the mug in her hands and raised it to her nose. Inhaled the richness of the beans that gave their all for her satisfaction.

"So you knew Dad is coming this weekend, didn't you?" Brianna smirked.

"Yes. Where is he staying?" Patty struggled to keep her stomach calm. The thought of the four of them together choked her. There hadn't been enough time to emotionally prepare for a family reunion, but she promised to do her best.

"Not sure. He thought it would be a good time for the family to get together since Mom and I already planned to be here." Brianna folded her arms across her chest.

"So he knows that Mom is staying here, with me." Olivia sighed.

"I didn't tell him that. I assume he'd figured it out." Brianna grabbed a book from the nearest table and shoved a copy of *How to Raise Your Parents* in Olivia's hand. "Maybe this book can tell you how to fix it."

Patty shook her head and cracked a slight smile. Her oldest could be fun when she wanted.

"And you two do know that I'm sitting right here and am within earshot of what you're saying?"

"Mom, why don't we go shopping or something? Get out of Olivia's hair for a bit." Brianna turned to her sister. "Can you do without us for a bit?"

"Most definitely. Go." Olivia scooted them to the door. "Have fun. Don't spend too much money."

Patty stood and smoothed the front of her skirt with expertly manicured hands. The dark-plum polish wasn't too flashy but still caught the eye.

She walked toward the counter and caught a glimpse of herself in a mirror at the back of a bookshelf. Slight wrinkles hinted she was older than she looked. She watched everything she did since Alex had left her for a younger woman. And she prayed that her daughters weren't emotionally damaged to the point that it weighed heavily on their young relationships.

Patty stood in front of the counter and ran her index finger along the edge.

Olivia sighed. "Why must you inspect everything? I dusted yesterday, Mom."

"Try Led Zeppoli. The smell alone will make you hungry," Brianna offered.

Patty tugged at the sides of her skirt. "Don't need the calories, and I'm not inspecting—just admiring."

"Well, I'm starving. Cookies and coffee aren't doing it for me. You coming or not?" Brianna grabbed her purse.

Bitch factor creeping in.

"Go. I'll stop down there if I get a chance. Marcie's here and Lauren should be soon."

"You don't know your staffing schedule?" Brianna's eyes widened.

"Of course I do. I let Marcie handle that side, and she lets me know when she won't be in. But she practically lives here. It's a fight to get her to take a day off."

"You're too nice a boss, that's why. I know because I worked for some that were horrid," Patty said.

"Is that why you left the Boston job?" Brianna asked.

"Actually, it's complicated, and I haven't left. I don't want to go into it right now. Can we just enjoy being together?"

In spite of her situation, she made time for her daughters. But it would be nice if they came to visit her once in a while.

"You know what? I'm sure Marcie can handle things on her own for a bit." Olivia scribbled a note, stuck it on the front door, and texted Marcie in case she overlooked the message. "Okay, ready."

※ ※ ※

"You're here early." Patty poured a fresh cup of coffee at the snack table the next morning. The caffeinated boost helped her deal with Alex's impending visit. On second thought…she grabbed a peanut butter cookie as reinforcement.

He had been calling her for the most random reasons. Vacation spots. The best restaurants in Boston. She figured a divorce from Tiffany was imminent, but she'd be damned if she'd become his mentor on how to date in the twenty-first century.

"So how has it been going?" Brianna tossed her purse behind the bookstore counter and snatched Olivia's cookie.

"Oh, it's going. And Mom hasn't left me alone for a minute."

"I can hear you!" Patty yelled from behind a stack of books. She walked up to her daughters, fists on her hips.

"Don't talk about me like I'm not here. It's rude, and seriously, there's no reason for it." She didn't think the girls were intentionally being mean, but it wasn't right. "You two can talk about me all you want but not while I'm standing here."

"Mom, please." Olivia grabbed Patty's arm. "I want you here. I truly do."

Brianna threw her arms around them in a group hug. "We miss you, Mom. And we're worried."

Patty shook away their arms. "First of all, you two are about as sincere as an atheist in church."

"Mom, you're welcome here anytime. But sometimes I do feel like I have to entertain you."

Patty's mouth hung open. Never in her life did she want to be a burden to her children. Maybe it was a mistake coming to Havenport. She spun on her heel and stomped up the stairs.

What was her life going to become?

Hold it together. She'd been through worse. Maybe she was hormonal and being overly sensitive. She collected herself, her coat, and her purse, and headed downstairs. It wasn't time to feel sorry for herself.

Maybe they were simply spending too much time together. After all, it had been years since they'd been around each other for more than a few hours at a time.

"Listen, I'm going out." Patty pulled on her coat.

"Mom, we…"

Patty cut off Olivia, who she knew would give her some kind of so-sorry-mommy speech. She wasn't in the mood to hear it. "You do what you have to do, and I'll do what I have to do."

"Mom!" Brianna raised her voice.

"Stop." Patty raised her finger for silence. "I'm not angry, not mad. I need to be by myself. You two should understand that. You made sure you two took—what did you call them?—mental health vacations. Yeah, that's what I need."

She slung her purse over her shoulder and left the store.

Chapter Four

Patty glanced out the window as she straightened impulse items at the register. There was only so many times she could rearrange bookmarks, pens, and event postcards. Snow continued to sprinkle the pavement every few hours. The weather outlook hadn't changed, but the gray skies blocked the sun from revealing an occasional ray of sunshine. Patty needed a break from the past two dreary nights. Even night owls like her needed a dose of natural vitamin C every once in a while.

Maybe she was spending too much time in the bookstore. As much as she liked the atmosphere Olivia had worked so hard to create, she needed social interaction. Havenport wasn't like Boston, where she could stop in a pub on the way home from work. Royce's was the only business in town that had a bar she would even consider going into. The other local bars were dives frequented by fishermen and construction workers. Not that she was opposed to their choice of occupation, but she needed someone who understood her.

Olivia and Brianna would hang around for as long as they could, but she didn't want to be a burden on them and make them feel obligated to entertain her. She wanted someone her own age to have a conversation with.

"Do you need my help anymore today?" she called out to Olivia. Brianna had left an hour earlier and didn't say where she was headed. Probably back to her room at the Havenport Inn. After the dog bed fiasco, she made it a point to get her own place to stay.

That might not be a bad idea. She enjoyed staying with Olivia, but surely she was taking up too much space in an already-cramped living arrangement.

The store opened at eleven o'clock, and Olivia had informed Patty to enjoy a day in town. See the sights. Catch up with some old friends. That would be nice, but her old friends no longer lived there. They were as seasonal as she was, and once their parents sold off summer homes, everyone she knew headed for Boston, New York, or Florida.

With no one to visit, she helped the best she could in the bookstore, then headed upstairs to steal some quiet moments.

The sun threatened to break through dark clouds throughout the day, but never did. Still, she'd take advantage of the dreary November weather.

First, to connect with the outside world for a few minutes. Two days in isolation were enough mental therapy. She powered up her laptop and her mail tone rang furiously as the count climbed higher, each piece bombarding her inbox.

An email from Peter marked URGENT. She opened it first.

Call me.

Each notice had nothing more than *CALL ME* in the subject line. No message, and at a quick count, there were at least thirty.

She dialed his number and he picked up.

"Christ, the phone didn't even ring. What's the urgency?"

"You're a hard person to get in touch with. Don't you check your phone?"

She ignored his drama. "Yes, and I chose to ignore your messages. You know I'm on vacation."

"Permanently."

"Isn't everyone going to be? Though I haven't read anything in the news." She hadn't even checked.

"Nope. Here's what I know. Johnson is out."

"We figured that, and the company will be closed. So?"

"Not so. Someone from Baxter Associates paid us a visit."

Her heart sank. *No.*

"Are you sure?" She sat on the edge of the bed nearest the window and drew circles on the frosted glass. Each subsequent circle bigger than the last. "But how can that be? And you're sure the rep was from Baxter Associates?" A common surname. It could be any Baxter. *It better be.*

"I'm positive. I sat in on the meeting myself. Most of the advisors went elsewhere when word got out about Johnson."

Typical. That didn't surprise her. It used to happen to Alex all the time. The promise of a sign-on bonus was like handing a gazelle to a lion.

"Peter. Is this why you were trying so hard to get in touch with me?"

"Yeah. I didn't want to leave a voice mail and I wanted to get to you before someone else did."

"Like the national news." She laughed.

"Yeah, or Alex himself."

"You sure it's Baxter Associates from New York?"

"The one and only." Peter sighed. "And there's one more thing."

"What?" Like the thought of her ex-husband buying out her company wasn't enough? She knew Alex. He was after the client base. He would come in like the white knight and convince people that only he could get them through this horrible financial mess the previous owner got them into.

"Um, you're not on the retention list." His breath caught as the words came through the airwaves. "Maybe it's a mistake."

"I see. Thanks for filling me in. I'll talk to you soon. I'm going to finish out my vacation in peace. Later."

She hung up the call, not even waiting for Peter to say goodbye. It was no mistake. She knew exactly what her ex was doing. He liked his female financial advisors to be young, thin, and current. She was anything but.

He would age out women all the time, something she fought with him about. He denied that's what he did, but she knew he believed finance was a man's world. Women had no place in that environment. And it had pissed him off when she got her securities license.

She was the top producer. He couldn't let her go because of lack of production. It had to be something else. Ageism was the only argument she had.

She slammed her laptop closed and tugged her leather boots on over her jeans. She grabbed a cowl-neck sweater from Olivia's closet and pulled her shoulders back. The cowl-neck helped hide the subtle loose skin of her neck.

All about presentation. Deal with perception, not reality. Well, she'd absorb some perception of the Havenport social scene.

❋ ❋ ❋

Fog rolled up the sidewalk from the sea. Patty headed to Royce Tavern but changed her mind halfway down the block.

Streetlights reminding her of London lit up as if following her with each step. Led Zeppoli was still open, and she craved a jasmine green tea.

"Oh, thank you," she said to a man holding the bakery door open.

"My pleasure."

She missed that. It was nice when a man held a door for her. With all of Alex's shortcomings, he'd been ever the gentleman. Held her coat, her hand, the door. The only thing he couldn't keep to himself was his dick.

She shook her head, disgusted with how she thought sometimes. She'd been hanging around the boys too long and was beginning to talk like them. One of the drawbacks of working in a male-dominated field. Sometimes she forgot how to behave like a lady.

"Hmm, small jasmine green tea, plain."

"Anything else?" the young girl asked.

Patty scoped out the cookie case. "Yes. A black-and-white cookie, please. No need to wrap it."

The girl handed Patty the cookie with a sheet of wax paper. Didn't look the same as when she was a child. This one was more of a cookie base instead of cake, but the icing looked and smelled the same.

She took a small bite in the middle so she got chocolate icing with the white. *Hmm.* She took another bite. It was okay. Not as satisfying as the black-and-white cookies from the Jersey bakery when she'd been a kid, but everything changes.

Everything. Whether you want it to or not. Her conversation with Peter presented another life challenge. Definitely out of a job. What she couldn't understand was why Alex would do that to her. If he worried about her age, he could at least keep her on the inside. Most of her clients were handled by email or phone anyway. It didn't make sense. She didn't want to think the worst of her ex, but that was her first go-to considering how he'd left her.

"Thank you." She left a ten on the counter and took her tea to the wrought-iron table and chair by the window.

She pulled off the lid and dipped the teabag in the steaming water to hurry the steeping process so she could toss the bag and be on her way. A store like Led Zeppoli usually did well no matter how small the town. People needed their coffee and sweets.

With the tea steeped to her liking, she tossed the used bag and placed the lid back on her cup. She threw the black-and-white in the trash can, deciding the calories weren't worth the inferior cardboard-like taste of the cookie.

The streets were empty, but she felt safe, unlike Boston after dark. She walked down to the vacant store she'd noticed earlier.

She pressed her head against the glass with her right hand blocking out the glare from the streetlights. Dark. She couldn't make out much. It seemed to be one large room. Copper ceilings and plaster walls.

"What was this place?" Talking out loud helped her think. She struggled but couldn't remember what the space used to be. Then again, it was sure to have been twenty different places since she'd been a kid. She never paid much attention to things she didn't care about.

That was a fault of hers, and it got in the way of her marriage. That much she did take ownership of. Especially when Hayley—*no*. She shook her head violently. She didn't want to think about that.

She stepped to the left edge of the large window and tried from that angle. Still nothing. Except for the old ceilings and wall, which described half the buildings on the waterfront, it could have been anything.

A barbershop?

No, that wasn't it.

Food store?

Not likely.

What? What? What?

"Do you always wander around in the dark unescorted?"

She swung around, nearly spilling her tea on her ex-husband. "You bastard."

He grabbed her hand to keep her swing to a minimum. "What did I do?"

She wanted to hate him, but he was the father of her children and she had to deal with that for the rest of her life. But her heart still raced whenever she saw him.

"Good evening to you." His eyes twinkled in the moonlight. He got better with age. The sleek, dark hair with silver highlighting his ears made him more handsome. No matter how old he got, she was still attracted to him.

"The girls mentioned you would be here. I didn't know if you would show since you cut out the last time without so much as a hello." He'd never explained what happened, at least not to her. He was supposed to meet her and the girls in Royce's, showed up on his phone, and left. She chalked it up to work.

Speaking of work, did she dare bring up her company takeover? *Hmm. No.* She wanted to see how long it would be before he told her. Maybe that was why he made it a point to come to Havenport.

"Why aren't you at the store?" She sipped her tea, staring at him over the rim of the cup.

He held out a cup of coffee and pointed to the Led Zeppoli logo. "Coffee."

"This time of night?"

"Decaf." He held the bottom of the cup in his left hand, his right placed over the lid.

"Seriously? Since when?" Patty thought of how he made fun of people who drank decaf. *They're old. Soft. Can't drink coffee like a champion.*

She adjusted her cowl-neck under her chin. It all catches up. It was an opportune time to ask about his wife, but she hesitated. Let him offer the dirt. She felt like she was in competition with her even though they rarely saw each other, but would suck in her gut anytime she was around Tiffany. Even her name was cute and perfect. *Agh!*

Being left for a younger woman wreaked havoc on her self-esteem. Each year that passed meant she was one year closer to death. She hadn't even been on a date in two years.

The few disasters she'd experienced when she first got divorced left her gun-shy. As lousy as Alex turned out to be in the end, he was still the best man she had known. A gentleman, attentive. She missed that.

Tears lined the edges of her eyes.

"Are you okay?" He reached out.

She pulled back. "Yes, I'm fine. It's the cold getting to me. The salt air. You know how that is."

He nodded.

There was something different about him. Could be the lack of caffeine, but no, his eyes were tired. Sure, he had more lines at the corners than the last time, but his soul seemed more content than sad.

His usual agitated nature was absent. Maybe Tiffany dragged him along to the yoga classes she taught.

"Why don't we go see the girls? It's cold."

"The weather's not too bad." She shrugged.

"My coffee. I need a microwave to heat it up."

For a moment, she thought about staying with him and the girls. It was a nice night for a family dinner, but too many emotions stirred inside. He didn't have the *I'm keeping something from you look* about him.

There was something, but it wasn't that. Maybe it was the surprise of running into each other. They had been talking more because of the business investment with Olivia. Patty wanted to make sure her daughter understood everything that had to be dealt with. Even though she was a smart girl and the business was small compared to Alex's company, the same principles applied.

She'd been with Alex when he went out on his own and started Baxter Associates. His father had been a huge help and Alex did right by him, making him part owner and not just taking a loan. The family suffered when his father died, and Alex dove hard into the business more. With his father's ownership given back to Alex, it was what he needed to expand the company to a level he never thought possible.

Patty was suspicious of Tiffany, and so was Brianna. She knew this was why she could never let Alex go. She'd been with him when he'd fought hard to make the business a success, and she'd be damned if some young just-out-of-college *chippy* would come along and claim it as hers.

"How's the wife?" She nearly choked on the words, but someone had to bring it up. She didn't want to come across as the jealous ex. She had his children so their tie would never be severed—no matter how many years since the divorce.

"Tiffany?" He looked away.

"You have another that I don't know about?" She laughed, though she wouldn't be surprised. For the life of her, she couldn't figure out what he saw in that girl. Sure, she had perky tits and a firm ass, but Patty could pay for that if she wanted to. She just didn't.

"No. No other one. Never."

"Hmm. That sounds like there's trouble in Pleasantville."

"Nothing to talk about. She's…"

"Immature, and that's why there's nothing to talk about."

She knew she had him. One thing about Alex, he liked intellectual conversation. Nothing bored him quicker than a person with no opinion or facts to back up their argument.

"Don't start. You know I've always said she wasn't much for conversation."

"Oh, that's where you're wrong. If you want to talk about the newest line of makeup or how cute Internet kitten posts are, you've got the right girl. It's if you need to talk about retirement planning, or mortgages, or who the president is, then you have a problem."

She stepped back. That came out mean and wasn't her intention, however good it felt. Tiffany wasn't the one to blame. It was Alex. He'd been the married party, not that his current wife didn't take advantage of the situation. His fault.

Maybe she should have pushed harder for counseling—not that he would have made the time to go. He was barely home for dinner. But had she pushed him a bit more things may have turned out differently. It was a rough time in their marriage, and neither was consolable.

Patty could never bring herself to believe that losing Hayley was the reason for the end of their marriage. How could she put the blame on a stillborn baby? She couldn't, but sometimes when she cried in solitude, she felt guilty. That blame tried to grab her and tell her it wasn't her fault. Her youngest daughter wasn't meant to survive this world.

She struggled to push back tears. "Sorry about that. I didn't mean to…"

"Be mean?" He folded his arms across his chest and tilted his head to the side.

"Yeah. Sorry. Just went someplace inside me that I shouldn't have." She tossed her empty teacup in the trash can next to a bench. "Look, I don't mean to hold you up. I'm going to get on my way."

"Heading back to the store?"

"And then some. It's a nice night. Not too cold. Quiet." She started to walk away and stopped. "Listen."

She cupped her ear with her hand.

"What?" He shook his head.

"Ssssh. Listen. You can hear the ocean. And it looks like a full moon tonight."

"You always enjoyed listening to the waves." He smiled.

Yes, she did. Especially in the northeast. The Jersey Shore was nice, Florida was okay, but she found the New England coastline to have the best beaches and sturdiest waves. A constant flow of calm as the tide washed in and out. Each caress of the sand was a drop of water from somewhere else. She would go out early to hunt for sea glass.

"Are you helping out Olivia with the book signing?" She continued her stroll.

"No. I'd only be in the way. I'm here for moral support and to check the books. See how the business is growing. *If* it's growing."

"You should be proud of her. She's done a good job."

He grabbed her elbow. "Mind slowing it down a bit? I lost my New York walk years ago when I stopped commuting."

"Well, my time in Boston helped me keep mine up to date."

A sharp pang of needing to know surged through her body. She wanted to bring up the takeover, but promised herself she wouldn't be the one to do it. She wanted to see how long he'd continue before he addressed the issue.

He had to know she was affected. She'd told him where she worked. At least she thought she had. Maybe she was mistaken? They really didn't confide in each other. Their conversations focused on the girls, as it should.

She would see how the situation played out. In the meantime, her focus was on the vacant store. What could she do with it? What did Havenport need?

Chapter Five

Alex was surprised to run into Patty so soon. He figured he would see her at dinner, and the noise of the crowd would interrupt the conversation, or at least keep it on the girls.

They walked back to the store. Flurries picked up, fell faster and heavier.

"You know, maybe you should go in and see the girls. I'm going to head out on my own for a bit. See the town by myself. I haven't done that in a while."

"No, we can…"

"Go ahead. Have dinner with the girls. I'm not really hungry anyway."

"Pat…" He wanted her to go with them.

"Nah, really. Enjoy your time together. We'll catch up later. I'm sure Olivia is going to need help with the book signing. I know Brianna needed to talk to you also, and I'm sure it involves money."

He lowered his head. This wasn't the moment.

She was beautiful. Her green eyes still made him pause, and her hair was a deeper auburn than he remembered.

"If you insist."

"I do. I've had those two for enough hours. I *reaaaallly* need some time to myself."

"Would you let me know where you're going? I'm uncomfortable with my former wife walking around alone at night. Especially near the ocean."

A dull ache ran through the back of his neck. What a hypocrite he'd become. First drinking decaffeinated coffee, and now being concerned for Patty when he hadn't given her well-being a second thought when he'd left.

That night was a bad night for both of them. He figured out too late that he hadn't handled it well. He left Patty at her most vulnerable, when he should have been there to comfort her.

The years past brought her strength. He could see that. Never would she walk around in the dark by herself. He had no right to be her keeper now, when he was the one who'd forced her to grow into the independent, no-nonsense woman she'd become.

The pain would never go away. No matter how many drinks he had, or deals he closed, or women he slept with—nothing would bring peace to what happened those many years ago.

He knew he wasn't the same person, and neither was Patty. Could they even get along at this point without their daughters running interference?

"I'll be fine. I have my phone with me and I'll stay along a lighted path. I simply need some fresh air. Quiet, fresh air." She tugged at his coat sleeve. "Have fun with the girls."

He stood outside the bookstore and watched her walk away. She stayed under the streetlights like she promised. He sipped his coffee.

The snow let up, and he brushed a few flakes from his cashmere overcoat. The bookstore was closed, but Olivia putzed around inside.

He knocked on the window.

Her face lit up and she ran to the door, let him in. "Dad. You made it."

He hugged her tight, lifting her feet off the floor as she arched back with joy. He loved both his girls, but Olivia was the easiest to be around. Always pleasant, looking for the solution instead of dwelling on a problem.

Brianna, well, it depended on her mood. She had a giving heart, but sometimes her delivery put people off, including him.

"How's my girl?" He walked over to the microwave and warmed his coffee.

"Dad, I can make you a new cup."

"This is fine." He slipped off his coat and draped it across the wingback chair. "You've done a nice job with this place. Kept most of Susan's stuff, yet added your own touch."

Olivia sat on a plaid ottoman her uncle Matthew had brought from Scotland. "I love what I'm doing. I know you wanted me to go to school instead, but I have to tell you, this is by far a better education."

He sat on the chair opposite her. "You're still taking classes?"

"Yes, that was the deal. I'm taking one per semester. That's enough. I learned so much from you not even knowing what was happening. All those little jobs you gave me in the office during school breaks. That was time well spent. Those skills have come in handy."

"And you thought it was a waste of time." He spun in the chair and got his reheated coffee.

"Not me. Brianna. She's the one who used to complain. Can you imagine how annoying she would have been if she went to the office as often as I did?"

Alex thought back to when the girls had helped him at the business. Brianna was definitely the more difficult of the two. Selfish—that was her problem. He could never understand why. She wanted for nothing. Even after he left, he saw the girls and took care of them.

He knew it was Tiffany that got in the way. At least Brianna made it seem that was the problem. Apparently she was much smarter than he.

He shook his head and smiled in reaction to Olivia's statement about her sister. Two sisters so different, yet they were there for each other. It would have been different if Hayley—

No. Don't go there.

"So." He stood and yanked at the hem of his suit to smooth out the front. "How are things going with you and Max?"

Olivia grabbed a chocolate croissant and rested it on her knee atop a napkin. "We're good. He's still back and forth between here and his family home in Pennsylvania. I told you the story that brought him here."

"Yes. I can't imagine what it's like finding out you're adopted. How has he been handling it?"

"Good. His father lives in town, but Max isn't ready to confront him."

"Why not?"

"His adoptive parents are good to him. If he'd never found that letter, he wouldn't know he is adopted. He's been trying to reconcile his feelings for some time. I don't push. I've tried to encourage him, but he'll reach out when he's ready."

He leaned over and patted his daughter's knee. "I imagine that must be a difficult thing to do. He must be torn."

"Yeah, he doesn't talk about it much anymore. Must be a man thing. Keep everything tied up like a knot inside."

He laughed. "Guilty."

"Oh, I know. If it weren't for me and Brianna dragging words out of you, we wouldn't know half the stuff we do. It doesn't do anyone any good to hold feelings inside. Words mean nothing once someone is gone."

This kid is too wise.

The bell over the front door rang, catching Alex's and Olivia's attention. "What time did you get here?"

His oldest daughter slammed the door and tossed her purse on the floor in front of the counter, walking to them. Traits she'd displayed as a kid that he hoped she would grow out of. No such luck.

"You're in time for dinner." He stood to hug her.

"I have impeccable timing when it comes to food. Any idea where we're going?" Brianna splayed her hands near the hot embers. "You should kick this up. It's going to be cold tonight."

Olivia tossed a log onto the glowing remnants of dead wood. "I have enough wood stored. It shouldn't be too bad. The weather forecast calls for occasional flurries."

"That may be what the news said, but Lauren told me different." Brianna stirred the ashes with the fire poker.

"Who's Lauren?" Alex asked.

"She's one of my employees."

"She's great. She knows things." Brianna made a spooky sound.

"Ignore her. Lauren is tuned in to things more than most, that's all. Brianna thinks she's a metaphysical genius. Lauren is the first to tell Brianna she's wrong."

He stared at the dancing flames, wondering what kept Patty. Darkness made the safe streets of Havenport a little unsettling when the fog rolled down the road. Even though it was a safe town, one never knew what could happen.

"Have either of you heard from your mother?"

Olivia shook her head. "No, I was busy. She never came back?"

Brianna checked her phone. "Nope, nothing from her. Do you want me to call her?"

Alex stood and pulled down his suit jacket again. "No. Leave her alone. I thought maybe we should ask her to come to dinner. I don't want her to feel like she's being ignored."

He meant it. Besides, it was nice seeing her. He didn't get the opportunity to be alone with her. He'd been thinking about and hating what he did.

He had hoped to have them all together at dinner so he could tell them about Tiffany. Not that the news would make a difference or change the past, but it might give him a place to start over and make things right.

"Get your coats. I'm game for any place that has a hot meal. Don't care if it's a hamburger." Alex slipped on his coat.

"We have to go to Royce's. They have the best steaks. I'm really in the mood for one tonight." Brianna pleaded with her eyes.

He couldn't say no. He carried too much guilt for leaving his girls. Plus, Brianna could be a royal pain in his ass if he didn't give in. Most times it was easier to give in when something wasn't important to him. There were worse things in life to get upset over. Where he'd have dinner wasn't one of them.

"You sure you don't want me to call Mom?" Olivia asked as she threw on her jacket.

He rethought asking her. She seemed adamant about being left alone. Maybe she had a date and didn't want to tell him. As far as he knew, she hadn't been involved with anyone after their divorce.

What right did he have to judge her?

None.

It must be Saturday weighing on his mind. November fourth put him in a bad mood. Even marrying Tiffany on that date didn't erase the heartache. He may have been smart in business, but not so bright when it came to caring about people, especially those close to him.

Could Patty ever forgive him? Was he too late?

He let out a deep sigh. "Come on, girls, let's go." He held the door as Olivia and Brianna left the store. He shut off the lights and walked behind them toward the dock.

The street was empty and eerily quiet. He had gotten so used to the noise of the city that he had forgotten what silence sounded like. Except for the crashing surf as they neared the restaurant, not a sound pierced the night.

"It's going to snow. Can't you feel it?" Brianna stopped short and looked up at the sky. Her head craned back and she sniffed the night air.

"Whatever. Keep walking. I almost tripped because of your impromptu snow alert." Olivia picked up her pace.

Alex held back and watched his daughters banter like they were kids again. Some things never changed. He stopped and checked his phone. No calls. Good. Martha was handling things for him back at the office.

His thumb wavered over Patty's number on his favorites list. That was something that had always upset Tiffany. But Patty was the mother of his children and she would always be on speed dial no matter how much it annoyed his current wife.

Facts couldn't be changed.

"Ah, we must be close. I can smell that steak on the grill." His stomach growled. He hadn't eaten since he'd left the city earlier that day.

"Yep, right over there." Olivia pointed across the street.

He took in the quaint setting of the town. Very New England. He never paid much attention when he used to visit with Patty. His head was usually buried in work or thinking of how to manage their life plan.

He didn't do that with Tiffany. She spent money constantly, and he was getting tired of it. Maybe it was his stage in life, but he looked at things differently.

Olivia had helped him change perspective. When she told him she wasn't returning to college, he was furious until she sold him on a plan she believed would work.

And it did.

He could see her mood was lighter, content, and was proud of what she'd created. She would never be wealthy, but maybe she had the right answer. She found a way that filled her with joy, and no amount of money could be worth more than her happiness.

Alex opened the door to the restaurant.

"No wonder the streets are empty. Everyone is in here. Is this place always this crowded?" He shouldered his way through people blocking the door.

"Usually. It has everything. Liquor, food, legend." Olivia took off her jacket and hung it over her arm.

"Is there a coat check?" Alex scanned the room.

"Yeah. Your seat." Brianna laughed. "Dad, this is a fishing town on the verge of becoming artsy. Just keep your coat with you or I'll hold it."

"Thanks. I think I can manage." He moved to the hostess stand. "Three, please. Baxter."

"It will be less than ten minutes," the hostess said.

"No problem. Thank you." He glanced through the crowd.

"Looking for someone?" Brianna nudged him.

"No. Just trying to see what's here. I haven't eaten here since they changed ownership. I forget what it was called, but it wasn't as nice." His throat tightened. Crowds made him claustrophobic when he couldn't move. He didn't want to upset his daughters so he toughed it out. It wouldn't be the first time, but the older he got the higher his anxiety.

He attempted to elbow a space against the door. At least he could catch a breath of fresh air when the door opened.

What's happening?

He never had anxiety issues before. He thought about the last vacation he took. *Nope.* Tiffany dragged him to Florida, which he hated. Too hot. He spent most of the time in the hotel lobby on his computer and phone, while his wife ordered drinks topped with paper umbrellas and fruit.

His chest began to close, and his breathing raced. "I'm going to step outside. Get me when our table is ready."

Olivia waved him away.

"Phew." He steadied himself against the bench and cleared his head. "One...two...three."

Each gulp of fresh air opened his chest further. He'd make it a point to check with his doctor when he got back to New York.

It had to be a sign. Christ, he was thinking like Brianna with that new-age crap. The only sign he saw was that he needed to lose a few pounds and not stand in a room with shoulder-to-shoulder people. It didn't matter if there were a million people around him, as long as they kept their distance and were moving. Being idle made him antsy and irritable.

His pounding heart slowed and his breathing returned to normal. Once inside, a gin and tonic would help him relax.

This thing with Tiffany wasn't helping. What did they say? Karma's a bitch? With that, he would agree.

Many nights he lay awake, sorting through the mistakes he'd made in his personal life. There wasn't an eraser big enough to forget about his soon-to-be-ex-wife. Fortunately, Ben was giving him a break on attorney fees. Just as he should, considering Alex had made Ben enough money in the stock market.

His anxiety attacks had progressed over the past year. He hadn't told his daughters yet. He didn't want to hear lectures, character assassinations, or opinions. Not now. Once the chaos died down and he was completely out from under his marriage from hell, he would deal with his family.

"Dad?" Olivia's voice broke his train of thought. He turned to her. "Our table is ready."

Thank God. He followed Olivia to a table along the glass wall. Waves broke at the jetty that protected the building. Overspray speckled the window, warning how close Mother Nature was while they ate dinner.

"Nice table. In the back. I like that." He lay his coat over the back of the chair next to him and ran his hand down the material to keep wrinkles from setting in. Olivia and Brianna took the seats across from him.

"Liz! Nice to see you. Where have you been?" Olivia smiled.

"Arizona. Went to visit the kids. What'll you have to drink?" Her clown-red lipstick reminded him of his grandmother, may she rest in peace. She was even buried in her favorite color. She'd bought a dozen tubes when the shade was discontinued. He didn't remember much about Grandma Bella, except her red lipstick and Pall Mall reds.

"Girls?" He picked up the menu.

"I'll have a frozen margarita, and Brianna?"

"Blackberry vodka on the rocks."

"Gin and tonic with lime for me. Thank you."

"Be right back? Bread?"

"Yes." He nodded. The bread was necessary to soak up the gin. It was sure to be a long night. The drama was under control for the time being, but he never knew when it would blow. He gave Patty credit for dealing with the teen craziness. Even if he hadn't left her, he would have missed most of the tantrums because of work.

Liz placed the drinks on the table. "You ready to order?"

Olivia held up her hand. "Give us a few. We're expecting one more."

"Sure thing, dear."

He waited for Liz to leave the table. "What do you mean?"

"Oh, just wait. And don't worry, I'll cover the meal."

Maybe Olivia was surprising him with a visit from Max. He knew he would be back sometime soon. It would be good to get to know the man who got his youngest to settle down into a somewhat serious relationship.

"Well, whoever it is, I wish they'd hurry. I'm starving." Brianna tore a piece of bread from the fresh Italian loaf and smothered it with whipped butter. He rated the quality of the restaurant by the type of butter served. Fresh and homemade indicated that the food would be good.

"No sooner do you bitch than our final guest has arrived." Olivia motioned toward the door.

Alex struggled to recognize a familiar face in the crowd.

Chapter Six

Patty edged her way through the crowd to meet her daughters. Her night on the town was a bust. She loved Havenport, small and quaint. The walk along the dock excited her; the dinging sounds of buoys floating in the ocean let her know something lurked in the dark water. But it wasn't like strolling along Boston Harbor.

And considering her change in employment, she doubted she would stay in Boston.

"Excuse me." Patty squeezed her arms together to muscle through the crowd. She could see a break of bodies past the bar.

Damn!

She pursed her lips. Olivia was setting her up to have dinner with all of them. Olivia had fibbed and said it would only be the two of them. Now she had to deal with Brianna and Alex.

With her courage in check, she stood ready to get through a pleasant dinner, no matter how hard she had to bite her tongue. She wished her daughters hadn't manipulated, but it honestly didn't surprise her.

"So this is what's so important?" She smiled and put

her purse on the floor. Alex's mouth hung open, obviously just as clueless.

Whatever.

It had been a long time since the four of them sat together for a meal. She could manage to get through dinner. As long as Alex didn't bring up anything to do with her company.

As she'd walked around town and thought about what had transpired, she'd gotten angrier the more she thought about Baxter Associates putting her out of work. She helped build that company. She should have taken the partnership as part of her divorce settlement instead of a cash payout.

Hindsight was best. How was she to know the business would grow the way it did? *Stupid.* How could she not? She knew him and how he did things. Which was why her feelings were all over the place.

"I thought it was easier for us to get together instead, at least for one night. It's difficult to get Dad to sit still, and this one…" Olivia pointed to Brianna. "I never know what she's up to. She can tell me she's staying the entire weekend, then she's gone in the morning."

"Not this time. Lauren asked me to help out at the store so she could go to some wedding on Saturday." Brianna took the last piece of bread and pushed the empty basket to the edge of the table.

"That's the one I'm going to. That's why *I* asked for help at the store, so I can get out early." Olivia picked up her frozen margarita.

Patty shuddered at the thought of having such a drink on a November night. She grabbed the brandy snifter, tossed it back, and slammed it on the table. "Add another to his bill."

She sent an evil glance at her ex and shrugged her shoulders. Only one more drink or else she'd be in trouble. She was a lightweight when it came to alcohol.

"So how long will you be in town? And why?" That came out meaner than she'd expected. *The brandy.* Maybe the one would be her only drink for the night.

"I plan on staying until Sunday morning."

"No rush to get home?" She toned down her voice.

"I put this weekend aside to catch up with the girls. I'm not expected back until then." Alex drank his gin and tonic and looked straight ahead.

He was lying. She knew him too well and could feel his reluctance to go home. There must be trouble in paradise. Her lips curled.

It wasn't the time or place to get into a discussion with him. He was right—this weekend was about their daughters.

Plus, she had her own issues to work through. The more she thought about the vacant store, the more her mind ran wild with ideas. If her daughter could run a business, so could she. But what did Havenport need? It would have to be a business that could be sustained year-round, not just when the tourists were in town.

There would have to be a discussion with Olivia. She was bound to have a sense of what the town lacked.

"Did you order your food yet?" Patty placed her napkin across her lap. The salt air made her hungry.

❄❄❄

"No, we didn't. Steaks all around?" Alex asked.

Everyone at the table agreed. "Here. Let me take that."

He removed his coat from behind Patty's back and put it on his chair back instead. Liz came to the table, and he gave their order. He thought it was strange the way they all liked their steak medium-rare. Not Tiffany. She lived on a rabbit diet of green vegetables and water. No wonder she was always in a bad mood.

Soon that relationship would be history.

"What do all of you have planned after dinner?" He handed the menus back to Liz.

Brianna shook her head, as did Olivia.

"Patty?" He nudged her elbow.

"Oh, I thought you meant the girls." Patty fidgeted in her seat.

"No. We're still a family, right?"

Patty nodded.

Something was off. When Alex saw her earlier, he thought it was the cold. Maybe she was tired. She did drive in from Boston and wasn't a fan of the interstates. He had to do the driving whenever they traveled.

Divorce brought out many strengths in people. Hers was conquering the highway.

His?

Well, he was working on that. For all of his confidence and skill in business, dealing with his emotions was a weak spot.

Though he did learn something from the divorce. He learned how much he loved Patty. It had been a difficult time for both of them, and he handled it in the most cowardly way he could, a way he would always regret.

Once he knew the Tiffany divorce would be final, he'd cleared his schedule to come to Havenport. The fact that Brianna decided to come at the same time was a bonus. If he set his strategy on the right path, he could make amends with all of the Baxter women and they could move forward.

Patty would be his biggest challenge. For all of her caring and eager-to-please personality, he had dealt her a blow that would be hard to forgive.

She'd grown so strong. He saw the strength in her eyes when she challenged him on an issue. He—

"We have to leave the building," came an announcement through the PA system. "No danger. Please leave in an orderly fashion."

"What the hell? We haven't eaten." Brianna waved the empty bread basket in the air.

Liz stopped at the table. "Mario's got a small grease fire going. It's out. But the fire department needs to check it out. Sorry for the inconvenience."

"No problem." Alex stood.

"What about our dinner?" Brianna bitched.

"Don't know." Liz took the empty basket and walked away.

"Come on. We'll find someplace else." Olivia took her sister's hand and dragged her to the door.

Alex gently reached out to Patty. "How about me and you go somewhere else? Ditch the girls."

She twisted her lips and narrowed her eyes. *That isn't good.* He had witnessed her volcanic eruption once, the night he left.

He stood firm. They were getting older and could spend the rest of their lives hating each other, but he didn't want that. He struggled to muster up the nerve to deal with her head-on, and he wasn't going to walk away now.

He held her arm as they walked with the crowd outside into the smoke-free air.

Olivia walked over to them. "I got a call from Marcie. A late shipment came in and she wants to get it processed before tomorrow because we have the event and Christa's wedding the next day. So I'm heading back to the store."

She yanked on Brianna's arm.

"Hey."

"You're helping. We'll have something delivered. Come on."

Alex smiled as his girls walked away. Olivia, always quick to pick up on something. Brianna, bratty as expected. If he didn't know better, he'd think their birth order reversed.

"Well, it looks like just me and you." He pulled his coat collar up to his ears and rubbed his palms together.

"I don't know." Patty stepped away from him.

"You have to eat. It's not like we haven't eaten together before."

She shook her head.

He took her hand in his. "What's bothering you?"

Patty lowered her head. "I don't want to talk about it."

"Come on. If you tell me your secret, I'll tell you mine." He laughed. Okay, not the best comment considering what he'd done to her in the past. But he was never known for being politically correct, especially when it came to Patty.

She walked away. "I don't think I can do this. Not now. Not here, anyway."

Hmm. "We can go to my hotel."

She shot him a stare that nearly burst him into flames.

"I mean, jeez. Come on, give me a break. I'm not trying to pull anything on you. It's frigging November, I'm cold, starving, and frankly, walking on eggshells right now because I know something is wrong with you. Historically, I'm usually the reason for your misery. So I'm playing the odds."

Her lips curled slightly and she stifled a laugh. Something he'd seen many times during their marriage.

He placed his hands on her shoulders and pressed his forehead to hers. "Come on. Why can't we have a night by ourselves and talk?"

She raised her head. "I don't think your current wife would approve."

Should he tell her now? Would that make her more

agreeable to go to dinner alone with him? He'd gambled his relationship with her once; he wasn't going to do that again.

If he'd been man enough to deal with Hayley's death and stay with Patty instead of seeking solace with Tiffany, his life would have turned out differently.

He realized too late that he had abandoned Patty, and for that he could never forgive himself. At the time, his selfish nature took over and he didn't know how to comfort her. He would spend the rest of his life making things right with her, even if it meant groveling.

"I'm not taking no for an answer."

Patty narrowed her eyes.

He slid his hand from her shoulder down to her hand and gently squeezed. If only he had been there for her. Maybe it was middle age making him aware of how much time he had left. Maybe it was realizing how ridiculous he looked next to Tiffany. Or maybe it was as simple as Patty being the true and only love of his life.

She swallowed hard. "Okay."

❄ ❄ ❄

The night threatened more snow than the few flurries falling from the sky. A fire burned in the massive fireplace at the far end of the dining room at the inn. They were taken to a table for two, close enough to be comfortable from the warmth of the hearth.

"It's nice that this place isn't as crowded as Royce's." He pulled the chair away from the table for Patty to sit.

"It is nice. I've never been here—not for dinner, anyway." Patty placed her purse under the table. Her voice was softer and she seemed more relaxed than when they were in the madness of the tavern.

"True. I know Brianna was adamant about eating at the other place…"

"Maybe this happened for a reason." Patty smiled.

"My thoughts exactly. Steaks?" He opened the menu.

"Yes. I'm up to seeing how this place compares." She pulled the silverware out from the napkin and tapped the butter knife against the table. "Tell me something."

Here it comes. He knew something was on her mind and braced for her wrath.

"Why the hell would you take over my company and not retain me? You know damn well I am more than qualified. Hell, I learned the business from you."

He shook his head in confusion. "What are you talking about?"

"Don't play dumb with me." She waved the knife at him.

He took it from her and placed it at the edge of the table near him. "For my safety and to keep you out of jail. Too many witnesses here."

"Peter told me that Johnson was taken out and your company took over mine."

He emptied his glass of water. "Is that why you're anxious?"

She crossed her arms and pulled them tight into her chest. "How could you not say anything to me? Even if you were keeping me on staff."

He sighed, feeling like a blowfish as he exaggerated an exhale. This conversation could go one of two ways. He could explain the business reasons as to why things played out the way they did. Or he could tell her the real reason she wasn't on the list. Risky.

Making a vow to himself, he rolled the dice and hoped she bought his excuse, at least until he was ready to reveal his hand.

"I've had my eye on that firm for a few years, before you even started working there. When was that? A year ago?"

She nodded. "That shouldn't matter."

"Well it can. You know why anyone would want a boutique firm."

"Yes, to buy the accounts, not the employees." She sipped her blackberry brandy.

"I ordered ahead. Dinner also." He raised his glass in cheer. "And to your statement, correct. We want the accounts."

"But you'll need people to service them."

"To some degree. I've upgraded our systems, so paperwork is at a minimum."

"Still, Alex. It's not right. You know better than anyone what position that puts me in."

He rested his drink on the table and leaned back into the chair. He could come off as manipulative, but that wasn't his intention. He hoped things would work out as planned.

"Listen, I'll check with the conversion group and see what's taking place." That would buy him some time. Patty's anxiety brought up a good reason for him to ramp up his plan. He miscalculated how upset she would be. He didn't think the news would get out so fast. Then again, it wasn't like years ago when one could keep information quiet. Today, the news was out into the world before anyone left the building.

"I need a job."

"Does it have to be that job?" He spread his napkin across his lap as the waiter put their steak dinners on the table.

"No, it doesn't have to be that one. I mean, I love Boston. Don't have many friends there, but I focus on work anyway. But you know…" She pointed her fork at his chest. "My alimony stopped."

"I know that." He wanted to pay her longer because of how terrible he felt about what he did to her, but his attorney advised him against it, and he listened.

But he would make things right. *If she'll let me.*

"Why don't we forget about business for tonight? It's been years since we've had time alone, and I would like to make the best of it." He winked, then cut into a medium-rare porterhouse steak.

Patty put down her cutlery and planted her elbows on the table, her chin on her fists. "Give it up."

"What?" Chewing, he could barely get out the word without choking.

"What's going on? What are you planning? Are you going to jail and trying to make sure I don't testify against you? I can, you know. We're no longer married so you're not protected under whatever that law is."

He swallowed his food and covered his mouth with his napkin. She always made him laugh. He watched the fire in her eyes as he imagined his master plan being set into motion.

"No, nothing like that. But…"

"What? Here it comes."

She was right; he needed to put it on the line now. He pushed his plate aside and took her hand across the table. Surprisingly, she didn't resist.

"You're right. I do have something to say." He downed the last of his brandy and waved for another. "I haven't been nice to you…"

"Nice? You've been a dick! Nowhere close to nice."

"Can I finish?"

"Whatever." She slunk back into her chair, but he didn't let go of her hand.

"I have made some changes in my life…"

"Don't tell me you're dying. I'm not dealing with Brianna on my own. She's your nightmare. I'll keep Olivia."

He shook his head. "No, I'm not dying, and yes, I'll take Brianna. She can be a real bitch, can't she?"

"I tried my best." Patty smirked.

"Anyway, can I finish without interruptions?"

She passed her fingers over her mouth like she was zipping her lips closed.

"Thank you. The changes. The business is obvious. You figured that out. The biggest change is I am divorcing Tiffany. It's almost final."

He waited for a response.

Nothing.

He lowered his head and looked deeper into her eyes. Surely she'd have a reaction.

"Poor Tiffany." She pulled her hand from his. "I'm not very hungry now."

"Can we talk?"

She stood up from the table. "What's to talk about? You're getting divorced. I don't see how that affects me."

Patty threw on her coat and walked away.

He grabbed her hand. "Because I love you. You. You are the love of my life. I know I screwed things up and I'm trying to figure out how to fix it."

Patty yanked her hand from his and left the restaurant.

Chapter Seven

Patty watched the snow fall faster than the plow could keep up with it. Maybe it had to do with the fact that Havenport only had one plow and it didn't even belong to them. They had to wait until Downport finished plowing their streets and then the plow would make a pass through the seaport.

Fortunately, the snow held off until the day after the signing. They would have had to cancel if it were today. The crowd had been larger than expected, but they'd managed.

Brianna had done a wonderful job. She came through as promised and decorated the book signing section with merchandise from Serendipity, so that brought in extra sales.

Topped off by a surprise visit from Beth Alexander and Winnie Boyle, who signed copies of books, made for the best book signing ever.

With Olivia gone to Christa's wedding and Brianna off somewhere taking care of some things, Patty felt alone. The building seemed like it was watching her. Shadows bounced off the walls and it spooked her. She did a walk-through of Serendipity. She never really paid attention to what her daughter had on that side of the business. Patty wasn't one for that new-age stuff. Scented oils and incense gave her headaches.

The layout was smart and inviting, but the scents got to her, so she left and closed the door in between the stores. The bookstore was more to her liking. She stretched out on the worn, faded green couch. It wasn't in such bad shape when she was a kid, and she knew it was old then. But Olivia was keeping it no matter how ragged it had become.

Lauren and Marcie were also at the wedding, so there wasn't any risk of them popping in unannounced. She grabbed the fire poker and stirred the embers. Heat rushed through her body and warmed her to the core. She glanced at the cuckoo clock above the mantel. Nearly eight o'clock. She placed a log on the fire and flames leaped at her. She stood back, searching her sweater sleeve to see if it had caught fire. Nope, she was good and ready to settle into a quiet night. The girls weren't expected home for hours. Brianna even mentioned that Olivia could stay in her room at the inn if she needed.

She'd spent the past day thinking about what Alex said to her. But hadn't spoken to him since and wasn't ready to accept his apology.

Not today.

Hayley would have been twenty-two. The constant thoughts about her daughter never got easier, and her birthday was a mournful reminder that she was gone.

Patty sighed heavily and put the poker back on the stand next to the fireplace. She poured a cup of hot chocolate and wrapped her hands around the mug. Holding in the heat like she could feel Hayley.

For that scant moment, she thought she had felt life after the forced labor. It was all in her mind. She knew going into delivery that Hayley would not be going home with her and Alex.

Their marriage couldn't survive that. She crawled into herself and hid from the world. At first, Alex tried to help her from her self-imposed exile, but she wouldn't have it. Thank God her mother and Aunt Susan helped take care of Olivia and Brianna.

But who took care of the adults?

Alex eventually found comfort somewhere else, and Patty hadn't been strong enough to fight for her marriage.

They'd changed as they got older. She got stronger and didn't get upset as easily. Alex was kinder, more understanding. Yet she couldn't give in to trust him wholeheartedly.

It felt good the other night having the entire family together, without Tiffany being in the way. Patty wasn't even going to ask Alex why he was leaving his wife. She cringed when she thought of them together. Not because he was married to someone else, but that he was married to her, a woman so unlike his type and maturity level. His problems didn't matter to Patty. She worried about herself.

She kept thinking about the vacant store across the street. *Hmm.* Havenport didn't need another tourist shop. She hadn't had any intention of opening a business, but the location and vacancy of the store called to her. Every time she passed it, she'd stop at the window and stare. Something compelled her to inquire about the building.

She went upstairs. Each step creaked beneath her feet. She felt a moment of panic, realizing how alone she was.

Patty picked a floral-covered spiral notebook from the bookcase, grabbed a pen, and sat in the cramped window seat with her back against the wall in Olivia's bedroom. Frost collected on the glass as her breath hit the pane.

She reached overhead and flicked the light switch on the wall behind her.

Poof!

Darkness filled the room. "What the…"

She jumped from the snap and crackle of the burning fire logs. So quiet she could hear every noise downstairs.

Snow fell furiously. She brushed away the frost and couldn't see the streetlights. The entire street was dark. The expected snow raged outside her window. Some poor soul plowed into a lamppost. A full-blown blizzard. Five-foot mounds of snow in the street buried cars.

She rummaged through Olivia's dresser drawers. There had to be candles or a flashlight. Every New England home prepared for a power outage.

Nothing.

The closet? Nothing.

She wanted to spend a quiet night alone, but not so alone as to be a sitting duck in a B-grade horror movie waiting for something or someone to find her alone and scared.

I'm strong. Not afraid.

Bull.

Even though she'd lived alone for years, she kept the lights on in her apartment, and there was the comfort of knowing someone was on the other side of the wall. Here she was all alone, near the ocean at night.

She couldn't see anyone walking the streets, and the businesses were closed by now.

Knock.

Knock.

Knock.

Her heart lurched, but she gathered her courage and stepped cautiously down the stairs. She reached for the phone. Dead.

The glow from the fireplace provided some light while casting unnerving shadows throughout the store. She moved closer to the door with each pound.

❄ ❄ ❄

"Can you let me in all the way? It's freezing out here." Alex pushed against the door to make his way into the warm bookstore.

"Honestly, you can freeze to death for all I care." She pulled a blanket from the love seat and threw it around her shoulders, then tossed in another log to provide more light and heat, making sure she didn't set the blanket on fire.

"I understand you're upset."

"Upset doesn't begin to explain what I feel."

That he got. It was the anniversary of Hayley's death. "You left before I could talk to you about a few things. The steak was delicious, by the way."

"You ate without me?" She clutched the blanket into a knot at her chest.

"You left. I was hungry." He shrugged.

She rolled her eyes and turned away. "What do you want?"

He wanted to be considerate. Something new for him, but he had to give it a try. "Are you doing anything tonight? Going anywhere?"

"Seriously? It's a freaking blizzard out there." She pointed to the window, the blanket never leaving her fist.

"True. I didn't want to assume."

"Whatever. Have your say."

He cleared his throat. He had one shot to make this right. He had made too many mistakes, and it would take a lot to convince her of his sincerity.

"First, I love you." He reached for her.

She stepped back. "Don't hand me that shit. Do you even know what day it is? You're going to pull some insensitive crap today?"

He took a step closer. "No, Patty. I'm not. That's why

I'm here. I wanted to tell you the other night, but you left all upset. Well, I figured I'd give you a day to unwind. I knew I would get a chance to see you."

"And why is that? Because your company took my job from me? You know I have no place to go. You think I'm going to stay here and let my daughters take care of me?"

He shook his head. "Come on, be honest. Do you really thing Brianna would take care of you? We know these kids."

If her stare could send him up in flames, it would. *Okay. No jokes.* He laid his briefcase down on the coffee table and tossed his coat on the chair. Leaving no room for either of them to sit except for the love seat.

"Can I sit?"

"Whatever."

He sat and patted the seat next to him. "Come on. Join me."

Patty wrinkled her nose and pushed her lips to the side. He knew that look all too well. He got to her. She wasn't completely convinced to hear him out, but his badgering broke through her shell.

"Don't think I'm buying into your boyish charm."

Damn. Miscalculated. He'd forgotten that look of hers could also mean *no way in hell.*

She walked over to the front window. Snow piled against the glass until no light shone through. Even the moon was hidden by the storm.

"I don't think you're going to get very far if you're thinking of walking out on me again," he said with a slight smile.

She opened the door. Snow higher than her waist kept her from venturing out.

"Just give up and realize you're stuck here with me. We're alone and snowbound. It's like the universe is forcing us to be together tonight."

Patty laughed. "Where did you get that ridiculous line from?"

It did sound stupid. He must have heard Tiffany say it. Patty walked to the fireplace and stoked the embers. The rush of light temporarily lit up the room.

"Maybe we should throw a log or two on. It's going to be a long, cold night. I heard on the radio this area has never had a storm of this magnitude and the power could be out for hours. It's a good thing there's a fireplace." He got up, stood next to her, and placed three logs on the grate. "I meant what I said."

"Bull." She challenged him.

He spun on his heel and clenched her upper arms, holding her just inches from his face. "Listen, I know I screwed up royally. I don't know how to fix it, but I'm trying."

"Don't you dare upset me today. *Not* today. It's taken me years to wake up on this day without tears."

He squeezed her tighter. "Do you think that I don't hurt? Do you believe that I never think about that day? Watching your heartbreak as you were forced through that delivery, knowing Hayley wouldn't be alive. Do you think I'm so shallow that I can't hurt like you?"

Patty dropped her head on his chest and wept. "You deserted me at the time I needed you most."

He pulled her face closer and hugged her lovingly. "I know I did, and for that I will never have an excuse. My only rationale is that I was hurting, and even though it killed me to watch you fall deeper into your depression and distance yourself, I couldn't find a way to reach you."

"You should have tried harder." She wiped her eyes with his suit sleeve.

"At that time, I thought I was. I gave everything I had and I know it wasn't enough. I now know I took the coward's way out, and for that I'm sorry. One thing you have to know is, I've never stopped loving you."

"Tiffany?" She looked up into his eyes.

"The divorce is almost final. We haven't lived together for months. Fortunately, she found someone with more money and a shorter expiration date."

"I told you she was a gold digger."

He knew Patty considered his failing marriage a win, but she was mature enough to let it die a natural death.

"I don't know if I can ever forgive you." She moved closer to him. His heart pounded with her familiar touch and sweet smell.

"All I ask is that you try. You know we're good together."

"Yeah. Then why are you putting me out of a job?" She pushed away from him and headed toward the stairs.

"You're going to freeze up there. There's no heat."

"It won't be any colder than the past fifteen years of my life."

❄ ❄ ❄

Patty stormed up the stairs to Olivia's room and emptied the closet of blankets and pillows. Alex was right that it was colder upstairs, but she should have enough to keep her warm. She pulled back the comforter to find regular cotton sheets on the bed. The thought of sliding her body into those cold sheets made her teeth chatter. She found a set of flannels sheets and lay them over what was there. A comforter, woven blanket, flannel sheets, and pajamas should get her through the night without becoming a frozen casualty.

She crawled underneath the covers and tucked them under her chin. Patty never felt guilty or held Alex responsible for Hayley being stillborn. It was one of those unexpected things that happened, but she could never get past the hurt. Years withdrawn, even from the girls. With the help of her mother, they all got through the first year. Except for her marriage. The one time she and Alex couldn't make it work. Even if she wanted to help him through his mourning, she didn't have the strength.

Feeling sorry for him, she gathered up a blanket and pillow and carried them to the top of the stairs. "Alex?"

He came to the foot of the staircase. "Yes? Willing to talk?"

"No." She threw the bedding down to him. "Sleep well."

The blanket landed on his face. He pulled it away. "Wait. Wait. Do you still read before you go to bed?"

"Yes, but there's no electricity. Blizzard." She motioned outside.

"Here. Just take this and read it. It's not very long." He handed her a manila envelope and his keys that had a mini LED flashlight. "This should help you."

"What is it?"

"It's a story I've been working on. I don't have an ending, and that's where you come in. Please just give it a quick read. I value your opinion."

She rolled her eyes and stomped up the stairs. Hours had gone by, and she was tired. Midnight. The storm showed no sign of letting up.

She plumped the bed pillows and slid in under the covers. She held the small flashlight in between her teeth with the beam aimed at the envelope. With her free hands, she removed the typed papers.

Dear Patty,
I hope you find this to be a reasonable and fair proposition.
Love,
Alex (your favorite ex-husband)

She smiled at his attempt at humor. For a moment, she felt bad that he would be spending the night in a cold building on an old, raggedy love seat.

One night of suffering wouldn't begin to pay back what he owed her.

He was right—the package was very thin, only a few pages. Her eyes fell on the highlighted clause.

PARTNERSHIP AGREEMENT

The following persons agree to said terms. Alexander Joseph Baxter and Patricia Emily Baxter to hold equal shares of FIFTY (50) percent each in the newly formed partnership of Baxter Enterprises.

Why would he do this? She jumped out of bed in her flannel pajamas and ran down the stairs in bare feet, waving the papers.

Alex was asleep on the love seat.

"What the hell? Get up." She whacked him with the papers. "What is this crap?"

He sat up, barely awake. It always baffled her how he could fall asleep so fast.

"It's pretty straightforward."

"You're giving me half your company? Why?"

Alex ran his hand through his hair to comb it out of his eyes. "You deserve it. That's why you weren't on the retention list. I don't want you to be an employee. I want you to be where you should have always been, right next to me."

"Why the name change?" She jabbed her finger into the paper.

"The business is bigger, with different interests now. Baxter Associates will remain the brokerage firm, but creating a parent company leaves room for growth."

She nodded. "Makes sense."

He walked up to her and held her hand. "I thought the first new venture could be that vacant store across the street."

"I...I wouldn't even know what to do with it." She slid her fingers between his.

"You don't need to make a decision now on what you want it to be. The only decision you need to make is calling the owner of that building and buying it."

"I thought renting would be a better option."

He leaned in to her.

"Really?" She pulled him closer.

"Buy. Make the commitment," he whispered in her ear, and slid his hand under her pajama top.

Her skin tingled. She missed his touch. Her mouth invited him, and he lovingly responded. He held her tight, nearly lifting her from the floor. The flames danced at their feet.

She gently pulled away.

"I see you threw more wood on the fire." Her breath hushed.

"And then some." He smiled.

She took his hand and pulled him up the stairs.

"You sure we'll be warm enough up there?" he asked.

She stopped and looked down at him with a wink. "Oh, I'm sure we'll be plenty warm."

About the Author

LITA HARRIS spends her time between New Jersey and the Endless Mountains region of Pennsylvania, where she writes most of her books. She also lived in Alaska for a short time just for fun. An avid crafter, unused supplies clutter her basement and attempts at making pottery, jewelry, and stained glass are proudly displayed in her house, usually behind a picture or holding a door open. She also makes candles and homemade soap. With enough books to stock a small library she may need to construct a building to store her literary obsessions.

She writes in multiple genres, including women's fiction, contemporary romance, paranormal, and cozy mysteries.

❄ ❄ ❄

For more information about Lita, please visit her website at www.LitaHarris.com or at Twitter.com/LitaHarris and Facebook.com/LitaHarrisAuthor.